"Chapman is unmatched and unforgettable."*

Praise for the novels of Janet Chapman

"A romantic, funny, quietly intense story of wounded survivors reluctantly finding love." —*Publishers Weekly*

"Janet Chapman's *Dragon Warrior* is head and shoulders above any shape-shifting or paranormal romance I have ever read . . . A spectacular and brilliant novel for those who love the juxtaposition of the paranormal and the real world. A Perfect 10 is a fitting rating for . . . a novel which is both tender and joyful, but also has beasts looking for peace and a new way of life after centuries of struggle."

—*Romance Reviews Today*

"Delightful romantic series with a paranormal twist . . . Chapman brings plenty of warmth and fun to the story by enlivening it with a rich cast of characters. You can't go wrong with a Chapman story!" —**RT Book Reviews* (4 stars)

"If anyone can make me fall in love with a ninth-century warrior who also spent several centuries as a dragon, it's Janet Chapman. I always love her secondary characters . . . I love the humor that she injects [in *Dragon Warrior*]."

—*Fallen Angels Review* (Five Angel Review)

"The idea of a time-traveling warrior, who was once a dragon, courting a modern woman is steamy fun . . . As funny and steamy as can be expected from Chapman . . . Well executed!"

—*Fresh Fiction*

"From exceptionally moving scenes to delightfully amusing moments, the originality of *Dragon Warrior* keeps your total attention . . . Creatively innovative with inventive plots and particularly appealing characters." —*Single Titles*

"Readers will be enchanted with Chapman's love of Maine in her latest romance, a story filled with wit and tenderness."

—*Booklist*

"Lovable characters, a sweet romance, and the grouchy troublemaker dragon combine for a delightful read."

—*Publishers Weekly*

Jove titles by Janet Chapman

HIGHLANDER FOR THE HOLIDAYS
SPELLBOUND FALLS

Spellbound Falls

Janet Chapman

THE BERKLEY PUBLISHING GROUP
Published by the Penguin Group
Penguin Group (USA) Inc.
375 Hudson Street, New York, New York 10014, USA
Penguin Group (Canada), 90 Eglinton Avenue East, Suite 700, Toronto, Ontario M4P 2Y3, Canada
(a division of Pearson Penguin Canada Inc.)
Penguin Books Ltd., 80 Strand, London WC2R 0RL, England
Penguin Group Ireland, 25 St. Stephen's Green, Dublin 2, Ireland (a division of Penguin Books Ltd.)
Penguin Group (Australia), 250 Camberwell Road, Camberwell, Victoria 3124, Australia
(a division of Pearson Australia Group Pty. Ltd.)
Penguin Books India Pvt. Ltd., 11 Community Centre, Panchsheel Park, New Delhi—110 017, India
Penguin Group (NZ), 67 Apollo Drive, Rosedale, Auckland 0632, New Zealand
(a division of Pearson New Zealand Ltd.)
Penguin Books (South Africa) (Pty.) Ltd., 24 Sturdee Avenue, Rosebank, Johannesburg 2196,
South Africa

Penguin Books Ltd., Registered Offices: 80 Strand, London WC2R 0RL, England

SPELLBOUND FALLS

A Jove Book / published by arrangement with the author

PUBLISHING HISTORY
Jove mass-market edition / March 2012

Cover design by George Long.
Cover handlettering by Ron Zinn.

For information, address: The Berkley Publishing Group,
a division of Penguin Group (USA) Inc.,
375 Hudson Street, New York, New York 10014.

ISBN: 978-0-515-15036-0

JOVE®
Jove Books are published by The Berkley Publishing Group,
a division of Penguin Group (USA) Inc.,
375 Hudson Street, New York, New York 10014.
JOVE® is a registered trademark of Penguin Group (USA) Inc.
The "J" design is a trademark of Penguin Group (USA) Inc.

PRINTED IN THE UNITED STATES OF AMERICA

10 9 8 7 6 5 4 3 2 1

To Nick Chapman.
I swear I don't know whether to be proud
of the scary-awesome man you've become, or very afraid.
So go on now, son; go move some mountains!

Chapter One

Realizing the guy was utterly serious, Olivia bolted from the truck before she burst out laughing. Pretending not to hear Mark calling to her, she ran into the trading post—only to dart down the side aisle when she spotted Ezra waiting on Missy Maher at the counter in the back of the store. Finally stopping when she reached the alcove crowded with fishing gear, Olivia pressed her hands to her cheeks. For crying out loud, Mark was what . . . twenty? Twenty-one? She couldn't remember what his application had said, but she'd swear he couldn't be a day over twenty-two.

Good Lord, did she look like a cougar? Or even worse, did she come across as some lonely widow so desperate for sex that she'd hop into bed with a . . . a man-child? She was thirty-three, dammit; not old enough to be the audacious twit's mother but certainly too old to be his summer entertainment.

Olivia sucked in a deep breath and slowly exhaled. Now what was she supposed to do? Not only was her new employee—the sole applicant who'd had *any* camp counselor experience—about as proficient with a paintbrush as a two-year-old, the guy thought dawn cracked at ten A.M.

But it had been during this afternoon's hair-raising ride to town that Olivia had decided she'd have to dig out her small pile of applications and begin searching for a new handyman/counselor/activities assistant. Not five minutes after telling Mark there wouldn't be a small army of young women working at Inglenook this summer, the horny toad had boldly stated that he found *her* really sexy, and asked if she'd be interested in sneaking over to the bunkhouse tonight after she put her daughter to bed.

What in hell was it with young people today that made them blurt out whatever they were thinking? Had good manners and discretion gone the way of the passenger pigeon? Was *nothing* taboo anymore?

Olivia gasped. Oh God, she sounded just like her mother-in-law!

"Olivia? Where'd you run off to?" Ezra called out, his voice moving toward her from the back of the store.

"Boss?" Mark called from the opposite direction.

"You can come out now, girl," Ezra said with a chuckle. "Missy's gone next door to plague everyone at the Drunken Moose."

"Hey, boss," Mark said as he came to a stop beside the alcove, his youthful face screwed into a frown. "You jumped out of the truck before I could ask if I should drive around to the side of the store."

No, she'd jumped out before she got sued for smacking an employee. "I'm sorry, I just assumed you would. Hi, Ezra. Is my water heater out back on the loading dock?"

"Well, it ain't hiding back here behind the ice fishing traps." Ezra took the trap she'd distractedly picked up and slid it on the peg as he shot her a conspirator's grin. "You're safe for the next couple of days. Missy told me her brother's gone back to Chicago to close the sale on his house."

"Damn," Olivia muttered. "If Simon sold his house, that means he really is moving to Spellbound Falls." What was it about her that caught the attention of twenty- and fifty-year-old lechers, yet not one man around here her age gave her a second glance? "I need to order a case of bobbers and another dozen fishing poles," she continued, stepping out of the alcove. "And you might as well add a pack of size eight fish hooks, two reels of ten-pound-test line, and several top-water lures."

Ezra headed toward the rear of the store. "Maybe you should order *twenty*-pound line, so you won't have to keep buying so many lures and hooks every year."

Olivia fell into step behind him, walking along the front of the counter as he shuffled behind it, aware of Mark following her—probably ogling her backside. "Why in hell doesn't someone make indestructible bobbers? I swear the parents break more of them than the kids do."

"It would probably be cheaper to buy cork ones," Ezra said, his eyebrows lifting at her tone as his gaze darted from her to Mark. He looked down and tapped a few keys on his ancient computer. "Cork bobbers might cost more up front, but at least they still float after being bounced off the rocks all day."

"I tried some a couple of years ago, remember, but the toddlers kept eating them. Mark, why don't you go see about loading that water heater."

"By myself?"

"It's on a hand truck, young fella," Ezra said, glancing over his glasses.

"Just make sure you tie it down tightly," Olivia added, remembering that the twit drove as recklessly as he asked for sex. "I don't want it landing in the ditch the first time we hit a yes ma'am."

Mark had started to turn away, but turned back. "When we hit a what?"

Ezra looked up from his computer again. "Where you from, young fella?"

"Georgia."

"You don't have large dips in the roads down there in Georgia that bangs you up against the roof when you hit them too fast, making you say 'yes ma'am' every time your backside lifts off the seat?"

"We have potholes. And the name's Mark, not *young*

fella. I'm twenty-three," he said, puffing out his chest as he shot Olivia a lecherous grin.

Which meant he was still ten years too young. She gave him a motherly smile. "Ezra calls anyone under seventy *young fella.* Go load the water tank so we can get back in time to meet Sophie at the turnoff. I just had my road graded, and I don't want the school bus driving all the way in to Inglenook if I can help it."

But when Ezra silently nodded toward the small white box hidden behind a display of key chains, Olivia glanced at her watch and decided she had plenty of time. "Oh, Mark," she called out as the boy headed through the back door. "After you've loaded the tank, could you please go to the post office and pick up the mail?" She shot him a brilliant smile. "If you gave Inglenook's address like I suggested, maybe there's a letter for you from your *girlfriend.*"

That seemed to brighten his mood as he disappeared out back, her not-so-subtle reminder that he was already spoken for apparently going right over his head.

Ezra slid the box onto the counter between them. "I ran next door to the Drunken Moose right after you called. Vanetta was just pulling this batch out of the oven, so they should still be warm."

Olivia immediately opened the box. "Ohmigod, I love it when you spoil me. And your timing's perfect; I really, really need this right now," she said, grabbing one of the huge, warm, and gooey cinnamon buns. She took a bite and closed her eyes as she pressed the thick icing against the roof of her mouth, then chewed slowly before finally swallowing so she could take another bite. But she stopped with the bun halfway to her mouth when she saw Ezra gaping at her. "Don't you look at me like that, you old poop. These buns are better than taking up drinking."

"What's the matter? Did Eileen make you sit through another reading of her dissertation last night?"

"I don't know why that woman asks my opinion if she doesn't want my input on anything." Olivia licked icing off her finger, then shot him a grin. "At least she's given up discussing her latest theory on the role of grandparents with me, since I suggested she interview an expert living right here in Spellbound Falls, seeing how Bunkie Watts has sixteen and a half grandbabies." She sighed, nodding toward the back room. "No, Mark's the one making me want to take up drinking. That boy sleeps more hours than he's awake, and he eats like there's no tomorrow." She leaned closer and lowered her voice. "And I swear the inside of his truck smells like pot. I'm going to have to replace him before Inglenook starts up again, as I can't risk having a pothead around my campers." She straightened with a glare. "I think they should make it legal for an employer to ask right on the application if someone is a recreational drug user."

Ezra choked on his bite of bun and took a quick sip of coffee. "Doreen gave me hell when I told her she had to fill out a W-2 form in order to work here two days a week. She said her social security number wasn't any of my business, even after I spent half an hour explaining that's precisely *why* she was given the number. Speaking of Sophie," Ezra said, wiping his fingers on his pants, "you do know that ducking down aisles and running out the back door of the Drunken Moose ain't gonna serve you in the long run, don't you? One of these days Simon Maher's gonna wise up and be sitting in your van the next time you jump in it. Need I remind you that postponing the inevitable won't make it any easier?"

Olivia swallowed with a frown, wondering how they'd gone from employees to Sophie to Simon. "And you know the minute I tell her precious brother to get lost, Missy Maher will turn my life into a living hell again. She wasn't all that keen when Simon became interested in me in the first place, but once she got hold of the notion that Inglenook and I might be a package deal, she all but started throwing him at me. If I flat-out tell Simon to go jump in the lake, she'll start up her campaign to shut us down again."

Ezra waved that away. "You already fixed every infraction the inspectors found. The state can't close down a complying business just because some neighbor doesn't like the sounds of a camp full of families having fun."

"They can close down a business that causes the game wardens to initiate a massive search when I lose one of those families."

"That was several years ago, Olivia, and every damn last family member said it was the best three days they'd ever spent together. Hell, the Minks have been coming to one of your weeklong sessions every year since." Ezra leaned on the counter toward her again, his cloudy blue eyes filled with concern. "You got to set Simon straight the moment he gets back from Chicago; if not for yourself, then for Sophie. What are you teaching that girl about grown-up relations when her mama drags her out the back door of the Drunken Moose right in the middle of breakfast to avoid talking to a man? Hell, last Saturday when I tried to get her to come see the new kites I got in, Sophie told me she couldn't because she was keeping a lookout for Simon."

Olivia blew out a sigh. "I am such a phony. How do I have the nerve to run a camp that teaches parents how to connect with their kids when I stoop to bribing my own kid into spying for me?"

Ezra reached out and patted her hand. "Now Olivia, everyone knows it ain't easy being a single parent. Since way before Keith died you've been raising Sophie all by yourself and looking out for Eileen and John like a daughter. Hell, you've been single-handedly running Inglenook for them for years." He shook his head. "Why Keith couldn't be content to stay here and run it himself is beyond anyone's guess. Ain't no one in town gonna talk bad about our only war hero, but the man had no business getting himself killed in some desert half a world away."

"Keith loved being a soldier," Olivia defended, though only halfheartedly.

Ezra answered with a snort. "So, you asked Eileen about buying Inglenook yet? She should have her doctorate in what . . . another couple of months?"

"I can't just flat-out ask her; she'll fall over laughing. And besides, you know I'm hoping to get another six months of savings before I broach the subject." She touched his hand when he tried to interrupt. "I'm not taking any money from you. I feel guilty enough as it is that Doris left me her savings. That money should have gone to family."

"You're the closest thing to family Doris and I got," he said thickly, turning his hand to grasp hers. "And more than anything in this world, she wanted to help you realize your dream. Let me give you the rest of what you need for the down payment so you can buy Inglenook *now*, before Eileen gets it in her head she can sell to developers for more than you can afford."

"No one's going to pay big bucks for land way up here in the mountains; everyone's too busy developing the coast. As it is, our campers keep complaining about how far we are from the nearest large airport." She shook her head. "I need to wait until Eileen finds a position at a college, so she'll be desperate to sell Inglenook. That's the only way I'll get it for a reasonable price."

"I know. I know," he said, patting her hand again. "Everyone thinks Eileen's been taking advantage of you all these years, and I agree it's better to let them keep thinking you're in awe of your mother-in-law until you make your move. But I don't like that people believe you're a wimp for ducking down aisles to avoid them."

Olivia broke into a smile. "And just when have I cared what people think of me?"

"But they complain you're aloof."

"Good. That way they don't ask me to be on every committee in town. You know it took me all of Sophie's kindergarten year to get them to stop asking me to bake cookies every other week for some school function." She snorted. "When burning everything didn't deter them, I had to resort to adding too much salt."

"But that's just it, Olivia. You haven't let anyone see the real you since you were eight, when you finally decided your daddy wasn't coming back," he said gruffly, squeezing her hand. "You only let Doris and me and Sophie inside your world. Don't you think it's past time you showed everyone the real you?"

"I promise the real Olivia will make her appearance the day she hangs a new sign at the end of the road and opens up her own camp for families. Because I intend to climb Whisper Mountain and shout to the world that Olivia Naglemeyer Baldwin is *home*," she said, trying to lighten the mood. "I promised myself when Sophie was born that she would have *one* home growing up, and that she'd always know right where to find me." Olivia tapped the counter. "So it looks as if Spellbound Falls is where I'm making my stand. And come hell or high water, and God save anyone who gets in my way, by this time next year Inglenook will be mine."

"Now that sounds more like the girl I know and love," Ezra growled, stuffing the last of his bun in his mouth.

Olivia checked her watch, stepped behind the counter, and gave him a hug. "I have to get going if I want to catch Sophie's bus. Thanks for the treat. You just saved me from raiding the pantry for a bottle of wine," she said, stepping back into the aisle—only to nearly run into Peg Thompson. "Oh, hi, Peg." She looked down and ruffled the hair of the boy clinging to his mother. "Hello, Pete. Or are you Repeat?"

"I'm Jacob," the boy said as he pointed at his twin running toward them. "He's Peter." He then turned his pointing finger up at her. "You got white stuff on your chin."

"That wouldn't happen to be icing off one of Vanetta's buns, would it?" Peg drawled as she pushed Jacob's finger down. "Because I swear I smell cinnamon."

Olivia rubbed her chin with her sleeve. "Guilty," she laughed.

"Well, looky here," Ezra said, making Olivia turn to see him pull another box from under the counter. "I must have ESP, and knew you young fellas were coming in this afternoon. Why else would I have these gooey cinnamon buns smelling up my store?"

Peter and Jacob were at the counter before he'd finished speaking, their young eyes going wide when Ezra opened the box and held it down to them.

"Oh, for pete's sake, Ezra," Peg moaned. "You're spoiling them."

"That's right," he chuckled. "For Pete and Jacob's sakes. Go on, boys, take your pick." He held the box toward Peg. "You too, young lady."

"I'll be back for mine in a minute," Peg said, leading Olivia down the aisle. "Pete, Repeat, you stand right there and eat them. And don't touch anything."

"What's up?" Olivia asked as soon as they were out of earshot.

Peg let her go, her eyes turning troubled as she glanced at the counter, then back at Olivia. "I'm worried about Ezra," she whispered. "He's starting to . . . I'm afraid he's . . ." She shifted so she was facing away from the counter. "Dammit, I think he's getting senile. At first I blamed his ancient computer for messing up my bill every month, but now I'm worried it's *him.* He's made a few mistakes in the past, but lately it's been getting pretty bad. I called this morning just like I do every month when I get my social security checks for the children, figuring I owed Ezra about two hundred dollars, but he claims I only owe him ninety-five. I told him that couldn't possibly be—what in hell are you smiling at?" she growled.

"He's not getting senile, but he does seem to be getting more blatant," Olivia said with a sigh. "Ezra sort of . . . fudges the accounts of several people in town who buy on credit from him."

"He *what*?"

"Heck, he even messes with mine when he thinks I'm not paying attention." Olivia leaned closer. "He and Doris had been doing it for years, only Doris always made sure it wasn't obvious. Misplacing a few slips is their way of giving back to the community."

"But he's losing money!" Peg shot a glance toward the counter, then pulled Olivia behind a rack of potato chips. "Are you telling me he's undercharging me on *purpose*? That old goat," she muttered when Olivia merely nodded. Peg blew out a harsh breath, shaking her head. "I'll be damned if I'm going to be responsible for his going bankrupt. I'm writing him a check for two hundred dollars today, and from now on I'm keeping every slip to prove what I owe him."

Olivia grabbed her friend's sleeve when she started to turn away. "You can't, Peg. It'll devastate him if you do. Doris originally came up with the idea about a year after they bought the store, and Ezra *needs* to keep doing it in her memory. He feels so good about helping his neighbors, that if you call him out on it or tell anyone, he'll . . ." She squeezed Peg's arm. "He's been doing it for over ten years and hasn't gone bankrupt yet. Please, can't you just keep playing along?"

"But I can pay my own way. Let him help people who really need it." Peg shook her head, her shoulders slumping. "I can't possibly keep shopping here now, knowing he's not charging me for half the stuff I buy. I wouldn't be able to live with myself."

"Can you live with yourself knowing you'd break his heart? His customers are all he's got left." Olivia waved toward the back. "The minute he found out you were coming in this morning, he ran next door for cinnamon buns for you and the twins. And if I'm not mistaken, there are a couple of extra buns in that box for you to take home to Charlotte and Isabel. It's not charity, Peg; it's simple, old-fashioned, neighborly love." She shot her a grin. "And for Ezra it's a sneaky little joke he's been playing on everyone for years."

"Does he really do it to you, too?"

Olivia nodded. "And every so often I even get all huffy and complain that he's *over*charging me."

"You do? But you're the least confrontational person I know! For pete's sake, I caught you hiding in my minivan two weeks ago. You scared the living daylights out of me when I opened the door."

"I was hiding from Missy's brother, and thank you for pulling your punch at the last minute."

Peg gave a visible shudder. "Simon's gotta be old enough to be your father." She arched a brow. "You do know hiding isn't going to make him go away, don't you?"

Olivia sighed. "I know. But it's hard to flat-out reject a

guy to his face, especially when a supposedly lonely widow is doing the rejecting. I'm hoping Simon will come to his senses and decide I'm not worth the trouble." She touched Peg's sleeve again. "So you'll keep shopping here, and let Ezra keep up his pretense?"

"But where does he get the money to keep the store going?"

"I have no idea," Olivia said with a shake of her head. "Ezra and Doris had a modest lifestyle, but they always appeared to be financially comfortable." She shrugged. "They must have invested wisely."

Peg touched Olivia's sleeve. "I miss Doris, too."

Olivia nodded her thanks. "That's why it's important we continue letting Ezra think he's pulling one over on us. He *needs* to still feel needed. And if you feel compelled to do something nice for him in return, then haggle over his prices."

Peg just gaped at her, then suddenly burst out laughing, only to slap a hand over her mouth as she leaned around the potato chips to glance down the aisle. She looked at Olivia and shook her head with a lingering chuckle. "I don't know which is more outrageous: that Ezra's giving half his store away or that you're asking me to complain about it."

"Hey, everyone needs a good rousing argument once in a while, don't you think? Consider it your contribution to keeping his big old soft heart revved up."

"Mom! Peter wiped his hands on my shirt and now I'm all sticky!"

Peg closed her eyes on a sigh. "If I wasn't afraid his heart would *explode*, I'd leave Pete and Repeat with Ezra for the day." She headed down the aisle. "Peter Thompson, what did I tell you about minding your manners in here?"

Olivia stayed hiding behind the potato chips, breaking into a smile when she heard Jacob snicker in delight. Wouldn't she love to have a little son to plague Sophie. But God help her, not twins! Lord, she didn't know how Peg survived raising her four children alone since her husband had died three years ago.

"Ezra," she heard Peg drawl. "You gonna make me drive

all the way down to Turtleback to redeem my coupons, or you gonna get serious about being a *real* store?"

Olivia covered her mouth to stifle a laugh when Ezra gave a loud harrumph. "I'll have you know that Grant's Grocery prints those flyers to reel in unsuspecting chumps like you with ridiculously low prices on one or two items, only to jack up the price of everything else they sell by ten percent. And it'll cost you more for gas than you'd save to drive the sixty-mile round trip."

"But today they're offering double coupons."

Olivia leaned around the rack of chips to see Ezra glaring at Peg as he suddenly thrust out his hand. "Oh, give me those blasted coupons. But if you tell anyone I honored them, I swear that'll be the last cinnamon bun you get from me."

Peg clutched the coupons to her chest. "Double?" she asked.

"Jumped-up old monkey poop," he growled. "Are you trying to bankrupt me?"

Olivia crossed her fingers when she saw Peg hesitate, and gave a relieved sigh when her friend finally handed Ezra the coupons.

"Oh, okay," Peg said, sounding defeated. "I guess face value is worth saving me the drive to Turtleback. Um . . . can I have my bun now?"

"You can," Ezra muttered as he shuffled over to his computer. "But I'm adding it to your bill. Not the children's buns; just yours."

Olivia stepped into the aisle and shot Peg a wink when the woman gave her an uncertain look, and then headed outside to find her way-too-forward employee.

Or rather, her about-to-be-fired employee.

She stood at the edge of the road looking for Mark's truck and sighed. Dammit, she couldn't fire Mark until she found someone to replace him. Five families, totaling twenty-four people in all, would be arriving at Inglenook in three weeks, and even half a worker was better than none.

She was cutting it close as it was, considering all the work still left to be done. Next year she'd have to think about stretching her downtime between the winter and summer sessions, because five weeks just wasn't long enough to give every cabin a spring cleaning, paint and make repairs, and spruce up the grounds. She still had to plumb the new water heater into cabin six, replank the docks if she hoped to put them in the lake as soon as the ice went out, get the stables ready for the twelve horses arriving in three weeks, and go through every last linen and towel to decide how many needed replacing.

What had made her think she could get away with hiring only one helper for this year's mud season makeover, when it was obvious she needed a small army—other than the fact that her operating budget was nearly blown for this year, that is. Hell, she could barely afford the new water heater, much less pay someone to put it in.

That was the only reason she'd let Eileen talk her into allowing Mr. Oceanus and his son to arrive three weeks early; the outrageously large check he'd offered to give him a jump start on the other campers meant she could finally make the repairs she'd been putting off. And other than having to feed them, how much of a bother could a lone man and his six-year-old son be, anyway, considering the organized chaos she dealt with when camp was in full session?

Olivia saw Mark sitting in his truck parked in front of the post office and headed diagonally across the road instead of crossing to the footbridge that spanned Spellbound Stream. She did take the time to look both ways for traffic, considering that the thunder of the falls made it hard to hear even a large truck rumbling through town. On the ride home she'd give Mark a gentle but firm *no thanks* to his salacious offer, she decided, and then fire the twit the moment she found a replacement.

As for Simon Maher, well, considering how quickly it had brought the Minks to their senses, maybe she'd invite Simon to go on a pleasant spring hike when he got back from Chicago and accidentally lose him, too.

Chapter Two

Apparently Mark Briar wasn't used to anyone telling him no, be it the girlfriend who'd just sent him a Dear John letter or some lonely widow he was magnanimously offering sexual favors to. Hearing the aggressive edge creeping into his voice, Olivia wondered what terrible sin she'd committed to be finding herself stuck in the front seat of a tired little pickup with the employee from hell. Not only did Mark keep trying to point out what she'd be missing if she didn't come to the bunkhouse tonight, it appeared that her repeatedly gentle but firm refusals were making him angry.

Well, and the Dear John letter he'd crumpled into a ball and thrown at her feet after reading the more interesting parts to her. Added to that, his driving had gone from reckless to downright scary. What had she been thinking when she'd asked if they could use his pickup to go after the heater? If she'd taken ten minutes to pull the rear seat out of her van, she'd be in only half the mess she was in now; she might still be dealing with an angry young man, but at least the pine trees wouldn't be speeding by in a blur.

Olivia decided that when they met the school bus, she and Sophie were walking the last three miles to Inglenook.

"Look, Mark," she said calmly, even as she checked the buckle on her seat belt, "it's not that I'm not flattered by your offer, but I have a very firm rule about fraternizing with my employees."

"Employ*ee*. You have one. So it's not like anyone can complain the boss is playing favorites or anything."

"When camp's in session I have fifteen people on the payroll: seven who live at Inglenook—you, the cook, and several counselors—and eight locals who show up every day *at the crack of dawn*," she said, getting a bit angry herself.

His eyes narrowed menacingly. "What about the campers? You got any rules about fraternizing with them?" He snorted. "Or is that how you fill up your single-father sessions year after year?"

Olivia counted to ten to keep from smacking the belligerent snot, wanting worse than anything to get out of this damn truck. "Ohmigod!" she shouted, pointing out the windshield. "Quick, pull off the road!"

Mark hit the brakes in surprise, then veered into a small gravel pit before bringing the truck to a sliding stop and shutting off the engine. "What did you see?" he asked, looking around.

Olivia immediately undid her seat belt and got out. "A moose just crossed the road in front of us," she said, pointing toward the trees when he also got out. "And where there's one, there's usually more. Hitting an animal that size would total your truck."

"I didn't see anything." His complexion darkened, his anger returning as suddenly as it had left. "You just made that up," he said, storming around the front of the truck. "What in hell is it with you women, anyway? You think you can just dump me like yesterday's trash to go after some rich guy just because he's got a *career* and drives a Porsche?"

"Hey, wait a minute." Olivia started walking backward. "I'm not your girlfriend; I'm your *boss*."

"Not anymore, you're not, because I quit."

Well, that took care of that little problem. Now she just had to deal with being in the middle of nowhere with this idiot. Growing somewhat alarmed when he continued advancing, Olivia weighed her chances of making a run for it over convincing him she was considering coming to the bunkhouse tonight.

"Wait," she said, holding up her hand to stop him. "I . . . um, you have to give me time to consider your offer, Mark. I mean, I'm not opposed to getting together with you," she said, matching him step for step when he didn't stop. "It's just that you caught me off guard earlier."

He finally stopped and looked around the small gravel pit, then back at her, his eyes growing suspicious again. "So what say we get a little practice in right now, to help you decide?"

Was he for real?

Okay, maybe running would be wiser. Olivia bolted for the woods, figuring Mark would probably beat her in an open footrace down the road. Besides, maybe she could find a stick and beat some sense into the idiot.

Only he caught her before she made it ten feet. She shouted in surprise when he grabbed her shoulder and spun her around, and then yelped in pain when she stumbled to her knees and he landed on top of her.

For the love of God, this couldn't be happening. He was just a kid!

But his grip was as strong as a man's. Olivia tried shoving him away, but he stuck to her like glue; his fingers biting into her arms as he rolled her over to face him. The air left her lungs in a painful whoosh when he landed on top of her again, and she cried out when his mouth slammed against hers.

Okay, it was time to panic; they were in the middle of nowhere, she couldn't seem to get control of the situation, and the idiot was flat-out attacking her! Olivia kicked at his legs and squirmed to push him off as she fought to breathe. Trying to jerk her hands free only ended up wrenching her wrist in his unbreakable grip, but she did manage to twist away from his punishing mouth.

"Mark! Stop this!" she cried. "You need to stop!"

"What in hell kind of camp doesn't have girls?"

Olivia stopped struggling. Talking was good. If she could keep him talking, then maybe he'd calm down. "Th-there will be girls your age in town once college lets out," she said, panting raggedly as his weight crushed her into the gravel.

"That's more than two months away!"

Olivia shouted in outrage as she turned away from his descending mouth and put all her strength into bucking him off even as she drove her fist into his ribs. He reared up, his own shout ending on a strangled yelp as his weight suddenly lifted off her. Olivia rolled away, then stumbled to her feet, scrambling around Mark's truck—only to run straight into another vehicle.

She stumbled back to her feet just as she heard Mark shout again and started running toward him when she saw a stranger drive his fist into Mark's stomach. The boy hadn't even doubled over when the man's fist slammed into his jaw, tossing him into the air to land on the ground on his back, out cold.

"No!" Olivia cried, grabbing the stranger's arm to stop him from going after Mark again. "Don't hurt him any-more!"

The man shrugged her off and turned toward her, the dangerous look in his sharp green eyes making her take a step back. "Forgive me," he said gutturally. "I was under the impression the bastard was attacking you." He gestured toward Mark even as he gave a slight bow. "I will leave you to your little game, then," he said, turning away and striding to his truck.

Olivia ran after him. "No, don't leave! He *was* attacking me."

He stopped so suddenly she bumped into him and would have fallen if he hadn't grabbed her shoulders. And that's when Olivia's knees buckled, the magnitude of what had nearly happened turning her into a quivering blob of jelly.

Her rescuer swept her off her feet before she reached the ground. He carried her to a small mound of dirt at the entrance to the gravel pit and set her down, then shrugged out of his jacket and settled it over her trembling shoulders. But when he crouched down in front of her and started to reach toward her throbbing cheek, Olivia buried her face in her hands and burst into sobs.

"It's okay. You're safe now."

"I can't believe he a-attacked me. He . . . he's just a kid." She straightened to pull his jacket tightly around her as she took gulping breaths. "Oh God, I can't breathe!"

"You're safe now, madam." He cupped her jaw in his broad hand, his penetrating gaze inspecting her face before coming to rest on her eyes. "You have my word: The bastard won't ever hurt you again."

Olivia leaned away from his touch and glanced toward Mark, trying to slow her breathing in an attempt to calm her racing heart. But finding that the two vehicles were blocking her view, she looked back at her rescuer. "He's only a dumb kid, but I couldn't stop him. H-he just exploded. I tried to be gentle but firm, but I . . . he wouldn't take no for an answer."

She swiped at a tear running down her cheek. "I never should have hired him. If I'd listened to my gut and sent him packing the day he arrived, this wouldn't have happened." She wiped her eyes again, hoping a good dose of outrage would stop her from feeling like she'd just spent ten minutes in the spin cycle of a washing machine. "But not one other applicant looked as promising. Except that girl in Wyoming. She didn't have any counselor experience, but I bet she wouldn't have insisted I have sex with her—unless she's gay." Olivia covered her gasp with her hand. "Ohmigod, I can't shut up!"

"Henry, come here," her rescuer called over his shoulder.

The rear passenger door of the pearl-white SUV opened and a young boy got out. Olivia immediately tried to stand up, not wanting the child to see her like this, but the gentleman set his large hand on her shoulder. "Come here, son. This lady has just had a fright, Henry, and she needs comforting," he said, gesturing at Olivia. "Sit here and hold Miss . . . what's your name?" he asked, giving her a gentle smile.

She didn't know if it was his smile that did it, or the fact that she needed to pull herself together for the sake of the child, but Olivia took a shuddering breath and released her death grip on his jacket. "My name's Olivia," she told the boy—only to gasp. "You're Henry! And Mr. Oceanus," she cried, looking at the man. "You're arriving today!" She hid her face in her hands again, utterly humiliated. "Ohmigod, this is terrible. You shouldn't see me like this."

But when a small arm settled over her shoulders—the young hand at the end of that arm gently patting her—Olivia quietly started sobbing again.

That is, until she realized Mr. Oceanus was no longer crouched in front of her.

Olivia shot out from under Henry's comforting arm. "No, you can't hurt him!" she shouted, rounding the vehicles in time to see Mr. Oceanus hauling Mark to his feet.

"He's just a dumb kid."

"Go sit in my truck, Olivia. I merely intend to have a little discussion with him."

"Not in front of your son, you're not," she said, grabbing his arm. "Is this the sort of man you want Henry to see you as?"

Still holding Mark by the scruff of his neck, Maximilian Oceanus turned his lethal green eyes on her. "If you mean do I want him to see me as the sort of man who won't let a bastard get away with brutalizing a woman, then yes."

"And just what are you teaching him by beating up a defenseless kid?"

"I would hope I'm teaching the boy that he has a duty to rescue a woman who's being attacked."

"But you did that already," she said, keeping her voice low so Henry wouldn't hear them. Good Lord, Trace Huntsman hadn't been kidding when he'd told Olivia that his friend didn't have a clue how to deal with his newly discovered son. "Henry saw you rescuing me, but it's equally important that he also sees you acting in a civilized manner toward my assailant."

He arched a brow. "Would you prefer I let Henry watch *you* make this bastard wish he'd never been born?"

"I'm not going to beat up Mark!" Only Olivia wondered if that wasn't amusement making his eyes so vividly green now. "Look, Mr. Oceanus, this—"

"I prefer you call me *Mac*. And if by acting civilized in front of my son you are suggesting I do nothing, then I suggest you and Henry go for a little walk. You have my word: I will wait until you're out of sight to have my little discussion."

That had to be amusement, because he couldn't possibly be serious.

Mark finally stirred, letting out a dazed groan as he started to struggle against the iron fist holding him upright by the throat. And even though Olivia knew firsthand how strong Mark was, her rescuer didn't even acknowledge the boy's struggles other than to send Mark into a fit of choking coughs by tightening his fingers.

"Please let him go, Mac," she pleaded, her shoulders slumping as she pulled his jacket tightly around her. "I—I just want to meet my daughter's bus at the turnoff and go home before I fall down."

The sudden concern in his eyes disappeared the moment he looked back at Mark. "If I catch you within fifty miles of Spellbound Falls after sunset today, I will kill you. Understand?" he said ever so softly. He twisted the boy to face her. "But first you will apologize."

His eyes nearly popping out of his beet-red face, Mark made a strangled sound and tried to nod. "I . . . I'm sorry," he choked out.

Mac released him so suddenly that Mark fell into a listless heap on the ground, and Olivia didn't even have time to gasp before her rescuer lifted her into his arms.

"Henry, open the front door of our truck," he said, striding to the SUV and setting her inside. He reached in his pants pocket and pulled out a handkerchief. "Your lip is bleeding," he said, handing it to her. "Where is the turnoff you spoke of? You said you wish to meet your daughter."

She took the handkerchief from him and shakily dabbed at her mouth. "It . . . it's another couple of miles up the road."

He nodded and closed the door, then opened the door behind her. "Get in and buckle up, son," he said, closing the door once Henry climbed in.

But instead of walking around to the driver's side, he strode back around Mark's truck. Olivia started to go after him, but the door wouldn't open even after she pushed all the buttons on the handle. She was just about to start pounding on the buttons when a small, surprisingly firm hand clasped her shoulder.

"Father will be civilized," Henry said, giving her a nod when she turned to him. "I believe he's just making sure the bastard understood his instructions."

"You *heard* what we were saying?"

"I have very good hearing." He patted her shoulder. "You can get over your fright now, Olivia; Father won't let that bastard hurt you again."

She twisted around in her seat. "Henry, you can't keep calling him a bastard; it's a very bad word."

His eyes—as deeply green as those of the man who'd sired him—hardened in an almost mirror image of his father's. "Is it not appropriate to use a bad word when referring to a bad person?"

Good Lord, he even talked like his father!

But Trace Huntsman, a military buddy of Olivia's late husband who lived several hours away down on the coast, had told her that Henry had come to live with Mac only a few months ago, after the child's mother had died. And that up until then the two had never met, as Mac hadn't even known Henry existed.

"How come you call him *Father* instead of *Dad*?" Olivia asked.

Henry's tiny brows knitted into a frown. "Because that's

what he is. He calls me *son* and I call him *Father*." His frown deepened even as his face reddened. "And please forgive me, for I believe I'm supposed to call you *madam*, not Olivia. My mama would be quite upset with me if she knew I was calling a lady by her Christian name."

Olivia smiled warmly. "And what's your mama's name?"

"Cordelia. But when Father speaks of her, he calls her *Delia*. My last name used to be Penhope, but now it's Oceanus." He went back to frowning again. "Only Father is also thinking of changing my first name. I suggested we might change it to Jack or even Jake, only he said those names aren't noble enough."

"But what's wrong with *Henry*?"

The boy shrugged. "Father says *Henry* is too English."

"It's too—" Olivia spun toward the sound of a truck door slamming and saw Mark push down the locks before blindly fumbling with the ignition as he watched Mac through the windshield—who was standing a few paces away, his arms folded over his chest, staring back at him. The pickup started and the tires spun on the loose gravel as Mark sped onto the road without even checking for oncoming traffic.

"See, I told you Father would be civilized," Henry said, giving her shoulder one last pat before he hopped in his seat and fastened his seat belt. "He didn't kill the bastard even if he did deserve to die."

Despite meeting Mac and Henry less than thirty minutes ago, Olivia had a feeling they were going to be a tad more of a bother than merely setting two more places at the table. For as precocious and direct as Henry was, his father was even scarier. Maximilian Oceanus was an undeniably large, imposing figure; the sort of man who not only would stand out in a crowd but likely command it. He had to be at least six feet four inches tall, his shoulders filled a good deal of the front seat of his full-sized SUV, and he had picked her up—twice—as effortlessly as if he'd been handling a child. But it was when he looked directly at her with those intense green eyes of his that Olivia felt her world tilt off center. Kind of like when a person stood in a receding wave on a flat sandy beach and had the illusion of being sucked out to sea even while standing perfectly still.

She never should have let Eileen talk her into breaking her rule of no private parenting sessions. She should have at least recognized what she was getting herself into when Mac had summarily dismissed her repeatedly gentle but firm refusals to let him come to Inglenook three weeks early—much the same way Mark had dismissed them this afternoon. Only whereas Mark had attacked her, Mac had gotten his way using good old-fashioned bribery. Did *anyone* listen to her? Honest to God, she needed to throw *gentle* out the window and put a lot more emphasis on *firm*—preferably while she was holding a baseball bat.

Which meant she should probably start working out and take up running again, considering how easily Mark had overpowered her, and sign up for one of Inglenook's meditation classes, considering her emotional breakdown afterward. She was still shaking uncontrollably and fighting back tears, which was why she'd jumped out of the truck the moment they reached the turnoff, before she humiliated herself again.

Only Henry had shot out of the truck right behind her. At first it was obvious he'd felt duty bound to continue comforting her, but once Olivia had assured him she was feeling much better, the boy had taken off to explore the nearby woods instead.

That is, after he'd dutifully run back and asked his father's permission.

Mac had also gotten out of the truck but had merely leaned against the front fender, his feet crossed at the ankles and his arms folded on his chest, apparently content to let his son deal with the welling tears he'd seen in her eyes. She was still wearing his leather jacket, and should probably give it back since he was standing in the cool March breeze in only his shirt, but the warm security of its weight surrounding her simply felt too wonderful to relinquish.

She buried her hands in its roomy pockets with a heavy sigh. Now what was she supposed to do? Without Mark, there was no way she could get Inglenook fully functional in three weeks. And even though her father-in-law would insist on helping, Olivia would have to insist—likely while holding that baseball bat—that she wasn't letting John put his recently replaced knee at risk. Her mother-in-law wouldn't be much help, either, as Eileen already had a full plate, what with trying to finish her dissertation while developing several new programs for this summer's sessions, finding and then training a couple of interns to implement those programs, and working with their cook on a new all-organic menu for this year.

Dammit, what in hell did she know about plumbing in a water heater?

Assuming the heater wasn't sitting in the ditch between here and home, or still in the back of Mark's truck on its way out of town before sunset. Olivia slowly started walking back toward the main road but picked up her pace when she realized she couldn't see Henry anywhere. "Henry?" she called out, scanning the woods on both sides of the road. "Henry, where did you go?"

"He's fine, Olivia," Mac said, straightening away from the fender. "He climbed down to the brook and is throwing rocks."

"There are some deep pools in that brook," she said, trying to pierce the dense woods. "And there's still snow in places. He could slip and fall in, or wander off and get lost. Little boys have a tendency to follow anything that catches their interest without realizing how far they're going."

"He may get wet, but he won't drown," Mac said. He pointed downstream of the bridge that sat a hundred yards up from the entrance of the turnoff. "And I will call him back if he wanders too far. Is it not my son's job to explore the world around him, and my job merely to keep him safe while he does?" He frowned. "At least that's what I've surmised from the books I've been reading."

Olivia couldn't help but smile. "You've been reading books on parenting?"

Instead of returning her smile, his frown deepened. "At least a dozen—only I've discovered a good many of them contradict each other, and one or two had some rather disturbing notions about discipline."

"Parenting is more of a hands-on, trial-by-fire sort of thing, Mr. Oceanus. And though several people have tried, no one's been able to write a definitive book on child rearing because humans are not one size fits all."

Good Lord; there she went sounding like Eileen again.

He finally found a smile. "So I have your permission to ignore everything those books said, Mrs. Baldwin?"

Oh yeah, his eyes definitely turned a deep vivid green when he was amused. "Actually, you have my permission to throw them away. And please, call me Olivia."

Up went one of his brows. "Forgive me; you led me to believe we were no longer on a first-name basis."

"My mistake . . . Mac." She arched a brow right back at him. "Do you know where your son is right now?"

"Just downstream, crossing the brook on a fallen log."

Olivia turned, trying to locate Henry. "Where? I don't see him."

"Then I guess it's a good thing I have very good eyesight as well as exceptional hearing. He's just reached the end of his courage and is heading back toward us."

"Speaking of good hearing, apparently your son has inherited yours. You're going to have to watch what you say around him, Mac. He kept calling Mark a bastard."

"Is that not the appropriate term?"

"Not for a six-year-old boy, it's not." When she saw the sparkle leave his eyes, Olivia wondered if she'd ever learn to read this man. "I don't think you understand what Henry's doing. When Trace first called me, he said that in the course of only a few months your son's mother died and he came to live with you, even though the two of you had never met. Is that correct?"

Mac silently nodded.

"Well, coming to live with a complete stranger after suffering such a loss has been far more traumatic for Henry than for you," she said softly. "And from what I've seen in the last half hour, your son is trying very hard to be what he thinks you want him to be. Henry's like a sponge soaking you up: emulating your mannerisms, your language, and how you treat people." She smiled, gesturing at the road she'd been pacing. "Heck, he even walks like you."

"Excuse me?"

Still unable to read his expression, Olivia widened her smile. "You have a rather direct stride, Mac. You want to see what it looks like sometime, just watch Henry."

"Are you saying I should discourage him from emulating me?"

"No. That's a good thing. It means Henry is looking to you as a role model." She shoved her hands in the jacket pockets again. "You really should be talking to my mother-in-law about this; Eileen's the expert. I'm just trying to point out that when you call someone a bastard, even if he is one, Henry's going to call him one, too. And if you beat up that bastard, even if he deserves it, Henry's going to beat up any kid his young mind believes might deserve it. So I'm only suggesting that you be aware of what you say and do in front of him. All children are highly impressionable, but Henry's even more so, because not only is he trying to figure out exactly where he fits in your life, he's desperately trying to find his place in your heart."

Mac unfolded his arms to shove his hands into his pants pockets and turned to face the woods. "I have no business being anyone's role model, especially not an impressionable young child's." He glanced over his shoulder at her, then back toward the brook. "I am the worst son a man could have, and there's a very good chance I will be an even worse father."

"You already are a wonderful father, Mac."

"How can you possibly say that?" he asked without looking at her. "You know nothing about me."

"I know how completely focused you are on Henry. And your insisting on coming to Inglenook early and then staying through the entire summer certainly proves how determined you are." She started walking toward the main road when she heard the school bus approaching, but stopped and turned with a smile. "Parenting's not about you versus Henry, Mac; it's about you and Henry versus the world."

For the first time in nearly three months—since a mysterious, overly intelligent, pint-sized person had come to live with him—Mac felt a glimmer of hope that he might actually survive this. He hadn't even made it to Inglenook yet and already he was seeing his son in a whole new light, the most surprising revelation being that Henry was soaking up everything he said and did like a sponge. Which, now that he thought about it, was frighteningly true; within days of their tumultuous meeting, Henry had started mimicking him to the point that Mac realized he could be looking in a thirty-year-old mirror from when *he* was six. But maybe the most insightful—and reassuring—thing Olivia had said was that he and Henry were on this journey together.

And that simple notion intrigued him as much as the woman who'd said it did.

Which could be a problem. He was here to learn how to become a good father, and he really didn't need the distraction of finding himself attracted to the teacher, no matter how beautiful she might be, or how warm and inviting her smile was, or how compassionate she was to a fault. Damnation, he'd didn't know which had angered him more: that she would have been raped if he hadn't happened along, or that she had in turn protected the bastard.

"It's a good thing we were driving by when the lady was being attacked, wasn't it, Father?" Henry said. "It's too bad she wouldn't allow you to kill the bastard, though, because I think he deserved it. Your letting him go might lead him to believe he can attack another woman and get away with it again."

Mac looked down to find his son standing beside him, the child's arms crossed over his chest and his feet planted to relax back on his hips as he watched Olivia walk across the main road in front of the stopped school bus. Sweet Prometheus, how could the boy possibly know his very thoughts?

Mac unfolded his arms and shoved his hands into his pockets. "Apparently *bastard* is an inappropriate term for a six-year-old to use, son. So maybe you should cease saying it until you're older."

"How much older?" Henry asked, also shoving his hands into his trouser pockets as he frowned up at Mac. "Can I say it when I'm ten? Or fifteen? Or do I have to wait until I'm your age?"

The boy always took everything so literally! And if Henry asked one question he asked a hundred; every day, morning until night, one right after another. The problem was, Mac didn't have a clue how to answer him half the time. How in hell was he supposed to know how old a person should be to use certain words? As far as he was concerned, if the term fit it was permissible at any age.

"Maybe that's a question you should ask Olivia."

"And do I call her *Olivia* when I ask, or *madam*?"

Mac dropped his head in defeat. "You might wish to ask her that, too. And Henry, don't mention to her daughter what happened today," he said when he saw Olivia walking back across the road holding the hand of a girl who appeared to be a year or two older than Henry. "Olivia might not want her to know for fear of worrying her. Now go put your things behind your seat to make a place for her to sit," he instructed, looking toward the main road as Henry ran to the truck.

The two women could have been twins but for their ages, the younger Baldwin having wavy brown hair that fell over her shoulders to frame an angelic face, an effortless smile, and an energized beauty that seemed to swirl around her like liquid sunshine—exactly like her mother.

Mac shuddered, thanking the gods he'd sired a son,

knowing damn well he would have worried himself into an early grave if he'd had a daughter.

The young girl even took on Olivia's same expression of concern when she spotted her mother's swollen lip and puffy eyes. She stopped to ask a question once they reached the dirt road and the school bus started off again, and Mac saw Olivia's smile widen as she made a gesture, obviously concocting some tale to explain her injury. Only it appeared the young girl wasn't sure if she believed her, judging by her frown. She then tugged on the unfamiliar jacket her mother was wearing over her own and asked another question.

Mac watched Olivia glance guiltily toward him as she started unzipping it. But her daughter stopped her by grabbing her hand and pushing up the sleeve, exposing a bruise on Olivia's wrist that had darkened enough for Mac to see from where he was standing.

"Sophie looks just like her mother," Henry said, having come back from his chore to once again stand with his hands in his trouser pockets.

"Sophie?" Mac repeated, unable to remember Olivia mentioning her daughter by name. Probably because he'd been too angry that he'd been forced to release the bastard who'd brutalized her.

"Didn't you hear Olivia tell me her daughter's name is Sophie, and that she's eight years old and in the second grade?" Henry glanced up at him then looked back at the women. "Even from here I can see they have the same colored eyes as each other, just like you and I do. Olivia's eyes remind me of cinnamon, which is my favorite spice, and I bet Sophie's are the same." He suddenly frowned. "I don't think I would have let the bast—that man drive away if I had caught him hurting Sophie." He suddenly grinned menacingly. "I would have at least sent him home carrying his stones in his pocket."

Mac broke out in a sweat. Henry wasn't merely walking and talking like him; his son even *thought* like he did!

How could he have forgotten that people became who they lived with?

Especially impressionable young children.

There were a lot of things he'd forgotten, apparently, about the inherent nature of man—which, considering his line of work, could be hazardous. But indulging in the more pleasurable aspects of human desires for the greater part of his adult life, Mac realized he had obviously dismissed as unimportant many of the more mundane laws governing the universe.

Nothing like having a son to put everything into perspective.

Yes, for as much as he hadn't wanted to travel even this short a distance from the ocean, bringing Henry to Inglenook just might prove to be one of the wisest decisions he'd made in several centuries.

Chapter Three

The moment they crested the final knoll that brought Inglenook's main lodge into view, Olivia spotted Eileen helping John climb up into the passenger seat of their van. And judging by the look of relief on their faces when they realized she was in the SUV, it was obvious they had been coming to search for her. Giving them a wave to show that she was fine, Olivia directed Mac to continue along the narrow lane winding its way through the high peninsula studded with old-growth pines.

She had originally wanted to put Mac in cabin three nearer the main lodge, so he and Henry wouldn't have so far to walk before the dining hall opened in three weeks, as well as because the smaller cabin was a good fit for them. But considering the size of the check he'd sent—most of which was already spent—Eileen had felt Mr. Oceanus deserved their most secluded cabin that sat right on the lake, since it was going to be his and Henry's home for the next six months.

Only instead of heading out onto the peninsula, Mac pulled into the driveway leading up to the lodge, stopped behind the van, and shut off the engine. Olivia got out with a sigh, wondering why she bothered to open her mouth if no one listened to her.

"What's going on?" Eileen asked, rushing over as John followed on his crutches. "Livy! What happened to your face?"

"In a minute," she said, turning to grab the opening back door. "Sophie, why don't you take Henry over to cabin ten and show him where he's going to be staying?"

Sophie started to hand Olivia her backpack, but suddenly passed it to Eileen instead. "Mom hurt her wrist when she fell, Gram, so could you take this for me?" She turned as soon as she was relieved of the burden. "Come on, Henry. The grown-ups will probably talk forever, so we can stop by and see Tinkerbelle on the way." She headed toward the barn. "And if you promise to be gentle, I'll let you hold her babies."

Olivia watched young Henry start after Sophie but wasn't surprised when the boy suddenly stopped and turned to Mac, who was just walking around the front of his truck. "Father?" Henry asked.

"It's okay, son; you can go with Sophie. Just remember to assure the mother that your intentions are good before you pick up her kittens."

"And you two stay away from both of the lakes," Olivia called after them as they took off at a run. "The ice is already rotting along the shoreline of Whisper."

"What happened?" John asked the moment they were out of earshot. "Mark came flying in here like a bat out of hell and drove straight to the bunkhouse. He threw his things in his truck, shoved the water heater out of the back of it, and was gone before I could get over there to see what was going on."

"What happened to your face?" Eileen whispered, eyeing Olivia's swollen lip. Her gaze darted to Mac, then back to her. "You look like you were . . . did Mark hit you?"

"He tried to rape her," Mac said before she could answer.

Her in-laws turned to him, Eileen with a gasp and John's eyes hardening in anger as they both looked back at her.

"Eileen, John, this is Mr. Oceanus," Olivia said with a tight smile. "He and Henry were driving by when . . . while Mark . . . when he . . ." She stuffed her hands in the pockets of the jacket, unable to admit—even to herself—that she'd nearly been raped.

"And you just let the bastard go?" John growled, his question directed at Mac.

"Not by choice," Mac said. "It would appear your daughter-in-law doesn't believe in holding a 'dumb kid' accountable for his actions."

Eileen sighed so hard Olivia felt her hair move as her mother-in-law wrapped an arm around her. "Oh, Livy, you've always been too damned softhearted for your own good. Good Lord, you're shaking like a leaf." Only because she'd started shivering again when she'd spotted Mark speeding toward them from Inglenook, his face filled with fear as he'd nearly driven into the ditch when they'd passed each other on the narrow dirt road.

"Let's go inside and get some hot tea into you." Eileen tightened her arm around Olivia. "Please come in, Mr. Oceanus, so we can properly thank you."

Her rescuer fell into step with John hobbling beside her on his crutches. "I prefer you call me Mac. And could you also tell Henry how he should address all of you, as I'm unsure what to advise him."

Eileen stopped. "Everyone here is on a first-name basis, Mac, especially the children. All of our staff wear name tags, and the first few days of each session we encourage our guests to wear the conference badges we give them." Her smile widened. "We should probably have some name tags made for you and Henry, since the two of you will practically be permanent fixtures here for the next six months."

Mac bowed ever so slightly, though Olivia noticed his smile didn't quite reach his eyes. Apparently Maximilian Oceanus wasn't all that keen on running around with his name plastered on his chest.

Still hugging Olivia, Eileen headed up the walkway to the lodge. "I told you the moment I met him there was something odd about Mark," she said quietly. "And the worst part is you *agreed* with me. But you kept him on against my better judgment anyway, claiming you couldn't very well have him drive all the way from Georgia just to fire him." She gave Olivia a squeeze. "I can't believe you allowed that bastard to drive away after what he did to you."

Olivia let herself be led up the stairs like a child, wondering how they'd gone from Mark to *her* being the idiot.

Sitting on the bathroom floor of cabin six, a pipe wrench in one hand and an opened book on home repairs in the other, Olivia scowled at the pipes coming out of the leaky water heater crammed in the closet between the shower and equally leaky toilet. She'd given herself one hour to change out the heater, a half hour to replace the wax ring on the toilet, twenty minutes to tidy everything up afterward, and ten minutes to deal with any surprises. Only that schedule was blown to hell now, seeing how it had taken her thirty minutes crawling around under the cabin to find the water shutoff that some diabolical plumber had placed *under* the floor.

She glanced down at the step-by-step pictures in the book, then at the heater, then at the pictures again—not one of which looked anything like the maze of pipes in front of her. She snapped the book closed and tossed it on the floor, crawled onto her hands and knees and squeezed into the closet, and fitted the pipe wrench over the corroded brass . . . thingy on the bottom side of the tank. Maybe she'd have better luck figuring out how to plumb in the new heater after she got rid of the old one.

Of course it couldn't be simple; she couldn't see what she was doing because her body was blocking the light, the brass thingy wouldn't budge once she finally got the wrench adjusted over it, and she was pretty sure she was stuck. Twisting like a contortionist didn't help, and neither did cursing. And just when she thought nothing else could go wrong, Olivia realized someone was standing behind her.

"I swear to God, John," she growled, trying but failing to get unstuck. "You step one toe in this bathroom and I'm throwing your crutches in the lake."

She heard a masculine chuckle. "Maybe if you had used that tone on your employee yesterday you wouldn't have needed my help."

Olivia shot backward out of the closet so fast she would have slammed into the opposite wall if a large hand hadn't gotten between it and her head at the last second.

"I'm sorry; I didn't mean to startle you," Mac said, crouching down on his heels to smile at her. "You weren't at breakfast."

Olivia shuddered, though she was unsure if it was from the thought of breakfast or that new gleam in Mac's eyes she couldn't quite read. "I skipped breakfast this morning. I don't particularly like tofu pretending to be sausage, and I hope if you don't either that you shared your opinion with Eileen." She smiled, trying to disguise how disconcerted he made her. "I'm afraid the real reason we let you and Henry come early is because Eileen needed a couple of guinea pigs for her new menu." She shook her head. "It's one thing to serve all-organic food, but I don't know why she feels it has to be low-fat, too. I've warned her that we're going to have a rebellion on our hands the first week we're back in session if she insists on serving that stuff."

Good Lord; there she went talking nonstop again! What was it about this man that turned her into a nervous ninny?

"Don't worry," he said, that gleam intensifying. "Henry voiced his opinion. Eileen told me she thought you were cleaning cabin eight, but when I finally *found* cabin eight it was empty." He arched a brow. "Is there a reason all your cabins are numbered out of order?"

He'd been looking for her? "They're numbered according to when they were built. And I'm sorry I forgot to return your jacket yesterday," she flat-out lied, figuring he'd been looking for her because he wanted it back sometime before summer.

But as pathetic as it seemed in the stark light of day, she

had in fact slept with his jacket spread over her blankets, unable to resist the feel of its substantial weight holding her all night—even as she'd fantasized it had been the man who owned it instead.

So much for not being a lonely widow.

She tried getting to her feet. "It's on a peg at home. I'll go get it for you."

He placed one large hand on her shoulder to stop her. "There's no hurry. That's not the reason I was looking for you." He sat down on the floor beside her and gestured at the water heater. "John and Eileen spent most of breakfast worrying that you don't have anyone to help you get Inglenook ready for the upcoming sessions."

Olivia looked down, saw that her jeans were filthy from crawling under the cabin, and brushed at the dirt. "I plan to go into town this afternoon to see if I can find someone local who might be willing to work with me for a few weeks." She sighed. "Although anyone who would have been available is already helping the sporting camps' owners get ready for the summer tourist season."

He picked up the book she'd tossed on the floor, looked at its title and then at the water heater, then over at her. "John mentioned that might be a problem for you, so I said I'd be willing to fill the vacancy." He grinned. "Eileen immediately hired me, and after offering to take Henry to town with her and Sophie, she told me to report to work."

Olivia could only gape at him. Eileen had *hired* him?

He actually reached over, placed his finger under her chin, and lifted her mouth closed. "Should I assume from your expression that you can't quite picture me doing an honest day's work, Olivia?" he asked quietly.

"Huh? No, of course not. I just figured that for you an honest day's work would be in a boardroom, not down on your hands and knees in mud," she said, gesturing at her pants as she dropped her gaze. "And we can't even come close to paying what you're used to." She forced herself to look at him again and even managed to smile, albeit sheepishly. "I already spent the check you sent us, so I can't exactly give some of it back to let you work for room and board."

If her smile had been sheepish, his was downright smug. "What if I said I'd be willing to work for extra parenting advice?"

"I believe I mentioned when you called two weeks ago that we'd be hard-pressed to give you and Henry much attention as it was." She shook her head. "I have no idea what Eileen was thinking when she insisted on letting you arrive early, considering she's scrambling to finish her dissertation before camp starts up again. And next week she's heading to a couple of universities to interview interns for this year's program. Then she wants to work with our cook when he arrives, to figure out what we're going to feed everyone so he can stock the kitchen. I'm sorry; I just don't see how she can find any extra time."

"But that's exactly why my offer makes sense. My working with you throughout the day will give me access to all those wonderful pearls of wisdom on parenting you sprinkle around like a fresh gentle rain." He arched a brow when she started gaping at him again. "Which, I assure you, I'm eager to soak up like a thirsty sponge," he said, his eyes so vivid now they were practically glowing.

She burst out laughing before she could stop herself.

Was this guy for real? Or simply so determined to get his way that now he was stooping to good old-fashioned, *outrageous* flattery?

She held up the pipe wrench. "I'm not the brains of this operation, Mac, I'm just the brawn. Eileen is better equipped to answer your questions. Because the truth is, I've been known to turn tail and run when I see Sophie headed my way wearing a certain expression." She crawled back onto her hands and knees, hoping he'd get the hint and leave. "So if you're looking for something to do, maybe when everyone comes back from town you and Henry could walk to the main road and look for moose. And while you're at it, you could have a nice little chat about . . . oh, I don't know; maybe about him calling you *Dad* instead of *Father*."

Of course he didn't leave, because that would mean he'd actually been *listening* to her. Instead he swiped the wrench from her hand and shouldered her out of the way, then reached into the closet without having to contort so much as a muscle—although Olivia did see several of them bunch with seemingly little effort just as she heard a deep metallic squeak followed by a really loud snap.

Okay; because she wasn't a complete idiot, maybe she'd hold off a bit before *firmly* telling Mac the only thing he'd be soaking up like a sponge would likely be dripping from his cabin ceiling the next time it rained.

And if he still wouldn't take no for an answer . . . well, maybe a couple of days spent replanking two hundred twenty feet of docks would change his mind.

Because honest to God, if she wasn't careful, Olivia was afraid she might start wondering what it would be like to replace that big leather jacket with the big strong man who owned it.

Chapter Four

Olivia was so exhausted she could barely keep her eyes opened as she leaned against the bathroom doorjamb to supervise Sophie's bedtime ritual. Her daughter, however, was so wound up she hadn't stopped talking even while brushing her teeth.

"I wish you could have seen Henry's face when Gram let us go to the bookmobile and he found that book of baby names," the girl said from inside her pajama top. Her head popped out, sporting a huge grin. "He was so excited he wouldn't even look at anything else the librarian tried to show him. He said that one book would keep him busy for weeks while he tries out all the different names."

"Tries them out on whom? Are you letting Henry name Tinkerbelle's kittens?"

Sophie stopped with her hairbrush halfway to her head. "No, he's trying them out on himself. Henry said his father's thinking of changing his first name, too, just like he changed his last name from Penhope to Oceanus. Only his dad said it's got to be a noble name, befitting his . . . lineage or something."

"I hope you told Henry that *Henry* is a lovely name,"

Olivia said, plopping down on the hamper at the realization the boy had been serious yesterday in the truck. But what was wrong with the name his dear dead mother had given him—other than its not being *noble* enough? Was Mac trying to erase Cordelia from Henry's life completely?

"Mom?" Sophie asked, suddenly serious. "If you ever got married again, would I have to change my name, too, like Henry did?"

"No, sweetie. Until the day you get married you will always be Sophie Baldwin—and even then you don't have to take your husband's last name if you don't want to."

"You changed your last name to Daddy's."

Olivia took the hairbrush out of her hand, turned her around, and started working the tangles and several pieces of hay out of her hair. "Yes, I did, because I loved your daddy so much I wanted everyone to know I was his."

"And I love him so much that I'm never changing my name to some other man's," the girl said with all the conviction of a loyal daughter. She turned with a frown. "I don't think Mac should make Henry change *both* of his names, because that would be like his mama never even existed."

Olivia was too tired to stop herself from wincing; Lord, she hated hearing Sophie call adults by their first names. Growing up she had addressed everyone, even whichever foster parents she'd been living with at the time, as Mr. and Mrs. So-and-So.

But she'd lost that particular battle to Eileen when Sophie had started talking. Olivia wondered how she managed to stand upright, considering she didn't have much of a backbone sometimes. She'd certainly been lacking several vertebrae today—which is why a tall, ruggedly handsome man with short dark hair and intense green eyes was going around calling her *boss* now and was responsible for her wanting to fall asleep right here in the bathroom.

Spending the day hiding from a fantasy was exhausting.

"Mom, are you listening to me? I asked if Mac and Henry can come with us on our picnic tomorrow."

"But that's supposed to be our special you-and-me time, sweetie. I thought you looked forward to our time alone together."

"It would only be just this once," Sophie said. "When I told Henry I couldn't play with him tomorrow because we were going on a picnic, he suddenly got all teary-eyed and said he used to go on picnics with his mama all the time, too. But when he suggested going on one to his father, Mac said maybe they would sometime, only they never have. And I thought if Mac saw how much fun picnics are, he'd start taking Henry every Sunday just like you take me."

Heaven help her, Sophie was turning into Eileen!

The girl cupped Olivia's face in her tiny hands and looked directly into her eyes—exactly like Eileen did when she was primed for battle. "Please, Mom, can we take them with us just this once? Your big old sappy heart would have just melted today if you'd seen how sad Henry got. He misses his mama so much, and he . . . he asked me how I got over missing my dad."

"And what did you tell him?" Olivia asked past the sudden lump in her throat.

Sophie dropped her gaze to her hands on Olivia's cheeks, her own baby-soft cheeks turning pink. "I told him I was really little when Daddy died, and that before then I can only remember bits and pieces because he was gone most of the time." She looked up. "I asked Henry if he had any pictures of his mom, but he got all teary-eyed again and said he hadn't been able to bring anything from home because his uncles had stolen him out of his bed in the middle of the night." Her own big brown eyes grew misty. "Isn't that sad? Henry doesn't have *anything* to remind him of his mother."

"He has his memories, sweetie."

"But he's only six. He's going to forget if he hasn't got pictures. Sometimes I can't remember what Daddy looked like when he wasn't wearing his uniform, so I dig out our photo albums." Her tiny hands pressed deeper into Olivia's cheeks. "Please can we take them with us tomorrow? And when you have a chance, could you ask Mac to get a picture of Henry's mom for him so he won't forget what she looks like?"

Four hours. All she wanted—all she looked forward to all week—was four hours every Sunday alone with her daughter: away from Inglenook, away from John and Eileen, and away from anything that reminded her of Keith.

"Okay," she said with a quiet sigh. "Tomorrow at breakfast you can invite Henry and Mr. Oceanus to come with us."

Sophie threw her arms around Olivia's neck with a squeal of excitement. "Oh, thank you! He's going to be so happy!" She pulled away and ran into the hall toward her bedroom. "And we can fly the kites Gram bought us today." She hopped into bed, burrowing under the blankets when Olivia sat down beside her. "So the surprise place you pick out this week needs to have a really big field."

She had planned on disappearing for the entire day and driving down to Bangor to take Sophie to a movie and do some shopping, their picnic being in a really nice restaurant for a change. Only that plan was blown to hell now, thanks to the big old sappy heart Sophie had inherited from her.

And the don't-take-any-prisoners determination she'd gotten from the Baldwins.

Olivia gave her daughter a kiss on the forehead and stood up. "I'll make sure there's room for kite flying," she promised. She shut off the bedside lamp. "And don't take too long talking to your daddy tonight, okay? You're up at the crack of dawn with me tomorrow, so we can find a safe place for Tinkerbelle to raise her kittens. The hay truck is coming in a couple of weeks, and we need to move her out of the loft so she can get used to a new nursery for them."

"The kittens would be safe in my bedroom closet."

Olivia stopped in the doorway. "Tink's a barn cat, sweetie, and likes to come and go as she pleases. Even a beautiful home like ours would feel like a prison to her."

"Mom? *Are* you ever going to get married again?"

"Not in the foreseeable future, I'm not."

The young girl gave a soft snort as she folded her hands

on her stomach and looked up at the ceiling. "I guess you would need to get a *boyfriend* first in order to get a husband." Olivia saw the blankets shudder. "Just as long as it's not Simon Maher." Sophie lifted her head to make a face at her. "Ezra told Gram today that Simon is moving to Spellbound Falls. You know he's going to keep bugging you to go out with him if you don't just tell him to get lost." She bolted fully upright. "Or unless you got another boyfriend first. I know; maybe Mac could be your boyfriend."

"Don't even go there, young lady."

"But he's really big and handsome and strong looking, and a whole lot closer to your age. Simon wouldn't dare keep bugging you if Mac was your boyfriend."

"Sophie."

"And next time we went to the Drunken Moose, I'd get to finish my oatmeal."

"Sophie."

"And you wouldn't have to hide from everyone anymore." She beamed Olivia a brilliant smile. "Because Mac would protect you, just like he protected you from Mark the bastard."

"Sophie! You don't *ever* call anyone a bastard, young lady." She stepped back into the room. "Who told you about Mark?"

The blankets pulled up to her chin, Sophie's cheeks turned a dull red. "Henry did," she squeaked, her eyes widening as she slapped a hand over her mouth. "But you can't tell him I told you! And please don't tell Mac, either. It's my fault; I kept bugging Henry until he told me how you really hurt yourself yesterday. He said his father didn't want me to know Mark hit you because he was afraid I'd get upset, but I promised Henry I wouldn't tell anyone. Please, *please* don't tell him I told."

"I won't say anything to either of them. But you have to promise me you won't use the word *bastard* again, okay? And if Henry uses it again, you tell him to stop saying it because it's a very bad word."

"I promise, I will. Why did Mark hit you?"

"Because he's a really dumb kid. And he's gone home to Georgia, so you don't have to worry about him, okay?"

Her daughter went back to smiling. "That's because Mac told him to get out of town before sunset. See, having a strong boyfriend would be handy. Maybe tomorrow on our picnic you could ask Mac if he'd like to go on a date with you. I bet he'd say yes, because Henry told me his father thinks you're pretty."

Olivia let out a loud yawn, lifting a hand to her mouth to cover her blush. "Dawn cracks early; you need to go to sleep now."

Of course the girl didn't listen to her. "If you're too shy to ask him, I can. I asked Tristan if he wanted to be Zoey's boyfriend, and he said yes and now they're the hottest couple in the entire school."

Good Lord, she had to stop this. Olivia pointed a threatening finger. "I so much as *hear* the words *boyfriend* or *girlfriend* tomorrow on our picnic, young lady, and you'll be cleaning cabins with me from the moment you step off the bus until you go to bed for the next three weeks. Got that?"

The blankets pulled up to her chin again and her eyes huge—more likely from shock than fear—Sophie mutely nodded.

Olivia took in a calming breath. "You know we can't get emotionally involved with our guests," she said softly. "I realize that's usually not a problem for you because most everyone is here only a week or two, but Henry and Mr. Oceanus are staying through the summer and then they're *leaving.* So just like I can't have Mr. Oceanus as a boyfriend, you need to make sure you don't get too attached to Henry. I don't want your heart to get broken, Sophie."

When the girl only nodded again, Olivia smiled warmly. "I love you, baby."

"I love you, too, Mom," she said, dropping back onto her pillow with a miniature version of her mother's sigh.

Olivia quietly walked down the hall to the kitchen, her heart aching with remorse for losing her temper. She went over and locked the outside door, then pushed back the curtain and saw that the lights in the upstairs windows of the main lodge were still on in John and Eileen's private quarters. She rested her forehead against the cool glass, suddenly so close to tears it was scary. Sophie needn't worry about her getting married again, because the girl was right; she had to be somebody's girlfriend before she could be a wife. And the chances of that happening in Spellbound Falls were about as promising as someone catching a giant whale in Bottomless Lake.

She might go a bit weak in the backbone on occasion, but she sure as hell had enough pride not to settle. If she couldn't have a man who made her palms sweat and her heart race, who didn't see her as a prize that came with a ready-made family and six hundred acres of prime wilderness lake frontage, or who thought she was perfect just the way she was, then she'd rather remain a lonely widow the rest of her life.

Because she deserved a man who would move mountains for her.

Olivia straightened and started to turn but caught sight of Mac's jacket hanging on the peg beside her door. She really needed to return it, if only to get him out of her head once and for all. But truth be told, she hadn't even realized how much she missed a man's touch until Mac had swept her into his arms and placed his jacket over her trembling shoulders while promising the bastard would never hurt her again.

Oh, but she loved the feel of a man's strength; her last memory of her father was him holding her in his big strong arms when she was five, crushing her to his chest with his face buried in her hair as he'd promised he would move heaven and earth and any mountains that got in his way to get her back.

She'd waited three years for him to come back and get her, and finally forgiven him four foster homes later on her eighteenth birthday. Olivia pulled the jacket off the peg and pressed the soft leather to her face, remembering how she'd headed off in search of the security she'd lost at age four when her mother had died.

Only she'd found Keith instead. Or rather, Keith Baldwin had found her waiting tables in Orono his last year of college. The tall, handsome, determined man had literally swept Olivia off her feet, married her the week after he graduated, and settled her here at Inglenook one month before running off to join the military.

It had taken him two years of furloughs home to get her pregnant, and another four years to get killed protecting fallen comrades being airlifted to safety. At least that was what his commanding officer had said as Olivia had watched Sophie clutch the folded flag at Keith's funeral—which the girl now kept in her bedroom next to a picture of her war-hero daddy.

Olivia snapped off the porch light, undecided whom she was the angriest at: herself for hating a dead man, or Keith for dying before *he* had found the backbone to tell his parents they were getting a divorce. Her heart aching again for not telling them herself, Olivia headed to her bedroom—only to realize she was still clutching Mac's jacket.

Well, why the hell not? It wasn't as if she intended to attack its owner or anything; that's why it was called a *fantasy*. Because really, she wasn't looking for another tall, dark, handsome stranger to swoop in and rescue her, considering how that had turned out the last time. No, she was holding out for a man she could trust to honestly and truly love her, forever and ever.

A man who preferred her bed instead of some other woman's.

But until that miracle happened, there wasn't any reason she couldn't dream Mr. Right was out there somewhere. And while waiting for their paths to cross, what was wrong with pretending she was sleeping wrapped up in a pair of big strong arms? Considering she hadn't had sex in more than six years, shouldn't she think about having two or three passionate affairs before she turned into a dried-up old woman? It wasn't like she was looking for the perfect man or anything; she'd always thought perfection was overrated.

Olivia spread the jacket on her bed, left her clothes on the floor where she'd shed them, and carefully burrowed under the quilt with a soft hum of pleasure. Mr. Right didn't even have to be handsome, she decided, pulling the jacket-covered quilt up to her chin to breathe in the masculine scent. In fact, it might actually be better if he was flat-out ugly, having learned the hard way that a handsome face could just as easily hide a black heart.

He did have to have a sense of humor, though. And he needed to like children—especially little girls—and she'd really like it if he was really strong, because she really loved feeling all that carefully controlled strength moving over her, and beneath her, and deeply inside her.

Olivia finally fell asleep, her palms slightly sweaty and her heart beating a little bit faster, feeling safe and secure wrapped in the warmth of a fantasy.

Chapter Five

Standing on the porch staring out at the moonlight reflecting off the ice on Bottomless Lake, Mac listened to Henry sitting inside reading aloud from the book of baby names he'd gotten in town this afternoon. The boy had slowly been making his way through the alphabet and was up to the letter D; occasionally stopping to write some of the names down after repeating them with different inflections, sometimes adding *Oceanus* to see how they sounded together.

Sweet Prometheus, but he'd caught hell from all his friends' wives back in Midnight Bay simply for mentioning that he'd like to change Henry's first name along with his last. But his worst sin, apparently, had been to mention it in front of the boy, who had obviously taken it to heart.

But what had Delia been thinking when she'd given his son such an uninspiring, decidedly English name as Henry? From the day he'd met her, Mac had been totally honest about who he was—and despite not telling him she was pregnant, Delia had *known* she was giving birth to the grandchild of Titus Oceanus.

Mac snorted softly. Which was exactly why she'd kept her pregnancy a secret. It was also likely why she'd chosen such an unassuming name, hoping it would help keep the boy's parentage—and his heritage—free of public speculation.

Except her brothers had known who had fathered their bastard nephew. And after Delia's death five months ago, upon learning that her closest servants were plotting to bring their young charge to the child's father, the three Penhope men had mounted a campaign to kill Mac in order to keep control of the boy.

Thank the gods one servant had managed to at least reach Titus. And for that reason alone Mac was still alive, two of Delia's brothers were dead and one had staggered home carrying his stones in his pocket.

The cabin door opened. "What do you think of *Dorian*?" Henry asked as he stepped onto the porch. "It means 'from the sea,' so it's appropriate. And *Dorian Oceanus* has a noble ring to it, don't you think, Father?"

Mac walked over and picked him up, then sat down in one of the wooden porch chairs, settling Henry on his lap. "Let's start with *my* name, shall we? I'm thinking of changing it from *Father* to *Dad*. How does that sound to you?"

Henry's eyebrows lifted in surprise. "You want me to call you *Dad*?" Down went those brows into a frown. "Just while we're here at Inglenook, and then I should return to calling you *Father* when we leave?"

"Well, since I still intend to be your dad after we leave here, I thought maybe you could continue using the term."

"But you call Grandfather *Father*, and when you came to his ship and stole me from him, I also heard you call him *sir*."

Mac smiled to cover his wince. "That's because my father scares the hel—the daylights out of me. And I rather hoped that by your calling me *Dad*, I would know that *you* aren't afraid of *me*."

"I'm not afraid of anything." The boy suddenly looked away. "Except that something bad might happen to you," he whispered. "Like your getting sick and dying just like Mama did."

Mac cupped his son's chin to face him. "Nothing bad is

going to happen to me, Henry. I'm going to live for a long, long, *long* time." He tapped the boy's cheek with his finger. "And so are you. And for as long as I have breath in my body, even after you're grown and leave home, I will be here for you."

"Even if I do something really bad?"

"There's nothing you could ever do that would change the way I feel about you, Henry. Nothing."

Mac let go of his chin when Henry turned away again. "I disobeyed you, Fa—Dad," he said, staring out at the lake. "I told Sophie that bad man hit her mama yesterday." He looked at Mac, the moonlight revealing his apprehension. "I know you told me not to say anything because you didn't want Sophie to worry, but she suspected her mother hadn't merely fallen down. And she was imagining all sorts of bad things had happened, because . . . I think because she's afraid her mama could die and leave her just like her father did."

Mac cradled his son back against him with a heavy sigh. "Death isn't some big bad terrible thing, Henry, even though it feels like it is to those of us still living. But fathers and *mothers*," he said, giving him a squeeze, "don't ever leave their children." He placed his hand over Henry's heart. "Your mama's still right here inside you, Henry. And anytime you want to talk to her, just talk; silently or out loud, it doesn't matter. You have my word, son, your mama hears everything you say, and she knows everything you feel. And if you ask her something she will answer you, only instead of hearing with your ears now you must learn to listen with your heart."

Henry reared up, incredulous. "That's what Sophie told me! I asked her how she got over missing her dad, and she said she didn't miss him so much once she started talking to him every night when she went to bed. And she said sometimes if she listens real hard, she can almost hear him talking back to her."

Oh yeah, coming to Inglenook had definitely been one of

his better decisions. "It appears you have a very wise new friend." He turned the boy facing out again and wrapped him in a warm embrace. "I'm sorry Sophie's father died, but I'm glad you can talk to her about what it's like to miss someone you love."

"Did you love Mama?"

"I cared very deeply for Delia."

"Then how come you left her before I was born?"

"Because she asked me to."

Henry craned his head to frown up at him. "But why? Didn't Mama care as deeply for you?"

Mac nudged him back around. "I believe she did, but I also believe she loved you more," he said, tightening his arms for emphasis. "I think that when your mama realized she was carrying you, the notion of having my child frightened her, so she asked me to leave before I knew you existed."

"But what's wrong with your being my dad?"

"I believe it was your grandfather Delia feared most, Henry. Titus Oceanus is a very powerful man, and his reputation is . . ." Sweet Prometheus, how much should he reveal to the child? "Well, let's just say that everyone is afraid of my father."

Henry patted Mac's arm. "*You're* not afraid of him. When Mr. Trace blew that hole in Grandfather's ship, you stole me right out from under his nose. Why, you're not afraid of anyone."

No, only a pint-sized, six-year-old mirror image of himself.

"You know what, Henry? Instead of calling him Grandfather, I think you should start calling him *Grampy.* So the next time you give Trace a letter to take out to sea and toss overboard, go ahead and begin it with 'Dear Grammy and Grampy.' "

"And can you take a picture of me and Sophie so I can send it to them? I want them to see what a wonderful new friend I have."

Mac smiled. What he wouldn't give to be there when his old man opened Henry's letter calling him *Grampy*. "I'm sure they'd both like that very much."

"And can I also write to Aunt Carolina and invite her to come visit us?" Henry asked, craning around to look at him again.

Mac disguised his shudder by shrugging. He supposed he couldn't postpone the inevitable any longer, as Henry had been asking to meet Carolina ever since she'd sent him the giant stuffed whale and book of mythology. But knowing his sister, Mac had sneaked the whale out of Henry's arms when the boy had been sleeping, carefully taken it apart at the seam, and found Carolina's little . . . surprise.

Only upon realizing his brat of a sister—obviously in love with her new nephew sight unseen—was sincerely trying to help him, Mac had taken her inspired gift out of the whale, replaced it with something of equal weight so Henry wouldn't notice, and painstakingly restitched the seam and tucked the animal back into his son's arms.

"Yes, I believe it is time you met your aunt. And if we give Carolina an invitation that includes actual dates, at least we'll know when she's coming rather than just having her show up without warning."

Henry relaxed back against him again. "Next week, then?"

"How about next month instead? That way we'll have time to grow accustomed to our temporary home first."

"But all the campers will be here then."

Mac smiled over Henry's head. "Exactly, as I intend to sign Caro up for one or two of the sessions." He patted Henry's leg. "She's going to love the idea, because I happen to know she's quite determined to be your favorite aunt."

Henry frowned up to him again. "But she's my only aunt."

Mac lifted the boy off his lap and set him down facing the door. "And if you're a wise young man, you won't be too quick to point that out to her," he said with a chuckle, giving him a nudge to get him moving. "Not if you want her to keep sending you gifts. Now go brush your teeth and strip off for bed, and I'll be along to tuck you in."

Henry stopped at the door. "Are you sure Mama doesn't mind that I don't wear pajamas?" he asked, the moonlight revealing his suspicion.

"She never used to mind when I didn't wear any," Mac drawled. He stood up. "But if you're worried, tonight just before you go to sleep maybe you should ask her."

"But what if she doesn't answer me?"

"She will, son, I promise. Only remember you'll hear her answer with your heart instead of your ears. And in the morning, if your mama told you she prefers you wear pajamas, tomorrow we'll go into town and buy you some."

Henry's shoulders slumped. "Can we go to town even if she says it's okay if I sleep naked? That way I'll have something to do while Sophie's gone on her picnic." He took a deep breath. "I've decided picnics must be something only *mamas* do with their children. And dads do . . . they do something else with them."

"You mean like teach their sons how to handle a sword?" Mac asked quietly.

Henry's eyes widened. "A sword? Truly?" He stepped closer. "Will you teach me how to fight with *your* sword?"

Mac folded his arms over his chest, biting back a laugh. "I think we should start with one you can actually lift." He canted his head. "Perhaps you would enjoy wielding the small sword my father gave me when I was your age."

The one Carolina had thoughtfully hidden inside the giant stuffed whale.

Henry's eyes widened even more. "Grandfather gave you a toy sword when you were my age? And you're going to let me use it? Oh, Father, I promise to be very careful not to break it, as you must hold it dear to your heart. Can we start my lessons tomorrow while Sophie's gone on her picnic?"

Mac could feel the excitement humming through his son clear across the porch. "I'm not just letting you use the sword your Grampy gave me; I'm giving it to you to hold dear in your heart as a gift from your *dad*. One that I hope you will someday have the good fortune to pass down to your own son." He walked over and opened the door of the cabin. "And you needn't worry about it breaking; it's a true and lethal weapon, Henry, except that it's sized for a smaller hand. And for that reason alone you must always treat it with respect." He turned him around and gently shoved him inside. "Now go get ready for bed."

Henry took all of two steps and turned back, his young eyes filled with doubt. "We will begin my lessons tomorrow?"

Mac shook his head. "Not in the light of day; but I give you my word we'll have our first lesson tomorrow night. We'll go on a hike tomorrow instead, and find a clearing in the forest we can use." He leaned down to look Henry level in the eyes. "And you will give me your word that you'll not tell anyone, including Sophie, what we're doing, if you don't want to feel the flat of *my* sword on your backside. Understand?" he asked, stifling a smile when his son vigorously nodded.

Mac straightened. "The same rules apply to your lessons as to everything else we've talked about. The less people know about us, the better for everyone."

The boy nodded even more vigorously.

Mac shoved his hands in his pockets. "I know what a burden it is to keep secrets, Henry, especially at your age and especially when those secrets don't even make sense to you half the time. And I'm really proud of you for handling them as well as you have. A lot has happened to you in the last few months, and . . . well, I want you to know that every day I thank the gods you're my son."

Reading his intentions, Mac crouched down just as Henry charged toward him, catching him and straightening with an exaggerated grunt when the boy threw his arms around his neck in a bear of a hug.

"I'm glad you're my dad," Henry whispered. He leaned away just enough to look Mac in the eyes, his young eyes glistening with emotion. "I wished and wished for you to come for me after Mama died," he said, his voice quivering.

"Because she told me over and over how strong and powerful and good you were whenever I asked."

"If I had known about you, Henry," Mac said thickly, "I would have come for you immediately." He walked to the smaller downstairs bedroom and lowered the boy to the floor, then cupped his face in his hands to make him look up. "Nothing—not even your uncles—would have kept me from you. And remember that if we somehow ever get separated in the future, all you have to do is make your way to the ocean and you will find the help you need to get back to me."

Henry beamed up at him. "I know that now." He let out a yawn. "I understand Misneach belongs to Fiona, but I miss him terribly. Can I have a puppy of my own?"

For the love of Zeus, the child changed directions like the wind! Realizing that if he didn't get him in bed the boy was going to talk all night, Mac pulled back the blankets. "You can have a pet once we settle into a permanent home. Now strip off and climb in. It's well past your bedtime."

"But I haven't brushed my teeth," he said even as he pulled his shirt off over his head. "And you haven't read to me from Aunt Carolina's book." He shed his trousers and underpants and kicked them to the side. "Tonight I was supposed to learn how Athena took Athens away from Poseidon."

Mac stifled a sigh. "I'm afraid brushing your teeth six times a day isn't going to stop them from falling out, son. And as for that particular war between the gods, the people of Athens decided they liked Athena's gift better than they liked Poseidon's," he continued, lifting Henry into bed. He sat down beside him and tucked the blankets under the boy's chin. "And so they chose Athena as their goddess."

"What was her gift?"

"She planted an olive tree in the city, whereas Poseidon drove his trident into the ground at the Acropolis and created a spring." Mac shrugged. "And deciding an olive tree was more useful, the people chose Athena as their patron."

"Didn't they know that water is *necessary* for life?"

"They preferred Athena's gift because they could eat the olives, whereas they couldn't drink from Poseidon's spring because it was salt water."

The boy arranged his stuffed whale under the blankets beside him with a frown. "But weren't they afraid having a woman as their patron would leave them vulnerable to attack?" He snorted. "Because the gods were warring against each other all the time and people kept getting caught in the middle, they should have chosen Poseidon to protect them because he was stronger."

"Ah, but Athena was known for her wisdom. And wisdom is far more powerful than brute strength, Henry. Which is why being big and strong and knowing how to wield a sword isn't always enough; it takes wisdom to recognize if something is worth fighting over, so you can decide when to stand your ground and when to retreat to fight another day." Mac patted Henry's chest and stood up. "Now close your eyes and talk to your mama, and let me know in the morning if we need to buy you pajamas."

"Sophie told me her mama is always running away from people," Henry said just as Mac reached the bedroom door. "So does that mean Olivia is wise like Athena? Because I think Sophie believes her mama's just scared of everyone."

Mac could see he needed to start preparing for bedtime a good hour before he wanted Henry to go to sleep. "Why don't you wait until you know Olivia better, and then decide for yourself if you think she's wise or frightened? Good night," he said with all the authority of a man nearing the end of his patience, closing the door to a crack before Henry could ask another question.

He walked back out to the porch, leaving the exterior door ajar so he could listen for movement inside, and stood staring toward Olivia's home, which sat back in the woods well away from the main lodge.

Mac chuckled at how alike he and Henry truly were, since he'd found himself wondering the same thing about Olivia as he'd spent most of today trying to find her. But he hadn't sensed any fear in her this morning when he'd offered to help her get Inglenook ready for the upcoming sessions; more like . . . discomfort. Which made him think Olivia wasn't physically afraid of people but simply preferred to run away rather than deal with whatever they might want from her.

The woman did seem to have a hard time saying no. And Mac suspected she more often than not swallowed her anger to avoid engaging in open warfare. Which was probably why despite being a mere mortal, Olivia Baldwin had somehow mastered the difficult art of becoming invisible.

Even when she was standing in plain sight, it was as if she weren't there. More than once today when he'd been ripping rotten boards off Inglenook's endless spans of docks, Mac had looked up to find she'd disappeared. She walked with the stealth of a kitchen mouse, and when she spoke, usually only to give instructions, he'd found himself going very still and even having to cant his head to hear her.

He figured that following yesterday's attack, Olivia had been as talkative as she got.

Something was weighing down her shoulders, he decided: some deeply rooted . . . sadness that accounted for her not wanting to draw attention to herself. And though she kept saying Eileen was the brains of their business, Mac would bet his bottomless satchel of money that without Olivia, Inglenook wouldn't exist.

He wondered about her husband, and whether the sadness he sensed was because she missed him so much. When he'd carefully asked about Sophie's father at breakfast this morning, John had told Mac that his son had died four years ago fighting in the war in Iraq. John had also mentioned—somewhat angrily, Mac had noticed—that before his death Keith had spent most of his marriage to Olivia away from home.

Four years was a long time to mourn a husband who hadn't been around all that much to begin with, and Mac wondered why the beautiful and still-vital woman hadn't moved on by now. Was Olivia so dedicated to Inglenook—which was her daughter's birthright as John and Eileen's only grandchild—that she didn't dare make a new life for herself and daughter with another man? Or was she staying for some other reason?

Mac sighed, guessing that if he wanted to know what was going on behind those beautiful cinnamon eyes, he needed to know more about Olivia's past.

Only that little miracle wasn't going to happen anytime soon, was it?

Unless he could get Carolina to do a little snooping for him.

He folded his arms over his chest and scowled at the frozen lake. No; even if he could persuade her to help him, Carolina couldn't access enough of the knowledge. Because according to Titus Oceanus, sons were destined to become their father's heirs and daughters were destined only to provide those heirs to their husbands. Which was probably why, to this day, sons and daughters were still wrestling their fathers for control of their destinies—just as he and Carolina were continually fighting Titus for theirs.

Mac shoved his hands into his pockets. So far all he'd gained was a one-year reprieve from being forced to marry. And if in that time he couldn't prove he was capable of being a good father to Henry, Titus would take the boy away from him and raise Henry himself.

Only Mac hoped the old man realized that in order for that to happen, he would have to rip the child out of his cold, lifeless hands.

Chapter Six

His ears tuned to the conversation taking place in the backseat about the pros and cons of having a long tail on a kite versus no tail at all, Mac took note of Olivia's intrinsic grace as she crossed the street and disappeared into the trading post she'd asked him to stop at on the way to their picnic.

The picnic he'd ironically ended up having to persuade Henry to go on.

But upon seeing Olivia's poorly disguised relief at breakfast when his son had informed Sophie he couldn't go on their picnic because he was going on a hike with his dad, Mac had immediately decided they should spend the day with the ladies instead. So he'd taken Henry aside and assured him their sword lesson was still on for tonight, explaining they would have plenty of time to locate a suitable clearing in the woods if they left right after dinner.

Deciding two adventures in one day was almost as exciting as waking up to find a small sheathed sword hanging on his bedpost this morning, Henry had returned to the table and told Sophie they would love to go with her and her mama. Mac had bitten back a laugh as he'd watched Olivia's shoulders slump, and smiled openly when she'd pulled her disappearing act again after muttering something about needing to go home and pack the lunch basket.

Mac knew he should feel bad about intruding where he clearly wasn't wanted, but not only did the woman's elusiveness spark his primordial desire to pursue her, but Olivia Baldwin also aroused his instincts to possess and protect.

Which should have been a problem, considering he was here to prove he'd put his wild bachelor ways behind him. But sometime in the early hours of his restless night's sleep, Mac had started wondering why he'd assumed that parenting and pursuing women were mutually exclusive endeavors. He had to marry eventually, and he preferred to be the one choosing his bride. And there wasn't any reason he couldn't be a good father while he continued looking for a woman who wouldn't run away screaming when she discovered who—or rather what—was asking for her hand in marriage.

Delia had known the *who*; it had been the *what* he hadn't revealed to her.

So upon concluding that women were still fair game, Mac had fallen into a peaceful sleep—only to dream of pursuing a delectable little kitchen mouse with warm cinnamon eyes. And then this morning at breakfast, almost as if the gods were commending his reasoning by presenting him with the reluctantly offered invitation, he hadn't been able to resist the opportunity to take up his pursuit in earnest.

As for the possessive and protective instincts Olivia unwittingly brought out in him . . . well, could a tiger change its stripes? If Titus had managed to pass down only one indelible trait to his rebellious son, Mac would say it was his compulsion to protect anything or anyone that belonged to him—even if that possession was only temporary.

"Oh no, Simon's back from Chicago!" Sophie suddenly cried, staring at the car pulling into a parking spot several places ahead of them. She grabbed the door handle and looked at Mac. "I'll be right back. I have to go in and warn Mom that he's here."

"Wait," Mac said, hitting the lock button before she could get the door open. "You can't just jump out into traffic. Why do you have to warn your mother that this Simon gentleman is in town?"

"So she can duck out the back door if he and Missy decide to go to Ezra's before they go to the Drunken Moose for breakfast." When Mac only arched a brow at her instead of releasing the lock, the young girl gestured impatiently toward the car. "Simon keeps bugging Mom to go out with him, and she doesn't want to because he's old and stuffy and . . . and full of himself." She suddenly canted her head, her big brown eyes taking on a calculated shine. "Or *you* could go in and warn her instead. Simon wouldn't dare ask Mom for a date if he thought you were her . . . if you were with her."

The doors of the mud-splattered car opened, and Mac watched a middle-aged woman and gentleman get out. They stood speaking to each other for a moment, then both started walking across the street toward the trading post instead of the restaurant.

"Oh no, they are going to Ezra's! Please, Mac, if you don't want to pretend you're Mom's boy—that you're like her date or anything, then at least let me go in and warn her. I'll be careful crossing the road, I promise."

Mac released the locks. "I believe we should all go in," he said, getting out and opening Henry's door, immediately taking the boy's hand to hold him beside the truck.

Mac reached for Sophie when she got out behind Henry, but the girl tucked her hands behind her back. "I'm eight," she said, her chin lifting defiantly. "I don't need anyone to hold my hand to cross the road."

"You do when your mother leaves you in my care," he said, still holding out his hand. "If not for me, then do it as an example for Henry."

"Just do it, Sophie," Henry said. "We have to go save your mama again."

Mac guessed it was the *again* that got the young girl to take his hand; either that or so she could drag him toward the store.

"I suppose your mother has a lot of men . . . bugging her for a date," Mac said as they crossed the nearly deserted street. "Does she ever say yes to any of them?"

"Only Simon bugs her, because none of the other men around here are brave enough to ask her out." Sophie released him the moment they reached the other side. "Gram says it's because they don't dare."

Mac took hold of her jacket sleeve to stop her from opening the door and turned her to face him. "Why don't they dare?" He smiled. "Are all the men afraid of your mother?"

"No, they're afraid of my dad." She nodded at his confusion. "When I saw Mom was all sad at our town Christmas party this year, I asked Gram why nobody was asking her to dance. And she said it was because all the men are afraid they won't measure up to my dad because he was so handsome and strong and a war hero."

Sophie started to open the door but stopped and looked up at him again. "I bet you wouldn't be afraid to ask her out, but you can't because you're leaving in the fall. And besides, it's against the rules to fran . . . to *frantinize* with the guests. But if you didn't mind just pretending you're her—that you and Mom are sort of a couple for the summer, Simon would leave her alone and she wouldn't have to keep avoiding him."

Mac opened the door and ushered Sophie and Henry ahead of him so they wouldn't see his smile. Apparently he didn't need Carolina to dig into Olivia's past after all, since her daughter was such a bubbling fountain of information.

After whispering something to Henry, Sophie gave the boy a shove and the two of them ran off down separate aisles, clearly on a mission to find and subsequently save Olivia from her old and stuffy and full-of-himself suitor. The hunt might take them a while, though, Mac decided, as the store had quite a few aisles crammed full of everything from food to clothes to camping equipment, as well as—according to the sign in front of him—night crawlers, live bait, and ice-cold beer.

Another sign said this was also the place to rent ice fishing shanties.

Seeing only Simon's sister talking to a much older gentleman at the back counter, Mac stood very still for a couple of heartbeats and then headed toward the far right-hand side of the store—where he found Olivia trapped in an alcove crammed full of fishing gear, her escape cut off by his rival pursuer.

"Ah, here you are, sweetheart," he said, reaching past the startled man to take hold of her jacket sleeve. "Our kids were getting worried you were taking so long." He pulled her out of the alcove and wrapped his arm around her—ignoring her squeak when he snagged her against his side to keep her from bolting. "Did you find everything you need for our picnic?"

Only instead of trying to pull away like he expected, Olivia settled into him with a soft, feminine sigh. "I was looking for fishing line. Simon, this is Mac Oceanus. He and his son are guests at Inglenook. Mac, this is Simon Maher. He's staying with his sister, Missy, who lives across the cove from us on Bottomless Lake until he buys a place of his own here in Spellbound Falls."

Mac extended his free hand toward Simon. "Mr. Maher."

After a false start the man shook Mac's left hand. "Mr. Oceanus." He frowned at Olivia. "I was under the impression Inglenook was closed for the next few weeks."

"It is," Mac said before she could answer. "And I'm more Olivia's employee than her guest." He looked down. "If you're looking for line, does that mean our surprise destination involves ice fishing?"

Simon choked back a snort. "If your destination's a surprise, I hope you have a good sense of direction, Mr. Oceanus." He smiled tightly. "Olivia's been known to . . . lose some of her guests occasionally. Accidentally, of course."

Oh, yeah: Simon Maher was not at all happy.

Mac gave a chuckle. "I believe Olivia is discovering I'm not exactly an easy person to lose. It was nice meeting you, Mr. Maher. Maybe I'll see you on the lake this summer. Come on, sweetheart," he said, turning with her still tucked against him. "Let's find our kids so we can get going. I'm starved."

He was even more surprised when she still remained complacent as they headed toward the back of the store. And he'd swear she brushed her cheek on his jacket—the one she had finally if reluctantly returned this morning.

"Mom!" Sophie said, spotting them as she rounded the end of an aisle at a run. The young girl slid to a stop, her eyes widening and her cheeks turning a lovely pink at the sight of Mac's arm around her mother. "It's not what you think," she whispered, darting a quick glance at the woman and older gentleman at the counter. "I was coming in to war—to get you, only Mac decided we should all come in."

Olivia finally stepped out of his embrace and took Sophie's hand, and started leading the girl up the center aisle toward the door—her intrinsic grace a bit stiff.

"Olivia, aren't you going to introduce me to your gentleman friend?" the woman at the counter called after her.

When Olivia merely kept walking, Mac gave a slight bow. "Mac Oceanus," he said with a congenial smile. "I'm Olivia's new employee. And this is my son, Henry," he added when the boy ran up to him. "Henry, I believe this nice lady is Miss Maher. She and her brother, Simon, live just across the cove from us."

Henry also gave a slight bow. "Madam." He looked around and then up at Mac. "I couldn't find her, Dad. She must have slipped out the back door."

"It's okay, son, I found her. She and Sophie have already gone to the truck." He took hold of Henry's hand, then smiled at the seemingly speechless woman. "If you will excuse us, my boss doesn't like to be kept waiting and I don't wish to get fired." He gave a nod to the hugely grinning gentleman behind the counter, then turned and led Henry up the main aisle toward the door.

"Did you save her again, Dad?" the boy whispered up at him.

"I arrived just in the nick of time," he said, squeezing his hand, "and once again rescued the poor damsel from the clutches of an unwanted suitor."

Henry sighed. "This is becoming something of a habit for us, isn't it?"

Mac swung him up into his arms with a laugh. "Well, son, not all habits are bad."

Heaven help her, she was in trouble; feeling Mac's in-the-flesh arm wrapped around her had been way better than his empty jacket. Olivia had known by his grip that he'd expected her to get all huffy for manhandling her like that, but honest to God, she'd been too busy enjoying being plastered up against his big strong body.

The guy didn't have an ounce of fat on him. Only instead of being hard with pumped-up muscle, Mac seemed more classically athletic; like instead of working out at a gym he just plain *worked*. He was quite tall—a good three or even four inches taller than Keith—and beautifully proportioned and amazingly supple, his stride loose and confident as if every muscle in his body were working in harmony without even trying.

Olivia finally tore her gaze away from the scene outside the ice shanty window and started unpacking the picnic basket. For their entire walk to the truck from the store, Sophie had sworn she hadn't once mentioned the word *boyfriend* or *girlfriend* to Mac, yet the man sure had acted like a boyfriend.

And he'd called her *sweetheart*. Right in front of Simon. Twice.

Hell, her palms getting sweaty and her heart racing had been nothing compared to the perspiration she'd felt gathering between her breasts as she'd stood inside his embrace like an adoring, obedient girlfriend right there in front of God and Missy Maher.

And Ezra, the old poop, was probably still laughing his head off.

And now here she was smack in the middle of a frozen lake, hiding in one of Ezra's fully equipped ice fishing shanties so she could openly stare at Mac, getting all hot and bothered again just watching him effortlessly handle the heavy, powerful auger drilling holes in the ice. And damn if that leather jacket didn't look better on him than it did on her bed, just like it had *felt* better with a real live arm inside it.

Good Lord, being a lonely widow sucked.

Then again, being a lonely wife hadn't exactly been fun, either. In fact, it ranked right up there with being a forgotten daughter. Sometimes Olivia wondered that if she had yet to find a single man who could love her enough to stick around, why was she expecting one to move mountains for her?

Maybe she was aiming too high. Maybe instead of waiting to be loved forever and ever, she should be focusing on having just the first one of those steamy affairs.

Yeah, to hell with her stupid rule of not fraternizing with the guests; why should the campers have all the fun? How many times in the last eleven years had she watched some of the single parents hook up with each other for a discreet little affair? Heck, some of them had obviously kept the relationship going, and even come back in subsequent years married to each other, suddenly needing Inglenook's help to integrate their kids into a new family unit.

So why was it okay for the campers to sneak out of their cabins after their kids had gone to bed to meet on a moonlit beach, or in the gazebo, or down on the nature trail, or even in the backseat of their cars in the parking lot, yet it wasn't okay for her? Hell, she'd even watched one couple—two obviously very coordinated individuals—*do it* right there in the middle of the cove, in the moonlight, in a canoe!

Apparently Missy Maher was a very light sleeper, because less than two days after that particular incident a state inspector had shown up, claiming Inglenook wasn't licensed to run sex therapy programs.

In truth, a few of the single fathers had propositioned Olivia the first summer she'd stopped wearing her wedding band, only she'd still been too angry to consider their offers. And then as Sophie had gotten older and more aware, Olivia had been too afraid to let any of the men get close enough even to ask.

But Mac might not exactly be the best candidate for her first outing back into the world of dating, either. He seemed a little bit too . . . well, too *male*; too intense, too tall and strong and confident, and way too sexy for a woman who hadn't had sex in more than six years.

Maybe Simon Maher was a safer choice.

Except Simon wouldn't be leaving in the fall, so she'd have to go through all that awkward breaking-up business once she'd gained enough confidence to go looking for her next affair, and then she'd find herself running into an ex-lover in town all the time.

Hell, she was just like Goldilocks—only one bed had been too young, one was too old, and the one bed that was just right was too damn sexy.

"Sophie, we need to stop now. No, come back!" she heard Henry shouting. "The ice is getting thin. Stop!"

Olivia dropped the bag of chips and shot out the shanty door, heading after her daughter at a dead run when she spotted the girl chasing a runaway kite. "Sophie! Stop!"

The girl stopped and turned with a frown even as she pointed at the kite skimming across the frozen lake. "My string broke, Mom. I need to go catch my kite before it blows all the way to shore."

"You don't take one more step, young lady!" Olivia shouted as she ran toward her, only to squeak in surprise when Mac caught her sleeve and brought her to a halt beside him and Henry.

"But it's okay, Mom. See?" Sophie said, gesturing at the perfectly normal-looking lake between her and the kite sliding over the snow. "There's no puddles or darkening or anything. Henry's just not used to being on a frozen lake, so he doesn't want to go that far. Look, there's even fishermen over in the cove," she added as she started walking backward.

"Sophie," Mac said, stopping the girl dead in her tracks even as the hairs on Olivia's neck prickled at the quiet authority in his tone. "You will come back to us now."

Apparently Sophie felt it, too, because she immediately started toward them.

Olivia tried to go to her daughter, but Mac held her arm.

"Let her come to us," he said quietly.

She looked around, trying to see what had made Henry decide the ice was getting thin. They were about a mile from shore, surrounded by at least five other parties of fishermen spaced maybe one to two miles apart. And she had watched Mac drill through almost two feet of ice to set their five fishing traps. "I don't understand," she said, more to herself than either of them. She looked at Henry. "What makes you think the ice isn't safe over there?"

He gave her a quizzical look and then shrugged. "I just know." He looked at his father. "I could sense it was getting thinner as we were running after Sophie's kite." He suddenly looked doubtful. "You can feel it, too, can't you, Dad?"

"Yes, son, I feel it. There's probably a spring welling up under the ice, making it thinner in that one spot."

Olivia's neck hairs stirred again. How could either of them possibly know that?

Mac crouched to sit on his heels, bringing his eyes level with Sophie's as she came up to them, and smiled at her. "Henry and I will retrieve your kite when we head back to shore after our picnic. Until then, I'm sure he would enjoy sharing his."

"We can take turns," Henry said, turning to head back to the shanty. "Oh, look! We have a flag! We've caught a fish!"

Olivia started to take hold of Sophie, but noticing she was still shaking from her scare, she shoved her hands in her pockets instead. "Go on," she said, nodding in Henry's direction. "Go show him how to set the hook and pull the fish up through the hole. Just follow your tracks back," she called out when the girl took off at a run. "Maybe we should finish our picnic on shore," she said to Mac, glancing around again at what appeared to be a perfectly normal, solidly frozen lake. She looked at him. "There might be other places it's not safe."

"There's just that one spot in this area," he said as he stood back up. "But it does appear as if Bottomless is beginning to wake up from its winter's sleep." He placed his hand on the small of her back, urging her toward the shanty. "And Henry may have overreacted, Olivia; the ice covering the spring is still several inches thick. But I'm glad he had the sense to err on the side of caution rather than ignore his instincts."

"But how could he possibly know?" She frowned up at him. "Or you, for that matter. There's not one sign that anything is different in that area. Even a seasoned fisherman can't judge how thick the ice is without cutting a hole."

Mac gave her a somewhat arrogant smile. "It would appear my son's been listening to me after all. Since he's come to live with me, I've been teaching Henry that we all have the capacity to *feel* the world around us far better than we see it."

Olivia stopped walking. "You mean like ESP or something? You've been telling Henry you have extrasensory perception? And that he does, too?"

"No more than you do, Olivia. Nor any more than anyone else does. Have you never felt in your gut that something wasn't quite right?" He suddenly turned serious. "Tell me: The first time you met that bastard who attacked you, what was your initial impression of him?"

Olivia dropped her gaze to his chest, feeling her cheeks heat up. "There was something I didn't like about him, only I couldn't decide what." She looked up. "But I don't believe in being judgmental, so I gave Mark the benefit of my doubt."

"So your gut was telling you something wasn't quite right about the man, yet you ignored your instincts in favor of . . . what? Why did you hire him anyway?"

"I couldn't very well tell him I'd changed my mind and that he had to drive all the way back to Georgia just because I didn't like him."

"You were nearly raped because you would rather not hurt his feelings than follow your instincts?"

"So just like Eileen, you're saying it's *my* fault Mark attacked me?" Balling her hands into fists in her pockets, Olivia stepped toward him. "Well, let me tell you, Mr. ESP: I'd rather have a big old sappy heart than no heart at all." She spun toward the shanty, but he took hold of her jacket and pulled her back around.

He cupped her face in his large warm hands to hold her looking at him. "You are the embodiment of heart, Olivia," he said quietly. "And I apologize for implying you had anything to do with your attack." His thumb brushed across one of her scorching cheeks, and his eyes crinkled at their corners. "But I will not apologize for pointing out that our instincts are always stronger than our minds, or that I will still be reminding my son of that truth on my deathbed."

He dropped his hands so suddenly Olivia barely caught herself from staggering forward as he folded his arms over his chest and smiled at her. "Maybe while you're teaching me how to be a good father, there will be one or two things I can teach you. Would you not like to know your daughter will become a strong, confident woman for simply listening to her heart?" He canted his head. "What if she came to you one day and said a certain person made her uncomfortable? Would you tell her to ignore her instinct, or would you suggest she avoid that person?"

Olivia dropped her head with a heavy sigh. "I'd tell her to run like hell."

"Would you like me to go drill a hole in the ice where Henry believes it's thin?"

She snapped her gaze to his. "Why?"

"To see that even a young child knows enough to follow his instincts."

"So now we're back to Mark's attack being my fault."

His smile widened. "No, Olivia. We're back to finding

some way for you to follow your instincts without hurting a person's feelings. Other than ducking out back doors, that is," he said deadpan.

Of all the arrogant—Olivia turned on her heel and started marching toward the shanty again. Only instead of physically stopping her this time, his quiet laughter did.

Dammit to hell, she was not running away! She pivoted around and strode right back up to him, and when she got there she poked him in his big broad chest. "For your information, I was going to fire the idiot the minute we got back to Inglenook. So maybe *his* gut was telling him what was going to happen, and *that's* why he got so angry."

"No," he said, shaking his head. "I believe the bastard was too overwhelmed by your beauty to listen to anything but his raging hormones."

Her jaw dropped in—was he *serious*?

He used his finger to gently close her mouth. "Ah, Olivia; the men in this town are idiots. It's not your dead husband they should be afraid of, but you."

This time Olivia managed to close her gaping mouth before he closed it for her. "What in hell are you talking about?"

"While you were in the store this morning, your daughter told us that Eileen said the men in Spellbound Falls wouldn't ask you to dance at the Christmas party because they're afraid they won't measure up to your deceased husband." He took hold of her hand, which she only now realized was grasping his jacket instead of poking it, and pressed her fingers between his warm palms. "Except that Simon Maher doesn't seem to realize what a shrine you've become to the good people in town."

"Excuse me?" she whispered. "They think I'm a *shrine* to the dead bastard?"

Olivia slapped her free hand over her mouth, craning around to look for Sophie. Seeing her bent over one of the fishing holes with Henry a good fifty yards away, she turned back with a scowl and tried to tug free.

Of course he didn't let her go, because she wasn't holding a baseball bat.

Maybe she needed to get one of those taser-thingies instead.

Because judging by Mac's very stillness, Olivia knew he'd caught her mistake, and this time she didn't have any trouble reading that look in his deep green eyes.

Chapter Seven

Mac sat on the crystallized snow with his back against the shanty and his eyes closed against the sun, and decided he liked picnics. He'd never given much thought to dining outdoors in early spring, but he was finding it to be a rather pleasant experience—though that might have had more to do with his picnic companions than the time of year.

The location was equally unique. If just three short months ago someone had suggested he'd be basking in the sun on a frozen freshwater lake, with a beautiful woman and her daughter as well as a son of his own, Mac would have thought them insane. But here he was stuffed with simply prepared food, utterly relaxed and undeniably the most content he'd been in a long, long time.

Then again, that also might have had something to do with his immediate company.

Olivia was quite easy to be with, he'd discovered, once he'd stopped baiting her long enough to let her relax and enjoy their outing. But he'd been curious to see how she'd react when confronted when she had no place to hide, and . . . well, he certainly hadn't been disappointed.

In fact, he'd been caught completely off guard by the

realization that instead of pining for her dead husband, Olivia actually despised the man. The reason why was anyone's guess; Keith Baldwin could have been a bastard for any number of reasons, from being abusive to unfaithful to indifferent toward her. Which was baffling, really, as Mac couldn't imagine any man not treating Olivia as a prize to be cherished.

The woman was an enigma of beauty and grace and warm swirling energy just begging to engage life, yet she seemed to go out of her way to keep everyone but her daughter at a distance. She certainly had an intelligent if devious mind, he'd found out when she'd put him to work replanking the docks in hopes that he'd rescind his offer to help, and she definitely wasn't afraid to come out swinging—or chest-poking—when backed into a corner.

Mac cracked open his eyes to see her relaxing on the ice a good thirty feet away, reclined against a mound of snow she'd formed on a slant to catch the low-hanging sun. The woman also had a sharp sense of humor, which he'd caught a glimpse of when he'd invited her to sit beside him after she'd finished repacking the picnic basket. Looking him right in the eye while pointing off to her left, she'd said her *gut* was telling her she'd be more comfortable over there, then gracefully sauntered away, dropped to her knees, and started shaping the snow into a bed.

The lady should be thanking the gods they had an audience, as he'd been tempted to jump up and kiss that little smirk right off her face, and not stop until she melted into him. Or rather, into his jacket—the one he'd felt her *accidentally* brush her cheek against several times this afternoon in the close confines of the shanty, just before she would turn away with a soft sigh. The same jacket that now carried more of her scent than it possibly could have taken on in the brief time she'd worn it the day of her attack.

Oh yeah; Olivia was attracted to him, only the poor woman didn't seem to know what to do about it. But Mac supposed being a shrine for four years could get a person out of practice. And for that, the local men's loss was going to be his gain—at least for the next six months.

Mac sat forward just as Henry dropped down beside him with a groan. "Can you tell the fish to stop biting?" the boy whispered, pulling off his hat and wiping his sweaty brow. "Sophie and I just get a hook baited and reset the trap, and another flag goes up. And you drilled the holes so far from each other that we're spending more time running after flags than flying our kite."

"There's not really enough breeze anymore, is there?"

"Well, no. But ice fishing is a lot more work than flying a kite, so I thought you could ask the wind to come back up and the fish to stop being so greedy."

"Sorry, son; you're on your own on both counts," Mac said with a chuckle.

They both looked over to see Sophie flop down to cuddle up against her mother, and Henry released another heavy sigh. "How much longer is this picnic going to last?" he asked softly. "Because I've been thinking we could skip dinner and go find that clearing as soon as we get back to Inglenook. I'm still full from lunch, and if we get hungry you can just teach me what's safe to eat in the forest like you did at the ocean."

Mac leaned against the shanty again, pulling Henry with him. "Unlike tidal pools, the forest plants are dormant right now or buried under what's left of the snow."

"I saw fish in the brook while we were waiting for Sophie's school bus. If we found another brook on our hike, we could catch some and build a fire and cook them." Henry let out a yawn and relaxed into Mac's chest. "I'm glad we came here. I like that there's not as many people in Spellbound Falls as there are in Midnight Bay, even though I do miss Mr. Trace and Miss Fiona and Misneach."

Mac stifled a chuckle. Midnight Bay had a population of all of a thousand people, whereas Spellbound Falls had maybe three hundred residents this time of year. Not exactly metropolises, either one of them.

Henry tilted his head back to grin up at him. "But I don't miss your cooking," he said, covering his giggle with his gloved hand. "Miss Olivia and Miss Eileen don't burn everything." His eyes suddenly turned apprehensive. "Um, I asked Mama last night if it was okay to address adults by their first names like Miss Eileen said I should, but this morning my heart told me that it's just not right. So I decided to use *Miss* or *Mr.* in front of their names, just like I do with everyone in Midnight Bay. Do you think Miss Eileen will mind very much? Even if I tell her my *mama* said I should?"

"Ah, Henry," Mac said, pulling him back to his chest with a deep sigh. "You go right ahead and do what your heart's telling you to, son, and Eileen will just have to respect your decision." He rubbed his thumb along Henry's hairline. "Did you also ask if we need to buy you pajamas?"

Henry nodded without lifting his head. "Mama said that if I'm old enough for sword lessons, then I'm too old to be wearing pajamas like a baby."

Mac gave a quiet chuckle. "Delia is obviously proud of the man you're becoming, Henry. Why don't you have a quick nap with me here in the warm sun," he suggested when the boy yawned again. "And we can skip dinner tonight if you wish."

"But I have to keep watching for flags."

"I believe the fish are about to take a nap, too. So close your eyes, little man, and rebuild your strength for tonight. Though it might be sized for your hand, in the morning I believe your muscles are going to let you know your sword's no toy."

But instead of closing his own eyes, Mac allowed his gaze to wander over the scene before him; the five ice-fishing traps—flags obediently down—and Henry's kite half buried in the snow to keep it from blowing away. The ice auger he'd used to drill the holes lay next to the two empty and four full bottles of beer sitting in the carton Olivia had handed him when they'd first arrived, which was sitting next to the sled they'd used to haul everything out to the shanty. And Olivia with her daughter sleeping in her arms, both their cheeks kissed pink by the sun over the last few hours, and himself with his own child tucked securely against his heart.

To a neutral observer they could be any family out enjoying a beautiful early spring afternoon on one of Maine's more massive lakes.

The very idea stirred something deep inside Mac; a powerful sensation he innately knew was as ancient as the earth itself suddenly making his world shift slightly off center. The word *home* whispered around him on the dying breeze, drawing his gaze to the heavily forested mountains surrounding the lake, their rolling peaks lined up like sentinels charged with keeping the maddening world at bay.

And Mac understood why Olivia had stayed in Spellbound Falls.

He tried to wrap his mind around his contentment, as *home* for him was the ocean, the very womb that had given him life and now sustained it. And still he'd traveled inland for Henry's sake, two hundred miles away from the very essence that pulsed through his veins like blood.

Yet the awareness stirring deep inside him, the whispered litany on the breeze, the expansive lake and towering mountains, the familial scene—all of it triggering something deep inside him that he couldn't describe but desperately wanted to deny. A new and powerful yearning that suddenly scared him far more than having a son did.

"Can I take Henry to go see the falls, Mom?" Sophie asked as Olivia started to open her truck door. But before she could answer, her daughter addressed Mac. "I promise we'll stay on the bridge and I'll hold his hand."

"Or all three of you could go see the falls," Olivia suggest as she climbed out, "while I go in and return the shanty key to Ezra."

Mac opened his door and also got out. "Or we could all return the key and then all go see the falls," he said over the hood of his truck, dropping one of his provocative smiles on her like a loaded hand grenade. "That way we won't have to drag you out of some dark corner of the store again."

"Yes, I do believe Dad and I should go with you, Miss Olivia," Henry said before she could think of a snappy comeback. Only the boy's smile was more compassionate than challenging. "I could even hold your hand if you'd like."

Good Lord, did the child think she needed protecting?

Granted, their first meeting hadn't been under the best of circumstances, but it did seem to have left him with the impression that she was a damsel in distress. Especially since Sophie had ingenuously announced in the truck this morning that her mother had needed to be rescued from Simon.

"That's very chivalrous of you, Henry, but I think I can return the key without getting into any trouble. And besides, Ezra's pretty good at keeping a lookout for me." She checked for vehicles and started across the road without making eye contact with Mac, not wanting to see his amusement.

"My mama taught me that chivalry is the foundation of a civilized society," Henry said, catching up and reaching for her hand.

Olivia let him grasp it with a silent sigh; apparently the son had no more intention of taking no for an answer than his father did. "You have a very wise mama, Henry."

"I told her I was going to be a powerful knight when I grew up," the boy continued. "But now I guess I'm going to be a theurgist instead."

Olivia stopped in front of the trading post as Sophie and Mac crossed the road and stopped beside them. "Um . . . what's a theurgist?"

Henry looked at his father, suddenly uncertain.

"It's an ancient term for *wizard*," Mac said. He shrugged. "Or what you might think of as a magician. Rather than being a knight, Henry's decided he can help people with magic instead of weapons."

"But it's still important to grow big and strong and know how to fight," the boy added, "even though wisdom is stronger than brute strength. Because sometimes people just get contrary, and when both wisdom and warring won't work, then you need to use the magic."

Olivia gave him a warm smile. "Good for you, Henry, for wanting to help people. When I was your age I wanted to be a teacher."

"Teachers help people," he said, his expression conciliatory as he squeezed her hand. "And in a way, theurgists are teachers. We help everyone learn how to get along together." He looked up at Mac again. "Right, Dad?"

Mac opened the trading post door. "That's right, son. Come on, let's return the key so we can go see the falls before it gets too late."

Both children ran inside, and Olivia walked down the narrow aisle beside Mac. "Where would Henry have learned such a rare word as *theurgist*? I don't think *I've* ever heard it before. Oh, damn," she hissed, stopping when she saw Ezra bobbing his bushy eyebrows at her as he nodded to his left. Olivia immediately started backing up as she looked around. "Now who the hell's in here?" She shoved the shanty key at Mac. "You take this to Ezra, and I'll wait for you and the kids in the truck."

"It's locked," he said as he handed her the key fob. He went very still all of a sudden, his head lifted as if he were listening for something, then smiled. "There's a chance you'll make a clean escape if you're quick. But watch for traffic," he called after her as Olivia bolted toward the door.

Only she ran smack into Janice Crupp just as she reached the end of the aisle, and then had to catch the elderly woman to keep her from falling into a rack of clothing.

"Good grief!" Janice cried, grabbing Olivia. "I didn't see you!"

"But we're glad we ran into you," Christina Richie said as she helped steady her friend. "We've been trying to reach you for days, Livy. Didn't Eileen give you any of our messages?"

"She did," Olivia said, eyeing her escape route only to

decide she couldn't be so rude as to run out the door. "But I've been so busy getting Inglenook ready for the new season that I guess time got away from me. And I'm sorry, but I can't really chat with you right now. I'm with a couple of my guests."

"Olivia was about to show us the falls," Mac said, coming up beside her.

Just barely catching herself from leaning into him so he could put his arm around her, Olivia ended up sighing instead when he didn't. Apparently that only happened when he was rescuing her from *men*. Both women's gazes traveled up over Mac's broad chest to his handsome face, and Janice even had to step back to see him.

Mac gave a slight bow. "Mac Oceanus," he said, his tone as charming as his smile. "I'm actually more Olivia's employee than her guest."

God, she wished he'd quit telling everyone that. Nobody in their right mind could see her bossing him around—including Janice and Christina, judging by their shock.

But then Olivia suddenly went as still as a stone herself, at the realization of why the man kept telling people she was his boss. Good Lord, she hadn't been teased in so long she'd forgotten it even existed.

"I'm Janice Crupp, and this is my friend, Christina Richie," Janice said, making the introductions since Olivia was too busy trying to remember if teasing was the same as flirting. "We're co-chairs of the Spellbound Falls Memorial Day committee," Janice continued—just before grabbing Olivia's sleeve and pulling her away from the towering protector she'd been inching behind.

Because dammit, she had a pretty good idea why the ladies had been looking for her, and she really, really didn't want to talk to them.

"We've left at least four messages asking you to call us," Janice continued, "to tell you that we want you and Sophie to be the grand marshals of our parade this year."

And they wondered why she'd been avoiding them?

Olivia gave the women an appreciative smile. “Gee, that’s really sweet of you ladies, but I don’t think—”

“And all the funds we raise over the summer,” Christina broke in excitedly, “are going to provide you and Sophie with an all-expenses-paid trip to Disneyland.”

Olivia reared back in surprise. “What!”

Janice shook her head. “We know its way overdue, Livy, and we’re sorry. And we’re all ashamed of ourselves for letting four years go by without doing something to show you how much everyone appreciates your sacrifice.”

“My . . . what in hell are you talking about?”

Christina shot her a scowl. “Now Livy, there’s no need for profanity.” But then she reached over and patted her arm. “I guess the shock of our good news just got the best of you.”

“But what sacrifice are you talking about?”

This time Janice gave her arm a pat. “At our Grange meeting last month, Bunkie Watts mentioned a segment she saw on CNN about how people around the nation are doing different things to support our troops and their families. Bunkie said towns are having fund-raisers to send families on fancy vacations together.”

“But—”

“And you’re the only war widow we got, Livy,” Christina interjected. “And so the vote was unanimous that we should send you and Sophie to Disneyland. Thelma got on her Internet at the post office and found out there’s an entire organization dedicated to providing trips to our servicemen’s families.”

“And they even have special trips for people who’ve lost a loved one in the war,” Janice added. “We’re going to try and get you and Sophie on one of those, so you can meet others who know exactly how you feel.” She stepped closer. “It would be healing for both you and that precious little girl of yours.”

Olivia started backing away, shaking her head even as she looked around for her daughter. “That’s very kind of you ladies," she said, holding out her hand when they started following. "But Sophie and I don't want . . . I can't . . . really, we're doing just—"

"Mom, look what we found," Sophie said, running up the aisle with a box in her hand, Henry right on her heels. "It's a *magic* kit." She held the box up to Olivia. "It's got a book that tells how to do all the tricks, and a long scarf and some magic coins and even fake money to practice with." She held the box toward Mac. "Could you buy it for Henry, Mac? He wants to start being a thee— . . . a theer— . . . a wizard. And I can help him practice."

Instead of taking the box, Mac pulled out his wallet. He took out two twenties and handed them to Henry. "You can pay the gentleman, son. And here," he said, handing him the key to the shanty. "Return this to him, also."

"Sophie, wait," Janice said excitedly as the girl turned away.

"No!" Olivia snapped, stepping between them. "Go on, Sophie; go help Henry buy the magic kit. And thank Ezra for letting us use the shanty," she said while giving Janice a warning glare. "I don't want anyone mentioning this to her," she said when she heard Sophie running down the aisle. "Understand?"

Clearly taken aback, Janice flapped her jaw several times, trying to speak.

Olivia slashed her hand in the air to cut her off. "You can't just up and decide to send us on a trip without discussing it with me first. And you sure as hell can't get a little girl excited about something that is *not* going to happen."

"But, Livy," Christina said, her face darkening. "This is a great honor. Why *wouldn't* you accept it?"

"And just exactly what did I do to deserve this honor?"

"Your husband died in Iraq," Janice snapped, "leaving you to raise your daughter all by yourself. These trips are a town's way of thanking all the people left behind for their sacrifices, especially the lonely widows and children."

"And is Spellbound Falls going to thank Peg Thompson for her sacrifice?" Olivia whispered, shoving her hands in her pockets to hide her fists. "Are you going to send her and her children to Disneyland?"

"But Billy Thompson didn't die in the war," Christina pointed out.

"No, Billy died in a construction accident while working to feed his family. Does that make him any less of a hero in their eyes? Or does it make Peg any less of a widow?" Olivia sucked in a calming breath and released it slowly. "Look, ladies; I really appreciate what you're trying to do, but I'm afraid I'm not going to let you do it to me. Sophie and I have everything we need, and if I thought a trip to Disneyland would be good for her, I'm quite capable of getting us there on my own."

"But what about Eileen?" Janice asked.

"What about her?"

"She and John lost their only child, Livy. And when we told Eileen what we were planning, she was truly honored."

"We all lose people we love," Mac said quietly, *finally* wrapping his arm around her. "So I think what Olivia is trying to say is that yes, your brave troops and their families deserve to be recognized for their sacrifices, but that she would be uncomfortable being honored while Mrs. Thompson is not. How about if at your next Grange meeting you discuss a compromise? Maybe you could erect a plaque for your fallen heroes from all wars someplace here in town, and use what money is left to start a general widows' fund. That way you would be helping so many more people."

Once again, Olivia witnessed Mac's quiet authority work a magic of its own, and both women's expressions turned thoughtful.

"Well . . . I suppose that does make a certain sense," Christina murmured. She smiled sheepishly at Olivia. "We're truly sorry, Livy. I guess none of us stopped to think how this might open up an old wound that's obviously still painful for you. It's just that everyone knows how much you miss Keith, and we really wanted to show you that all of Spellbound Falls still loves him as much as you do."

Olivia felt Mac's arm tighten around her and realized she was trembling.

"If you ladies will excuse us," he said with a nod. "I believe we need to go check on the children."

"Yes, of course," Janice said, each woman giving Olivia a sad smile as they left.

"Easy now," Mac whispered, turning to wrap both of his arms around her. He chuckled. "I'm beginning to understand your propensity for ducking out back doors."

She really shouldn't be standing in the center aisle of the Bottomless Mercantile & Trading Post wrapped up in the arms of her *employee*, but Olivia simply melted into him with a groan.

Forget the baseball bat and taser-thingy, because really, she just needed to wear *Mac* whenever she came to town.

Chapter Eight

"If you'd like, I can give you folks the key to cabin three, seeing how it's a lot more private than the middle of my store."

Mac looked over Olivia's head at the man shuffling down the aisle toward them and immediately knew two things: the gentleman was her friend, since she didn't stiffen and try to step away, and judging by the twinkle in the old man's clouded blue eyes, the storekeeper was rather pleased to see her in Mac's arms.

"Ezra Dodd," he said when he reached them. "And if you don't mind, I'd like to shake your hand, big fella."

"Mac Oceanus," Mac said, taking his offered hand. "Olivia's employee."

"So I understand. Eileen told me how you saved Olivia from that idiot punk the other day, and I want to personally thank you for that." The twinkle in the old man's eyes intensified. "I've been noticing a pattern of you pulling our girl here out of the pickles she keeps getting herself into," Ezra said, still pumping Mac's hand as his gaze traveled to Olivia, who still had her face buried in his jacket.

Mac gave a chuckle when the man finally let him go.

"Yes, I believe I may have to change my job description from handyman to bodyguard."

"Well, big fella, you seem to have the qualifications, your size being the most obvious. You gonna hide in there till closing, Olivia, or you want me to run back and fetch that key to cabin three? I just got it scrubbed up and aired out yesterday."

Mac felt Olivia take a deep breath, and when she finally lifted her head, she was wearing a sassy little smirk. "Last I knew, cabin three only has short double beds," she said, stepping out of his embrace and turning to her friend. She nodded over her shoulder. "And I don't think this 'big fella' will fit in any of them."

She then gave the old man a warm hug, confirming for Mac that Ezra Dodd held a special place in her heart. "Thanks for trying to warn me." She shook her head. "I swear I didn't see that one coming. I'd caught wind they wanted Sophie and me to be in the Memorial Day parade, but I had no idea they planned to send us to Disneyland."

"They meant well, girl." Ezra gestured toward Mac. "But your fella there ended up giving them an even better bone to gnaw on."

"You heard that from way down back?" she asked, clearly surprised.

"I might be half blind but my ears still work," he said, his grin implying he wasn't offended. "So, how was your picnic? Were the fish biting?"

"They were until around one o'clock, then just suddenly stopped."

"You might wish to pull your rental shanties from the lake soon," Mac interjected. "I believe Bottomless is getting ready to shed its winter coat of ice."

Ezra sighed. "I was hoping to get another two or three weeks out of that lake, but seeing the shoreline's already starting to rot in places, I made plans for Grundy to drag them off for me. How's Whisper holding up, Olivia? That's usually the first lake around here to go out."

"Its edges have softened and the center's already darkening."

"Mom, look," Sophie said, running up with a pair of boots in her hands, Henry right behind her clutching his magic kit to his chest. "Mr. Ezra got in some new mud boots just for girls. See, they're pink."

"*Mr.* Ezra?" Olivia asked.

Sophie darted a glance at the storekeeper and then frowned up at her mother. "When Henry heard me calling his dad *Mac*, he said his mama told him that children shouldn't call adults by their first names. So he puts a *Mr.* or *Miss* in front of them, and he calls strangers *sir* or *madam.* I think it sounds kind of neat so I'm trying it out, because Henry says people like kids better when we act respectful to our elders. Do you think it'll make Missy stop scowling at me every time I say hi to her?" The girl's eyes suddenly widened. "*Miss Missy*'s gonna sound funny."

"But better than just plain *Missy.*" Olivia shot Mac what appeared to be a grateful smile, as if this were somehow his doing. "I think it's a wonderful idea, Sophie. What do you think, Mr. Ezra?"

"Sounds like a fine plan to me."

"So, can I get the boots?"

"You already have a perfectly good pair of mud boots. I bought them a whole size too big last spring, remember?"

"But these are *pink.*"

"They won't be the first time you wear them outside."

"Please, Mom."

Mac started to reach for his wallet. But when Ezra cleared his throat and gave him a barely perceptible negative headshake, Mac shoved his hands in his pockets with a thankful nod. Yes, knowing Olivia, she wouldn't want him to think she couldn't afford to buy her daughter a pair of boots, just as she'd refused his offer to contribute to their picnic, not even letting him pay for the beer she'd thoughtfully brought for him.

"Next year, sweetie," she said, passing the boots to Ezra.

"Come on, let's go show Henry and Mr. Mac the falls." She took Sophie's hand and started toward the door. "We don't want them to be late for supper, as Eileen is serving veggie burgers and bean sprouts tonight. See you around, Ezra," she said with a wave over her shoulder.

Mac felt Henry give a shiver when he took the boy's hand, and after a nod to Ezra, they began following the women. "I assume by that shiver you don't care for veggie burgers and bean sprouts?" he asked.

"I'm not exactly sure what they are," Henry said, shuddering all over again. "But I am glad I don't have to find out tonight." He frowned up at him. "I wasn't supposed to tell Miss Olivia I'm going to be a theurgist, was I?"

"It's okay, son. I explained it's just another word for a magician."

"But it's not, really." He stopped at the door and held out the magic kit. "Only Sophie was so excited when we found this, I didn't want to disappoint her by explaining that theurgists don't do tricks with coins and scarves. We use the magic to *help* people."

Mac crouched down to be level with him. "But first a theurgist must learn how to control the magic." He tapped the kit. "And though this is nothing more than a toy, there's no harm in you and Sophie playing with it. Nor is there any harm in letting her and Olivia believe that you intend to be a magician." Mac straightened and opened the door, ushering him outside. "Just try to remember to use modern words from now on. And especially not the Latin your old tutor taught you; except in the sciences you'll be studying in school it's considered a dead language. And I'm not going to be able to explain that one away quite so easily."

"I'll try to remember, I promise."

"That's all I ask, Henry." He stopped at the street and checked for traffic, once again noticing there was barely a car in sight, and led Henry over to his truck. Since he'd given his key fob to Olivia, Mac set the magic kit on the roof, then followed Henry over to the narrow bridge where the women were standing.

Though it was a constant sound in the background, the roar of the falls grew louder as he approached. Once Mac reached the bridge he saw the powerful surge of water pushing through the spruce forest floor towering above him, first appearing back from the road several hundred yards. The water tumbled in a boiling froth before spilling over a granite ledge at least sixty feet straight down no more than a stone's throw away from where he stood. The thunderous crash of the falls pummeling the narrow gorge shook the bridge beneath his feet, the force of it sending spray flying upward into a mist, creating a microclimate of cooled air and swirling breeze. The rushing stream then settled into a deep churning pool before continuing under the two side-by-side bridges, where it pushed into Bottomless Lake, cutting a long open channel far into the ice.

The main road through Spellbound Falls effectively cut the tiny town in half, the stream bisecting the town in half again. The buildings, some more than a century old, appeared to be clinging to the mountain responsible for the falls, as if to keep themselves from tumbling into Bottomless Lake.

Mac stepped closer to Olivia to be heard over the thunder of the pounding water. "Do you know how the falls got its name?"

"Legend has it a group of surveyors plotting out townships set up their base camp here," she explained, leaning against the metal rail as she shoved her hands in her pockets. "It's said they arrived in the dead of winter and could hear the falls, but the fog from the spray was so thick they didn't actually see it for several days." She shrugged. "One rumor claims they named it Spellbound because they kept staring at it as if mesmerized, captured in the spell of the changing rainbow the spray created."

A sassy smirk appeared, lifting one side of her mouth. "But another rumor, dating back to when this was no more than a logging camp, claims that the women who came here looking for husbands are the ones who named it Spellbound Falls." Her smirk grew into a full-blown grin. "Seems the women decided a magic spell was cast over any couple who kissed while standing in the spray, causing them to fall head over heels in love with each other."

She nodded across the street. "The first permanent building to go up was the church. Then some single-family homes, a general store where Ezra's store now sits, a large boardinghouse for the bachelors and another one for the women, a livery, and a train station." She pulled a hand out of her pocket and gestured toward Inglenook. "The road ends about ten miles up, at an old lumber mill. The railroad tracks used to end there, too, and there's an old roundabout house where they turned the steam engines around. The timber was either rafted down the rivers or hauled by horse-drawn sleds to the lumber mill, sawed into boards, then the boards taken by train down to Bangor where they were loaded onto schooners bound for Boston."

"So that's why there's so little traffic," Mac said, leaning against the opposite railing facing her. He folded his arms over his chest and crossed his feet at the ankles, gazing around the town. "This is literally the end of the road."

"We get more traffic in the summer. Logging roads continue up into the mountains all the way to Canada, only they haven't been cutting much back there for several years. Now the traffic headed through town is mostly people going to their camps on the lakes farther north, and fishermen and hunters."

"I don't see a school," Mac said.

"That's the only thing I don't like about living here; the kids have a forty-five-minute bus ride every morning and afternoon. There are about thirty kids in Spellbound, from kindergarten through high school, who get bused to Turtleback Station." She shrugged. "That's the closest we have to an actual town. Turtleback doesn't have any big-box stores, but there's a wide variety of shops and restaurants, an elementary and high school, a decent-sized grocery store, and even an old movie theater."

Mac looked at the bridge they were standing on, which was a separate structure from the road bridge. "I take it the train no longer comes through here? This appears to have been a train trestle that's been converted to a footbridge."

"The mill at the end of the paved road closed about forty years ago and the tracks were abandoned." She shot him a smile. "And the Grange ladies declared that the tracks and trestle were town property not a year after the last train went through. They ripped up the rails for several miles in each direction to create a nature path, turned the trestle into a footbridge, and built the park around the stream in hopes that Spellbound Falls would become a tourist destination."

"It appears the Grange women have always been rather busy."

"Oh, yeah. Only about twenty years ago the snowmobile clubs in several of the towns along the abandoned tracks started using the old rail beds for snowmobile trails in the winter and ATV trails in the summer." She gestured both right and left of the trestle. "Which actually worked out better for Spellbound; people travel from all over New England to snowmobile here, which gives the stores and camps and inns a steady stream of winter business. The trails are groomed so perfectly they're smoother and faster than most roads. In fact, we have a fleet of ten snowmobiles at Inglenook, and during our winter sessions we take families out on trail rides."

Mac remembered something Simon Maher had said. "What was Simon referring to this morning, about your losing some of your guests?"

That sure as hell wiped the smile off her face. "It was only a problem *once*, and then it ended up being the best thing that ever happened to the Minks. And it was the dead of summer, so it's not like they were going to get frostbite or anything. We haven't lost anyone since, because Eileen went ballistic when she realized I was losing them on purpose."

Mac arched a brow. "Any particular reason why?"

Her grin returned. "It all started when I got so angry at one family that I just up and ditched them to keep from shoving them all off a cliff. But I stayed close by, waiting for them to realize they didn't have a clue how to get back to

Inglenook." Her smile widened. "I guess there's nothing like the fear of being eaten by a bear to get teens and parents talking to each other. Instead of constantly bickering, they quickly formed a cohesive group with the common goal of getting back before dark." She shrugged. "So without saying anything to Eileen, I started accidentally losing any family that couldn't seem to get their act together."

But then she scowled. "Only when I ditched the Minks, I ended up losing them for real. There was a mom and dad and a teenage boy and girl, and I swear I hadn't left them more than fifteen minutes. But the Minks got their act together quicker than most and started hiking in what they thought was the direction of Inglenook, and I flat-out lost them. It took eighty searchers three days to finally locate them, as they'd covered nearly twenty miles in the exact opposite direction."

She went back to smiling, though sheepishly. "All four of them were good sports despite being tired and bug-bitten, and thankfully they didn't sue us. But even though they've come back every year since, Eileen still won't let me take families on excursions anymore." She straightened away from the rail. "We should probably head back so you don't miss supper," she said, looking around. She suddenly grew alarmed. "Sophie! Henry!" she shouted over the sound of the falls. "Where are you!"

"They're okay, Olivia. They're sitting on the bench next to one of the pines in front of the pool, talking."

Mac watched her take a calming breath. "I swear that girl's been getting so independent lately she's starting to scare me. She's been asking me to let her go sleep over with some of her classmates who live in other towns, but I simply can't stand the thought of her being twenty or thirty miles away at night." She looked up at him, her eyes darkening with that underlying sadness—which had all but disappeared today out on the lake. "She's growing up so fast, and Eileen's been pushing me to let Sophie go spend the night with her friends, but that's one battle she's not going to win."

Apparently realizing she'd revealed too much to him

again, Olivia started walking down the trestle toward the children.

So, the woman not only despised her dead husband, it seemed she wasn't all that enamored with her mother-in-law, either. But Mac didn't think Olivia felt the same way toward her father-in-law, and he knew from his short conversation with John at breakfast yesterday that the man certainly had a soft spot for her.

"There's no rush," Mac said, catching up. "I called Eileen earlier and told her Henry and I won't be at dinner tonight. We have other plans."

She stopped in surprise. "When did you call her? And from where?"

He reached in his pocket and pulled out his cell phone. "I called this afternoon, when we were on the lake."

"But there's no service out here because of the mountains."

He flipped it open and held it facing her. "I have a strong signal."

She actually took the phone from him and scowled at the screen. "But that's impossible," she said, handing it back.

"Check yours for a signal," he suggested.

She looked up with a crooked grin. "Why would I own a cell phone if there's no service up here? And who would I call, anyway?"

"Your family?" he hazarded to guess.

She snorted and started walking toward the children again. "I live a stone's throw away from them; all I have to do is step out my door and shout."

"Not the Baldwins; *your* family. Do they live here in Maine?"

Without breaking stride, she reached in her pocket, pulled out his key fob, and handed it to him. "Last I knew I was an only child and am probably an orphan by now."

Mac stopped at the end of the trestle, watching Olivia make her way down the path winding through the park. She didn't have a family, other than the Baldwins? Maybe that was the reason she was still here, as the woman literally had no place else to go. He gave a sharp whistle to Henry just as Olivia reached them. His son said something to her, and after a slight bow he headed toward Mac at a run.

"Sophie says I should be going to school," Henry said when he reached the trestle. "Is that true?"

"Yes," Mac said, starting back toward the truck. "But we need to be in a permanent home before I can enroll you in school."

"Will that be in Midnight Bay?"

"Yes. When we go back I'll purchase a house on the ocean, and you'll likely go to the same school that Maddy's daughter, Sarah, goes to."

"Based on what Sophie and Sarah have told me, I believe I'm going to like school instead of being tutored. The lessons should be fun with other children around."

Mac stifled a shudder, trying to imagine Henry in school all day, out of his reach and definitely out of his control. "I'm sure it will be enlightening for both of us." He unlocked the truck, took down the magic kit, and opened the back door. "Hop in and buckle up." Mac took off his jacket and hung it on the back of his driver's seat, then walked around and opened both doors on the other side for the ladies.

The drive to Inglenook was made in relative silence but for the soft murmurs coming from the backseat as the children thumbed through the magic book.

"You and Sophie only eat breakfast with Eileen and John?" Mac asked into the silence of the front seat. "What about when camp is in session?"

"We only have breakfast with them on the weekends and an occasional Saturday night supper. I've always tried to keep a normal routine for Sophie at home." She gave him a quick glance, then stared out the windshield again. "That's why I moved out of the main lodge and into what was originally the groundskeeper's cottage when I realized I was pregnant." She shot him a smile. "You'll notice there's a fence and small gate halfway down the path, which I put up when Sophie was four because she'd started dragging home camp kids. The rule is no guests beyond that gate."

"Child or adult?"

"Yup. That little cottage is home, and if I didn't make it a steadfast rule, people would be showing up every time they wanted to ask me a question. I had a bit of a go-round with Eileen," she said, glancing over her shoulder to make sure the children were engaged in their own conversation, "when I put up a bell at the gate, and a sign that said to ring it instead of coming to my door." Her smile turned smug. "She wasn't real happy when I explained that she was only welcome as Sophie's grandmother, not my boss. I pointed out that I have an office in the main lodge, and she could talk about Inglenook to me all she wanted in there."

"Surely Eileen understood your need to create a sanctuary away from your work for you and your daughter?"

She looked back out the windshield with a snort, and they fell into companionable silence again. Mac finally drove up the lane leading to her house, but stopped next to the fence rather than following the driveway all the way to her door. He walked back and opened the rear hatch and started unloading their picnic remains—including Sophie's torn kite that he and Henry had retrieved from shore—and set everything beside the fence post. Olivia grabbed one of the large canvas bags, then ducked into the backseat to gather up what Mac assumed were her daughter's hat and mittens.

"What time should I report to work tomorrow?" he asked.

She handed their trash bag to her daughter with instructions to put it in their shed, and then turned to him. "I take Sophie down to meet the bus just before seven." She shot him a devious grin. "But you can finish replanking the docks without me."

"Olivia," he said when she'd taken several steps inside her private sanctuary. "Thank you for sharing your day with us; I know Henry had a good time, and I can't remember when I last spent such an enjoyable day in such good company."

Her beautiful cinnamon eyes turned a bit sad again, even though her smile was genuine. "You're welcome." She hesitated. "Um, maybe we can do it again sometime."

"I'd like that." He canted his head. "When was the last time you and Sophie visited the ocean?"

She hesitated again, her eyes growing distant. "It's been a few years."

"Then what if before Inglenook starts up, the four of us sneak off for the day and head down to the coast?"

When she didn't immediately answer, Mac guessed his invitation might be a little too much too soon, or maybe a little too far away from home for her.

But then he saw her take a deep breath and her shoulders went back. "Eileen and John will be gone next weekend, but Sophie and I are free the following Sunday."

Making sure neither his surprise nor his elation showed, Mac merely nodded. "And dinner will be my treat."

"Just as long as it's not tofu lobster," she drawled. And this time when she walked away, Mac noticed that a good deal of Olivia's intrinsic grace had returned.

He shut the rear hatch and got back in his truck. "You ready to go learn how to slay dragons?" he asked, smiling in his rearview mirror at his son.

"Not dragons," Henry said with a shake of his head, utterly serious. "That would hurt Mr. William's feelings." He puffed out his chest. "You need to teach me to slay demons." But then the boy's eyes suddenly turned haunted. "They can't . . . you won't let them get near me again, will you, Dad? Not until I'm all grown up and strong enough to fight the demon bastards myself?" he whispered.

Mac turned in his seat to look at him directly. "As the gods are my witness, you have my word that nothing and no one will ever get close enough to harm you again, Henry. And by the time you're a grown man, I promise you the demon bastards will run in fear at just the sound of your roar."

Henry's expression turned fierce, his hand slashing the

air as though wielding a sword. "And they will dissolve into dust when I chase them down and cut them in half. And then I'll go after whoever created them, and send him crawling home with his stones in his pocket like Grampy did to Uncle Jarlath."

Mac gave him an equally fierce grin before turning around to hide his own haunted eyes as he started the truck and headed for their cabin. "I want you to go in and put some warm clothes in your backpack. You're going to need them for our hike back, so you don't get chilled after getting sweaty."

He shut off the truck when they reached their cabin, then got out and opened Henry's door. Crouching down to look the boy level in the eyes when he got out, Mac took hold of his small shoulders. "You understand why Grampy did what he did, don't you, Henry?"

The boy nodded solemnly, his eyes growing haunted again. "Mama's brothers wouldn't have stopped until you were dead and they had control of me. But I don't understand why Grampy didn't kill all three of them. How come he only maimed Uncle Jarlath and then let him go?"

"He wanted Jarlath to be a living reminder of what happens to anyone who incurs the wrath of an Oceanus. What we do is serious business, Henry, and all of humanity depends on us to keep the knowledge out of the hands of those who would abuse it." Mac gave the boy's shoulders a reassuring squeeze. "It's not always a pleasant task we've been called to, but . . . well, it is what it is. Once your Grampy Titus made the decision to champion mankind by planting that first Tree of Life, his fate—and mine and someday yours—was sealed."

Mac pulled the wide-eyed boy into a hug. "And so it's you and me and Grampy against the world now, son; and we will keep all the powerful drùidhs, who protect the Trees of Life now growing all over the world, safe from the evil." He leaned away to smile at him. "We are theurgists, Henry, and it's very important that you see our calling as a blessing rather than a curse, and embrace it completely."

"Is that why mama sent you away before you knew about me—because she didn't want me to grow up to be just like you and Grampy?"

Mac shook his head. "Delia knew she couldn't stop your destiny, but I believe she wished to give you a normal childhood until you became a man." He hugged the boy to him again. "And I will honor your mama's wish for as long as I can, Henry. We will stay here in Maine, in this century, and you'll go to school with children your age and discover all the wondrous, *everyday* magic this world has to offer." He held him tightly for several heartbeats, then set him away and stood up. "But that doesn't mean you can't start learning the skills that will serve you in adulthood." Mac gave him a gentle nudge. "So go prepare your backpack and get your sword."

Henry took all of two steps and turned back, gazing around before frowning at him. "But it's still daylight. What if someone sees our swords on our backs?"

"Then I guess your first lesson should probably include becoming invisible."

Though Mac figured Olivia could teach Henry that little trick as well as he could.

"But you can't waste your powers on something that trivial," Henry said in surprise. "At least not for the next hundred years."

"Ah, but becoming invisible isn't so much magic as a state of mind. Does a brooding partridge not become invisible to the hawk when she sits on her nest in the dried leaves? And do a tiger's stripes not conceal it in the tall grass from its prey?"

"Then tonight we will be tigers!" Henry said, pivoting and running to the cabin. "And we will have rabbit for dinner!"

Mac walked to the rear of his truck with a laugh, mentally warning all the rabbits in the area to be on guard for a young theurgist with a tiger's appetite.

He lifted the rear hatch, then went very still as he scanned the grounds of Inglenook, making sure he wasn't being observed before he reached in and opened the false panel on the inside of the fender. He pulled out his own sheathed sword—which was nearly as long as Henry was tall—and settled the sheath's harness over his shoulders so that the hilt was within easy reach of his left hand. He closed the panel and hatch, then walked to Henry's open door to grab his jacket off the back of the front seat.

Only it wasn't there.

He straightened, snapping his gaze to Olivia's home. She hadn't been getting Sophie's belongings out of the backseat; she'd been filching his jacket!

Mac dropped his forehead to the cold metal of his truck with a groan. Sweet Zeus, that was going to raise hell with him tonight as he lay in bed picturing Olivia sleeping in his jacket—even as he wished she were in his arms instead.

Chapter Nine

Olivia was finally ready to admit that her little obsession with Mac's jacket was getting out of hand; not only had she actually stolen it from him yesterday, but here she was freezing her tail off this morning, skulking from tree to tree trying to return the damn thing before he discovered it was missing.

She peeked around the towering pine to squint through the predawn light at cabin ten, deciding she really needed to stop this foolishness before she ended up completely humiliating herself. She couldn't exactly spend the summer ducking in and out of buildings to avoid Mac, now could she, considering he actually *lived* here.

Why couldn't the man be short and fat and poor and . . . effeminate or something? He could at least be obnoxious or loud or a coma-inducing bore.

But, oh no, Maximilian Oceanus was *perfect*; perfectly tall and handsome and unbelievably strong, as well as charming and attentive and apparently richer than God.

Olivia pressed her back against the tree with a snort. He was also a flirt and a tease and so damned self-confident she wanted to smack him.

Why in hell wasn't he married? How had such a perfect man managed to reach his age without some beautiful, confident, perfect woman scarfing him up?

Olivia gave a silent gasp. Maybe there was an ex–Mrs. Oceanus. Or two or three or half a dozen! Hell, the guy probably changed women like she changed television channels.

Damn. Maybe he wasn't so perfect after all.

But wait: If Mac was a womanizer, wouldn't that make him perfect for *her*? Because if she knew right up front there wasn't going to be any forever and ever, then she couldn't get her heart broken. She could just sit back—or rather *lie* back—and enjoy herself, and finally end her sexual drought by having an affair with the real thing instead of his stupid jacket.

Olivia peeked around the tree again, scanning the darkened windows of cabin ten and the surrounding area. Deciding the coast was clear, she scurried over to a giant maple and pressed her back against it, crushing his jacket to her pounding heart.

So really, what did she have to lose by having an affair with him?

Well, other than her dignity if she made a complete fool of herself—which sure as hell was possible considering she hadn't had sex in more than six years.

What if she'd forgotten how? Or worse, what if he flat-out rejected her before she actually found the courage to try?

Olivia stared down at the jacket. Was giving up her fantasy to go after the unknown worth the price she might end up paying? Hell, even if she could remember how to flirt, she'd never been very good at it. To this day she didn't know how she'd caught Keith's interest, only that she hadn't been able to hold it more than a few years, and then likely only because he'd rarely been home.

Olivia clutched her bathrobe closed at the neck against the frosty chill in the air and peeked around the maple. She was putting this stupid jacket in Mac's truck and leaving it there, and if he continued flirting with her, she . . . she would just flirt back, dammit! Because even making a fool of herself had to be better than turning into a dried-up old spinster.

"Please be unlocked," she prayed as she made a dash for the truck—only to go perfectly still when its lights suddenly flashed and its doors clicked locked. She closed her eyes on a silent curse, so embarrassed she couldn't move, much less breathe.

"Did you forget something in my truck?" he asked from somewhere behind her.

Apparently she wasn't the only one skulking around in the dark this morning. "I . . . your jacket must have fallen into my tote bag," she said without turning around.

"And you felt compelled to get up before dawn to return it?"

"Well, yeah. I didn't want you to spend the morning looking for it, or worry that you'd left it in the ice shanty or . . . or something."

"I appreciate your concern."

"You're welcome." She reached out to hang the jacket on the truck's side mirror, only to gasp when he took hold of her shoulders and turned her around. And not only did she stop breathing again but her heart stopped beating.

God, he was big and strong and broad-chested.

"All you need do is ask, Olivia. I promise I will say yes."

Knowing damn well he wasn't referring to his jacket, her heart resumed pounding so hard she was afraid he would hear it. And she sure as hell couldn't lift her gaze to his, knowing his deep, dark eyes would be just as serious as his tone, and so imposing her knees would probably buckle.

And then he'd catch her before she hit the ground, and she would get lost in all that wonderful masculine strength, and . . . and she would ask.

"I—I can't. I'm too scared."

He cupped her face between his strong warm hands and lifted her gaze to his. "You have my word I will be gentle," he said quietly, lowering his mouth to within inches of hers. "And very careful with you, and . . . unrushed."

She didn't know if he moved or if she did, but suddenly their lips were touching. And once again Olivia found herself standing in a receding wave, her world tilting so far off center she had to drop his jacket and clutch his arms to keep from falling.

She nearly wept at how good it felt to be kissed.

Olivia pressed her mouth to his, needing to make sure this was really happening, that all the controlled strength in this towering mass of testosterone wasn't merely a fantasy that smelled of the forest and tasted divine.

Because all she had to do was ask, and he'd become real.

She parted her lips to test her courage, surprising herself by not retreating when his tongue gently eased inside. Bolstered by the fact that her knees were still holding up against the riot of sensations sweeping through her, she gave a soft hum of pleasure.

He broke the kiss to rest his forehead against hers. "Ask me, Olivia."

"I . . . it's been over six years, Mac. I've forgotten . . . I don't know . . . I'm afraid."

"You're not afraid of *me*," he said, wrapping her up in his big strong arms with a heavy sigh. "We both know it's going to happen," he said against her hair, the authority in his voice washing through her like warm, liquid heat. "And I prefer it be sooner than later, as I'm not sure I'll survive another night like the one I just spent envying my jacket. Ask me, Olivia," he whispered. "Give me permission to act."

"I don't want to disappoint you."

He tilted her head back and brushed his thumb across her cheek. "You could only do that by not asking." He canted his head. "Did your husband leave you with a bad taste for lovemaking?"

She tried to push away. "That's none of your business."

He held her looking at him. "Yes, it is. If it's not me you're afraid of, then it must be something else."

"What makes you so sure I'm not afraid of you?"

The smile he gave her was so arrogant, the ground beneath her tilted again. "That you spent the last three nights sleeping with my jacket tells me that whatever you feel toward me, it's not fear."

She would have fallen when he suddenly released her if he hadn't steadied her as he bent down and picked up his jacket. He settled it around her shoulders and pulled it closed across her chest. "Why don't you keep this for now, and return it to me when you're ready to replace it with the real thing." He placed a finger over her lips when she tried to speak. "I only ask that you not wait too long. Though I may be known for my patience, few have dared test its limits." He used the lapels to pull her toward him even as he leaned down. "And those who did were very sorry."

He kissed her then, his unbreakable hold on the jacket only accentuating the gentleness of his coaxing lips. And once again Olivia nearly wept at the simple contact, his mouth moving over hers with such tender intensity that her knees finally buckled and she melted into him.

Just ask, her mind whispered even as her heart pounded in fear. *He promised to say yes. And he said he'd be gentle and . . .*

But if just his kisses made her go weak in the knees, what would his lovemaking do to her? Heaven help her, she'd probably faint dead away and miss the whole thing.

Olivia's small sound of protest got muffled in his shirt when he broke the kiss and pulled her to him with a growl. "We will stop now, before I forget my noble intentions."

Thank God one of them still had a firing brain cell.

But then, Mac obviously had more experience at this sort of thing. Hell, she couldn't even remember what she was doing out here at the crack of dawn, wearing only her bathrobe, being kissed senseless by her *employee.*

She pressed her face to his chest, stifling the urge to giggle. So much for not fraternizing with the help, considering all she wanted to do was rip open his shirt and press her lips to his bare chest.

He set her away, his gaze narrowed in suspicion. And despite knowing her cheeks were blistering red, Olivia somehow managed to give him a smile. She did not, however, have the courage to address the unholy gleam that suddenly sparked in his eyes. So she gathered his jacket around her, stiffened her spine, and started walking home—doing her damnedest not to let him see how badly her knees were wobbling.

"Olivia."

Finding that her world was righting itself in direct proportion to her distance from him, she turned and mutely arched a brow.

"I really do prefer that you ask."

"And if I don't?"

His eyes all but glowing in the first rays of the rising sun, he gave a deceptively negligent shrug. "I will still be gentle and careful with you, and unrushed."

He turned away then, leaving her staring at his impossingly broad shoulders as he strode onto his porch and disappeared into his cabin—even as she tried to decide if he had just made her a promise or delivered a threat.

Mac stood in the lodge kitchen scowling down at the note in his hand, half tempted to go after its author so he could rip it into little pieces in front of her, and then let her watch them fall like snowflakes when he tossed them in the air.

About the closest he'd gotten to Olivia in the last four days were these damn notes he kept finding on the table every morning when he and Henry came to breakfast, each one a list of tasks she wanted him to do that day, accompanied by succinctly impersonal instructions. And on the bottom of every note she always politely suggested he should address any questions and concerns he had to John or Eileen.

Even though he didn't regret his actions the morning he'd caught her trying to return his jacket, Mac knew he should at least feel guilty for sending Olivia into hiding; but in truth, their sunrise encounter had only left him all the more determined to have her. Upon discovering he was likely the first man to kiss her soft, sweet lips in more than six years, Mac's interest in Olivia had gone from pursuing a casual affair to an overwhelming need to possess her completely. Especially once he'd done the math and realized her marriage had ended a full two years before her husband's death.

Though he understood the many reasons women stayed in loveless marriages, particularly when children were involved, Mac was forever in awe of the fortitude and determination that the everyday reality of remaining in them required. The irony being that where most people judged such women as cowardly fools for staying, Mac considered them braver than many battle-hardened warriors he knew.

"Is our list of chores very long this morning?" Henry asked just before cramming a spoonful of cereal in his mouth.

Mac scowled down at the note in his hand. "It appears we'll be spending today in the stable, getting last year's hay out of the loft and readying the stalls for the twelve horses that will be arriving in ten days."

Henry swallowed, his face brightening. "Sophie told me there would be horses here this summer, and that we'll get to go on trail rides." His expression turned sad. "Mama and I used to go riding every day, sometimes even if it was raining. And though he was just an old carriage horse, Champ seemed to enjoy my riding him." He smiled sadly. "Sometimes when I'd start to lose my balance, he would stop and wait for me to right myself so I didn't fall off."

Warming up to his memories, Henry snickered. "He didn't like it when I used to grab an overhead branch and swing off him, though. He always stopped and turned around, looking for me on the ground." Unshed tears pooled in his eyes again. "I'm never going to see him again, am I? Champ's been dead for hundreds of years now."

Mac crouched down beside him. "You will have many pets come and go in your lifetime, Henry. And you can only cherish them while they're here and hold fond memories of them when they're gone." He tapped the boy's chest. "And just like your mama, Champ is with you as much today as he was back in your original century."

"Would he be upset with me, do you think, if I enjoy riding other horses?"

"Far from it, son. Your old friend is proud that you're using the skills he taught you, and expects nothing less than for you to become an expert horseman."

Henry drove his spoon into his cereal. "Then we must do an excellent job on the stable today, as Champ always insisted on having the freshest hay from the loft and a spotless water bucket." He stopped with the spoon halfway to his mouth. "When we buy our house in Midnight Bay, will it have a stable?"

Mac straightened. "If it doesn't, we will certainly build one."

"And maybe when we leave here in the fall, Sophie will want us to take a couple of Tinkerbelle's kittens with us," Henry added, his expression calculating. "Every barn needs plenty of cats to keep the mice out of the grain."

"I'm sure we won't have any trouble finding some cats," Mac said. He pulled out a chair and sat down, dropping Olivia's note on the table and picking up the one Eileen had left him. "It appears we're on our own for the next week, as Mr. and Mrs. Baldwin have gone on a trip." He smiled at Henry's sudden concern. "Eileen says the kitchen's all ours, and that we are free to raid the pantry and fridge for our meals."

"I noticed there's a restaurant in town," Henry said. "Or maybe Miss Olivia can cook for us." His expression turned calculating again. "It would be nice if the four of us took our meals together, don't you think?"

"What I *think* is that we should start looking through those recipe books," Mac said, gesturing at the bookcase at the end of the counter. "And finally get serious about learning how to feed ourselves."

Henry stopped with his spoon halfway to his mouth again. "But why would we waste our time learning how to do women's work? Once we move to our new home we'll have servants to do all our cooking and cleaning."

Mac nearly choked on the sip of juice he'd just taken,

setting the glass on the table with a chuckle. "I suggest you refrain from using the term *women's work*, young man," he said, forcing himself to look serious. "Especially in front of Madeline and Eve when we get back to Midnight Bay. And I doubt you would endear yourself to Olivia and Sophie if they hear you saying it. The distinction between men's work and women's work is nearly nonexistent in this century, Henry. Today women can even be warriors if they want, and some of the world's best cooks are men."

Henry set his spoon in his empty bowl. "But that's just not practical. Most women would barely be able to lift a sword, much less fight an entire battle with one."

"Swords are ancient weapons," Mac explained. "Have you not seen both men and women on television using handguns and rifles? Guns and explosives and something called missiles are the weapons of choice today, and quite often warriors don't even see the enemy they're fighting."

"But that's not right," the boy said, his eyebrows rising into his hairline. "It's not very noble to kill a man without looking him directly in the eyes."

"Last I knew, nothing about war is noble," Mac said quietly. "Which is why as theurgists, we endeavor to find peaceful solutions."

"Then how come Grampy doesn't just use his powerful magic to stop the wars?"

"We can't actually interfere in humanity's right of free will, Henry. In fact, it's our job to protect that very right." Mac leaned forward on the table, wrapping his hands around his juice glass as he wondered how they'd gotten on this subject. Hell, was it even possible to have such a philosophical discussion with a six-year-old? "What's the point of being born if we're to be nothing more than puppets on a string, with no control over our lives? Every decision a man makes and every action he takes, large or small, has consequences, Henry. And those consequences—good or bad—spread out like waves on the ocean, sometimes traveling great distances to affect others."

"What kind of decisions?" he asked, his brows knitting

into a frown. "Let's say I decide to stop brushing my teeth? How would *that* affect anyone else?"

Sweet Prometheus, he could see it was going to be a long day.

Where in hell was Olivia when he needed her?

"You don't think your wife will mind being married to a man whose teeth suddenly start falling out?" Mac snorted. "Assuming you could get a woman to marry you with such foul breath." He leaned back in his chair and folded his arms on his chest. "Let's consider a more serious decision a person might make. What if I had decided *not* to stop and help Olivia when I saw that man attacking her?"

Henry went very still. "But she could have been badly hurt or even killed."

Mac shrugged. "Why should I have cared? I didn't know Olivia, so wouldn't it have been better to simply drive by and not involve us in some stranger's trouble?"

"But, Dad! If anything happened to Miss Olivia, Sophie would be an orphan."

"So?"

The boy glared at him so fiercely, Mac was surprised they both didn't burst into flames. But then Henry took a deep breath, and Mac stifled a smile when he saw a twinkle appear in the boy's eyes.

"I know you would never walk away from someone in trouble," Henry said with all the authority of a loyal son. "You're just trying to make me see what would have happened if you hadn't stopped to help Miss Olivia."

"No, I'm trying to point out that I had a *choice*, and how my decision to stop had consequences that affected not only Olivia and her daughter, but also you and me."

"How did it affect me?"

"You and I have known each other what . . . three months?" Mac leaned forward on the table again when the boy nodded. "And did you not form an opinion of me within a few days, which has shifted and deepened in the time we've been together?"

Henry nodded again, now looking confused.

"So were you surprised that I stopped to help Olivia?"

"No. I would have been surprised if you hadn't. And . . . and disappointed."

"Even though I have constantly been telling you that as theurgists, it's not our place to meddle in people's lives?"

"But you meddle all the time. You gave Miss Fiona and Gabriella their lives back and brought them to this century, and you told all the big juicy lobsters to crawl into Mr. Trace's traps so he could sell them for lots of money."

Mac once again found himself wondering how they'd gotten on this subject, and how in hell he was going to get off it. Hadn't it started with horses or something?

No, it had started with Henry's distaste for burned food.

He gave the boy a tight smile. "And now Fiona and Gabriella have to live with the consequences of *my* actions, don't they? And so must I." Mac leaned back in his chair, folding his arms again. "So the point of this little discussion, I believe, is that I've decided there will be no servants cooking and cleaning for us when we settle into our permanent home."

Henry gasped. "But we'll starve!" His face suddenly darkened and his eyes filled with guilt. "I need to tell you that every morning you left me with Miss Fiona, she would make me a big, delicious breakfast. And she let me sneak cookies and tarts upstairs, which I hid in my bedroom for later."

"You ate a *second* breakfast every morning?" Mac asked in disbelief.

"Um . . . no, not a second one," Henry admitted, looking down at his cereal. "I sneaked the food you cooked for me under the table to Misneach."

Mac stood up with a burst of laughter and snatched Henry up in his arms. "You made that poor pup eat burned toast and rubbery eggs?" He shook his head. "Either Misneach is a very good friend or the beast doesn't have one discerning taste bud."

His eyes level with Mac's, Henry blinked at him. "You're not angry?"

Mac shifted the boy to one arm and picked up the bowl and glass from the table and carried them to the sink. "No, I'm not angry. In fact, I'm touched that you wanted to spare my feelings." He turned serious, giving Henry a squeeze. "But it only proves how much work there is ahead of us if we have any hope of surviving until I get back in the good graces of your Grampy Titus."

"*Then* can we have servants?" Henry asked as Mac strode outside with him in his arms. "And we'll go live in Atlantis, and I can travel back and forth through time with you to all the different centuries?"

Mac stopped in the middle of the driveway. "We're not going to live in Atlantis, because . . . well, because I've outgrown my father's home. And even after my powers are restored, we'll still spend most of our time in Maine in this century. We need to put down roots, son, and I can't think of a better place for us to call home. We have many good friends here, and I find the technology of this century to be rather enjoyable."

"But what about the women?"

"What about them?" Mac asked, setting the boy down.

"Do you find the women in this century enjoyable, too?" Henry frowned up at him. "Because if you don't pick out a wife soon, Grampy's going to pick one for you." The child gave a shudder. "And I'd rather *we* chose her, because the lady Grampy had picked out for you before he decided on Miss Fiona instead was . . ." He shuddered again. "She scared the hell out of me, Dad," he whispered. "I don't think Gadzalina would have any problem lifting your sword, and I never once saw her smile."

"What are you talking about? Who's Gadzalina?"

"She's the woman Grampy sent for right after he stole me away from my uncles. He brought Gadzalina to the ship to take care of me so he could finish slaughtering the demons trying to kill you. And I heard him telling her how honored she should feel that he'd chosen her over all the other beautiful women on the island to be your bride." The boy scrunched up his face. "If Gadzalina is Grampy's idea of a beautiful woman, maybe instead of learning how to cook we should put our energies into finding you a bride, as I certainly understand how *that* consequence will affect me."

Mac scrubbed his hands over his face, trying to wash away the image of just how close he'd come to being married to an Atlantean . . . beauty. Sweet Prometheus, some of those women were bigger than warriors and a whole lot scarier than he was.

And Titus wondered why Mac had spent the last several thousand years fighting his matchmaking efforts.

"Does your bride have to be a virgin?" Henry asked. "Or will any woman do?"

Mac dropped his hands in surprise. "Do you even know what a virgin *is*?"

Henry's cheeks turned a dull red. "I think it means a woman who hasn't had any children, especially any bastards like . . . me."

"You are not a bastard," Mac growled, looking around before he dropped to his knees and took hold of the boy's shoulders. "You are *my son*." He took a steadying breath and even managed to smile. "And your definition of a virgin is incomplete. She's actually a woman who has never . . . who hasn't . . . who . . ."

Dammit, where in hell was Olivia? Mac took another deep breath, trying to remember what the books had said about explaining sex to children. He sighed. "Why don't you go find Olivia, and while you spend the morning helping her work through her own list of chores, you can ask *her* what a virgin is."

"She can explain it better because she's a woman?"

"Partly. But mostly because she's likely already had this discussion with Sophie."

"Then why don't I just ask Sophie when she gets home? And that way instead of scrubbing and painting the cabins I can help you get the stable ready for the horses."

Mac stood up, shaking his head. "I don't think you should be discussing virgins with Sophie. Now quiet yourself to see where Miss Olivia is right now."

Henry went very still, his hands balled into fists at his sides and his forehead wrinkled in concentration as he slowly gazed around the grounds of Inglenook. He pointed toward the peninsula. "There. I believe she's in the cabin farthest out." He looked up with such an arrogant smile that Mac actually winced at how familiar it was. "Miss Olivia's energy is really quite beautiful, isn't it?" Henry suddenly frowned again. "Only this morning it's . . . something's bothering her, I think, because the air around her is swirling with both fear and anger." His eyes turned uncertain. "Maybe I shouldn't bother her."

Mac felt the back of his neck heat with guilt, knowing damn well what Olivia was angry and afraid of. "Or maybe this is a good time for you to see how a decision you make will affect someone else," he suggested. "Which do you think is the better choice: avoiding a person because you're unsure how to deal with what might be bothering her, or trying to bring her comfort?"

"You believe *I'm* capable of comforting Miss Olivia?"

"Did you not make her feel better after she was attacked by distracting her with simple conversation?"

Henry's face brightened. "I did," he said, nodding. He took off at a run toward the peninsula, but suddenly stopped and turned around. "You didn't answer my question. Does your bride have to be a virgin?"

"No, Henry. She only need be brave."

The boy arched a brow in question, but then suddenly grinned before Mac could elaborate. "I know: Tonight we'll sit down together and make a list of the qualities we want in a wife." He shook his head. "As I have some requirements of my own, since I'm going to be living with her, too." He started walking backward. "She's got to like little boys, and be a good cook, and enjoy flying kites and fishing and hiking. And, she needs to smile a lot." He stopped. "I think we better put that she likes animals at the top of the list. And she must also like the ocean."

Mac arched a brow, trying not to laugh. "Any requirements on what this paragon should *look* like?"

Henry started walking backward again. “We took care of that by saying she has to smile a lot. All women are pretty when they smile.” And with that the boy spun around and headed up the narrow lane at a run.

Mac headed toward the stable, wondering how long it would take Henry to realize that Olivia met every requirement he’d listed.

Well, except maybe one. Which was the most important, considering that if Olivia couldn’t even find the courage to return his jacket, there was a very good chance she would run screaming in terror if he did propose to her—because likes and dislikes and beautiful smiles aside, only a very brave woman would agree to marry the beast hidden inside the man.

Chapter Ten

Olivia was so ashamed of herself that she walked out of cabin four leaving it only half cleaned, determined to spend the rest of the morning focused completely on Henry. Mac had paid a small fortune to come early for some one-on-one help with his son, and she was guilty of neglecting the poor child in order to avoid his father.

Obviously at a complete loss as to how to answer Henry's question about virgins, and likely at the expense of his pride, Mac had sent the boy to her in hopes *she* could explain the birds and bees in terms a six-year-old would understand. Which she had to admit was very admirable of Mac, as Olivia was afraid he would have gone too in-depth, not realizing that children Henry's age didn't need—or particularly want—to know the details of what Mom and Dad were doing behind closed doors.

Come to think of it, neither did teenagers, Olivia thought with a smile as she patted the newly replanked dock for Henry to sit beside her.

"Dad believes you probably already told Sophie what makes a woman a virgin," Henry said. "But that I should ask you instead of her, because . . ." He scrunched up his shoulders. "I guess he thinks you might be a virgin, so you could probably explain it better." He glanced up when Olivia started coughing. "But I don't believe you are because you have Sophie. I think virgins are women who haven't had babies."

"Well, you're partially right. Women who've had babies definitely aren't virgins."

"That's what Dad said. But what's the other part?"

"Before I answer that," Olivia said, stalling to get her thoughts in order, "let me ask you where you heard the term *virgin*. Is it something your father said?"

Henry glanced up again, his expression guarded, then looked out at the lake. "No. Uncle Reginald said it when I heard him yelling at Mama once. He told her that no man would ask for her hand in marriage because she wasn't a virgin anymore, especially because she had a bastard child." Two red flags colored his cheeks as he leaned toward her. "He was referring to me," he whispered. He took a deep breath, squaring his young shoulders. "Only when I just mentioned it to Dad, he got angry and said I wasn't a bastard because I'm his son." He leaned closer again. "But I think I really am, because I think it means something besides just being a bad person. Please, Miss Olivia, will you tell me what a bastard really is?"

Olivia also took a deep breath in an attempt to ease the growing ache in her chest. "If you look up the word in a dictionary, a bastard is the child of a mother and father who aren't married to each other. And in olden times that used to be a bad thing, and that's why calling someone a bastard is considered an insult. But today," she rushed on when his expression fell, "it's more acceptable for a child's parents not to be married, so now the word mostly refers to a bad person."

"But if Mama and my dad weren't married to each other, that means I really *am* a bastard," he said thickly, his eyes welling with tears.

Feeling her own eyes growing blurry, Olivia pulled him

against her side in a fierce hug. "It's a very old term in the literal sense, Henry," she said past the lump in her throat. "And now it doesn't really have anything to do with the circumstances of your birth. Today it's just what we call a no-good, rotten person." She lifted his chin so he'd see her smile. "Want to know a secret? I'm a bastard, too," she said, nodding when his eyes widened in surprise. "My mom and dad weren't married to each other, either."

"They weren't?"

"Nope." She brushed a finger across his cheek, wiping away a tear that had spilled free. "And my mama died when I was four, so I also know a little something about what you've been going through these past few months."

"And did your dad come take you to live with him, too?"

Olivia hugged him to her again so he wouldn't see her expression. "He came when he eventually found out my mother had died, but he couldn't take me to live with him because of the kind of work he did. He did stay in town a couple of weeks, though, and visited me at the home where I was staying. But he eventually had to return to work."

"And did he come back and get you later?"

"No. I never heard from him again." She gave the child another fierce hug. "Your father is a very good man, Henry, and he loves you very, very much; so much that I know he'd move heaven and earth and any mountains that got in his way to be with you." She rubbed her hand up and down his arm, warding off the chill she was feeling. "So I don't ever want to hear you refer to yourself as a bastard, especially in front of him, okay? The word only means a bad person now." She patted his knee. "And you, young Mr. Oceanus, are one of the nicest persons I know." She swiped her eyes with her sleeve and nudged him to sit upright. "So, back to the definition of a virgin," she said with forced levity. "A virgin is a woman—or a man—who . . . well, it's someone who's never had sex."

There, she'd said it. And if Mac got mad at her, then he could just deal with it.

She looked down when Henry said nothing, only to find him frowning up at her. "That's it?" he asked. "Just never having sex makes a woman a virgin?"

"Do you even know what having sex *is*, Henry?"

He snorted. "Of course I do. Mama explained it to me when I saw our stableman fornicating with her maid in the hayloft. It's how babies are *made*." He beamed her a brilliant smile. "Animals have sex, too. That's how *all* babies are made."

Well, Olivia guessed that took care of that little problem, didn't it?

That is, until Henry frowned again. "Only that's what has me confused. Uncle Reginald told Mama no man would marry her because she wasn't a virgin anymore, but when I asked Dad if the wife we have to find him needs to be a virgin, he said no, that she only needs to be brave."

Olivia sucked in a surprised breath, pressing a hand to her suddenly pounding heart. "Your dad is looking for a wife?"

Henry snorted again. "We certainly don't want Grampy picking her out for us." He made a face even as he shuddered. "Gadzalina scared the hell out of me."

"Gadzalina?" Olivia repeated, deciding not to point out that saying *hell* was just as bad as saying *bastard*.

"She's the lady Grampy brought to his ship so Dad could marry her." He smiled again. "But then Grampy changed his mind and decided to marry us to Miss Fiona instead. Except Mr. Trace said he had first dibs on her. That's when I got really scared, because I thought that meant we were stuck with Gadzalina. But Mr. Trace blew a hole in the ship and Dad stole me right out from under Grampy's nose, and we all escaped." He looked out at the lake and sighed. "Only Dad has just one year to settle down and become a good father or Grampy's going to take me back and raise me himself. But now we've only got nine months left." He looked up at her, smiling again. "That's why we came here, so you can help us."

Olivia realized her mouth was hanging open and slowly closed it.

Because really, not one thing this boy was saying made a lick of sense.

"Henry, where did you live with your mother?" she asked, trying to unravel his fantastical tale by starting at the beginning. "In what country?"

"England."

"And your mother was wealthy enough to have a stableman and a maid?"

He puffed out his tiny chest, looking somewhat imperial—rather like his father did sometimes. "Briarsworth had a staff of ninety-six servants just for the manor house and stable alone, and I don't know how many more working the land."

"*Ninety*-six?" Olivia repeated in a squeak.

Henry arched a brow—again looking so much like Mac it was scary. "It takes a lot of people to run a dukedom, you know. Only when Uncle Reginald inherited the title he lost some of the lands in a game of chance, and so Mama had to let several of the servants go. I remember how angry she was with him, saying Grandfather Penhope was probably rolling over in his grave. That's when Reginald told Mama she'd better get used to his rule, because no man would have her now that she wasn't a virgin—especially since she'd given birth to Maximilian Oceanus's bastard."

Oh God, they were back to that.

"So, Henry, what's your favorite cartoon?" she asked lightheartedly, determined to move away from bastards and virgins by finding out what sort of television shows the child watched, or what books his father was reading him.

Because really, the boy's imagination was way over the top.

He blinked up at her, clearly confused. "I don't watch cartoons. They're silly."

"Then what do you read? Or what does your father read to you?"

His face brightened. "Every night Dad's been reading me the book Aunt Carolina sent me. It's a compilation of ancient mythology. I'm learning who all the different gods are and their roles in creating the modern world." His eyes suddenly widened. "Come to think of it, all the gods kept having sex with each other and even with mortals they weren't married to, and most of them are bastards, too."

Olivia sighed. "Let's try using the term *illegitimate*, Henry. It's far less offensive."

"Okay; most of the gods are illegitimate." He brightened again. "Did you know that besides being the god of the sea, Poseidon is also in charge of horses and earthquakes?" He nudged her with his elbow. "So if you ever feel the ground shaking, don't be scared, okay? It's probably just my dad moving heaven and earth and any mountains in his way to get to me."

Good Lord, the boy really was a sponge, soaking up what *everyone* said.

He also had a surprisingly well-developed sense of humor for a six-year-old.

"So what does your father do for a living?" she asked.

He blinked up at her. "Do?" he repeated.

"What does your dad do for work?"

"But you know that already. He works for you."

Olivia couldn't quite stifle a laugh. "No, I mean *before* he started working for me. Does he run a business? You mentioned your grampy had a ship; do your father and grandfather run some sort of shipping business together?"

"No, they don't do anything together except argue over Dad getting married."

Oh, that's right; she'd forgotten about Mac and Henry's quest for a wife—and the woman's state of virginity not being as important as her bravery.

"Are you angry at Dad and me?" Henry asked.

"No. What makes you think that?"

"Well, you've been avoiding us ever since our picnic on Sunday. So I guessed we must have done something wrong or said something to upset you." He reached over and took her hand in his and patted the back of it with his other hand. "And I could sense that you were afraid and angry earlier this morning, and if it has something to do with me or Dad, then I wish to apologize for the both of us." He gave her a tentative smile. "Because we both really like you, Miss Olivia, and we'd feel bad if we upset you."

Good Lord, did this child know how to tug on her heartstrings, or what?

Much the same way his father did.

"I'm not upset with either of you," she said in all honesty, since she was upset with herself. Which meant she certainly didn't have to worry about Mac asking *her* to marry him, did she, since she wasn't even brave enough to return his stupid jacket. "I've just been really busy trying to get Inglenook ready for its new season." She reversed their grip and patted his hand. "And you and your father have been a really big help. In fact, I'm so close to getting everything done, I believe the two of you should take tomorrow off and do something fun together."

"Like what?"

"Well, maybe you could drive down to Turtleback Station—that's a town not too far from here—and do some shopping and go see a movie."

"Will you and Sophie come with us? Tomorrow's Saturday, so she doesn't have school. Hey, I know," he said, his expression turning eager. "Dad and I can take you ladies to dinner at a restaurant in Turtleback Station. It'll be our treat."

Oh yeah, this boy had been soaking Mac up like a charming sponge, and Olivia found herself pitying the woman this formidable father-son team decided was brave enough to marry them.

"I'm sorry, but Sophie and I have other plans for tomorrow."

His face fell. "I understand. And Dad and I will probably spend tomorrow in the kitchen learning how to feed ourselves." He sighed so hard Olivia was surprised he didn't hurt his chest. "If we don't figure out how to run a stove we're going to starve soon, because Dad's decided we aren't going to have servants when we buy our house in Midnight Bay." He gave her a sidelong glance. "Does Inglenook have cooking classes when the guests are here, so people can learn how *not* to burn everything so badly it tastes like charred wood?"

"Sorry," Olivia said with a laugh. "We only specialize in helping parents and children get along with each other."

He looked out at the lake. "Maybe when we get our new home we can build a fire pit in the backyard. Dad seems to do better when he can see the actual flame."

"Or you could make sure your new house has a propane stove instead of an electric one," she suggested. "The burners have a flame he can see. And if the food starts to burn he just has to shut it off and the heat's gone instantly."

"That's it?" he asked, brightening. "They make stoves that use fire instead of electricity? Is the stove in the lodge propane?"

"It is," she said, nodding. "And there's a barbecue pit out back on the patio for building a wood fire you can cook on. I'll tell you what: If it's warm enough tomorrow evening we'll have a campfire, and I'll bring everything we need to make s'mores."

"S'mores?"

"What? You've never had s'mores?"

"I don't even know what they are. Is it something you eat?"

"They're graham cracker and chocolate and marshmallow sandwiches. You roast the marshmallows over the fire until they're all soft and gooey, set them on a graham cracker that has a piece of chocolate on it, and then squish everything down with another graham cracker on top. Sophie is an excellent s'mores maker, and I'm sure she'd love to show you how much fun they are to make. And we'll have hot cocoa and—" She stopped when Henry suddenly perked up and cocked his head, as though he were listening to something.

"There's a big truck coming up the last hill to Inglenook," he said, scrambling to his feet. He stilled again. "No, I believe there are two trucks."

Olivia also scrambled to her feet with a quick glance at her watch, worried that Sophie's school had let out early and no one had been in the office to answer the phone. But then she jumped off the dock and started running down the lane when she heard the distinct sound of air brakes releasing.

"Come on, let's go see what's being delivered," she said, looking back to make sure he was following as she racked her brain trying to remember what she'd ordered.

Or had Eileen ordered something without telling her?

Olivia skidded to a stop at the sight of two big tractor-trailer rigs pulling into the lower parking lot. "No!" she cried, taking off at a run again.

"The horses are here!" Henry shouted, sprinting past her.

Yes, they were—ten days early! What was she going to do with twelve horses for the next two weeks when she hadn't even found a wrangler to tend them yet, not to mention the cost of the extra hay and grain they were going to eat that she hadn't budgeted for?

Mac was already standing next to the first truck when she ran into the parking lot, and shaking Caleb Roy's hand by the time she reached them.

"Caleb," she said, pressing against the stitch in her side as she tried to catch her breath. God, she really did need to start working out. "What are you doing here? You're not . . . supposed to bring the horses for . . . another week and a half," she panted, glaring at the amusement in his eyes.

"Hell, Livy, I've got a tired old gelding in the trailer that's in better shape than you are." The sparkle in his eyes intensified, his gaze traveling down the length of her, then back up. "You do look like you've put on a pound or two over the winter."

"I did not," she growled, uncomfortably aware of Mac standing just off to her left—probably checking out her backside and rethinking his offer to have an affair. "What are you doing here *today*, Caleb?" She gestured at the trailer behind him. "I don't have a staff in place to take care of the horses until April fifteenth. What am I supposed to do with these eating machines for the next two weeks?"

That sobered him. "Didn't Eileen tell you I called? I explained we had a small barn fire Sunday, and asked if I couldn't bring these guys to you a little earlier than we'd planned. We need to tear down what's left of the barn and get a new one built."

"Oh no, did you lose any horses?"

"Naw. We got them all out in time." He shook his head, his eyes pained. "A couple of them got beat up, though, when they busted through a fence. It took us two days to round everyone up, and we still haven't found old Zeb." He suddenly grinned. "He's probably halfway to Canada by now."

Olivia glared at him. "Are you bringing me traumatized horses? Caleb, you know I need calm, gentle animals. I have children riding them."

He gestured at the trailer. "Trust me; this crew is so bombproof they wouldn't care if you put ten screaming kids on their backs. As for feeding them, I threw in extra hay at no charge, and I'm willing to take a few hundred bucks off our original deal as thanks for letting me bring them early."

"That still doesn't take care of my staffing problem."

"I got that covered, too." He gestured for the man standing beside the truck to come over. "This is Sam Waters, and he'll be your horse wrangler for the summer. Didn't Eileen tell you that I'd offered his services?"

"No, she didn't."

"Sam, this puffing lady is Livy Baldwin," Caleb said as the middle-aged man limped over to them. "Now don't let her being out of shape fool you none. From my past dealings with Livy, I happen to know for a fact there's a tigress lurking behind those big brown eyes of hers."

"Olivia," Sam said as he held out his hand, his slate-gray eyes also filled with amusement . . . and something else she couldn't quite identify. "If it eases your mind any, boss, I can vouch that the horses are bombproof."

Oh, lovely; another big strapping male calling her *boss.*

Olivia shook Sam's large callused hand, and still reeling in shock at once again being blindsided by Eileen, the best she could do was give him a smile and a nod.

But no sooner had she ended the handshake when Mac stepped forward and thrust out his hand. "Mac Oceanus," he said. "Olivia's only other employee at the moment. Welcome to Inglenook, Sam."

"Mac," Sam said as the two men shook hands—which, she noticed, lasted an inordinate amount of time as they eyed each other.

"And that excited young man is my son, Henry," Mac said, breaking the handshake to gesture at Henry watching two of Caleb's workers lowering the big heavy ramp. "And though I haven't seen him ride yet, the boy tells me he's quite a horseman already."

"Caleb, could I talk to you in private, please?" Olivia said tightly, walking to the side of the parking lot.

"Uh-oh, I'm afraid the tiger's about to show me her claws," Caleb said with a laugh, following. "Sam, go ahead and take the horses to the barn, will you?"

"What's going on?" she asked the moment they were both out of earshot. "You can't just up and bring me a wrangler without discussing it with me first."

"I did discuss it—with Eileen. Didn't she tell you?"

"No, she didn't. And I don't have it in my budget to pay an extra worker."

"But Eileen told me you were shorthanded this summer because the guy you hired didn't pan out."

"Mark was also supposed to double as a camp counselor." She waved toward the trailer. "And Sam doesn't look like he's . . . he doesn't look particularly suited for the job, Caleb. He has a pretty bad limp," she whispered, feeling her cheeks heat up again. "He might be able to head up the trail rides, but I can't exactly see him taking campers on mountainous hikes or helping out with the obstacle course. Which means," she said, cutting Caleb off when he tried to speak, "I have to fill my empty position with someone who can. Which means *I can't afford Sam*."

"But didn't Eileen—" He held his hand up to stop himself. "No, I forgot, Eileen doesn't tell you anything." Caleb smiled. "Sam's working for just room and board, Livy. And when he's not tending the horses, he'll do anything you ask him to—that he physically can, of course."

Alarm bells started going off in her head, and Olivia glanced over her shoulder to see Sam leading a horse toward the barn. She stepped closer to Caleb, her obvious anger wiping the smile off his face. "Inglenook is not a halfway house, or a rehab center, or a place to hide out from . . . whatever. I have families here. And *children*. And you know I need to do background checks on every member of my staff."

"It's not like that, Livy," he said, actually taking a step back. "You've got my word; Sam's so clean he squeaks."

"Then why is he willing to work for only room and board?"

"He . . . um . . ." Caleb sighed. "Sam and I have been buddies since we were five, Olivia. But he joined the military right out of high school, and I only saw him once over the last thirty years until he showed up on my doorstep a couple of weeks ago."

"Then how can you give me your word that he's not an alcoholic, or a convicted felon, or some pervert or something?"

"He's not, I swear!" He darted a nervous glance toward the barn, then back at her. "We've been doing business together for what . . . eight or nine years? So you know me well enough to realize I understand your liability concerns when it comes to your guests. Look, I know Sam doesn't drink—other than the occasional beer—and I trust him with my own grandchildren. Hell, my two-year-old granddaughter thinks the guy was put on this earth for her entertainment alone."

"Where has he been all those years, Caleb? What did Sam do in the military?"

"I can't rightly answer that. I think he was special ops or

CIA or something before he got busted up." Caleb held up his hand when she tried to say something. "I do know he's been out of the country most of that time. He stopped to see me about thirty years ago and said he'd give his right arm to move home to Maine. But then he just suddenly disappeared again a couple of weeks later."

She touched his arm. "I can't take the chance he might go crazy all of a sudden, Caleb. What if he has a flashback or something?"

"No, it's not like that. Sam's not shell-shocked or unstable. I think he's just tired more than anything. And he's still healing from whatever caused that limp." Caleb glanced past her shoulder, his face suddenly smoothing in relief. "And your other employee seemed to size him up quickly enough and decide he was okay. Didn't you see the look that passed between them?"

"I saw it."

"It appeared to me as if they sort of . . . recognized each other. You know, like that band-of-brothers thing military men share? Please, couldn't you just give Sam a chance? For me?"

"Is there a problem?" Mac asked—which explained Caleb's look of relief.

"Livy's just worried about my dropping Sam off here without her knowing anything about him. Especially because she didn't get to do a background check on him. But I've given her my word he's okay, which she'll see for herself if she gives him a chance."

"Would you excuse us a minute, Caleb?" Mac said with a slight bow, taking hold of her elbow and leading her away.

She pulled free but continued walking until they were several paces away and then turned. "I am quite capable of making my own decisions regarding Inglenook."

He folded his arms over his chest. "I am well aware of that. I'm just wondering if you took the time to consult your gut on this particular decision."

"Excuse me?"

"Did you not say that your gut told you there was something not right about your previous employee—even though you must have done a background check on him?"

Dammit; Mark was *still* haunting her.

"Which makes me curious, Olivia, as to what you felt when you shook Sam's hand."

She scowled, her eyes trained on his folded arms because she couldn't lift her gaze to his. "I didn't feel anything," she muttered.

"Excuse me? What was that?" he asked, bending to see her eyes. "Did you say you felt *nothing*?"

She thrust out her chin. "What did you feel when *you* shook his hand?"

"I felt a guarded and very tired soul with a deeply wounded heart."

"You read all that in a three-second handshake?"

"Sam is not a threat to Inglenook, Olivia," he said quietly. "Believe me, if he were you would have at least felt *something* when he took your hand in his. No matter how skilled a person may be at hiding his true nature, inherent evil cannot be masked. Your guests will be completely safe with Sam. You, however, may not."

"What do you mean?"

"You might not have felt anything when you shook his hand, but I certainly did." He smiled, though it didn't quite reach his eyes. "I believe your new employee was rather eager to meet you, but he was equally determined to guard his emotions." He canted his head. "You didn't find it strange that he called you Olivia even though Caleb had introduced you as Livy?"

Was he for real? Mac couldn't possibly be jealous. Could he?

Good Lord, Sam was old enough to be her father!

"So do I let him stay or not?" she growled.

Up went a brow. "I don't believe that's my decision to make." He unfolded his arms and stepped closer, making Olivia have to tilt her head back in order to continue glaring at him. Only the look she saw in his eyes made her stop breathing.

"Are you planning to return my jacket anytime soon?" he asked quietly. "Or are you hoping I'll make the decision for you and simply come . . . take it?"

"I . . . um, I . . ."

He placed a finger over her lips. "I, too, can see the tigress lurking behind those beautiful cinnamon eyes, Olivia. Do you not think it's past time she slipped her leash?"

"I *think*," she said, stepping away from his touch, "that it's time we put that truckload of hay in the loft." She walked over to Caleb. "I'll give Sam two weeks. But if I don't feel comfortable having him around by the time my first guests arrive, you're driving up here and taking him back."

"Fair enough," Caleb said, his smile instant. He fell into step beside her, heading toward the trailers. "I promise, you won't regret it."

Chapter Eleven

Finding her new employee in the barn filling water buckets, Olivia gave the giant nose a pat when the horse it belonged to stuck its head out to nuzzle her shoulder. “Sam, could you saddle up two of your most docile horses and another one for yourself? I need to go meet my daughter’s bus at the turnoff, and I thought I’d surprise her with a horseback ride. And if you don’t mind, I’d like for you to come with me.”

“Sure, boss,” he said, twisting the hose nozzle to shut off the water.

Olivia stepped out of reach of the persistent horse with a soft laugh. “If you want us to start off on the right foot, then let’s drop the *boss* title, okay? *Livy* will do.”

“Would you mind if I call you *Olivia*?” Sam asked, smiling hesitantly. “It’s just that I used to know an Olivia, and have always been partial to the name.”

“I’ll answer to most anything but *boss*. And you’ll find some child-sized saddles in the tack room, so could you put one on your smallest, gentlest horse for my daughter? Sophie’s eight and fancies herself a horsewoman.” She shook her head. “I know Caleb won’t bring me ponies because he claims horses are really safer, but I prefer that Sophie doesn’t have so far to fall.”

They headed toward the tack room, and Olivia slowed

her pace in deference to Sam's limp, which appeared to be more stiff than actually painful.

"Caleb's right," he said. "Ponies are often smarter than the kids riding them. And because adults don't handle them as much, the little beasts can turn into brats."

"Makes sense, I guess. And put my saddle on your *next* gentlest horse," she said when he stepped into the tack room. "Preferably one that can't muster the energy to do more than plod along."

His bottomless gray eyes crinkled half closed with his grin. "I believe you and Molly will make a good fit. She's about as fast as molasses running uphill in the winter. I'll have the horses out front in ten minutes," he said, disappearing into the tack room.

Olivia turned to stare down the aisle at the dozen various-sized heads sticking out of their stalls, and sighed. She really didn't know how much of a draw having horses at Inglenook actually was, but she couldn't bring herself to cancel the program—much to Eileen's dismay—because summer camp just wasn't *camp* without horses. And she felt it was important for parents to see their children controlling the large animals all by themselves, especially the overprotective parents who hovered like helicopters trying to keep their babies safe and sheltered and little forever.

Olivia snorted. Maybe she should sign up as a guest at her own camp and learn how to stop hovering over Sophie before the girl reached puberty and flat-out rebelled. She walked down the aisle, having to exit the barn through the opposite end because Mac and Caleb and his crew were filling the loft with enough hay to last through June, when Caleb would return with this year's crop. She ducked down to crawl between the rails of the paddock fence, only to hear Henry call to her when she straightened.

"I just saw Mr. Sam saddling one of the horses, and he told me you're going to ride down to meet Sophie's school bus," he said, climbing up on the rail to look her level in the eyes. "Can I go with you? I know how to ride. I've been riding since before I could walk."

"That would be up to your father."

His face fell and he hopped down off the fence. "Then I guess I'll have to wait for another time. I forgot I'm supposed to be keeping all the men supplied with ice from the kitchen and fresh drinking water." He started back toward the door. "Maybe I can go for a ride tomorrow, after the men leave."

Olivia stared after him, wondering if it wasn't time she addressed Henry's little habit of not questioning his father's dictates, because . . . well, because it simply wasn't right for a child to be *that* obedient.

"Henry, wait," she said, stepping up onto the bottom rail. She waved him back over to the fence. "When your mama told you to do something, did you always do it without protest? Or if you wanted to do something and she said no, did you always accept what she said as her final answer?"

"I tried to do whatever she asked me to," he said, giving her a confused look. "Especially if Uncle Reginald was around, because he didn't like it if I complained when Mama wouldn't let me do something. He often gave me a smack, saying I was at least half Penhope, and that whining was vulgar and unbecoming of my station."

Lord, she'd like to have five minutes alone with Uncle Reginald. "Are you afraid of your father, Henry?" she asked softly.

"You mean am I afraid he'll smack me?"

Olivia nodded.

Henry shook his head and even gave her a cocky grin. "I'm only scared of his cooking." He turned serious. "Dad wouldn't ever hurt me, Miss Olivia. In fact, he's going to make sure no one ever hurts me again, and he's promised to protect me until I'm old enough to fight my own battles."

She ruffled his hair. "That's a powerfully good promise." She canted her head. "So how come I've never seen you protesting something he's told you to do?"

He frowned up at her. "Because he's my *father*."

"And does your father do everything *his* father tells him to?" she asked, remembering Henry's fantastical tale about how they were trying to find a wife before Grampy found one for them.

The boy's frown deepened. "Well, no." But then his eyes suddenly widened. "Are you saying I'm *not* supposed to do everything my dad tells me to do?"

Knowing she was wading into murky waters, Olivia picked her words carefully. "No, I'm only saying that maybe it would be okay to *question* his orders once in a while. Like right now. I realize unloading a truckload of hay is hard work and the men need cold fresh water to keep them going, so it's definitely an important job your father's given you. But *you* need to understand that there's nothing wrong with asking if you could go meet Sophie's bus with Sam and me."

"But who's going to bring them water if I leave?"

"They're grown men, and there are at least three water spigots in the barn. There's no reason they can't drink out of a hose when they get thirsty."

"Am I paying extra for you to teach my son to question my authority?"

Olivia snapped her gaze up to the loft door only to tumble off the fence in shock, still gaping at the half-naked man even as she landed on the ground.

"Dad, you scared Miss Olivia!" Henry cried, ducking through the fence to get to her. "You surprised her."

"Not as much as she just surprised me," he said quietly—the growl in his voice contradicting the laughter in his eyes. He rubbed a big broad hand over his big, broad, sweat-glistening chest, and arched a brow. "Well, *Miss Olivia*? Is my hearing faulty or were you just encouraging my son to shirk his duty in favor of going riding?"

God, he was gorgeous. And damn if he didn't look even bigger half naked than he did fully clothed. Hell, the guy wouldn't have any trouble moving a few paltry mountains that got in his way.

"Miss Olivia," Henry whispered, bending down to peer into her eyes—which thankfully blocked her view of Mac. "Did you hurt yourself when you fell?"

"No, I'm fine, Henry." She rolled onto her hands and

knees, realized she was giving Mac a bird's-eye view of her butt, and quickly grabbed the rail and pulled herself to her feet. She started to crane her neck to look up again, but realizing her mistake about the time she reached his waist, Olivia spun around to put her back to the fence to look at Henry instead. "Ask him," she whispered, nudging the kid's shoulder when he frowned up at her. "Go on. Ask him if you can come with me to meet Sophie's bus."

"Can I ride with Miss Olivia and Mr. Sam to meet Sophie at the turnoff?"

"No."

Henry dropped his gaze to her, his expression saying he'd told her so.

"Whine," she whispered. "Pout. Say *pleeease*."

After an uncertain glance at her, the boy hesitantly stuck out his bottom lip and looked back up at the loft. "Pleeease, can I go with Miss Olivia?"

"If you leave, who's going to bring us water?"

Oh yeah, that was definitely amusement in Mac's voice.

"There's water in the barn," Henry said. "You and the men can drink straight from the hose."

"Is this whining and pleading going to become a habit?"

"Oh no, I assure you it's just this once." Henry caught her frowning at him, and looked back up at his father, one side of his mouth lifting. "Well, maybe more than just this once, but definitely not *every* time."

She heard Mac sigh. "Do you give me your word you will at least not question *Sam's* authority concerning the horses?"

"You have my word," Henry said, his eyes brightening at the realization that Mac was going to let him go. "I will follow Mr. Sam's instructions to the letter."

"Then you may go ask if he would saddle a horse for you, also."

Henry snapped his gaze to Olivia and beamed her a smile that put the one she was giving him to shame. "Go on," she said, nodding toward the barn. "Tell Sam I said to give you the *third* gentlest horse, and that way he'll know your request came directly from me."

Henry shot through the fence and disappeared into the barn.

"Olivia," Mac said, stopping her before she could also disappear. "Look at me."

"I'd rather not," she said, knowing it was safer to look anywhere *but* at him—afraid that if she did, she'd never find the courage to return his jacket.

"Then at least tell me what just happened here."

Olivia started walking, lifting her hands with her palms facing up. "Why, I do believe you just had one of my wonderful pearls of wisdom on parenting sprinkle down on you like a soft gentle rain."

Only the moment she rounded the side of the barn, Olivia immediately slumped against it. Holy hell, if Maximilian Oceanus were any more perfect he'd be one of those bed-hopping gods Henry was learning about!

Olivia plodded back toward Inglenook on the slower-than-molasses Molly, following her silent new employee and positively ecstatic Henry and Sophie as she wrestled with her decision to return Mac's jacket instead of following up on her plan to get to know Sam. But honest to God, she couldn't stop seeing Mac's strong, beautiful, sweat-glistening chest, or stop imagining how really nice it would feel to have all that wonderful male strength moving over her, and under her, and so deeply inside her.

Because if she had any hope of ending what she was beginning to realize was more than just her sexual drought, then it had to be now—before it became *never*—and she couldn't come up with one single reason why it shouldn't be Mac who finally helped her get back into the game of life.

Except maybe that instead of *easing* her back in, there was a good chance he might shock her out of her self-induced stasis like one of those heart defibrillators they used to bring people back to life. And she'd always wondered if that wasn't a painful experience.

He had promised to be gentle and careful with her, though, hadn't he?

Oh, and also unrushed.

Just the idea of getting naked with a man—especially one as perfect as Mac—who intended to take his time making love to her left Olivia a little breathless. Which was why she was still afraid she'd flat-out faint, and could only hope he'd catch her before she hit the ground—something he already had experience at, she decided with a smile.

But then she frowned, thinking about the actual logistics of having an affair. They each had children, so it wasn't like they could just hop into bed whenever the mood struck them. Olivia suddenly went back to smiling, realizing that a single parent must have invented sleepovers to get rid of their kids in order to have a sleepover of their own.

But even if she did let Sophie stay the night at a friend's house—a close friend, preferably only a few miles away—that still left Henry. And although Inglenook had the occasional pajama party for the kids in the dining hall so the parents could have some time alone to reconnect with each other, Olivia didn't think *occasionally* connecting with Mac constituted an actual affair.

No, that felt more like plain old sex for the sake of scratching an itch. And even if she was powerfully itchy, what she really wanted was to feel passion and excitement and desire, and experience all the emotional trappings that came with a full-blown affair.

Basically, *she* wanted to move a couple of mountains with someone.

So, if she was going to do this, then she had to find a way to do it right. And that meant more than just hooking up occasionally, or feeling sneaky and frantic when they did, because she wanted to be gentle and careful with Mac, too, and unrushed.

Maybe, since the man seemed fairly knowledgeable about this sort of thing, Mac might have some idea how they could make it work. And come to think of it, wouldn't she be advancing his skills as a single parent by helping him figure out how to court the future Mrs. Oceanus with Henry always being around?

Wow, the man certainly couldn't complain that Inglenook hadn't delivered on its promise to give him the one-on-one help he was paying a small fortune for, could he?

Oh God, that sounded just flat-out wrong. "Mom. Mom. Mommm," Sophie said, repeatedly tapping her leg. "Are you going to sit up there all day? Mr. Sam's waiting to take Molly back to the barn."

Olivia realized her new employee was standing in front of Molly, holding the reins of the other horses while silently waiting for her to dismount. And damn if his eyes weren't crinkled in amusement.

"You probably should start wearing a hat outside, Miss Olivia," Henry said. "Your cheeks are really pink."

Sophie held up her backpack. "Can you take this, Mom? I want to go see all the new horses and learn their names."

Olivia finally dismounted—only to grab the saddle horn with a groan when her knees buckled. "No, you go change your clothes first," she said, shifting her weight from leg to leg to stretch her aching thigh muscles.

"I told you old Molly is a good camp horse," Sam said as he slid the reins out of her hand. "She doesn't even need anyone in the driver's seat to do her job."

His grin as contagious as a yawn, Olivia shot him a sheepish smile. "I guess I have a lot on my mind right now."

"Yeah, I suppose running a facility this size isn't easy." His grin widened. "You have a beautiful daughter, Olivia." But then it disappeared altogether. "Caleb told me your husband died in Iraq a few years back. I'm sorry for your loss."

"Thank you," she murmured, letting go of the saddle to test her legs. Only just when she thought they were going to hold, Caleb and Mac appeared—making her knees nearly buckle again at the sight of Mac's big broad glistening chest peeking out of his unbuttoned shirt.

"Henry's right, Olivia," Sam said. "You might want to start wearing a hat before that sunburn gets any worse."

Worse? If it got any worse she was going to spontaneously combust!

And Mac—the sweat-glistening, smug-smiling, eyebrow-raising jerk—knew *exactly* why her cheeks were pink.

"You're still planning to put me and my crew up for the night, aren't you, Livy?" Caleb asked, his gaze darting between her and Mac. "We brought sleeping bags to bed down in your bunkhouse." He gestured toward the grounds of Inglenook. "And seeing how it's your off-season, I'll even provide the steaks and beer for a barbecue tonight."

"Only if you also spring for s'mores for the kids," she said, letting go of the saddle again and giving a silent sigh of relief when her knees held. "And you also agree to let Mac cook the steaks," she added, hoping to wipe that grin off Mac's face.

Only it widened as he ran a lazy hand over his naked chest. "I've found the best way to bring the flame to full heat is by being . . . unrushed."

Caleb clapped his hands and rubbed them together. "I knew there was a reason I was looking forward to coming up here this year," he said, his eyes dancing with amusement, "when Eileen told me she was going to be away this week. No offense," he said, his voice lowering to a conspirator's whisper, "but your mother-in-law has a way of putting a damper on a party, if you know what I mean." His eyes took on a distinctive twinkle. "You ever consider taking Eileen on a hike and losing *her* instead of your guests?"

"I've come close a time or two," Olivia said as she headed toward her cottage. "But I—" She stopped at the sound of a car cresting the final knoll and turned to see Peg Thompson's minivan pull to a stop at the end of the lodge driveway. The woman shut off the engine, turned to speak to her children in the back, and then got out.

"You got something against poor people, Livy Baldwin?" Peg growled before Olivia even reached her. "Or you just got something against *me*?"

"Good Lord, what are you talking about?" Olivia whispered, trying to lead the angry woman farther away from the men.

Peg pulled free, glaring through her welling tears. "I was able to overlook you not letting Sophie come spend the night with Charlotte, figuring you thought I already had a house full, but just where do you come off painting me as a *charity case*? I got my p-pride, you know," she cried, her voice breaking when she slapped her chest, causing her tears to finally spill free. "I don't need those busybody Grange women making me their new pet project!"

"Oh, Peg, I'm sorry," Olivia said in a horrified whisper, grabbing her friend's arm. "I didn't mean . . . I had no idea . . . I'm *sorry*."

Peg pulled free again and angrily wiped her cheeks. "They want to have a bunch of fund-raisers. And Janice Crupp said they're putting up signs with my kids' pictures on them at the Drunken Moose and Ezra's, and in *all the stores in Turtleback*."

"I swear, Peg, I never thought they'd do anything like that. I was only trying to make them realize that Billy is just as much a hero to you and your children as they make Keith out to be." Olivia pulled Peg into a hug, holding on despite her protests. "I'm sorry. I never meant to imply you needed their charity. I was just pointing out that instead of sending Sophie and me to Disneyland, that maybe they should . . . that they . . ." She sighed. "Oh hell, Peg, those women are just a bunch of busybody old twits with more time on their hands than brains."

Peg rested her forehead on Olivia's shoulder with a shuddering sob. "I know," she rasped. "It's just that I thought . . . hell, things might be tough right now, but I am *not* a charity case." She leaned away. "Then why do you let Charlotte come here for sleepovers, but you never let Sophie come to our house?"

"It has nothing to do with you, Peg. It's *me*. I get a little crazy at just the thought of Sophie not being in her bed at night. She's been bugging me to let her go on sleepovers, but I just can't. Not to *anyone's* house." She shrugged. "And you're right; I did think I was doing you a favor by not adding another kid to your chaos. I don't know how you manage four when I have all I can do not to let *one* drive me insane."

Peg blinked at her. "But you have dozens of kids here at any given time."

"And an entire staff to manage them," Olivia reminded her.

Peg scrubbed her face with her hands, then ran her fingers through her curly blond hair in an attempt to smooth it down. "I'm the one who's sorry," she said thickly. "I've just been so frustrated looking for decent daycare for the twins so I can at least *try* to find a job, that when Janice and Christine cornered me at Ezra's just now, I just snapped." One side of her mouth lifted. "And you were the only target I felt safe enough to aim my anger at."

"We'll fix this. I promise I'll go with you, and together we'll tell those twits to mind their own damn business and send *themselves* to Disneyland."

The other side of Peg's mouth lifted into a full-blown smile. "Or you could offer to take the entire Grange on a hike deep into the woods." Peg's eyes suddenly widened as she glanced past Olivia's shoulder, and she covered her face with a gasp. "Oh God, I can't believe I just made an ass of myself in front of your guests." She spread her fingers to expose one horrified eye. "Oh, Livy, I'm *sorry*!" she cried, pivoting around and running toward her minivan.

Olivia caught up with her halfway there and pulled her to a stop. "Please don't leave. They're not guests; they're just some of my workers." She gestured toward the van. "Let the kids go to the barn and see the horses, and you and I will go inside and have a cup of tea."

"I can't. I'm too embarrassed."

Olivia laughed at that. "You can't possibly be more embarrassed than I was when I had to face all those news cameras after I lost that family. Please stay." She leaned closer. "Don't leave me to entertain these men all by myself this evening."

Peg glanced toward the lodge. "Eileen's not here?"

"She and John are gone for the week." Olivia started toward the minivan. "And the guy who delivered the horses is springing for steaks and beer, and we're going to have a cookout and campfire. And s'mores," she added for good measure. "Stay and help us celebrate."

"What are you celebrating?"

Olivia stopped. "That Eileen isn't here!"

Peg laughed at that, and slid open the side door on the van. "Okay, everyone out. We're staying for supper. Charlotte, Isabel, you two are in charge of Pete and Repeat. You can take the twins down to see the horses, but you make sure they don't get eaten or stepped on."

Seat belts clicked open and arms and legs went flying as Charlotte and Isabel gave a whoop and started helping Peter and Jacob out of their booster seats. Peg grabbed each of the twins as they came scrambling out the door.

"You hold your sister's hand," she told Peter—or maybe Jacob. "And no running in the barn, and no screaming," she said first to Peter and then to Jacob—or vice versa. "I said no running!" she called after them as all four children headed for the barn at a dead run, Henry chasing after them. Glancing toward the men, Peg's face reddened again and she gave Olivia a nervous smile. "You're sure about this? We can stay just long enough for the kids to see the horses and then leave. I really don't want to intrude on your cookout." She stepped closer. "A couple of those guys look a tad overwhelmed by my little tribe of heathens."

"Which guys?" Olivia asked, checking out the men. She laughed when she saw that Mac was smiling, Caleb looked like *he* was a little shell-shocked, and Sam looked rather pale. "Oh no, if you stay for dinner you'll actually be doing me a favor. I'm trying to decide how my new horse wrangler is around children, and I can't think of a better test than a cookout with six kids making s'mores." She slipped her arm through Peg's and started toward the lodge. "And I don't know about you, but it's been ages since I've kicked back with a glass of wine and watched a bunch of men do all the work."

Chapter Twelve

Mac decided that the age-old adage that *the more things change, the more they stay the same* still held true, as he could see no discernible difference between an eleventh-century festival meal and a twenty-first-century cookout. In fact, this evening's gathering could be taking place when man lived in caves, as fire and food and family and friends appeared to be a timeless mix.

Accompanied by drink, of course; only this evening that meant juice for the children, beer for the men, and wine for the two women, who seemed quite content to sit back and let the men do all the work and the children entertain themselves.

Mac was afraid he could get used to this way of life.

He suspected Olivia could get used to it, too, as she appeared to be an entirely different person in Eileen's absence: quite boisterous actually, and relaxed and talkative and even flirtatious. Although that may have more to do with the wine she was liberally consuming than the thrill of having Inglenook all to herself.

Throughout the ages Mac had seen more than one woman's exuberance squelched by a domineering mother-in-law, and though he couldn't quite fathom *how* they endured years of such familial trouncing, he did understand why. For as timeless as it was to gather around an open flame, generations of young women had patiently waited their turn to become the matriarchal power that ruled the roost. Yet even after all they'd experienced at the hands of their mothers-in-law, a good many of those young ladies would in turn become the very women they had spent years disdaining.

As for children, they too were timeless creatures, mostly concerned with enjoying life to the fullest despite what twists and turns they might encounter on their way to adulthood. And tonight, Peg's four and Henry and Sophie were doing a fine job of being children: making a mess of their clothes by eating everything their sticky hands could reach, running around the raised campfire pit like banshees, and engaging in minor skirmishes over whose turn it was to roast the next marshmallow under Caleb and his crew's watchful guidance.

Mac was almost startled to realize that children seemed to have a knack for living in the present moment, and he wondered if many grown-ups couldn't benefit from their example. He took a sip of beer—which was really nothing more than watered-down mead—and decided that maybe one day soon he could have a little discussion with Olivia to see what other pearls of wisdom *he* might share with *her* about living in the present moment.

That is, assuming he could ever get her alone.

And also assuming he could keep his hands off her when he did.

Which made him wonder if at least part of the reason Olivia was taking her time returning his jacket was that she couldn't decide how to actually be alone with him. They couldn't very well set their children on a shelf and tell them to stay put while Mom and Dad ran off to have a little tryst in the hayloft, could they? Maybe Olivia had realized the same thing and was trying to figure out how to make it happen.

Sweet Prometheus, he hoped that was why she was taking so long.

Crossing his ankles after Jacob raced by on his way to his mother, Mac stilled with his beer halfway to his mouth when Olivia jumped to her feet with a loud gasp.

"Ohmigod, I'm such an idiot!" she cried; apparently too busy pointing her glass at Peg to realize she'd sloshed wine on herself. "Peg, you're perfect!"

Peg stopped in the act of wiping her younger twin's nose. "Excuse me?" she said, straightening to glance at the men as she tucked a stray curl behind her ear. She gave Olivia a questioning look. "Why are you an idiot, and . . . um, how am I perfect?"

"I can answer that one," Caleb interjected, using a flaming marshmallow to point at Olivia. "Livy here just realized she's an idiot for putting up with a mother-in-law who thinks she knows anything about running this business." He then aimed the stick at Peg. "And you, my dear, are perfect because you don't take any crap from anyone." He pointed the blackened marshmallow at one of the workers he'd brought with him. "Including my idiot nephew, who I intend to have gelded the minute I get him home."

Mac thought Peg had handled the young man's awkward advance quite well, considering she'd had a crying child in her arms when the fool had given her backside a pat on her way by. Peg had merely stopped, sat the crying child on his lap, and continued on her way as if nothing had happened.

"No!" Olivia cried. "Well, maybe some of what Caleb said, but mostly no. I'm an idiot for not seeing what a perfect counselor you'd be." She smiled crookedly. "And I just happen to be looking for a perfect counselor, and you just happen to be looking for a perfect job." She shrugged. "Which makes it perfect."

Peg finished wiping her child's nose and sent him off with a pat on his rump. "And you are either too drunk to know what you're saying," Peg drawled, "or insane." She snorted, Mac presumed to cover her blush. "Unlike your perfect mother-in-law, I don't know the first thing about what you people do here at Inglenook. But I'm pretty sure all your counselors have college degrees, while I just barely got through high school by the skin of my teeth."

Olivia snorted right back at her, again spilling some of her wine as she made a dismissive gesture. "Good Lord, Peg, I don't know anything about what we do here, either. I'm just a glorified gofer. And I dropped out of college after four semesters to get married. But you," she said, thrusting her glass out again, "you probably know more about what makes a family work than all of my counselors and Eileen's boatload of books put together."

Mac suspected Peg was right in that Olivia had had a bit too much wine, as he noticed that her intrinsic grace was a bit unsteady on her walk over to her gaping friend.

"Come work for me, Peg. The pay's better than anything you'll find around here, we have a health care plan you can sign on to, and the job is full time and year-round."

"But I can't find daycare for the twins," Peg countered. "And in the summer I'll need to find someone to watch all four of my kids."

Once again Olivia waved her wineglass. "For crying out loud, *we're* a daycare. Just bring them to work and stick them in the craft and swimming programs and all the other activities going on here. What do you think Sophie does all day in the summer? Heck, I've got enough clay thingamajig-gies in my house to have the mother of all yard sales. Come on," she urged, nudging Peg with her glass. "Come work for me."

Mac saw a tiny flame of hope ignite in Peg's eyes. "Are you serious?" she whispered, looking around at each of her suddenly quiet children before slowly bringing her gaze back to Olivia. "I can bring them to work with me?" But then the light snuffed out as quickly as it had appeared, and she shook her head. "Eileen would never go for it." She stepped closer to Olivia, her cheeks darkening again. "She never did like me, you know, especially when I . . . um, when I was dating Keith back in high school," she said softly enough that Mac guessed he was the only one who could hear her.

Well, and Olivia, who suddenly slapped a hand to her chest with a gasp. "You dated Keith?" she cried. "Oh Peg, I'm *sorry*."

Yes, the woman had definitely had too much wine.

Though it did appear to help bolster her courage, judging by the way Olivia suddenly threw back her shoulders and smiled at her confused friend—who obviously couldn't decide if Olivia was sorry she'd dated Keith or that Eileen didn't like her.

"I don't let Eileen win *all* the battles," Olivia declared. "Only the ones I don't mind losing. Come work for me, Peg, and I'll include lunch for your little tribe of heathens."

"Miss Olivia," Henry said, running up to her. "You can't call them *heathens*," he whispered, eyeing Peg before tugging on Olivia's arm to make her bend down to him. "She's never going to agree to work for you if you call her children bad names."

"Yes, *Miss Olivia*," Mac said, drawing her attention. "Are you too far into your wine, or is this another one of your pearls of wisdom?" he asked, stifling a smile when she sucked in her breath—hopefully because she was remembering her afternoon encounter with his bare chest.

Looking confused again, Peg laughed. "But Henry, they *are* my tribe of little heathens. Olivia hears me calling them that all the time, because that's what their daddy always called them."

Henry frowned up at her. "And did he also call his sons Pete and Repeat, even though their names are Peter and Jacob?"

Peg crouched down to be level with him. "It was his term of endearment for them, Henry. After having two wonderful girls my husband also wanted a son, only God decided to surprise us with two boys at once. We thought we were having only Peter, and when another son suddenly showed up, Billy shouted 'Pete and Repeat!' right there in the delivery room." She stood up and ruffled his hair. "And it just stuck. But you can call him Jacob. He answers to both."

Peg then thrust her hand out to Olivia. "And if you still

feel the same way in the morning when you are *perfectly* sober," she said with a grin, "then I accept your offer of employment." She used their handshake to pull Olivia closer. "But only if I get to take the guests on hikes," she added over the eruption of her suddenly excited children.

"Yippee!" Charlotte shouted, grabbing Sophie's hands to jump in place. "We're going to be campers at Inglenook!"

Isabel grabbed Henry and hugged him so fiercely he yelped. "Henry-Henry-Henry!" she sang, nearly knocking them both over as she jumped up and down. "We're going to see each other *every* day!" The girl kissed Henry right on his startled mouth. "You can be my boyfriend, and I can bring you to school for show and tell!"

Henry suddenly looked like *he* needed a good dose of wine.

And though Mac doubted young Pete and Repeat understood what all the excitement was about, the boys refused to be outshouted and started running around the patio like screaming little banshees again.

"I think this calls for a celebration," Olivia said over the cacophony of screaming children and laughing men as she walked back to her seat and picked up the bottle of wine. "Damn, it's empty." She headed for the lodge, waving over her shoulder. "Don't anyone move; I'll be right back."

Mac beat her there, but then had to grab her shoulders when she bumped into him. "Excuse me," she murmured, clutching his arms—only to flex her fingers on his muscles as she blinked up at him. One side of her mouth lifted. "You want me to bring your jacket back tonight?"

Mac disguised his smile by sighing. "I wouldn't mind getting it back sometime this century, but I'd rather have it returned when *you* are making the decision and not a bottle of wine." He took hold of her chin and lifted her gaze that had dropped to his chest, which she was now kneading. "And I expect you to be wearing it when you do, and nothing else."

He swept her up in his arms when she suddenly collapsed against him, and carried her into the kitchen. "Why

Miss Olivia, I do believe you just swooned like a *virgin*," he said with a chuckle as he sat her on the island counter. He slipped between her thighs and took her face in his hands. "Do you have any idea the hell you've put me through this week, making me lie in my bed at night picturing you lying in yours wearing nothing but my jacket?"

She smiled smugly and nodded solemnly.

"If I finally kiss you, will you stop digging your tigress claws into my chest?"

She nodded again even as she pulled him closer.

But Mac stopped just short of kissing her. "Tell me what you want, Olivia."

"You," she whispered thickly, pulling on his sweater again.

And still he held himself away. "Have you decided yet what it is you're afraid of?"

"You."

He sighed, resting his forehead against hers.

Olivia slid her arms around his waist, pulling his hips more intimately against her as she brought her mouth up to just touch his. "But not nearly as much as I'm afraid of being lost in the shadows forever. Please, Mac, don't let me disappear."

Instead of kissing her, he took a step back but had to grab her arm when she nearly fell off the counter as he turned toward the door.

"Henry just announced it's about to start raining," Caleb said as he strode into the kitchen—only to come to an abrupt halt. "Oh, sorry," he muttered, his face darkening even as his eyes lit up. "Um, if you could just tell me where the keys are to the van, I'll get out of here and let you folks get back to whatever you were doing."

"We weren't doing anything!" Olivia cried.

"Yeah, okay," Caleb said with a snort, giving Mac an apologetic look. "Are the keys in the van, Livy?"

"Why?"

"I'm going to follow Sam while he drives Peg home, so I can bring him back."

"Why?"

He stepped closer. "Because Sam and I decided she shouldn't be driving after drinking wine all evening. She's not even close to drunk," he rushed to say, "but we'd feel better making sure everyone got home okay." He frowned at Mac. "Your kid just said we needed to get everything inside because it's going to start raining in a few minutes." He shrugged. "I hadn't heard rain was predicted. But Peg said she needed to get going anyway, as it's past her kids' bedtime."

"I believe we have a good half hour before the storm arrives," Mac said, letting go of Olivia now that she was steady enough. "Only it's going to snow, not rain."

Caleb's frown deepened. "How do you know that? Listening to the radio on the way up here this morning, I never heard a word about a snowstorm tonight." He waved at the door behind him. "And it's too damn warm to snow."

Olivia answered before he could respond. "Mac and Henry just know that kind of stuff," she said, hopping down off the counter only to stagger forward, forcing Mac to catch her again. "And if they say it's gonna snow," she continued, clutching his arm, "then you guys better take Peg home. The keys are in the van."

"Maybe you should have someone take you home, too," Caleb drawled.

She stepped away, smoothing down the front of her wine-stained jacket. "I'm not drunk, either." She grinned. "And even if I were, I only have a short *walk* home."

"I've heard those sneaky trees can jump out in front of a pedestrian as well as a vehicle," Caleb countered with a chuckle.

The door opened and his crew came in laden down with the remains of their cookout. "The wind's come up," the backside-patting nephew said, setting his burden on the counter. "And I swear the temperature just dropped twenty degrees."

"Mom, can I go sleep at Charlotte's tonight?" Sophie asked, barreling through the door with Charlotte in tow.

"Not tonight, sweetie." Olivia looked past her daughter when Peg walked in behind the girls. "But one night very soon."

Sophie clutched her young chest with a gasp. "You *promise*?"

"I promise," Olivia assured her, though she was still looking at Peg. "Because I do believe you're old enough to go spend the night at a friend's house."

"And Henry can come for a sleepover, too!" Isabel cried as she darted out from behind her mother and ran up to Mac. Her bright blue eyes grew huge as she slid to a stop and craned her neck to look up at him. "Wow, you're as tall as a tree."

Mac immediately crouched to his heels. "And you're as pretty as a mermaid."

The girl's eyes widened even more. "You know Ariel? I got her movie. Do you know Sebastian and Flounder, too?"

That should teach him to give a girl a compliment. "Sorry, I don't know any of them personally," he said with a chuckle. Though he did know the panicked look in his son's eyes, as the boy stood behind Isabel silently pleading to be saved from his zealous young suitor. Mac gave Isabel a gentle smile. "Unlike Sophie, I believe Henry is still too young."

The girl snorted. "I'm six and I've been going on sleepovers for years."

"Come on, Isabel," Peg said, picking up her sleepy-eyed older twin and setting him on her hip as she held out her hand. "We need to get home ahead of the weather."

"But Mommmm," Isabel whined, not budging an inch even as she wiped her own sleepy eyes, further smearing the chocolate that had missed her mouth. "If Henry can't come to our house, then I want to stay here."

"Move it, young lady," Peg growled, pointing at the floor in front of her.

"Pssst, Henry," Olivia whispered loudly. "You paying attention? *That's* how real whining is done," she said, gesturing at Isabel.

Mac stood, scooping Isabel up in his arms. He carried

the girl to Caleb's nephew and handed her off just as thunder rumbled down over the mountains.

Caleb glared at Mac. "You're joking, right? You were watching the weather channel earlier, and that's how you knew a storm was coming."

"The only televisions with satellite are in my and John and Eileen's private quarters," Olivia said, even as she also looked at Mac in awe.

He shrugged. "I didn't create this storm, I just felt it coming."

Sam walked in. "Are we leaving sometime tonight? There's a distinct smell of snow in the air, and judging by that thunder I'd say we're in for a wild night, so I'd just as soon get Peg home before it hits."

Everyone moved at once: Caleb grabbing up Peg's younger twin, Sam taking hold of Charlotte's hand, Sophie running to her mother, and Henry giving a heavy sigh of relief as they all headed outside.

"It looks like everything got cleaned up," Olivia said, glancing around the patio. She held her hands over the dying fire against the chill in the air. "Good-bye, Peg!" she called as Peg and her tribe and entourage of men headed down the path around the side of the lodge. "I'll see you Monday morning."

"I'll be here bright-eyed and bushy-tailed!" Peg called over her shoulder with a wave. "Along with Pete and Repeat."

Olivia plopped down in a chair next to the fire pit. "Good Lord, I swear this evening was more chaotic than when camp's in full session." She pulled Sophie onto her lap and smiled when Mac sat down in a chair next to them and did the same to Henry. "So, young Mr. Oceanus," Olivia said, "did you see how whining and pouting is really done? I do believe you had the pleasure of witnessing a professional in action."

Henry stopped in midyawn and blinked at her. "I really didn't think it was the appropriate time for whining, Miss Olivia. Not with a storm coming. And I can't quite see myself pleading and pouting in front of others. It's not very manly."

Mac pulled his son against his chest with a laugh, tucking the boy's head under his chin as he shot Olivia a smug smile. "That's right, Henry; Oceanus men do not plead or pout or beg—especially to women."

"You don't have to be Isabel's boyfriend, Henry," Sophie said as she melted against her mother, her feet dangling nearly to the ground. "Isabel's only chasing after you because she's already scared off all the boys in her class. The next time she tries to kiss you, just— Mom! You're hugging me too tight."

"I'm sure Henry is quite capable of dealing with Isabel in his own gentlemanly way," Olivia said. "And if he needs advice, he can get it from his father."

Lightning flashed in the distance, silhouetting the mountains in a halo of white heat, followed shortly by a deep rumble.

"Mr. Sam said the air smelled like snow," Sophie said, her gaze trained on the looming mountains shadowed by bursts of lightning. "Can it thunder when it's snowing? I thought that only happened in the summer."

"It can happen any time of year," Olivia said. "Am I right, Mr. Mac?"

"I believe the conditions that cause lightning have to do with opposing pressure systems rather than with the time of year. It's just more common in the summer, when a cold front bumps into a humid air mass."

"But don't all of our storms come from over there?" Sophie asked, pointing to the west. "That's where the sky always gets dark in the summer and we have to get off the lake in a hurry."

"This one is coming from the Gulf of Maine," Mac said before Olivia could answer. Lightning flashed again, filling the sky overhead as it bounced off the roiling clouds. "I do believe it's time Henry and I walked you ladies home," he said, the last of his words lost in the ensuing thunder that gently shook the ground beneath their chairs.

Olivia set Sophie on her feet and stood up. "I do believe you're right." She grabbed the poker and stirred the dying embers, then placed a heavy screened dome over the top of the pit. "I don't think this will last much longer once the snow hits it." She took Sophie's hand and headed toward the side of the lodge, but stopped next to the door and peered inside. "I've got a mess to clean up, but it's nothing that can't wait until morning," she said, moving along.

Mac fell into step beside her, holding Henry's hand and then taking hold of Olivia's when she tripped in the darkness. "Your eyes will adjust in a moment," he said, smiling when she curled her fingers around his and refused to let go.

"Mom, are you drunk?" Sophie asked, her tone curious rather than accusing.

"Almost, sweetie. How about you? Are you drunk?"

Sophie giggled. "How come you told Miss Peg that you don't let Gram win every battle? You make it sound like you and Gram are always fighting."

"It was a figure of speech. And you're aware that Gram and I often butt heads when it comes to running Inglenook. In fact, you've been agreeing with me about our having horses, even though Eileen doesn't think they add anything to her programs."

"But they're fun. And the campers like them."

"Exactly. And that's why keeping the horses was one battle I refused to lose."

"Were you surprised Miss Peg dated Dad?" Sophie asked as they neared the line of privacy Olivia had literally drawn in the dirt by putting up the fence.

"Not really. After all, they did go to school together. I imagine your daddy dated many of the women around here before he went off to college."

"But you hired her anyway. Aren't you jealous?"

Olivia pulled Mac to a stop by refusing to let go of his hand. "Do you expect to be the first girlfriend of the man you marry, or that your daddy was *my* first boyfriend?"

"Well, no."

Olivia started walking again. "And the fact that Miss

Peg is such a nice person only shows what good taste your father had."

"But he married *you*, Miss Olivia," Henry interjected. "That shows Sophie's dad had *really* good taste."

Olivia looked up at Mac and smiled. "Why, thank you, Henry, for noticing."

This time it was Henry who stopped walking, pulling all of them to a halt. "Miss Olivia, how come you haven't gotten married again?"

Mac sighed, guessing the boy had finally figured out he'd just found a candidate to replace Gadzalina. "Yes, Miss Olivia," Mac said. "Why haven't you?"

"Because she needs a *boyfriend* first," Sophie answered, moving around Olivia in order to speak to Henry. "And all the men in Spellbound Falls are too afraid to ask my mom out on a date."

"My dad wouldn't be afraid to ask her. He's not afraid of *anything*."

"Then how come *he* doesn't ask her to go out with him?"

"Sophie!" Olivia snapped just as lightning flashed, exposing the thunderous glare she was giving her daughter. "What did I tell you about sticking your nose in someone else's business?"

"Henry brought it up," the girl countered, having to holler over the thunder.

Olivia let go of Mac's hand. "Thank you for walking us home," she said, leading Sophie down the path.

Mac rang the bell on the fence. Olivia stopped and turned to him, another round of lightning revealing her blush. Yes, she might be getting close to initiating an affair, but the woman obviously was far from ready to openly date him.

"We had a good time at your cookout, Olivia. Thank you for inviting us," Mac said, giving Henry a nudge.

"Yes, thank you, Miss Olivia. I enjoyed making the s'mores as much as I liked eating them."

"You're welcome," she answered softly, hesitating a moment before turning and heading off again with her daughter in tow.

Henry started toward their cabin, but Mac stopped him. "We will wait until the women are inside and we see the lights come on."

"How come Miss Olivia got upset when Sophie suggested you should ask her mom on a date?" Henry asked.

"I believe it's because Olivia doesn't think children should be playing matchmaker for their parents." He crouched down to be level with him. "And it likely embarrassed her that Sophie put us both on the spot by suggesting I should ask Olivia out."

"But you like Miss Olivia, don't you?"

"Yes, I do."

"Then why *don't* you invite her to go to dinner?" He frowned. "Only it really wouldn't be a date if Sophie and I go with you, would it?"

"No. I believe when children are involved, a babysitter must be hired."

"I know: Mr. Sam could babysit us while you take Miss Olivia out to dinner."

"Or your auntie Carolina could watch you and Sophie," Mac said, scooping Henry into his arms and standing up. "Maybe tomorrow night."

"Auntie's coming?" the boy said on a gasp, a series of blinding flashes exposing his surprise.

Only Mac had to wait until the ensuing thunder died down to answer. "Does this feel like a natural storm to you?" he asked. "Or something more . . . oh, let's go with melodramatic, shall we?"

Henry clasped Mac's face in his hands, his grin as wide as a river. "Tonight?" he whispered. "Auntie's coming in with the storm?"

Mac glanced toward Olivia's house to see several of the lights on and started walking to their cabin with a heavy sigh. "Caro never was one to wait for an invitation, and she certainly does enjoy making an entrance."

Chapter Thirteen

"When was the last time you saw something that precious?" Carolina whispered.

"Oh, about twenty-eight years ago, if memory serves me," Mac said, wrapping his arms around his sister when she leaned back against him as they stood just inside Henry's bedroom door. "Though I still have a bone to pick with the gods for not telling me what sort of hell I was in for when you were born."

"Your son's beautiful, Mackie." She craned to the side to smile up at him. "He's the best thing that ever happened to you."

Mac nudged her back around with a sigh. "Yes he is, assuming he doesn't kill me first." He tightened his embrace. "He scares the hell out of me, Caro. I don't know the first thing about being a father."

"Sure you do; you just have to be the opposite of ours."

"He's not really that bad, you know," Mac whispered. "Since Henry showed up, I've developed a whole new appreciation for our old man."

She snorted softly. "Did you *see* Gadzalina?"

Mac smiled over her head at his sleeping son. "No. But

Henry filled me in on what's waiting for us back in Atlantis if we don't get our act together soon."

She stepped out of his embrace and walked into the cabin's front room, and Mac followed after stopping to close Henry's bedroom door.

"Are you really going to settle in this century, here in Maine?" she asked, going to the hearth and holding her hands to the fire. She turned to him. "It's so . . . rural."

"Which makes it perfect," he said, sitting on the couch. He patted the cushion for her to sit beside him, and then shifted to face her. "I don't want to add too many people into the mix until Henry becomes comfortable with me and his eventual destiny."

Carolina shot him a brilliant smile. "See; you're already thinking like a daddy." She turned serious. "But why have you come up here?" she asked, gesturing at the cabin. "Spellbound Falls is too damn far from the ocean, Mackie."

"I can handle it for a few months. And we're only a three-hour drive from the Gulf of Maine. In fact, I'm planning on taking Olivia to visit Midnight Bay next weekend."

"Olivia?" she asked, arching a delicate brow.

"Olivia Baldwin. She's the widow of one of Trace's military friends who was killed in the line of duty four years ago. It was Trace's idea that I sign on as a guest here for the summer, as Inglenook is designed to help parents and children connect with each other." He smiled. "And Olivia is bubbling with insightful pearls of wisdom on parenting. She has an eight-year-old daughter named Sophie, and Henry has taken quite a liking to the both of them."

Up went his sister's other brow. "And is Mackie liking *both*?"

Mac gave a negligent shrug. "He's definitely interested in one of them."

"Is she pretty?"

"According to Henry, any woman who smiles is pretty."

Carolina smiled. "Oh, I knew there was a reason I already loved that boy."

"Olivia's beautiful," Mac said quietly. "And funny and

charming and capable, and she's a lot smarter than she lets on to people." He frowned. "And she's nearly mastered the art of becoming invisible."

"Sweet Athena, you sound as if you're halfway in love with her."

"No," Mac said with a shake of his head. "I can't let it go that far even if I could think in those terms. Better than anyone, you know that love is an elusive affliction for me, Caro. And Olivia deserves better than a man who's willing to settle for merely being . . . content." He shot her a grin. "But that doesn't mean we can't enjoy each other's company for the next six months, as I believe she's not looking for marriage, either, considering she didn't have very good luck with her first husband. Thank you for sending Henry my training sword."

Accepting his cue that their discussion of Olivia was over, Carolina flopped against the back cushion with a laugh. "Believe it or not the sword's actually from Father, as he figured boys and weapons are a timeless match, and that it would be a good way for you to bond with Henry." She turned her head to him. "The book of mythology was Mama's suggestion, as she believes every child needs to sit on a loving lap and be read to." She snorted. "As for the toy, Leviathan refused to deliver my package unless I included that giant stuffed whale, the vainglorious old lug."

Mac lifted a brow. "Then in all that you sent Henry, what was from *you*?"

Carolina threw up her hands with a laugh. "Me! I've just sent myself to Henry as a present. The other things were just to get him looking forward to my arrival."

"And did you have to arrive in a damned blizzard? We're trying to get Inglenook ready for its new season, and two feet of snow is going to put us behind schedule."

"Us?" she repeated, arching a brow. "I thought you were a *guest* here."

"Olivia needed help, and I needed something to do for a few weeks."

"Like what? Are you helping her test all the cabin mattresses for lumps?"

Mac stood up and headed for the larger downstairs bedroom. "You have your pick of mattresses upstairs, princess," he said over his shoulder. "Mornings come early here at Inglenook, and I intend for you to help Olivia cook breakfast for everyone while Henry and I help clear away all your pretty snow."

Within half an hour of meeting Carolina Oceanus, Olivia decided she wanted to become a theurgist just like Henry, so she could snap her fingers and instantly change herself into a gorgeous, sexy, imposing, and obviously richer-than-God person, too.

There really should be a law against two people in the same family being so perfect. Hell, not only was Carolina beautiful, she was sincerely nice and eager to help.

And that's why Olivia decided the Oceanuses must be richer than God, as they'd obviously grown up having servants to handle all the mundane details of their everyday lives. Because the moment Carolina started helping prepare breakfast, Olivia saw that Mac's sister knew her way around a kitchen about as well as he did. Carolina couldn't even make a pot of coffee because she'd finally admitted she'd never actually *seen* a coffee maker before, right after which the woman proceeded to fill all the glasses on the table—including Henry and Sophie's—to the brim with the boxed wine Eileen kept in the fridge for when her dissertation efforts were flagging.

Maybe Inglenook really should start offering cooking classes. It would certainly help out all the newly divorced fathers who suddenly found themselves having to take care of their children on the weekends, as well as the mothers who thought home-cooked meant frozen pizza cooked at home.

"It's quite a unique concept you've developed here at

Inglenook," Carolina said as she folded napkins into swans on each of the plates she'd set around the table. "I imagine you're overrun with requests from families looking to . . . how did Mackie put it? Ah yes, for parents and children wishing to connect with each other."

Olivia turned the heat down under the pan of home fries and covered it with a lid. "It's not my concept; Inglenook is the brainchild of my mother-in-law." She headed to the fridge to get the eggs. "I just handle the day-to-day operations."

"And yet Mac told me that *you've* been quite integral in helping him with Henry," Carolina said, walking over to the range and opening the oven door to filch a piece of bacon. "In fact, he claims it was you who told him not to see parenting as him versus his son, but rather as *him and Henry* versus the world." She smiled warmly. "And I can't tell you how much that one simple . . . pearl of wisdom resonated with him," she said just before popping the bacon in her mouth.

Olivia ducked her head in the fridge so Carolina wouldn't see her blush. "I must have heard Eileen once say something to that effect. She is the expert, after all."

"More than he cherishes life itself, my brother desires to become the best possible father he can be to Henry," Carolina said quietly from right beside her, making Olivia straighten in surprise. "And there are no words to express how happy I am that Mac's found you to help him transition from bachelorhood to parenthood," she said, holding up her hand when Olivia tried to speak. "Because within minutes of arriving last night I discovered that it's *your* advice Mac is sopping up like a thirsty sponge," she finished with a knowing smile.

Olivia sighed, dropping her gaze when she felt her cheeks heating up again. "I don't know why. I told him from the beginning that I don't know what I'm doing with my own child half the time, and that I've been known to actually hide from Sophie when she gets in one of her moods."

Carolina turned away with a laugh. "But isn't hiding

better than confronting a problem that would otherwise work itself out?"

Olivia rushed after Carolina, her heart thumping at the realization that she may have just met a kindred spirit. "So it's not just me?" she asked in surprise, setting the eggs down and turning to her. "You also think there are times when doing nothing works better than facing something head-on?"

Carolina leaned against the counter and folded her arms under her breasts as she crossed her feet at the ankles. "Are you kidding? I once spent several cent—several months avoiding the man my father intended me to marry." Her mouth curled up on one side. "And the bastard's relentless pursuit showed what an ugly human being he truly was, and my father—along with Mac—took care of the problem for me." She shrugged. "I've found that riding out a storm from a distance is likely the reason for the saying that retreat is often the better part of valor. Which, I believe, is why my mother taught me the value of silence over arguing with pigheaded men."

"Or pigheaded women," Olivia drawled. She laughed. "Ohmigod, I feel the same way, but I always thought I was just being a coward. I would love to meet your mother. She sounds wonderfully wise."

Carolina's vivid green eyes danced in the sunshine reflecting off the new snow outside the windows. "Be careful what you wish for, my friend, or you just might find her popping in here one of these days, as I do believe Mama has been hounding Father to bring her to meet Henry."

Olivia gasped. "She hasn't met Henry yet?"

Carolina straightened away from the counter to open the oven, and filched another piece of bacon. "No, Mac stole Henry away first." She grinned. "And despite our father's agreeing to give my brother a year alone with his son, Mama said *she* didn't agree to any such thing. She's dying to meet her only grandchild, so don't be surprised if you find yourself overrun with Oceanuses one day soon," she warned just before shoving the bacon in her mouth.

Heavy footsteps sounded on the porch as the men banged snow off their boots. The door opened and Henry and Sophie ran in, followed by Caleb and Sam, Caleb's nephew Dale, and his other worker, named Tom, with Mac bringing up the rear.

"I don't know what's going on," Caleb said to no one in particular, "but I swear the snow's melting faster than we're shoveling it."

"The plow blade was pushing only a few inches of slush by the time I reached the main road," Sam said, also sounding bewildered. "At the rate it's melting, it will probably be gone in a couple of days."

"I promised Henry hot cocoa," Sophie said, shedding her coat and hat and mittens. She kicked off her boots, then used her foot to shove them toward the wall. "Do we have any marshmallows left from last night?"

"In the pantry," Olivia said, grabbing another pan off the hanging rack. "Sit down, gentlemen, and don't worry about taking off your boots. There's fresh coffee on the sideboard, and I'll bring over some toast to get you started."

"Oh no, you all just sit down," Carolina said, going to the sideboard. "I'll bring the coffee to you."

"Be careful, *gentlemen*," Mac said with a laugh as he headed for the stove instead of the table. "Anyone patting any backsides might get a lap full of coffee."

Olivia saw him go perfectly still for two seconds, then bend down and open the oven door to grab a piece of bacon, popping it in his mouth and giving her a wink before he sauntered over to the table.

Mac had looked . . . different this morning when he'd shown up in the kitchen with Carolina just after dawn. He'd seemed peaceful, or maybe *relaxed* was a better word, his eyes positively vibrant as he'd let Henry—whose excitement had been nearly uncontainable—introduce his Auntie Caro to Olivia and Sophie.

And yet nobody, including Carolina, seemed to have a good explanation as to how she'd gotten here in the middle of the night in the middle of a blizzard. Especially considering there were no strange vehicles around, or tracks that one might have made when she'd been dropped off.

Carolina had said she'd ridden in on a snowflake, whereas Mac had said she'd flown in on her broom. Henry, ever the gentleman, had boldly admonished his father for that remark, and told Olivia his aunt must have walked in from the turnoff.

The entire three miles, in the dark, in the middle of a blizzard?

Which was only one of the reasons Olivia couldn't decide what was bugging her this morning about Carolina. Nobody that beautiful was as nice as she was—and Olivia was talking *serious* beauty. But according to her *gut* feeling, which she'd found herself consulting more often lately, she honestly liked the woman.

Even if Carolina was a bit . . . strange—her sudden, unexplained appearance at Inglenook notwithstanding. Mac hadn't even mentioned he had a sister, much less that he was expecting her to visit him here.

It was obvious Mac and Carolina were quite close to each other, making it even stranger still that she hadn't met her nephew until this morning, considering Henry had been living with Mac for more than three months. Or that Henry hadn't met his grandmother, but only his marriage-minded grandfather, whom Carolina and Mac seemed to both fear and respect with equal dedication.

And really, what was all this talk about virgins and bastards and dukedoms and bed-hopping gods? And what sort of aunt sent a book of mythology to a six-year-old? For that matter, what six-year-old thought cartoons were silly?

Yes, the Oceanuses were an imposing and decidedly strange family of beautiful people. And for as much as she honestly liked Henry and Carolina, Olivia flat-out couldn't stop obsessing over Mac.

Heck, last night she'd actually fallen asleep wearing nothing but his jacket after he'd put that image in her head just before he'd *almost* kissed her. Lord, but she craved to feel all that wonderful male strength moving over her and beneath her and so very deeply inside her.

"Caleb just took me aside and mentioned that you're handing out jobs like cookies this weekend," Carolina said as she walked over. She nudged Olivia out of the way and opened the oven to get out the plate of bacon and platter of toast. "And he suggested I should ask if you might be interested in hiring a babysitter." She leaned in, her eyes dancing with mirth. "Specifically for this evening, while your mother-in-law is away. Caleb seems to think it would be a perfect time for you to go out to dinner and maybe dancing." She leaned even closer. "Did you know Mac is an excellent dancer?"

Olivia opened her mouth but for some reason couldn't utter a word.

"And I am a much better babysitter than I am a cook," Carolina drawled. "And I just happen to be free tonight."

"I . . . but . . ."

"Ask him, Olivia," she said quietly. "He will say yes."

Chapter Fourteen

Ohmigod, she'd asked! Right after breakfast, just before Mac had walked out the door, Olivia had pulled him aside and asked if he would like for the two of them to drive down to Turtleback this evening and go to dinner at a nice restaurant she knew of.

Only instead of his eyes lighting with lust—or at the very least triumph—she'd been left staring through the kitchen door at his big broad shoulders when Mac had turned away with a shrug, saying he needed to think about it and would get back to her.

And then he'd made her wait *all* day—through sending Caleb and his two drivers on their way, through her spit-shining the rest of cabin four with Sophie's help, and through a lunch that never did make it past the lump in her throat before he'd finally "gotten back to her" at three. And then the maddening man had sent Henry to inform Sophie that *she* was invited to their cabin tonight for a sleepover with his Auntie Caro—complete with popcorn and a movie in the lodge first. Because, he'd then said to Olivia with a familiar-looking wink, his dad would like the honor of taking her on a date tonight.

But after spending a good deal of the day vacillating between confusion and anger, Olivia had nearly sent the boy back with the message that she and Sophie had already made other plans for tonight. And yet here she was standing in front of her closet, staring at her ancient wardrobe and wanting to throw up. Because apparently she was so pathetic, Olivia didn't care if she *had* stooped to asking a man to go out with her—only to stoop even further by going out with him after he'd put her through hell all day waiting for his answer.

And Sophie wasn't helping matters. "Isn't Miss Carolina the most beautiful woman you've ever seen?" her daughter asked from the bureau, where she was studying Olivia's collection of costume jewelry. "She's so tall, I bet she's a model."

Just what she needed: a reminder that she was going out with an equally beautiful man who would definitely complement her shabby lonely-widow look.

"Here, I think you should wear these," Sophie said, walking over with her hand outstretched. "Didn't you say your dad gave these to your mom before you were born?"

Olivia plucked one of the tiny white pearls out of Sophie's hand and pushed the stud through her ear with a sigh. "Yes, he did. But they still don't help me decide what to wear," she said, taking the other earring and putting it on. "Everything goes with tiny white pearls, even jeans."

"I think you should wear this," Sophie said, pulling out the hem of a deep red dress for her to see. "It makes your eyes stand out."

It was also the dress she'd worn when she and Keith had left on their honeymoon a lifetime ago. "No, I think it's got a couple of buttons missing," she said, grabbing the only thing in her closet that wasn't even remotely connected to him. "Here, what do you think of this?" she asked, holding the tailored blue blouse under her chin. "With my black wool slacks and pumps? It says clean sophistication, doesn't it?"

Sophie frowned. "Isn't that your funeral outfit? I was

with you when you bought it to wear to Miss Doris's funeral last year."

"That doesn't make it a *funeral* outfit," she said, slipping the blouse on over the only lace bra she owned. "Dig around in the bottom of my closet and find those black pumps, would you, sweetie?"

Olivia then pulled her wool pants off the hanger and slipped them on over her only pair of sheer knee-highs that didn't have a run in them. God, she really needed to drive to Bangor and update her wardrobe. No wonder nobody asked her out; she *dressed* like a shabby lonely widow.

"They're here!" Sophie cried, tossing the pumps on the floor and running out of the room when a vehicle drove up next to the house. She stopped in the hallway and looked back. "Hurry up and finish dressing, Mom. You don't want to keep Mr. Mac waiting," she said, running off again at the sound of a knock on the door.

Olivia tucked her blouse into her pants—several times, actually, because for some strange reason her hands had started trembling—and turned to look at herself in the full-length mirror. When she noticed her shoulders were hunched, she took a deep breath and threw them back.

She could do this. She just had to get through tonight without embarrassing herself, and then she could relax and *enjoy* the rest of their affair.

Because right now it wasn't the least bit fun.

Olivia practiced her smile in the mirror, aiming for a confident look—only what she got was a deer caught in the headlights of an impending disaster.

"Mom!"

"I'm coming," Olivia called softly, trying to sound calm and aloof. No sense appearing too eager for her *let me think about it and I'll get back to you* date.

"Mom, he's waiting," Sophie hissed from the bedroom doorway. "And he looks really handsome." She suddenly smiled. "I bet Mr. Mac could be a model, too. His shoulders are almost as wide as our doorway."

Good Lord, when had her daughter started noticing men's shoulders?

Sophie waved her along. "Come on, Mom. You're pretty enough."

Olivia headed after her fleeing daughter but stopped when she saw Mac's jacket lying on her bed. She stuffed it under the pillow, then squared her shoulders and headed down the hall with what she hoped was a confident smile by the time she reached the kitchen.

Heaven help her, he was tall and imposing and impeccably dressed in black pants, the collar of a crisp white shirt accentuating the V of his blue sweater. His hair was still damp, his jaw clean-shaven, and his eyes . . . Olivia felt her smile faltering when his eyes ran up the length of her, hesitated at the base of her throat—where her pulse was pounding so hard he could probably see it—and then locked on hers.

She jumped when Henry took hold of her hand. "Miss Olivia, you look quite beautiful this evening," he said, his own eyes sparkling. "And isn't it a coincidence that your blouse matches Dad's sweater." He pulled her down toward him. "Auntie Caro helped me pick out what he should wear, and she said that particular blue is the color of the ocean surrounding the *mythical* continent of Atlantis. Did you know that?"

"No, I can't say that I did," Olivia whispered before straightening and going over to take her long wool coat off the peg. She really should have a talk with Carolina about this mythology thing, considering how Henry soaked everything up like a sponge. Then again, could bed-hopping gods be any worse than the violent cartoons on TV today?

Mac took the coat and held it up for her to slide her arms into its sleeves, then wrapped it around her shoulders, his arms encompassing her in a circle of heat. She stepped away and grabbed her purse off the counter.

"Shall we go, then?" he said, taking one last curious look

around her tiny kitchen before opening the door and waving Sophie and Henry ahead of him. "Henry didn't wish to cross your fence," he said as Olivia walked past, "but I told him that a gentleman meets his date at her door. Was I right to do so?"

"Yes, of course."

He closed the door behind him. "Do you lock up your house?"

She laughed at that—though she was afraid it sounded more nervous than humorous. "No. If anyone came to Inglenook looking to steal anything, they'd likely hit the main lodge instead of the groundskeeper's cottage. Sophie," she called out as Henry and her daughter headed toward cabin ten. "You will behave for Miss Carolina, and you let Henry pick out which movie you watch tonight. Oh, and don't forget I put a couple of bags of microwave popcorn on the counter. Remember, three minutes a bag, and you watch that they don't burn," she said, remembering Carolina's proficiency in the kitchen. "And there's soda in the fridge."

"I *know*, Mom," Sophie said, walking backward. "You told me already."

"I . . . I'll see you in the morning, then."

"Yeah. Good-bye. Have a good time," the girl called over her shoulder.

"She'll be fine," Mac said with a chuckle, placing his hand at the small of her back to usher her toward his truck.

"The house will feel so empty tonight, knowing she's not just down the hall."

He stopped before opening the passenger door, giving her a strange look.

"Even when we have pajama parties in the dining hall, I only let her attend if I'm at them, too." She stepped back with a laugh so he could open the door. "I really need to stop hovering and let her grow up."

No, she needed to shut up!

Or maybe what she really needed was to stop letting Mac rattle her. She jumped into the front seat the moment he opened the door, then fastened her seat belt before he did it for her. Honest to God, every time he touched her she panicked.

And that's why they were going to a restaurant that *didn't* have dancing.

He walked around and got in behind the wheel. "All set?"

"Mm-hmm," she returned with a nod, afraid she'd start rattling off again.

Were all affairs this disconcerting?

Or was *who* she was trying to have an affair with the problem?

God, he was beautiful.

Okay: If she survived tonight—an everyday, no-pressure dinner date—without making a total fool of herself, then maybe she *would* give him back his jacket and let him take over from there.

She frowned out the windshield as he pulled onto the lane leading past the main lodge. That is, assuming he wanted to take over, considering he'd balked at just going to dinner. Maybe Mac was having second thoughts. Maybe seeing his sister again had gotten him thinking about his family obligations and marriage-minded father. Hell, maybe he'd taken one look at her standing next to Carolina this morning and realized good old invisible Olivia Baldwin wasn't worth bothering with. Not when Daddy had a beautiful candidate sitting in the wings back home.

What in hell kind of a name was *Gadzalina*, anyway?

It sounded an awful lot like *Godzilla* to her. And apparently to Henry as well, judging by the look on his face when he'd mentioned her to Olivia the other day.

Wait; maybe Mac had every intention of marrying his father's hand-chosen bride when he left here in the fall, and just wanted to sow some wild oats before he tied the knot. Yeah. The man was obviously bored to the point that he was working for her, so maybe he figured a little summer fling with one of the natives might be fun.

Olivia used the excuse of looking for something in her purse to cover up the awkward silence—only to go perfectly still when she touched the condoms she'd found in an old box in the back of her closet. Granted, they were over six years old, but she'd stuffed them in her purse for . . . for just in case.

Did condoms have expiration dates?

"I couldn't help but notice you didn't bring my jacket," he said into the silence as they finally pulled onto the main road. "Any particular reason why?"

She set her purse down by her feet to disguise her flinch, and then clasped her hands on her lap to disguise her trembling. "I guess I assumed you no longer want me to give it back. I don't understand, Mac. You said that if I asked you'd say yes, but this morning when I did, it took you all day to decide if you even wanted to go out to dinner with me tonight." She tried to shrug nonchalantly. "So I figured you'd changed your mind about our . . . our being together."

He slowed the truck rather suddenly, pulled to the side of the road and put it in park, then shifted against his seat belt to face her. But when she continued to stare down at her hands, he took hold of her chin to make her look at him.

"I haven't changed my mind," he said quietly, his stare so intense she had to drop her gaze to his mouth. He splayed his fingers along her jaw and gently lifted her eyes back to his. "But I do seem to have grown a conscience. I find myself liking you more than I intended, Olivia, and you deserve better than what I can offer you."

"But . . ."

He slid a finger over her lips. "I've yet to meet a woman who can give herself to a man without her heart eventually becoming engaged, and I'm starting to care too much for you to let that happen."

Oh God, he *had* changed his mind. "But I promise I won't fall in love with you!" She jerked away and buried her face in her hands. "Dammit, I just want to feel alive again. To feel *something*."

Utterly mortified, she unfastened her seat belt and opened her door, escaping his grasp as he snarled a curse when his own seat belt pulled him up short. Ignoring his calling her, Olivia ran toward the turnoff, stumbling onto the pavement when she couldn't see because of her threatening tears.

Dammit, they hadn't even made it to the naked part and she'd already embarrassed herself. She wasn't so dense that she couldn't recognize a flat-out rejection when she heard one. The jerk had been taking her on a consolation date!

Olivia came to such an abrupt halt that she screamed, and was swept off her feet and thrown bottom side up over his big broad shoulder before she finished gasping.

"I believe Turtleback Station is in the other direction," he said quietly, his arm around her thighs tightening against her struggles. "Which is where I have every intention of taking you."

"Don't do me any favors!" she snapped, only to go perfectly still. Wait; weren't there supposed to be more words at the end of that sentence? Like, *to dinner*? She started struggling again. "Because *I've* changed my mi—" Olivia gave another yelp when he unceremoniously stuffed her in the front seat of his truck, then leaned in to slip the seat belt around her and click it shut.

"You will stay put," he said, backing out and gently closing the door, then slowly walking around the front of the vehicle.

She immediately grabbed the buckle to jump back out again, only it wouldn't release. She twisted to look down, shoving again and again on the red rectangular button, but the damn thing wouldn't release!

Mac got in behind the wheel, put the truck in gear, checked his mirror, and started off down the road again as calmly as if they were taking a Sunday drive.

"My seat belt buckle is jammed," she said, continuing to push the stupid button. "It won't release."

He said nothing, only smiled.

"Did you hear me?" she said a bit louder. "My seat belt's stuck."

"It's likely only tension making it uncooperative. I'll see

what I can do to alleviate the problem when we arrive at our destination."

Uncertain of his mood, Olivia silently sucked in a shuddering breath and clasped her hands on her lap. "You said I deserve better," she whispered.

"Yes."

"And that your newly discovered conscience doesn't want us to have an affair."

"That's what I said."

"Then take me home, Mac."

"I intend to . . . first thing in the morning."

Olivia took another steadying breath, trying to figure out how things had gone so terribly wrong so quickly—as well as how her invitation to dinner had turned into breakfast. "I don't need sympathy sex."

His foot jerked on the accelerator as he made a sound: sort of half snort, half growl. "Trust me, Olivia; it's not exactly sympathy I'm feeling at the moment."

She fell silent at that, wondering if in her wildest dreams she'd ever thought she would need to bring a baseball bat on a date. Olivia spent the rest of the interminably long thirty-mile drive to Turtleback staring out the window, only to realize that the farther away they got from Spellbound Falls the less snow there was from last night's storm, until it disappeared completely at the town line. The sun was setting later now that they were well into April, and the unusually warm spring had already started showing up in the form of sinking culverts and expanding potholes.

Not that Mac's truck seemed to notice, as it appeared to practically glide over the road with the same quiet determination to get them to their destination as its driver.

What in hell had she gotten herself into? For crying out loud—which was still a possibility, she was afraid—all she'd wanted was a simple, no-frills, unemotional affair. Well, except for passion. She really wanted to experience some honest-to-God passion at least once before she died.

Instead she'd found a man who *liked* her too much to give her some.

She stifled a snort; apparently not too much to listen to his conscience, because he intended to *take her* to Turtleback anyway, and not bring her home until morning.

Oh, what the hell. At this point even sympathy sex was better than none at all. And really, she'd put on her sexiest underwear, dabbed her ancient perfume in all the appropriate places, and shaved her legs and everything. So why not simply relax and go with the flow, seeing how she couldn't be any more embarrassed if she tried?

"Um, that was the restaurant," she said, craning to look over her right shoulder as she pointed at the building he was driving past.

"We'll order in room service . . . later," he said, pulling into the parking lot of the only upscale resort on Bottomless Lake—which she knew charged the highest rates in the entire county, even in the off-season.

He stopped under the portico. "Stay put," he said, shooting her a smile that said he wasn't worried she was going anyplace. "I'll be back in a minute."

Olivia waited until he disappeared into the office before she started pushing the red button again. Not that she intended to go anyplace, but it was the principle of the thing. What in hell was wrong with this stupid buckle? Because the more she pushed and tugged and cussed at it, the tighter the damn seat belt got.

She yelped in surprise when his door opened and he got in, causing him to raise an eyebrow as he put the truck in gear.

"There are laws about holding a person against their will, you know," she said, arching a freshly plucked eyebrow right back at him.

"I am aware of all the laws in your country." He clicked something in his hand and guided the truck through the electronically opening gate, and then idled down the pine-studded lane past an array of flawlessly detailed, utterly charming cabins.

Olivia slunk down in her seat and watched the gates automatically close behind them in her side-view mirror. Oh yeah; if Mac wasn't richer than God he was damn close, because she knew for a fact this illusion of Maine woods camping cost more for one night than she charged for an entire week at Inglenook.

"Several of which make no sense, and most of which I prefer to ignore," he continued, though for the life of her Olivia couldn't remember what they'd been talking about. "Oh, look," he said, his tone provoking. "All their cabins are numbered in sequence. Here we are," he murmured, turning into the driveway of the very last cabin on the point of land jutting into the southernmost cove of Bottomless Lake.

He shut off the engine, but instead of getting out he set his hand back on the steering wheel and stared through the windshield at the cabin—which looked big enough to sleep ten and had smoke coming out of its fieldstone chimney.

He'd made reservations?

"Ask me, Olivia," he said quietly. He looked at her, his eyes revealing nothing. "I would prefer to be invited."

She pulled in a fortifying breath, held it for five pounding heartbeats, and then slowly released it. "I . . . I want to be with you, Mac."

Other than his eyes seeming to grow darker and slightly more imposing, she still for the life of her couldn't read his mood.

"Then go on," he said, nodding toward her door. "Back your words with action."

"I—I can't. My seat belt's stuck, remember?"

He smiled. "I believe it will unfasten now, if you truly wish it to."

She frowned, reaching down and pushing the button, only to gasp when the buckle slipped free of the lock. "What the—" Her gaze shot to his. "I swear the damn thing was stuck."

"Something certainly was," he muttered, opening his door and getting out.

Olivia opened her own door to get out, but before her feet hit the ground she gave a squeak of surprise when he swept her up in his arms.

"You've gotten very noisy all of a sudden for a kitchen mouse," he said as he carried her up the cabin steps. He stopped at the door and arched a brow. "Which has me curious as to what other sweet little noises you might make," he murmured thickly, nudging open the door and stepping inside.

Had he just called her a *mouse*?

Only instead of setting her down, he pushed the door closed with his foot, strode over to the large fieldstone fireplace, and set her on her feet in front of it. And then he had to grab her heavy wool coat to hold her steady when Olivia suddenly turned to jelly at the realization that this honest to God was going to happen.

Using his grip on her lapels, he pulled her closer and leaned down, his mouth stopping just shy of hers. "I would know you trust me if you stopped trembling," he said, his lips brushing hers. "I won't hurt you, Olivia, I promise."

She couldn't stop trembling. "I'm not . . . I don't . . . it's been a long time for me, Mac." She gave him a self-deprecatory smile. "And I'm not afraid *of* you but *for* you."

Instead of kissing her—even though she rose up on her toes to meet him—he cupped her head to his chest with a groan. "Ah, Olivia; sometimes I wonder if you're not your own worst enemy."

"Yeah, well, just so you know, I lied to Sophie last night," she muttered into his sweater. "I didn't exactly have a whole bunch of boyfriends before I met Keith. And the guys I did date never felt compelled to write *See Olivia Naglemeyer for a good time* on any bathroom walls. Is it hot in here?" she asked, stepping away to unbutton her coat as she finally looked around the cabin. "Good Lord, this place is a museum!"

"Olivia."

"Everything looks authentic," she said, tossing her coat on the couch as she rushed to the kitchen alcove. She stopped and brushed her hand over the table with a semihysterical laugh. "This sure as hell isn't a reproduction."

"Olivia."

"Everything we have at Inglenook is junk," she whispered, turning to him even as she felt her eyes fill with tears. "You're used to five-star establishments and service, and I can't even give you . . . one star," she finished lamely, spinning away. "Everything we have is just j-junk."

What *had* she been thinking? She was a nobody bastard orphan from a three-car town down on the coast who didn't have any business obsessing over a man who paid more for a room for one night than she earned in a month. And she'd stuck him in a forty-year-old cabin with creaky old beds and tilting floors and a roof that leaked every time it rained.

She sure as hell didn't have any business being *here*, pretending she was pretty and sexy and . . . and worldly enough to have an affair with him. Hell, she hadn't even been able to hold Keith's interest more than a few years before he'd gone looking for a prettier, sexier, worldlier woman.

She flinched when Mac encircled her from behind, and dropped her head when he locked his hands together below her breasts, effectively pinning her arms at her sides. "Are you through?" he whispered against her ear.

She shuddered. "Oh yeah, I'm done."

"Then I suggest you hold yourself as still as possible," he said, his hands moving up to the top button on her blouse.

She immediately reached up to stop him. "W-what are you doing?"

"Hush, Olivia." He pulled her hands down and pressed them to her sides. "I'll let you know if I need your help."

She sucked in a deep breath, causing his fingers to brush her breasts on their way back up to her neck, the intimate touch making her shudder again.

"Not knowing anything of your past," he said, his tone conversational as he undid the top button of her blouse and moved down to the next, "I have no idea when you first developed the notion that hiding in the shadows was preferable to standing in the light." He moved on to the next button. "And I do hate to destroy your illusion, Olivia, but you haven't quite managed the art of becoming completely invisible—at least not to me." He pulled her blouse from the waist of her slacks and finished undoing the last two buttons. "Your inner light gave you away, little one, and the only star here tonight is glowing with the brilliance of ten thousand suns."

He pulled her blouse off her shoulders, letting it fall to the floor between them. Using his jaw to move her hair out of the way as his hands dropped to the waistband on her slacks, he kissed her neck, making her legs buckle as she moaned in pleasure.

"No, you will stand for me."

She locked her knees against the onslaught of sensations coursing through her, feeling the zipper on her slacks slide down so slowly she nearly stopped breathing.

"Um, could you be a little less unrushed?" she groaned, trying to push down her slacks and panties at the same time. Because really, now that it was actually happening, she was going to just die if he didn't hurry up so she could feel all his wonderful strength moving inside her.

He captured her hands again and pressed them against her hips. "Sorry, but I keep my word," he murmured against the racing pulse on her neck, sending tremors of delicious heat straight to her groin. "Don't move," he said, straightening away—though his hands hovered next to her shoulders momentarily before disappearing completely.

Lord, she wanted to spin around and throw herself at him.

No, she wanted to confidently turn around and undress him.

Slowly. Eagerly. Maddeningly unrushed.

Dusk had fallen, the only light in the cabin coming from the blazing fire in the hearth behind them. Olivia watched the shadow of Mac's body on the wall she was facing as he pulled his sweater off over his head—even as she noticed that her own shadow was completely swallowed up by his. She jumped when she felt the back clasp of her bra suddenly open, and held it to her breasts when he slid the straps off her shoulders.

"Let it fall away, Olivia."

God help her, she couldn't. Granted, she was otherwise naked but for the bra covering her breasts and her knee-high socks and slacks gathered at her ankles, but . . . oh, God, they were at the totally naked part.

Only problem was, no man had seen her naked in more than six years.

She heard Mac sigh, saw his shadow shrugging out of his shirt, and then felt the crisp material settle over her shoulders.

"Slide your arms into the sleeves."

But that meant she'd have to let go of her bra.

"Are you a tigress or a kitchen mouse?" he whispered.

Did mice and tigers have boobs that headed south on their thirtieth birthday? Because honest to God, she'd swear she'd looked in the mirror one day and found the damn things two inches below her elbows. Why in hell did he think she'd worn such heavy lace armor tonight, anyway?

"Here's an idea," she said, addressing his shadow on the wall. "How about if I go into the bedroom and get in bed"—where gravity wouldn't be an issue—"and you come in two minutes later . . . um, without *your* clothes on?"

She heard him sigh again, this time hard enough that she felt her hair move.

She gasped when he swept her off her feet and plastered her against his big broad naked chest, just as her shoes fell to the floor followed almost immediately by her dangling pants and panties. Only instead of heading for the nice dark bedroom, he carried her over to the big bright blazing fire. Or more specifically, over to what looked like a thick feather bed topper positioned on the floor in front of it, covered in a deep hunter green sheet.

How in hell had she missed that earlier?

Olivia still continued clutching her bra as he laid her down, worried that instead of going south her boobs would head east and west the moment she let go. She quickly canted one leg over the other, remembering she was naked from the waist down.

Well, except for her stupid, *unsexy* knee-highs.

But she'd had their first time together all planned out, intending to undress in the bathroom, slip into bed while he was doing . . . something else, and shutting off the beside lamp before he came in, because . . . well, because she was pretty confident she *felt* a lot better than she looked. Only he'd ruined everything.

God, was that fire bright or was it just her?

He settled on the feather bed between her and the hearth—conveniently putting her in the shadow of his body—and slowly ran a finger down her scorching cheek. "Touch me, Olivia," he said quietly.

She stopped breathing. Ohmigod, she'd been so self-absorbed with her flaws and insecurities she'd completely forgotten about *Mac*.

She wasn't the only one who needed to get naked for this to work, and she sure as hell couldn't be the only one feeling unsure of themselves. Why else would the man have paid a small fortune to give her a romantic evening—right down to a feather bed in front of a blazing fire—if he wasn't feeling equally desperate to impress her?

And she was ruining the plans *he* had obviously spent the afternoon concocting.

She sat up and let go of her bra, immediately slipped her arms into the sleeves of his shirt, then quickly shed her knee-highs. She lay back on her side facing him, only to go slightly dizzy at the sight of his broad, wonderfully naked chest—the one that she'd just been given the go-ahead to *touch*.

"You're so beautiful," she whispered, running her fingers through the soft hair covering some really impressive muscles as she worked her way toward his belt.

He stopped her. "There really is no rush. We have all night," he said, the deep timbre in his voice sending a shiver of anticipation through her.

She suddenly dropped her head onto his chest with a groan. "My purse is in the truck," she muttered, even as she brushed the soft down on his chest with her lips when she turned to look at him. "I—I don't suppose you have a condom on you?"

The torso she was leaning on rose and fell with a heavy sigh, making her suck in her breath when it brushed against her sensitive nipples. "I've seen to that particular problem," he said, gesturing toward the hearth—where Olivia saw a bowl carved from a burl of wood, full of . . . good Lord, there had to be two dozen condoms in there! She pressed her face to his chest in utter and complete awe at the service money could buy.

Oh God, she hoped Sylvia Pinkham hadn't seen her in the front seat of the truck when the resort owner had given him the gate key. Because if she had, it would be all over Turtleback Station and eventually Spellbound Falls that Livy Baldwin was having a flaming affair with a man who had ordered a romantic seduction complete with a feather bed in front of the hearth and a bowl full of condoms.

Mac smoothed down her hair. "Touch me, Olivia."

Seriously, she had to get over herself. If she wanted to have an affair, it was nobody's business but hers. Well, hers and the half-naked guy she was sprawled over.

Dammit, she needed to stay focused before another six years went by!

Only just as she decided to have another go at his belt buckle, she heard him mutter something about wanting five minutes alone with . . . somebody, just as he reared up, rolled her onto her back and settled rather intimately between her naked thighs.

And this time she didn't have any problem reading the look in his eyes.

Chapter Fifteen

For the love of Zeus, he'd known simpering virgins less shy than Olivia. Mac couldn't tell what was going on inside that beautiful head of hers, but he'd let her stall long enough. He'd almost gotten her engaged by asking for her touch, but even that hadn't seemed to get her out of her head and into the room with him.

"W-wait," she stammered, pushing against his chest to hold him at bay.

By the gods, if he waited any longer Henry would be a grown man by the time they left this room. He gently pressed his groin into hers. "No, don't close your eyes. I want you to see how you affect me, Olivia. Watch how my skin tightens and shudders at your touch."

That seemed to get her attention as she snapped her gaze to his chest. She hesitantly combed her fingers through his pelt of hair with a feathery touch, her eyes widening when his muscles reacted with an involuntary tremor. Her other hand moved to trail one single finger down to his nipple, drawing a circle around it before moving even lower to his ribs, causing every muscle in his body to tense in response.

And still Mac held himself perfectly still against her

sweet torture, drinking in the sight of her flushed cheeks, her deep round eyes sparkling like mulled wine, her lips parting as her plump, feminine breasts rose and fell with her quickening breaths. He finally bent at the elbows just enough to lower his mouth to hers, pressing against her inviting lips even as she rose to meet him.

Sweet heaven, he'd promised he wouldn't rush, but he could see now that he'd made the vow in haste as her sometimes hesitant, sometimes bold explorations drove Mac a little frantic himself. He moved his mouth along her cheek, down to her jaw and then to her throat, pressing on her racing pulse to suckle a moan from her.

"Are you keeping your eyes open?" he asked as he trailed a moist path down over her collarbone, shifting so that he was even with her breasts. "Watch your own response, cinnamon eyes."

He pulled one of her nipples into his mouth, causing her to arch up with a gasp. Her fingers dug into his back, her legs wrapping around his as if she were afraid he'd suddenly disappear.

By the gods, she was definitely in the room with him now.

He suckled gently, then lifted his head and blew on her delicious nipple, watching it respond before returning to it again as she gave a deep moan and quivered in response. Her hands became bolder, slipping inside his trousers then sliding all the way up his back to his shoulders.

Her breath quickened when he trailed his lips across the valley of her chest to lavish attention on her other nipple, pulling it inside and then worrying its responsive peak with his tongue. She grew restless beneath him, her legs sliding along his as she at first pulled and then pushed at him with building frustration.

He captured her directionless hands and held them to her sides as he shifted again to bring his head lower still, dipping his tongue into her delicate navel as he repositioned his grip on her arms when she reared up with a gasp.

"Ohmigod, you can't," she rasped, straining against his

hold. "I'm not . . . you shouldn't . . . Ohhhh," she keened when his mouth closed over her delicate bud in an intimate kiss.

He immediately felt the storm begin to gather inside her, her body tensing with pulsing heat even as he realized her raggedly panted protests were no longer aimed at him but at herself. His own body shaking with need, Mac continued his loving assault as he fought his urge to be inside her when she crested, afraid if he took even a moment to put on a condom she'd slip back into the shadows. So he pressed on, sliding his forearms under her bottom to lift her to him.

He felt her straining toward release, her body growing damp with her efforts. And then she suddenly stilled but for the shuddering tremors coming from deep inside her, her shout of pleasure sending Mac precariously close to the edge of his control.

With his mind all but screaming that what he was about to do could very well be the end of him, Mac nevertheless rose to his knees, undid the buckle of his belt, and pushed his pants down. He quickly sheathed himself in a condom, then lifted Olivia's hips—only to stop just as he was poised to enter her sweet, welcoming heat. He spanned his thumbs across her belly, his fingers flexing into the soft flesh when she raised her hands to his shoulders—not to hold him at bay but to urge him inside her.

"Yes, Mac, come into me," she rasped, her body writhing with lingering pulses of pleasure. "Now. I need to feel you moving inside me *now*."

Yet still he hesitated, his mind asking for reason even as his heart pounded with the need to claim her. "Open your eyes, Olivia," he commanded. "And say you want to be mine."

"Oh, for the love of— No more games." Her fingers dug into his arms and she lifted her hips toward him. "I'm pretty sure I've been yours since the day we met."

Fully aware that she didn't have a clue what was really happening between them, and knowing he was already damned either way, Mac carefully eased inside her to finally and irrevocably claim Olivia as his.

Only it seemed she had no intention of letting him be gentle. The moment he slid past her entrance, the woman wrapped her legs around his thighs with a long, keening moan and arched up to seat him fully inside her. "Ohmigod, *move*," she cried.

He wasn't sure, but Mac thought she muttered something about a baseball bat just as her fingers dug into his biceps and her heels pressed him forward. He retreated ever so slightly and thrust forward, and she clenched around him with another moan—this one ending with a whispered plea that he do it again.

And so Mac moved, his eyes locked on Olivia's as she met each of his slow rocking thrusts with eager anticipation. He watched in fascination and no small amount of satisfaction as her gaze followed her hands roaming over his arms and chest and torso, until she finally threw back her head with a deep, guttural groan.

Feeling her tightening around him, Mac reared up and grasped her hips to lift her more deeply against him when she demanded he quit being so damned unrushed.

She was unbelievably abandoned in her response, her eyes locked on his as she arched her glistening body up to meet his increasing rhythm, her sweetly panted mews growing urgent as Mac let go of one hip to press his fingers intimately between them.

She crested again, her breathless cries finally pushing him over the edge.

He gave a shout of pure pleasure and went perfectly still, and allowed Olivia's contractions to pull him into the maelstrom with her, only remotely aware of the cabin filling with searing white light as the power of his own release shook him to the very core of his being. And with blinding clarity Mac knew he had just handed Olivia his fate—whether or not she wanted it or could even understand what it meant to hold that kind of power in her delicate hands.

Not that he intended to explain to her what had just occurred between them, at least not until *he* came to terms with what he'd just done.

Olivia slowly stirred beneath him, her ragged panting becoming stifled and her cheeks flushing crimson as she lifted her hands to cover her beautiful breasts. Mac watched her lids drop to hood her eyes, and she tried to turn away despite his still being embedded deeply inside her.

Realizing she was embarrassed by her wild abandon and afraid he was losing her into the shadows again, Mac carefully eased down beside her. He then rolled her into his embrace when she tried to get up, and settled a thigh over hers as he smoothed her damp hair off her face.

"Who made Olivia the child feel she had no value?" he asked quietly, desperate to keep her in the room with him. He threaded his fingers through her hair when she stiffened and tried to squirm out from beneath him. "Tell me where you first learned that becoming invisible was your only means of protection. Your husband may have made you all the more determined to perfect the illusion, but you learned the trick of disappearing long before you met him. Who first sent you into hiding?"

"Life did," she snapped, even as she gave up the fight to get free. Her eyes grew distant and Mac watched Olivia pull her defenses around herself like a cloak of thick ocean fog. "Quiet, invisible kids got to stay," she said with complete lack of emotion. "And troublemakers didn't last six months."

"They got to stay where?"

"With their foster families."

Mac shielded his unease by focusing his gaze on the racing pulse in her throat. "How old were you when your parents died?"

"Four when my mother died. And . . . and I don't know when my father died because the last time I saw him I was five."

"And you had no relatives to take you in, and were raised by a foster family?"

"Families, plural. I lived in four different homes over

the fourteen years I was a ward of the state." She tested his hold on her, only to take a shuddering breath when he refused to let her go. "What's your point, Dr. Oceanus? What does analyzing my childhood have to do with our having an affair?"

He stroked a thumb over her pale cheek. "Do you have any idea how hard it is to make love to a shadow, *marita*?" he whispered. "One minute you're here with me and the next you disappear into yourself."

"What does *ma-REE-tah* mean?"

He smiled down at her. "I promise I'll tell you one day soon. So, you discovered that if you were an invisible little girl, you . . . what? You weren't packed off to another foster home?" But then he frowned. "You said your mother died when you were four but that you last saw your father at age five. Did you live with him for that year?" He gave her a gentle squeeze when she said nothing. "You may recall my mentioning that I'm known for my patience?" he asked, stifling a smile when her eyes widened at his tone. "Well, if you wish to leave this bed sometime before Inglenook's new season begins you might want to start talking again."

The look she gave him should have extinguished the fire in the hearth, until she realized he wasn't bluffing. "My parents weren't married to each other, and my father didn't hear about my mother's death for nearly a year. And when he suddenly appeared out of the blue, that was the very first time I ever remember seeing him."

She shrugged one delicate shoulder, apparently wanting him to think she didn't care. "My mother told me he would come see me whenever he was in town, but I was too young to remember. Anyway," she said dispassionately. "When he finally showed up after she died, he visited me every day at the place I was staying for a couple of weeks. But then one day he told me he had to leave." She dropped her gaze to his chin. "He said he couldn't take me with him because of the work he did, but that he would . . . he told me he'd move heaven and earth and any mountains that got in his way to come back for me," she said in a whisper.

"And you never saw him again?"

Her eyes welled with tears. "Every night for almost three years I'd lie in bed waiting to feel the earthquake created by the mountains he was moving. Until I was eight and realized he . . . that he wasn't ever coming for me," she finished, her tears spilling free.

Mac rolled onto his back, pulling her with him and tucking her against his side. He stared up at the ceiling, holding Olivia through the storm he'd brought to the surface, and recalled something Henry had said to him on Friday. His son had come back from his morning talk with Olivia about virgins—and apparently bastards—and proudly told Mac that being illegitimate was not a bad thing in this century, and that Olivia had also said she knew his father loved him so much that Mac would move heaven and earth and any mountains that got in his way to be with him.

Unlike her own father, apparently, who had kept a little girl waiting three years to feel the earthquake that would signal he was coming for her.

Was she still waiting? Or had the eight-year-old child, who'd learned to vanish to keep from being moved from one home to another, simply decided she wasn't worth the trouble it would take to rearrange heaven and earth? Or could that be why she'd stayed in Spellbound Falls, to be close to the mountains if they ever did start moving?

She'd promised Mac she wouldn't fall in love with him when he'd told her she deserved better than he had to offer, and for that he did put some of the blame on her late husband. Had she loved Keith Baldwin only to have him also abandon her, which in turn had only added to her sense of little value?

Sweet Prometheus, he felt as though he were still missing parts of the puzzle. What had happened *six* years ago, when her marriage had ended two full years before her husband's death?

But more important, how could he prove to Olivia that she was worth not only rearranging heaven and earth and a few paltry mountains for, but also the very fabric of life?

Because whether she knew it or not, that was exactly what she'd done tonight, as the earthquake *she* had created had rocked Mac to his very core, and the whisper of home he'd heard out on the lake last Sunday had grown to a deafening shout.

His only question now being how to keep the woman from disappearing completely when he finally introduced her to the real Maximilian Oceanus.

Chapter Sixteen

Olivia was so flat-out proud of herself that she practically floated across the cabin and into the bathroom, where she softly closed the door and immediately did a silent little happy dance. She'd done it! She'd survived the first night of her very first affair!

And she'd only embarrassed herself a tiny bit.

Well, maybe a tad more than a bit, but at least she hadn't fainted and missed the entire thing. So really, things could only head uphill from here. She covered her giggle, thinking Mac didn't seem to care which direction anything headed—including her boobs. He just went chasing after them with either that very talented mouth of his or those big, strong hands that had done all sorts of amazing things to her.

Oh yeah, the guy was far more experienced than she could ever hope to be.

But she was a quick study, and she'd eventually caught up to him when it came to driving a person insane with pleasure; she knew because she'd actually made him shout a couple of times. And one time he'd even roared loud enough that she hoped Sylvia Pinkham heard it all the way to her house beyond the gate.

Olivia quickly used the facilities, then went to the mirror, only to gape at the wild woman staring back at her. Holy hell, she looked like she'd just spent all night thrashing around in a tumble dryer!

"Okay, get a grip on yourself," she whispered, trying to flatten out her smile. But it kept right on coming back, completely ruining her lonely-widow look. "Stop acting so proud of yourself, young lady. Remember foster-mother-two's warning about pride going before a fall. And besides, confident, *sexy* women do not go around crowing about getting laid by sexy, really talented men," she said, trying to look aloof—only to grab her neck as she leaned closer to the mirror.

Was that a hickey? She tilted her chin up and smoothed down the skin on her throat. Well, maybe not exactly a hickey, but it was damn close. She dropped her hands and stared straight ahead, trying to decide if it was low enough for her blouse to hide, or if she was going to have to wear a turtleneck for the next few days.

Wow. Mac had left his mark on her.

She started smiling again, noticing as she gazed at herself in the mirror that he'd left several marks, actually, in some rather interesting places.

The last time she remembered getting anything resembling a hickey had been on prom night, when David Bratham had thought dinner and an orchid and a fancy limousine had bought him entrance to her panties. Keith certainly hadn't ever given her a hickey, seeing how he'd been about as demonstrative as . . . well, as Eileen.

Olivia turned to check out the bathroom with a snort. What she'd mistaken as impeccable manners and respect for her had been nothing more than an elaborate mask hiding a cold fish. So where in hell had her *gut* been eleven years ago?

She took down one of the unbelievably plush bathrobes from the back of the door and pressed it to her face. Her gut must have been hiding under the silver-lined cloud she'd floated onto, she decided, when she'd dumped chowder on some jerk who'd patted her ass in the diner she'd been waitressing, and Keith had come to her rescue.

And she'd still been floating somewhere up in the clouds when he'd returned the next day and asked her out. Only she'd finally come down to earth after one month of marriage, when Keith had abandoned her at Inglenook with a mother-in-law who blamed her for his running off to join the military.

Olivia slipped into the bathrobe with a hum of pleasure, wondering what it would cost to outfit all her cabins with nice robes once she bought Inglenook. That is, until she remembered she was providing a *family* experience, not running a camp for lovers. She walked back to the mirror as she belted the robe and checked out all the fancy toiletries on the antique porcelain pedestal sink. The tiny bottles appeared to be brown apothecary glass like in the olden days, with little pinecones etched onto them.

She set the bottle back with a sigh. These wouldn't work, either, because of the children. And everyone brought their own toiletries anyway, because they were *camping*. Olivia eyed the deep, spacious claw-foot bathtub in the mirror, and sighed again as she ran her fingers through her hair to make it look less tumbled. Maybe in her next life she could have an honest-to-God antique soaking tub.

No, she wanted a *marble* soaking tub, just to one-up Sylvia.

Olivia opened the door, burying her hands in the deep plush pockets as she sauntered into the main room with all the confidence of a well-tumbled hussy—only to come to an abrupt halt. Mac was still on the feather bed, but instead of sleeping he had his head propped on his hand, watching her.

And all of her sexy confidence went flying out the window.

Because that wasn't lust she saw in those deep dark eyes but determination, as if he were primed for battle. She actually looked behind her to see what had him so riled, and then turned back with an equally determined smile.

"Good morning."

"Good morning," he returned, the timbre in his voice resonating all the way down to her toes. He patted the empty space beside him. "Come here, *marita*, and let me show you how lovers properly greet a new day together."

Oh God, he wanted to do it again? She really wasn't sure she'd survive another tumble in the dryer being driven insane with pleasure. She didn't think they'd set any world lovemaking records last night, but they'd certainly set a record for *her*.

"Olivia."

Hell, she hadn't done it five times on her entire honeymoon. And really, she wasn't all that confident she had the strength for another trip around the sun and back.

She felt a warm breeze brush across her hair at about the same time she heard a heavy sigh, and jumped in surprise when Mac pressed his big broad talented hands to her face and lifted her gaze to his.

"Are you tender this morning?" he asked, his thumbs caressing her scorched cheeks as his eyes searched hers.

Well, come to think of it she was a bit sore.

She nodded, feeling her blush kick up a notch.

Or maybe that was just the heat of his hands. No, it was definitely her cheeks, she realized when he encircled her in his big strong arms and held her head to his chest—which was at least a couple of notches cooler than her face.

God, he smelled good.

Maybe she was game for another tumble.

And just maybe she'd give him a hickey, too.

She gasped when he swept her off her feet and carried her over to the couch, only instead of setting her down *he* sat down with her on his lap, her head cupped against his chest again, making her acutely aware he was totally naked.

She sighed. Mac was so strong. And his carrying her around as if she didn't weigh more than a feather was so romantic.

No, wait; it wasn't romantic, it was condescending. His sweeping her off her feet was just another way for him to get what he wanted. Like if he wanted her back in the truck he just picked her up and put her there; if he wanted her up on the kitchen counter he just plopped her on the counter; and when he wanted her sitting on his lap he picked her up and then sat down.

The guy actually had a control issue.

"You really need to stop picking me up and lugging me around everywhere," she said, though she chose to say it against his chest rather than to his face.

"Why?" he asked, his growl quite loud against her ear.

"Because it's condescending to the person being picked up." She finally straightened to look him in the eye, only to see . . . well, he was definitely disgruntled but also curious. "You do it to Henry, too. You lug the kid around like a sack of potatoes half the time rather than simply asking him to come with you."

Curiosity left and disgruntled remained. "He doesn't seem to mind."

"Only because he doesn't realize what you're doing."

Up went a brow. "And exactly what am I doing?"

"You're controlling people."

"No," he said a bit too softly. "I'm being expedient. Do you want to take a bath before we head back to Inglenook? I believe there's time for you to still be home when Sophie returns from her sleepover, as I told Carolina not to let her leave before nine."

Apparently their discussion about sweeping people off their feet was over. Olivia looked down at her own feet, only to jackknife forward and pull the bathrobe up her leg—making Mac grab her hips with a grunt as he shifted her on his groin.

Olivia touched the thin gold chain encircling her right ankle, then straightened—making Mac jerk again—and pointed at her foot. "When . . . what . . . did you put that on me while I was sleeping?" she whispered, feeling her cheeks fill with heat again.

Oh God, he'd given her *jewelry.*

"It's a token of my affection, for you to remember our night together."

Olivia snapped her gaze to her foot; as in their first of many nights together or their *only* night together?

Wait; didn't guys give jewelry to women they were breaking up with?

But they'd just gotten *started*. And she'd had a really, really good time, and she thought Mac had had a really good time, too.

He took hold of her chin and turned her to face him. "It would please me to have you constantly wear it while we are lovers, Olivia. And that way when we're separated through all the long nights we can't be together, I'll know you're wearing a part of me. Constantly," he repeated softly.

She slumped against him in relief, canting her right foot back and forth to admire his . . . token of affection. "Thank you," she whispered even as she wondered what sort of token she could give him.

"You won't take it off, then?" he asked, his hand caressing her arm. "It appears to fit perfectly, so it shouldn't be in your way."

"But it looks so delicate, I'm afraid it might break," she said, lifting her foot to admire her ankle. She sat up in surprise. "What's the stone?" she asked, making him grunt again when she reached down to touch the tiny stone embedded in the clasp. "It's almost the same blue as your sweater." She straightened with a smile. "Or as Carolina told Henry, the same color as the ocean surrounding Atlantis."

He shrugged. "The stone is aquamarine, and you don't have to worry about the chain breaking. It's a lot stronger than it looks." He smiled. "Much like you."

Gee, maybe he really was a romantic.

And she was glad the stone wasn't expensive.

"Your sock and pants will keep it hidden if you wish for our affair to remain a secret," he said, urging her to lean against him again.

She took a deep breath. "Yeah, about that; I think we *should* keep this to ourselves. Not that I think it's bad or anything," she rushed to say, straightening again to look at him. "It's just that I don't want Sophie getting her hopes up that our being together will become permanent or anything." She collapsed back against him with a snort. "And I certainly don't want her thinking she can sleep with a man she doesn't intend to marry until she's old enough to know the difference between love and lust."

He started rubbing her arm again, and rested his chin on the top of her head—likely to keep her from bouncing around. "Do you know the difference between lust and love, Olivia?"

She patted his big strong naked chest in front of her nose. "Don't worry, I also keep my word. I won't throw a dramatic scene when you leave in September."

His hand stopped. "We'll just kiss and part ways? And not look back?"

She sat up with her best confident smile. "But I'm keeping the ankle bracelet," she said, pushing off him and heading to the bathroom. "And the bathrobe. Sylvia can just add it to your bill," she said over her shoulder.

Only she slumped against the door the moment she closed it, and covered her face with her hands at the realization the romantic fool had completely ruined her when it came to other men. After spending only one night with him, Olivia knew she'd never be satisfied with any man who wasn't bigger and stronger and sexier than Mac.

Because really, the earth might not have actually moved, but Mac sure as hell had given her sappy old heart a good shaking.

Popping the last of her bagel in her mouth, Olivia dug around in the bag for another one. She set it on the napkin on her lap, then reached for the plastic knife in the container of cream cheese on the dash and began sawing the bagel in half. "I don't know what that lady's problem was," she said after swallowing. "There wasn't any reason she couldn't have cut these before she stuck them in the bag like I asked her to. You want another one?"

"Give it to me without the cheese," Mac said, glancing

over as she brushed the bagel crumbs off her lap. "I'll eat it like a doughnut."

Seeing the lake's west outlet running under the bridge they were crossing, Olivia knew they were about halfway home. She handed Mac a sesame seed bagel, then brushed several crumbs off his beautiful chest—that she now felt rather proprietary of—before she went back to slathering cream cheese on her bagel. This wasn't exactly the dinner date she'd envisioned, and it was a tad late, but she wouldn't trade this morning for anything, not even a deep claw-foot bathtub like the one she'd just spent half an hour soaking in.

Olivia decided having an affair with Mac was finally starting to be fun, and she couldn't wait until they got together again. Which reminded her; "Um, I don't know how we're going to get away from our kids, much less Inglenook," she said, slapping the two halves of her bagel together. "John and Eileen will be back Thursday or Friday, and I haven't been able to figure out the logistics of having an affair, especially once camp starts back up."

"Since the beginning of time, lovers have found ways to sneak off together. We'll just have to be creative," he said, giving her a wink as he sank his teeth into his bagel.

Olivia shivered, remembering everywhere that mouth had been last night. Honest to God, she hadn't realized how sensitive the back of her knees were. And the inside of her *elbows*, for crying out loud. Who knew? She rested her hands on her lap without taking a bite of her bagel, wondering if she couldn't put Carolina on a permanent retainer as their official babysitter. Like, maybe again tonight.

"I guess sneaking around is supposed to be part of the fun," she said. "Hey, I know; I'll just take you on a hike and get us lost for three or four—Ohmigod!" she cried, bracing her hand on the dash when Mac braked to a sudden stop right in the middle of the road. "What *are* they?"

Three monstrous birds several feet tall were standing in the center of the road, their big dark eyes blinking against the harshness of the headlights. Mac shut off the engine with a muttered curse, then immediately turned on the parking lights, creating a soft yellow glow on their big white bodies.

"Stay put," he said with a distinct growl in his voice as he opened his door.

Olivia grabbed his arm. "Wait, you can't just go walking up to them. You'll scare the poor things. What do you think they are? They look sort of like seagulls, but they're *huge*. They're even bigger than turkeys."

"They're albatrosses," he said, gently pulling away from her grasp to get out. He turned back to lean inside, the interior dome light illuminating his seriousness. "Are you going to stay put?"

Oh yeah, he was still miffed that she'd refused to fasten her seat belt this morning. "Maybe you better leave me your cell phone so I can call 911 and report a man being mauled by a gang of albatrosses," she said, holding out her hand.

He softly closed his door.

Olivia jumped when she heard all the truck doors lock, and then she laughed. "That only works to keep people *out*," she shouted through the windshield—only to sober when she pushed the unlock button on her door and nothing happened. "You've got to be kidding!" she cried, jamming her finger again and again on the stupid button, and then trying the handle before pressing every damn button on the door.

That is, until she realized Mac had reached the birds and was crouched down on his heels in front of them. Was he insane? The albatrosses had long thick beaks that could poke out an eye, and the scruffy-looking things might be scared enough to be dangerous. Where could they have come from? Spellbound was a good hundred and fifty miles from the ocean as the crow flew—or rather as the *albatross* flew.

Did albatrosses even live in the Gulf of Maine? Weren't they southern birds?

Olivia placed her hand on the horn. She didn't know any animal that liked sharp, blaring noises, and she intended to blast away if they started attacking Mac. She watched him reach out, and the birds immediately waddled closer, the largest one shoving its head under Mac's open hand. The other two immediately crowded the first one out of the way to also be petted, and Olivia slumped back in her seat with a sigh.

Apparently she wasn't the only one who liked Mac's touch.

She straightened when she saw him stand up with one of the birds in his arms. "Hit the release button on the dash to open the rear hatch," he said as he walked past.

Yeah, right, like that was going to work. She hit the button on the dash anyway, and the rear hatch popped open. Olivia grabbed her door handle, but it *still* wouldn't open, even after she pounded on the stupid release button. "Dammit to hell," she growled, tossing her bagel on the dash and twisting onto her knees to see him set the giant albatross in the cargo area of the truck.

"Bring me that bathrobe you filched," he said.

"I can't bring you the robe because my door's stuck," she muttered, crawling over the console into the backseat. "The dealership sold you a lemon." She grabbed her beautiful plush robe and handed it to him. "Either that or this truck is possessed. Oh, is he hurt?" she asked in a croon, looking at the bird lying on its side, its dark watery eyes blinking at her as Mac examined its feet.

"*She* seems to have worn the bottoms of her feet raw on the pavement."

"You know it's a girl?" she asked just as two more heads appeared at the rear of the truck. "How do you know about albatrosses?"

He looked up with a smile. "I know females. Grab those water bottles in the pouch on the back of my seat." He lifted the two other birds into the truck. "Hand me one of the bottles, then open the other one and give those two a drink."

"How?" she asked, handing him one of the bottles while eyeing the nearest bird curiously eyeing her. "Do I pour some in my hand and let them slurp it, or do I hold the bottle up and try to pour it directly in their mouths?"

He looked up from the bird's feet he'd been pouring the

water over. "I don't know; I've never bottle-fed an albatross before. Try both ways and see which works."

She opened her bottle but then quickly leaned away when the two birds crowded toward her. "Good Lord, their breath is foul," she said over the soft humming sounds they were making. "Other than what are they doing in Spellbound Falls, a good question might be why were they walking down the road? Why aren't they flying?"

"I asked what they're doing here, but they refused to give me a straight answer," Mac drawled, tucking the bathrobe around the injured bird like a nest. "And I believe they're walking because this one has grown weak from their long journey north, and her friends refuse to abandon her."

Olivia poured water into her hand and hesitantly held it under the nearest lethal-looking, rose-pink beak. Only she figured the poor bird didn't get more than a drop or two in its mouth, as most of the water ran onto the carpet or up her arm. She held the bottle in front of it, only the bottle's neck was too narrow.

She looked around for something to pour the water into, but apparently Mac was a clean freak. "Wait," she said, turning around and lying over the console to reach her purse on the floor. She pulled it into the backseat, then dug around inside it, her hand emerging with one of the sleeves of condoms she'd stolen from the cabin—just to give Sylvia something to think about when she discovered only three packets left in the bowl when she cleaned. "What if I pour the water into one of these," she asked, holding it up for Mac to see, "and they can drink out of it? Their beaks won't fit in anything else."

The look Mac gave her was priceless, and she'd swear his cheeks darkened as he glanced at the birds. "Can you not find something else?"

"That wouldn't be a problem if we were in my van. You got a multitool or saw or something? We could cut off the top of one of the bottles."

He shook his head. "What about your juice bottle?"

She ripped open the packet with her teeth. "Its neck is

too small. Maybe if you drank coffee like any normal red-blooded male, we'd have a paper mug this morning."

"I don't like coffee," he said tightly, watching her unroll the condom.

"Um, maybe I should double them up," she said, eyeing the bird eyeing her. Could albatrosses smile? Because she'd swear its beak hadn't been curved up like that before. "I'm afraid just one will be too thin and it'll break."

"It will hold, Olivia," he hissed. "Just do it."

Oh yeah, the man was definitely blushing. She carefully started pouring the water in the condom, watching it grow longer and fatter with the weight of the liquid. Only she nearly dropped it when the closest bird let out a deafening squawk followed by a cacophony of chatter from its buddies—followed by Mac's sudden burst of laughter.

"Apparently those things accommodate any size man or beast," he said, only to suddenly go perfectly still as he stared at her, his eyes so imposing she nearly dropped the condom. What in hell had she been thinking!

"Sylvia provides her guests with nothing but the best," she muttered, ducking her head to hide her own blush. She held the distended condom out to the nearest bird, which dipped its beak inside and drank. "Hey, it's working!"

"Then I guess you're creative enough to find ways for us to be together," Mac said softly. "So let's get Inglenook's new guests hydrated so we can get them home."

"Guests?" Olivia repeated, moving the condom to the next bird. "You sound like you think we're keeping them. They're *albatrosses*, Mac. I'm pretty sure they belong *south* of the equator. When we get home I'll call Inland Fisheries and Games and see if they can figure out what to do with them. Heck, the poor things might even be on the news already if someone else spotted them. Three albatrosses lost in Maine are definitely as newsworthy as lost campers."

Mac caressed the injured bird as he leaned down to whisper something to it, then stepped back and closed the hatch, walked around and got in behind the wheel, and started the truck.

"Hey, how'd you get in?" she asked over her shoulder as she moved the condom back to the first bird when it started insisting on taking another sip. "The doors were all locked and I didn't hear them unlock."

Only she jumped in surprise before he could answer when the bird gave a loud screech and pulled the condom out of her hand and started shaking it, spraying water all over Olivia, the windows, and the carpet. And then the others joined in, the three of them sounding like a bunch of laughing loons.

"Ungrateful birds!" Olivia shouted over the cacophony as she scrambled back into her seat. She grabbed a napkin and wiped her face, wrinkling her nose at the stench. "You do know you're never going to get the smell of dead fish out of your truck," she said when they all suddenly quieted down. She looked over her shoulder to see that one of the albatrosses had settled down next to the injured bird, and the third was squatted with its head propped on the rear seat facing forward, the flaccid condom dangling from its beak.

"Would you consider not contacting anyone about them?" Mac asked as he lowered the rear windows to let in fresh air. He put the truck in gear and started for home again. "They could stay in the barn while the female recovers, and then we'll let them continue on their journey."

She blinked at him. "Are you serious?"

He nodded.

"But continue their journey to where? I'm pretty sure albatrosses belong at the opposite end of the world. And I know it's illegal to hold wild birds without a permit, even temporarily. And besides being a freshwater lake Bottomless is frozen solid, so what are we going to feed them?"

"Ezra sells live bait that should sustain them for now. And I'll take them down to the coast in a couple of days, after we're sure the female has had a chance to recover." He glanced over at her. "They can stay with Trace Huntsman until she's strong enough to fly, and then find their way home from there."

Good Lord, he *was* serious. "But they can't be wild,

Mac, considering how docile they are. They must have been born in captivity and escaped from some zoo. I know Quebec has a large zoo, and it's only a couple of hundred miles away, so they could have flown here from there. Aren't you worried letting them go might actually be a death sentence?"

"They're not from a zoo; none of them are banded."

"But . . ."

He reached over and took her hand. "I would ask that you trust me, Olivia."

"And what about Sophie, and Sam, and Eileen and John; how are you going to explain these guys to them?" She shook her head. "There's no way Sophie can go to school and not mention something as exciting as albatrosses living in her barn."

"Then we'll find a place nearby to hide them for a few days." He gave her hand a squeeze, the dash lights bright enough for her to see the concern in his eyes. "We could take them to the far end of Whisper Lake, over by the cliffs."

"I don't understand," she said, curling her fingers around his. "Why are you so concerned about these three lost birds? And why are you so adamant that we not tell anyone about them?"

He pulled his hand away and brought the truck to a stop directly in front of Ezra's store and shut off the engine. Shifting in his seat, he glanced back at the birds before looking at her. "I guess you could say I'm a man of the ocean. And our three smelly friends here," he said with a smile, gesturing toward the rear of the truck, "are Wandering Albatrosses, a magnificent species with the largest wingspan of any bird on the planet, capable of staying airborne for weeks at a time." He shrugged. "They are like old friends to me, Olivia, as I've spent many voyages with only a lone albatross keeping me company. And I would ask that you help me return the favor to these three now. Calling the authorities would put them through an ordeal, where at the least they'll be crated up and shipped back below the equator, or at worst held in captivity."

Olivia looked back and saw the one bird still resting its head on the seat staring at them—as if it were actually listening—as the other two sat nestled together behind it. "But one of them is injured. What if she can't ever fly again? Maybe we should at least hand her over to someone."

"Her mate and their friend won't leave her behind," he said with a shake of his head. "And all she needs is a few days to get her strength back." He took her hand again, rubbing his thumb over her palm. "I realize what I'm asking may seem strange, but my heart tells me it's the right thing to do. So can you not only trust me but stretch your imagination to consider that maybe we've just been given a gift."

"What kind of gift?"

"Since the beginning of mankind, whenever an animal showed up where it didn't belong, people have considered it an omen. Animals are usually messengers, Olivia, and that *you and I* are the ones who found three albatrosses walking down a road in Maine is not a coincidence. Do not send them away without hearing what they've come here to tell you, as it may be something you've been waiting a very long time to hear."

"But I don't speak albatross," she said with a smile. "Do you?"

He lifted her hand and kissed her open palm, then folded her fingers closed. "Some languages are universal, *marita*," he said, just as the bird resting its head on the backseat made a snorting noise.

Olivia laughed, and just because she could, she patted Mac's big broad chest. "Okay, you big sentimental softy, I won't call anyone. But I'm not—"

He pulled her to him, catching her gasp to slowly and quite thoroughly kiss her.

Their feathered audience started chattering loud enough to wake the dead.

Mac turned to them. "Enough!"

All three birds immediately went silent.

He gave her a crooked smile. "It appears they understand English," he said, just before kissing her again. Except that he stopped the moment she wrapped her arms around his neck, his eyes serious. "So can I assume this means you trust me?"

"I'm pretty sure I trusted you last night with a lot more than just keeping a few birds a secret," she whispered. She batted her eyelashes. "Isn't there some syndrome where captives become enamored with their big, strong, sexy captors?"

"And have I captured you, Olivia?"

She pulled away with a laugh, grabbing her door handle. "If you haven't, then your stupid truck sure has," she said, giving the handle a yank to show him she was locked in, only to have the door pop open.

She immediately jumped out and started backing away. Because really, this was getting downright eerie.

Mac walked around the front of the truck and gently closed her door before heading toward her.

"I swear that stupid door was *locked*. I pushed every button I could find and it still wouldn't open." She bumped into Ezra's store and slowly lifted her gaze to Mac. "I'm not kidding; I think your truck is possessed. And . . . and I think it doesn't like me."

"I like you," he said, taking her hand and leading her around the side of the building in a hurry. "What time does Ezra usually open up?"

Olivia heard the vehicle approaching just as they rounded the corner of the store, and recognized Vanetta's pickup crossing the bridge. She pulled Mac behind the rack of propane tanks. "He opens at eight but comes in around seven. That's Vanetta. She owns the Drunken Moose, which opens at six on Sundays. No, she's still on winter hours, which means she opens at seven."

Vanetta drove past and pulled into the narrow lane between the Drunken Moose and the Grange hall, and shut off her truck. "It's what . . . around six?" Olivia whispered. "She's probably in early to start making the best cinnamon buns this side of the Canadian border," she told Mac, smiling up at him. "They're the biggest, gooiest, most decadent buns you'd ever hope to taste. Maybe we could get the birds settled and bring Carolina and Henry and Sophie back for breakfast."

"Stay focused," he said, pulling her toward the back of the building. "Do you have any suggestions as to how we can get inside?"

"Why don't we just wait for Ezra?"

He stopped to raise a brow at her. "And just how do you plan to explain your sudden need for several dozen baitfish?"

Olivia gaped at him. "You intend to break in and *steal* them?"

"We'll leave cash," he said, reaching for the handle on the door next to the loading dock. And some strange reason, Olivia wasn't the least bit surprised when it opened the moment he touched it.

Rather like she had last night.

"Wow, do you know how to show a girl a good time or what?" she said, following him inside. "I can't wait to see what you've got up your sleeve for our next date."

Chapter Seventeen

"Is there a reason that instead of appearing happy and sated this morning you're so tense the forest is about to go up in flames around us?" Carolina asked just as Mac helped her across a brook in the overgrown road. She stopped, her sharp green eyes searching his. "Oh, Mackie, please tell me you didn't blow it last night. You knew Olivia hadn't been with another man since her husband, so where in hell was your legendary patience?"

Mac continued walking toward the cliffs at the end of Whisper Lake. "Olivia certainly gave it a good workout, but my patience prevailed."

"Then what's got you so uptight this morning?"

"I need to visit the Trees of Life, but I can't because Father has made that impossible. And without being able to access their knowledge, I have no hope of figuring out how to proceed with Olivia." He gestured at nothing. "Something in her past has been keeping her hiding out here, and I suspect her inability to move on with her life involves more than just her marriage to Keith Baldwin." He stopped walking. "Olivia has been a true orphan since age four, and all that she faced growing up has led her to believe she has little or no value." He folded his arms over his chest and shook his head. "Have you ever tried making love to a shadow, Caro? I vow I spent more time last night working to keep Olivia in the present moment than I did pleasuring her. It appeared as if she kept having conversations with herself in an attempt to create a distraction from all the conflicted emotions she was feeling. Only I swear she ended up persuading herself that she should be anyplace but where she was." He shook his head again. "Can you image Olivia believes *she* doesn't deserve *me*?"

"Personally, I'd be more worried by how much you deserve *each other*," Caro said with a cheeky grin as she started down the path his truck tires had made earlier. She took his hand when he fell into step beside her. "And I also think your not being able to access the knowledge might actually be a good thing in this instance."

"Excuse me?"

"Look at it this way, Mackie; for the first time in your overindulged life, you're going to have to actually work to get the girl. Like any other man, you'll have to learn who Olivia is the old-fashioned way: by getting to know her likes and dislikes, what her hopes and dreams are, and what fears are keeping her locked in the shadows."

Mac walked in silence for several minutes. "Hell, you make it sound as if by using the magic that I've been taking advantage of the women I've been with."

Carolina laughed at that. "You do have a rather annoying habit of using it to control people. And you sincerely believe that any means justifies the end result *you* think is best for someone." She stopped walking to glare up at him. "And I'm not only talking about your dealings with women; I've seen you start *wars* because you were so bloody angry at the people involved."

"I did that once, and then only because the evil had imbedded itself so deeply on both sides that those bastards deserved to kill each other." He shoved his hands in his pockets as he continued walking. "And I don't know if you happened to notice, but those two particular nations have been living peacefully beside each other ever since." He pulled her to a stop. "Olivia claims my carrying her in my arms is controlling. And that I do the same to Henry."

Carolina gave him a playful poke in the chest. "Which only proves that Olivia is already learning you." She started walking again, shaking her head. "And yet the woman obviously likes you anyway. Don't worry, you'll learn everything you need to know about Olivia without using your magic—assuming you want to badly enough." She broke into a jog. "Now come on, I'm anxious to meet our lost feathered friends."

Mac followed at a walk. Dammit, he wasn't controlling, he was expedient. And he carried Henry because the boy's stride was so short it would take them forever to get someplace if he didn't.

As for carrying Olivia, he *liked* the feel of her in his arms—and he needed to know everything about her past to ensure that she remained in them.

"Oh, Mackie, they're exhausted," Carolina whispered when he rounded the small cliff. She stroked the female's head on her lap. "She's in mourning, isn't she?"

"Yes. She and her mate lost a son to a longline fishing rig floating off the South American coastline a couple of months ago." He gestured toward the second male bird. "And he lost his mate last year the same way."

"Is that why they've sought you out—to ask you to return their loved ones?"

Mac sat down on the ground beside her. "No, actually, they've accepted their losses. They volunteered on behalf of all the sea creatures to come ask me to stop the practice of longline and open-water net fishing that causes many of their friends, both finned and feathered, to get entangled and drown when the lines break free and drift away to continue ghost fishing."

Caro snapped her gaze to his. "But you can't stop how mankind harvests the oceans. And the three of you are well aware of that," she said, addressing the birds. "You know Maximilian can't do anything that directly interferes in people's free will."

"But they also know I have the power to influence that will," he said. "They want me to draw attention to what's happening out in the open ocean, so the fishermen will freely address the problem themselves."

"But you don't have that kind of power right now, Mac. And you won't have it for the next hundred years unless you prove you're a fit father to Henry."

He arched a brow. "Do you honestly believe I didn't have the foresight to tuck away some of the energy, considering we both know Father's the one with the control issue?"

"You still have some of the magic?" she asked on an indrawn breath. Her eyes suddenly narrowed. "How much?"

"Enough for two, possibly three . . . epic events."

Carolina stilled. "But are you willing to use it to help them?" she whispered, nodding toward the silent birds. "Because it would take a powerful amount of energy to change nearly every culture's way of doing something they've been doing for centuries. People want progress, only they fight tooth and nail against *change*. So short of tangling all their nets and lines into useless knots, how can you possibly get them to stop filling our oceans with trash?"

Mac stood up with a grin, holding out his hand to help her up. "Start watching the news right along with the rest of the world, and see just how creative your big brother can be." He turned to address the birds. "And rest up, my valiant emissaries," he said, "because you are about to experience the flight of your lifetimes."

"Henry's going to be so excited to see his daddy in action," Carolina said as he led her back around the narrow ledge.

"I'm afraid he can't come on this trip, as I need to travel light and fast."

Carolina pulled him to a stop, then tried to shrug free of his grip to back away. "You can't think to leave him with *me*!" she cried when he wouldn't let go. "I don't know any more about being an aunt than you do about being a father."

Mac started toward Inglenook again with a laugh. "Don't worry, princess, I'm sure Olivia will share some of her wonderful pearls of wisdom with you."

Olivia made it back just in time to put on her pajamas and crawl into bed, where she rolled and thrashed around to make it appear as if she'd spent the night at home instead of rolling and thrashing around on a feather bed with her lover all night. Having an affair was a lot of work, she decided, just as she heard the kitchen door open and slam shut.

"Mom, I'm home!" Sophie hollered as her shoes hit the wall and her backpack thumped to the floor. Her daughter raced down the hall, ran into the room, and jumped on the bed. "Did you miss me?" the girl asked, her grin reaching ear to ear. "Did you bring me back a doggie bag from the restaurant? What did you eat? Did you and Mr. Mac go dancing?" she continued, her eyes dreamy. "I bet he's a great dancer."

"Sorry, but I ate everything on my plate," Olivia said, fluffing her pillow to lean against the headboard. She rubbed her eyes, then stretched her arms over her head with a yawn, remembering that she was supposed to just be waking up. "How about you?" she asked, diverting Sophie's other questions by firing off some of her own. "What movie did you watch? Did you guys make a big mess in the kitchen?" She swept the girl into a giant hug and gave her a noisy kiss on her cheek. "And how did you sleep, baby," she whispered, "away from your mom all night?"

Sophie sat up with a groan. "I'm not a baby anymore, and we didn't get to sleep until after midnight. After we watched *The Little Mermaid*, we went back to Henry's cabin and Miss Carolina read us stories about all the different mythological gods. Did you know the horse Mr. Sam let me ride on Friday is named Pegasus, and that Pegasus is a winged horse who's actually Poseidon's daughter?" She nodded when Olivia just gaped at her. "Pegasus rose out of the sea when Med . . . Med-somebody's head got lopped off and dripped blood on her. Isn't that cool? I think I'm going to ask Mr. Sam if Pegasus can be my horse for the summer."

Wonderful; now Mac's sister was teaching *Sophie* all about the bed-hopping and apparently head-lopping, blood-dripping gods. "Um, what happened to Henry's book of names?" Olivia asked. "I haven't heard any talk of him changing his first name lately."

Sophie's eyes widened. "Oh, wow! You should have seen Miss Carolina last night when Henry showed her that book and told her he was thinking of changing his name to Dorian, because he thought Dorian Oceanus sounded very noble. When she asked what was wrong with the name his mother had given him, and he explained that his dad didn't think it was noble enough, I thought Miss Carolina was going to explode." She covered her mouth. "She told Henry that hell would freeze over before she'd let anyone, especially her dumb lug of a brother, change his first name to anything. But she quickly apologized for saying *hell*," Sophie rushed to assure her. Her eyes widened again. "And then she tossed the book of baby names in the fire before I could tell her it was from the bookmobile."

Olivia threw back the blankets and got out of bed with a laugh. "Then I guess Carolina can go with Henry next week and explain to the librarian what happened."

"Are we going on a picnic today?" Sophie asked, following her down the hall to the kitchen. "I told Miss Carolina about our Sunday picnics, and she said it's been at least a *thousand years* since she's been on one," she said with a giggle. "Can she and Henry and Mr. Mac come with us again today?"

Olivia smiled out the window as she took a drink of water, not at all surprised that their just you-and-me time had turned into you-and-me-and-the-Oceanuses.

Her *guests* did seem to have a thing for fraternizing with the help.

"I hadn't planned a picnic today, sweetie, because Gram and Grampy's being away means we need to stay here and feed everyone, including Sam now."

"Then let's have a cookout on the patio again like we did Friday night. That was so much fun." She tugged on Olivia's sleeve. "We hardly ever do stuff like that when Gram's here, so . . . maybe we should . . ." She shrugged, looking guilty. "I just thought we could have a cookout every day until she comes back," she whispered.

Olivia pulled Sophie into a hug to hide her own guilt. Oh God, what had she been doing to her little girl by staying here under the shadow of Eileen? "I think that's a wonderful idea. Why don't you go down to the barn and find Sam, and tell him lunch will be served out on the—" She stopped when she heard the bell at the fence gate clang.

Sophie pulled away with a gasp. "Oh no, I forgot!" she said, running to the door and flinging it open. "I'm coming, Henry! I just need to put on my mud boots!"

Olivia walked to the door and looked out to find the boy standing at the gate, his hands in his pockets as he stared toward the house. She grabbed Sophie by the sleeve. "Has he been standing out there this whole time?"

Sophie nodded.

"But why didn't he come in with you? You don't just leave your friend standing outside waiting for you and then forget him."

"I told him to come in with me, but he said he's not supposed to 'enter our sacred domain' unless he and his dad are coming to get us for a date."

"Good morning, Miss Olivia," Henry called from the fence, waving hugely. "My dad told me you and he had a wonderful time last night."

It was all Olivia could do not to fall to her knees. Oh God, how many times had *she* been Henry: standing on the outside, not feeling welcome in someone else's sacred domain? "Henry, come here," she said, waving him over as she stepped onto her stoop in her bare feet. And then she did drop to her knees when he reached her and took hold of his shoulders. "Honey, it's okay for you to come to the house. That gate is for Inglenook's *regular* campers, not you."

He looked skeptical. "Maybe I should check with my dad first, as he said it was only okay last night because of your date."

"Not going beyond the gate isn't your father's rule, it's mine. Which means *I'm* the one who decides who crosses the fence and who doesn't. And you are always welcome in my home. Always," she repeated as she pulled him into her arms. "You belong here just as much as I do." She leaned away with a loud, exaggerated sigh. "And I suppose your father can cross the fence, too, because I like him *almost* as much as I like you."

Henry's eyes widened. "You do?" But then those vivid green eyes suddenly took on a calculated gleam—not unlike the way his father's did sometimes. "Do you like him enough to go out with him again? Because you're obviously brave, seeing as how you said yes the first time."

Having a pretty good idea where this was heading, Olivia sat down, figuring she'd better set the kid straight before he decided he'd just found a replacement for Godzilla. "Sophie, go change into your barn clothes, would you?"

As soon as her daughter disappeared down the hall, Olivia took both of Henry's hands in hers. "Looking for a husband or wife isn't the only reason people go on dates, Henry. Sometime a man and woman simply enjoy each other's company, and go out to dinner as *friends*."

He looked so crestfallen that Olivia couldn't stop from pulling him into her arms again. "Ah, honey, you leave finding a wife up to your father, okay?" She gave him a squeeze. "I promise he won't marry a woman who doesn't love you, too. Trust your daddy, Henry; he's big and strong and brave enough to stand up to your grandfather."

Henry hugged her back just as fiercely. "But what if the woman only pretends to like me?" he asked thickly. "W-what if she wants to marry us just because my dad's rich and powerful, and she . . . and she tricks him into thinking she likes little boys and animals and the ocean?"

Olivia leaned away to frown at him. "Hasn't your father been teaching you how to *feel* what you can't see and hear?"

He swiped at the moisture gathered in his eyes and nodded.

"Well then, don't you think he would immediately realize what she was doing?"

"But why can't *you* just fall in love with him?" he blurted out, throwing himself against her and wrapping his arms around her neck. "Because I really, really like you, Miss Olivia. And my dad does, too. I *know* he does."

"Henry," she whispered past the lump in her throat, trying to gently pull him away.

His arms tightened around her. "And you and Sophie could move to Midnight Bay with us, because I just know you'll like the ocean. And we could build a fire pit in the back and have cookouts and make s'mores all the time."

His tiny body was shaking so badly that Olivia also started shaking.

"I promise, I won't ever whine or pout and I'll do everything you tell me to."

Oh God, what a mess. "Shhh, honey." She stopped trying to move him away and simply hugged him. "Please don't get all worked up over this, Henry. You have my word: Your daddy's not going to marry anyone who doesn't love you as much as he does." She gave a forced laugh as she patted his back. "And I know your auntie Caro will certainly have something to say about who he marries." She leaned away enough for him to see her smile. "She's not letting him change your first name, is she?"

Henry sucked in a deep breath, trying to get control of his sobs. "Sh-she said hell would freeze over first, only I don't think that's possible because Hades is in charge of hell. He's Zeus and Poseidon's brother, and that means he's powerful enough to keep the fires burning so bright the ice would just melt."

Wonderful; another dastardly god for the boy to look up

to. Olivia cupped his cheeks in her hands. "That's why Carolina said what she did, to tell you it's never going to happen. What I'm trying to point out is that you have me *and* your auntie Caro to make sure your dad doesn't fall in love with the wrong woman."

Henry's eyes widened. "Oh no, he doesn't intend to *love* his wife; he only needs to like her enough to get married before Grampy forces us to marry Gadzalina."

"Ah, I see," Olivia said with a nod, afraid she did see. God, she hoped Mac didn't suddenly decide *she* would make a good replacement for Godzilla.

"Miss Olivia."

She gasped. What if that's why he'd tried so hard to impress her with the expensive cabin and . . . and all-night sex marathon?

"Miss Olivia."

Oh God, what if last night had been an *audition*?

She stood up, looking toward cabin ten. "Where's your father now, Henry?"

"He and Auntie went for a walk around Whisper Lake. Miss Olivia," he said, tugging on her pajama sleeve only to take a step back when she looked down at him.

Olivia quickly turned her glare to a smile.

"I was going to ask if . . . um, never mind," he said, taking another step back when Sophie came barreling out of the house.

"Come on, Henry," the girl said as she continued past them at a run. "Let's go see if Mr. Sam will let us brush our horses."

Henry started after her, but stopped and turned back to Olivia. "You won't tell Dad that I cried, will you?"

"There's nothing wrong with having a good cry once in a while, Henry," she said, considering she had every intention of making Mac cry the very first chance she got. He might have been taking casting calls on the couch for the role of Mrs. Oceanus, but she hadn't been auditioning for anything but a temporary lover. "Don't worry; I won't say anything to him. What was it you wanted to ask me?"

He shoved his hands in his pockets. "I was going to ask if you think I need to wear pajamas to bed. Because last night Auntie got all upset when I just stripped off and crawled under the covers." He made a disgusted face. "She made me wear one of her shirts and my underpants because I don't own any pajamas. Well, I used to have pajamas because Miss Maddy bought me some with Sesame Street puppets on them, but Dad left them in Midnight Bay because he said men are born naked and we're supposed to sleep naked. He says our bodies need to breathe at night." He took a step toward her. "Dad told me to ask my mama if it was okay, because he said she didn't mind when he slept naked with her. So I asked, and my heart told me Mama said that if I'm old enough for sword lessons then I'm too old to wear bedclothes like a baby."

How . . . wonderful.

Henry suddenly ran up to her, his face having gone as pale as new snow. "I meant *music* lessons, Miss Olivia, not sword lessons. Okay? *Music* lessons."

"Okay, Henry."

He squinted up at her, color springing back into his cheeks. "So, do you think I need to wear pajamas?" He touched her sleeve. "I can see that you do. And Sophie wore some last night." He frowned when Olivia sat down on the stoop again as she wondered what to tell him. "Are pajamas only for women and babies? And men are supposed to sleep naked?"

"Well," she said, trying to come up with an answer. "I suppose both your father and your aunt Carolina are correct," she said, giving a negligent shrug to make this a small problem in his mind. "If your dad says men sleep naked, then he should know, seeing how he's a man. But your aunt knew it wasn't appropriate since you had a guest staying with you, especially a girl guest. So maybe your father can buy you pajamas for when you have a sleepover or spend the night at a friend's house. That way nobody gets offended."

"Henry!" Sophie hollered from the lane. "I thought you

were right behind me. Come on! Sam's bringing out our horses so we can brush them!"

"I'm coming!" Henry hollered back. He gave a slight bow. "Thank you, Miss Olivia. I think that's a perfect solution." He shook his head, looking quite sad again. "It's too bad you couldn't just fall in love with my dad. I think you would make a good theurgist's wife."

And with that he headed down the path, leaving Olivia gaping after him.

Henry thought his father was a theurgist?

Olivia set her elbows on her knees and rested her chin in her palms with a frown. And what was that thing about sword lessons, anyway? Was Mac teaching Henry how to fence but had told him not to say anything, afraid she'd think it was too dangerous for a six-year-old?

But didn't fencing involve a foil or something, not a sword?

She snorted. She couldn't quite see Mac waving a sissy foil around. But she certainly could see him wielding a long, thick sword like King Arthur's Excalibur or one of those highland swords on the covers of the romance novels she liked to read.

And the scary thing was, the idea of Mac coming here from some long-ago century wasn't all that disturbing to her. Because really, the man certainly walked and talked and acted like a throwback to the bygone age of chivalry, right down to his giving her a token of his affection.

Olivia leaned over and pulled up her pajama leg to touch the thin gold chain. What had made him choose an ankle bracelet? And come to think of it, when had he chosen it for her? He hadn't left Inglenook all week except for last Sunday's picnic, and she'd only suggested they go out to dinner yesterday morning.

Oh God, had he asked his sister for something to give his date, and Carolina had given him one of her bracelets?

Olivia turned the chain to the clasp so she could take it off to see it better. Only there wasn't a clasp. Nothing. The thin gold rope went directly into the setting holding the stone, making the bracelet impossible to get off without breaking it.

"You've got to be friggin' kidding me," she growled, sliding the chain around her ankle, looking for some sort of clasp. Only there wasn't one. Nothing but a tiny gold medallion with an aquamarine stone set in the center of . . . she lifted her ankle onto her knee to study the medallion.

What in hell *was* that? Because honestly, it looked like the stone was set in the center prong of a pitchfork or a . . . a trident, maybe?

She sat up, her gaze going to cabin ten. Didn't Poseidon carry a trident?

Mythological bedtime stories. Formal mannerisms. Arranged marriages. Swords. Odd terms and old-fashioned speech patterns, like how Mac and Henry and Carolina posed their questions sort of backward and rarely used contractions—although she supposed that was common if English wasn't a person's first language. But that didn't explain words like *theurgist* instead of *wizard* and . . . and what in hell did *ma-REE-tah* mean, anyway? She didn't even know if it was French, Greek, or Swahili.

And why couldn't she get this damn ankle bracelet off?

For that matter, how come Mac's truck was out to get her?

And three albatrosses walking down a road in the middle of the night in Maine?

Really? *Tame* albatrosses?

Albatrosses that Mac didn't want her turning over to the authorities.

So, had she been living out here in the woods so long that anything foreign or different was suspicious? Or was she getting semihysterical over nothing because she had stepped way, way outside her comfort zone last night?

Hell, maybe she was drunk on too much sex all at once!

Olivia slid her foot off her knee and took a calming breath. Could she stretch her imagination, Mac had asked her this morning, enough to see the gift they'd been given? And could she listen to the message of the albatrosses, as it might be something she'd been waiting a very long time to hear?

Except the only thing she was hearing right now was her gut telling her there was something very weird about the Oceanuses.

And that more had happened last night than just the beginning of an affair.

Olivia dropped her face in her hands on her knees. Honest to God, Mac hadn't left just a few small marks on her body or placed a pretty shackle around her ankle last night; he'd somehow managed to sneak past her carefully guarded line of defense and make her want something she hadn't even dared to hope for.

But the really scary part was that even Mac's strangeness wasn't enough to scare her off. Because if there was one thing Olivia's mama had taught her young daughter before she'd died, it was that the most powerful and precious gifts often come out of nowhere, usually when least expected and almost always the last thing expected.

Which rather described Mac, didn't it?

Chapter Eighteen

He was so intent on trying to figure out why he'd gotten the cold shoulder from Olivia at dinner that evening, Mac nearly missed the fact that they were being followed. He lifted Henry off his shoulders and set him down on the moonlit path, putting a finger to his lips to signal they needed to stay quiet. He took Henry's hand and put it in Carolina's, then urged them to continue walking toward Inglenook ahead of him.

Had whoever was out there been stalking them all the way from the clearing and seen Henry's lesson? With Carolina noisily cheering the boy on, coaching him when to attack and when to retreat from his father's advancing sword, there was a good chance Mac wouldn't have realized they were being watched.

Whoever it was had the skills of a hunter, as he sensed rather than heard the footsteps touching the forest floor with deliberate care a good fifty paces behind them. Carolina looked over her shoulder, and Mac nodded over his own shoulder as he moved his fingers like walking legs to let her know what was happening.

"Caro, why don't you tell Henry how Prometheus gave man the gift of fire, and how angry that made Zeus," Mac said in a normal tone, gesturing at her to keep walking. "Tell him how that led to Zeus ordering the creation of woman to plague man," he added with a chuckle.

Carolina gave a very loud snort and began swinging Henry's hand between them so he'd face forward as she and boy continued down the path. "Well," Carolina began, "Zeus was so angry that mortals had been given the powerful gift of fire, he ordered Hephaestus to mold a woman out of water and clay and give her the even more powerful gifts of beauty and grace and charm."

"And seduction and guile and deceit," Mac drawled as he slowly widened the distance between them. "With which to tempt us poor, weak-minded men."

Carolina slapped her hands over Henry's ears even as she kept walking down the path. "Don't you dare listen to your father, young man," she said, shooting Mac a frown over her shoulder, then giving a nod as he fell back even farther. "Except the part about men being weak-minded," she continued, taking hold of Henry's hand again. "Sorry, nephew; I'm afraid you were born the weaker sex."

"But you make it sound as if Zeus wanted woman to be a punishment to man," Henry said, clearly confused. "Only I *like* women. You're all soft and huggable and . . ."

Mac focused on what was going on behind him instead of the conversation now taking place a good distance in front, even as he reached over his shoulder and pulled his sword from its sheath. He halted beside a giant pine tree, used his foot to make a mark in the dirt to indicate someone had gone behind the tree, and then stepped off the path on the opposite side, blending into the shadows to wait.

Within two heartbeats he recognized the stilted gait of their stalker, and smiled. As he'd surmised with only a handshake, Sam Waters was a seasoned warrior who apparently even crippled had the stealth of a lethal predator. The man also had good instincts and eyesight, Mac decided when Sam stopped about three paces before reaching the pine and studied the mark in the ground.

And still Mac waited, watching Sam take a step back and slowly reach down and pull up his pant leg, his eyes never leaving the tree. He silently slid a knife out of his boot, then turned, still half crouched, putting his back to the pine to face Mac's side of the path, his weapon held with the blade running along his arm.

"I'd rather not have to explain to Olivia why I killed her lover," Sam said softly. "So come out, Oceanus, and we'll have us a friendly little chat."

"About what you're doing here at Inglenook?" Mac asked from the shadows.

Sam moved in a blur, feinting to the right but diving in the opposite direction. Only when he ducked into a roll to come up behind Mac, Mac landed a blow across the man's back with the flat of his sword, then used the hilt to catch him in the jaw, flinging Sam back into the path. Yet despite what should have been a debilitating blow, Sam merely grunted and continued rolling, springing back to his feet facing Mac again, his knife poised to slash—that is, until he felt the sword tip pressing into his chest.

"Son of a bitch," Sam snarled, going perfectly still.

"I believe my mother would take exception to that, Waters. I would ask what you're doing out here on this beautiful night following us."

Sam slowly straightened, his hands dropping to his sides. "I guess you weren't just playacting with your boy tonight, and now that I'm seeing it up close, I guess this thing *isn't* a toy," he said, looking down at the sword just below his chin. His hand holding the knife rose slightly and fell. "Maybe I should look into getting a longer knife."

"I believe your weapon is equally lethal in your experienced hand. What exactly were you hoping to learn by following us?"

Sam started to shrug but apparently thought better of it, seeing how he had a sword tip resting on his chest. "I was hoping to get a feel for the man who didn't bring Olivia home from her dinner date until after sunrise this morning."

"I believe that's something only a woman's *father* need concern himself with."

"And if Olivia's father happened to be asking what your intentions are toward her, what would your answer be?"

Mac pressed the sword a little more heavily against Sam's chest. "I would tell him that I will never abandon her like he did. So maybe instead of discussing my intentions toward Olivia, we should talk about yours."

Sam looked down at his chest, his eyelids hooding his expression. "You've already decided I mean her no harm, or I wouldn't be alive right now."

"I believe you're right," Mac said even as he pressed his sword deeper. He felt Sam's flesh tighten against the tip, though the man held his ground. "I have been known to change my mind, however," Mac continued, "when I can't seem to get a straight answer. What are you doing at Inglenook, Waters? Or more specifically, why have you shown up here now, twenty-eight years too late?"

Sam lifted his steel-gray eyes, his glare as solid at the moon reflecting in them. "I never abandoned her. From the day my little girl was born, I've known every detail of her life. I can tell you the color of the frosting on all thirty-three of her birthday cakes, I know who the first boy was that she kissed, who took her to the prom, and the exact minute Sophie was born. Hell, I was the goddamn photographer at her wedding."

"Yet you weren't there to help her blow out the candles on those cakes, or walk her down the aisle at her wedding, or to once hold your granddaughter in your arms."

Mac felt Sam's shudder travel up the length of his sword. "My being a part of Olivia's life would have gotten her killed. There's a price on my head in more parts of the world than I've even set foot in, and if any of my enemies knew I had a daughter they'd go after her to get to me."

"Then what are you doing here now?"

Sam eyed him in silence for several seconds. "I'd be more inclined to answer that question if I knew exactly *who* was doing the asking. Because from what I've been able to gather from my sources, *you* don't actually exist."

Mac set the tip of his sword on the ground to rest his crossed wrists on the hilt.

Sam took a heavy breath and rubbed his chest. "What gave me away?" he asked, gesturing at the path behind Mac. "I know damn well you didn't hear me."

"Why have you come to Inglenook?" Mac repeated.

Sam bent to slide his knife into his boot before limping over to a rock and sitting down. "What nationality are you, anyway?"

"I was born at sea, actually."

Sam glared at him. "You need to call someplace home, because you need a passport issued by a *country* in order to enter the United States."

"Apparently not."

"Dammit, you don't *exist*. How the hell do I know you're not one of my enemies?"

"Because you're still breathing. Why are you here, Waters?"

When all he got was stubborn silence, Mac moved too fast for the man to defend himself, striking Sam's old injury with the flat of his sword and knocking him to the ground before placing its blade on Sam's neck. *"Why now?"*

"Because for as strong as she is, I can't be certain Olivia will survive the storm headed her way *now*," Sam growled, cradling his ribs. "And I wanted to . . . if she needs . . . hell," he snarled. "I felt I needed to be here for her in person this time."

Mac pulled away and sat down on the rock. "What storm?"

"Olivia's been planning and saving for years to buy Inglenook, but Eileen put it up for sale last week without telling her. And instead of looking for interns for this summer's sessions, she is right now accepting a position at a think tank in California." Sam relaxed back into the moss with a groan. "She and John intend to close this place in September and move to California."

"And Olivia knows nothing of this?"

"She's been expecting Inglenook to go up for sale, but not until after Eileen gets her doctorate at the end of August."

"And you believe . . . what? That Eileen is assuming Olivia and Sophie will move to California with her and John?" He arched a brow. "Considering all the storms Olivia has weathered that you *haven't* felt the need to attend in person, I ask again, why now?"

"Because putting Inglenook up for sale without telling Olivia is only a rain shower compared to the hurricane that's about to hit." Sam dragged himself backward and settled up against a tree. "The child Keith Baldwin fathered six years ago needs a bone marrow transplant, and the only likely candidate left is Sophie."

Mac stilled. "Baldwin fathered another child?"

"The bastard had an affair with a woman named Jessica Pilsner about six years ago when he was stationed in California." Sam shook his head. "Olivia refused to let him drag her around to wherever he was stationed, especially after she had Sophie." He looked up at Mac again. "I guess Baldwin didn't mind too much, seeing how a wife and kid would have cramped his style. Pilsner wasn't the only woman he cheated on Olivia with; just the only one he got pregnant."

"Does Olivia know about the child?"

"That's something I haven't been able to find out." He looked past Mac's shoulder and gestured at nothing. "Hell, she's been squirreled away in these woods for eleven years; there's a good chance she doesn't." He brought his gaze back to Mac. "John and Eileen do, though. They make two, sometimes three trips a year to California to see their grandson and have been supporting the mother. And I know for a fact that John and Eileen were screened as marrow donors, but were eliminated."

"And you've come to be with Olivia when they tell her

they're selling Inglenook as well as about the child, and that they want to test Sophie to see if she's a match?"

Sam snorted. "Olivia's not going to like telling Sophie her daddy was a no-good cheating bastard who fathered a half brother."

Mac slid his sword into the sheath on his back, then stretched his legs out in front of him and folded his arms over his chest. "I have no idea if Olivia knows about the other child, but I do believe she knew her husband was unfaithful, as her marriage to Baldwin ended six years ago instead of with his death."

Sam shrugged. "That's around when I heard she intended to divorce the bastard, only my source couldn't find out any more than that." He shook his head. "She must have known about his being unfaithful but kept it to herself."

"Then why didn't she follow through with the divorce?"

"Baldwin got deployed to Iraq just about then. Could be Olivia decided to wait until he got back." Sam snorted. "She probably didn't say anything to John and Eileen because she didn't want to risk her position here. And then when the bastard died it became a moot point, didn't it? How do you know Olivia's marriage ended six years ago? Did she tell you?"

Mac didn't answer him. "I don't understand why the Baldwins are assuming Olivia will move to California. They know how much this place means to her. There's no reason she wouldn't want to stay and run the camp for the new owners."

Sam shook his head. "Eileen's not about to let her programs continue if she's not here to oversee them; she's taking the concept with her. And Olivia knows it, and that's why she's been planning to advertise the new place as a family adventure camp, knowing the goodwill she's built with the campers all these years will keep them coming back. But considering the asking price, I'd say Eileen is hoping a developer buys the land, which puts Inglenook out of Olivia's reach." He shook his head. "That girl's too damned stubborn to let anyone help her financially."

"Who's your source?" Mac asked. "Who's been feeding you information on Olivia and Sophie and Eileen these last eleven years?"

Apparently figuring he didn't have to answer every question any more than Mac did, Sam grabbed a small tree and pulled himself to his feet with a grunt of pain. He stared at Mac for several seconds. "I'd appreciate it if you didn't tell Olivia who I am. I don't want to stir up old emotions, considering she'll have enough on her plate."

Mac also stood up. "I see your daughter's preference for living in the shadows comes naturally. You intend to quietly slip away after the storm, and not only continue to let Olivia believe she was abandoned but abandon your granddaughter as well?"

"I did what was necessary. And both Olivia and Sophie are better off without me. What in hell's up with the three albatrosses, anyway?" Sam asked, apparently done discussing his daughter. "They're a bit far from home, don't you think?"

"I'll be returning them in a couple of days. Anything else I should know about the coming storm?" Mac asked. "Such as when you expect it to arrive?"

Sam shrugged. "My guess is when Eileen and John get home. They've been in California finalizing the details of Eileen's new job and visiting their grandson. And Jessica Pilsner is getting desperate to find a match for her son. Riley's a little over five years old now, and from what I've been able to gather he's not going to see his seventh birthday without that transplant. So you might want to prepare yourself, Oceanus; Olivia's going to either explode when all this gets dumped on her, or pull so far inside herself that no one will be able to reach her."

"Olivia will not disappear," Mac said quietly, "because I won't let her. And *when* she explodes, I will clean up whatever mess she makes." He folded his arms over his chest. "She's on my watch now, Waters. You gave up all rights to your daughter when you made the choice not to return for her."

"Dammit, I tried moving heaven and earth to come back for her, but I *couldn't*. So I did everything in my power to keep her safe instead." He snorted. "Hell, I even hijacked one of our military satellites about three years ago to search for those idiot campers everyone claimed she lost."

Which told Mac two things about Sam Waters: the man was an entirely new breed of warrior, and he apparently had access to more than just an amazing network of information. "Is there anything else I should know?"

"Yeah; you break my little girl's heart or let any harm come to her or Sophie on *your watch*, I'll kill you."

"You'll be too late. The only way any harm will come to them is if I'm already dead." He stepped closer. "And now I have a warning for you. You think long and hard and be very sure before you tell Olivia who you are. Because if you come into her life only to abandon her again, I will hunt you down to the ends of the earth and make you wish your enemies had found you first."

"Fair enough," Sam said with a nod just before heading down the path, his limp more pronounced though his steps remained silent.

"Henry! Dammit, Henry, get back here!" Carolina shouted, the sound of her voice moving closer. "Mac! I've lost him!"

Sam stepped off the path and disappeared into the shadows with a wave over his shoulder just as Mac folded his arms across his chest and went very still. And despite being furious, he couldn't help but also be proud. Instead of charging headlong into trouble, Henry was sneaking back parallel to the path like a stalking tiger.

And Sam, thank the gods, continued on to the bunkhouse—probably having had enough of the Oceanuses for one night in favor of protecting his abused injury.

"Sweet Athena!" Caro said as she ran up, bending over to set her hands on her knees as she fought for breath. "The little brat ran off just as we reached the cabin, saying something about needing to guard your back." She straightened, sucking in heaving breaths. "I wasn't ten steps behind him when he suddenly just *vanished*." She turned in a circle, trying to pierce the forest before looking at Mac in horror. "He doesn't have any powers, does he?" she whispered, clutching her throat. "Henry can't actually shape-shift or anything, can he?"

"Not successfully," Mac said, listening to the distressed breathing coming from the bushes ten paces away, where the boy had stopped. "So now what is your plan, little man?" Mac said in a normal tone. "Exactly how are you going to guard my back with no hands to hold a weapon, as I don't believe those claws will inflict more than a scratch."

"He turned into an animal?" Caro whispered on an indrawn breath.

"A tiger cub," Mac drawled. "Henry, come out here. Now."

"I—I don't want to," a tiny voice said from the bushes. "I'm stuck. I—I don't know what happened but I can't . . . I don't want to come out right now."

"He shouldn't know how to change into anything," Caro hissed.

"He doesn't," Mac assured her. "It was an accident." He chuckled softly, keeping his voice low. "I scared the hell out of myself and Mama when she was teaching me Sanskrit when I was four. Wanting to be anyplace but in the classroom, I started imagining myself swimming with my friends in the ocean, and all off a sudden I was flopping around on the floor as a young shark." He shook his head. "I remember Mama screaming and running out of the room, and Father coming in and sitting down in her chair, where he just watched me gasping for breath." Mac unfolded his arms and lifted Carolina's mouth closed with his finger. "And that, baby sister, was my first lesson on being careful what I wished for."

She made a disgusted sound, her hands balling into fists at her side. "I hate that you got all the neat powers. That is so unfair."

"Apparently only *males* need them, seeing how we're the weaker sex. Henry, come out here."

"Are you going to punish me?"

"Yes."

"But I didn't *mean* to."

"Now, Henry."

A small, scruffy tiger cub stumbled out of the bushes onto the path, its head hung low as it approached. Stifling a smile, Mac turned him back into a little boy—though he was naked—by the time Henry reached them. Mac then slipped his sword sheath off his back and handed it to Carolina, and dropped to his knees. He shed his shirt and wrapped it around his trembling son, then held the boy's pale face in his hands and used his thumbs to brush the tears off his cheeks.

"I'm not going to punish you for shape-shifting, Henry, but for disobeying me. If I had been battling an enemy and realized you had come back here, I would have been distracted by fearing for your safety. And that would have put me in a defensive position instead of remaining on the offense. Do you understand?"

Henry nodded, his eyes so full of shame and a good deal of terror it was all Mac could do not to hug him. Sweet Prometheus, he'd been dreading this day. And for the first time in his life Mac realized that the true curse of fatherhood was having to punish someone whom he loved more than life itself.

"You will spend the next three days in your room, and be served nothing but bread and water," he said, shooting Carolina a warning glare when she gasped. He tilted the boy's head to bring Henry's eyes to his. "And during that time you will contemplate the danger you put us all in tonight by disobeying my order to stay with Carolina. And you will also consider the fright you just gave your aunt, and apologize to her."

Henry tried to turn to her, but Mac held the boy looking at him. "Just saying you're sorry is not enough, considering you put her life in jeopardy as well as yours and mine. So not only will you give Carolina your apology in three days, you will spend the following week serving her every need."

"Mac," Caro whispered.

He shot her another warning glare before turning it on Henry. "And the next time you disobey me, you will feel the full force of my wrath. Understand?"

His eyes wide with renewed terror, Henry nodded. Mac stood up and swept the boy into his arms, and started for the cabin. Carolina followed in silence, giving an occasional grunt as she carried his sword.

"Just leave it on the side of the path," Mac told her. "I'll get it later when I come back for Henry's clothes and sword. Henry, did you have a conversation with Olivia today that I should know about?"

"I—I don't know," he whispered, looking away.

Mac gave him a squeeze. "I've had enough evasiveness for one night. And one cold shoulder too many this evening has pushed my patience dangerously close to the edge," he said in Caro's direction. He went back to addressing Henry. "What was your conversation with Olivia about?"

"I asked if she thought I should sleep in pajamas," Henry said, still facing away—which told Mac that far more than nightclothes were discussed. "And I might have said something about sword lessons to her. But I quickly said I meant *music* lessons," he added in a rush.

"What else?" Mac snapped, giving him another squeeze. "Something upset Olivia, and I need to know exactly what you said to her."

Henry glanced at him, his eyes swimming in guilt, but quickly looked away again. "I asked if she might want to fall in love with you and marry us, and move to Midnight Bay," he whispered, only to suddenly throw his arms around Mac's neck. "I'm sorry, Daddy," he sobbed. "But I really like Miss Olivia, and I told her she'd make a really good theurgist's wife because she always knows just the right thing to say."

Mac stopped walking. "Did you use that exact term? Did you tell Olivia she'd make a good *theurgist's* wife?"

Henry nodded against him, his tears burning Mac's neck like flaming embers. "And what did Olivia say?" he asked softly.

"She . . . she said . . . she promised me she wouldn't let you marry any woman who didn't love me as much as you love me," he said, his tiny body shuddering with sobs. "And that you'd know if the woman was only pretending, and . . . and that you're big and strong and brave enough not to let Grampy make you marry Gadzalina."

Mac started walking again, rubbing Henry's back as the three of them made the rest of the trip in silence. When they reached the cabin he set Henry on his bed without saying a word, said nothing to Carolina standing in the middle of the main room glaring at him, and walked back outside.

Only instead of going after his and Henry's swords, Mac headed to the main lodge and let himself in the front door. He silently walked through the darkened kitchen to the window, and saw Olivia sitting in front of the dying fire with her daughter on her lap, the two of them snuggled up in a blanket, softly chatting and occasionally giggling.

Mac soaked in the domestic scene for several minutes before walking back into the main room of the lodge to stand in front of the floor-to-ceiling map of Maine.

The question wasn't if Olivia was strong enough to weather the coming storm, Mac realized, but if *he* was. He ran a finger over the map from Midnight Bay to Spellbound Falls. Because once he set things in motion there'd be no turning back, as the energy he was about to unleash was going to do far more than alter the fabric of life for everyone in the vicinity; it could very well start a battle between him and his father that would make the wars of the gods seem like minor skirmishes.

Yet it would be nothing compared to the battle Mac knew he would face when he finally told Olivia why he called her *marita*.

Chapter Nineteen

Olivia was just cracking her third egg into the frying pan when Carolina came barreling into the lodge kitchen and ran up and grabbed her arm. "You have to help me," she said, darting a frantic glance over her shoulder. "You have to stop Mac from punishing Henry."

Olivia dropped the egg in the pan, shell and all, and headed for the door. "Where are they? I swear if that man touches one hair on that boy's head, I'm going to run him through with a *real* sword."

Carolina pulled her to a stop. "No! Mac's not *physically* punishing him. He's making Henry stay in his room."

Olivia took a calming breath. And then she smiled, patting Carolina's hand still clutching her arm. "That's a perfectly acceptable punishment," she assured the frantic woman. "I send Sophie to her room all the time to mull over what she did wrong."

"For three days? Giving her nothing but bread and water?"

"Three *days*?" Olivia shook her head. "Three hours is too long for a six-year-old. What did Henry do, kill someone?" She pulled away and flung open the door to go save the poor child from his ogre of a father, only she ran into Mac's chest as he strode through the door—obviously in pursuit of his tattletale sister.

Ignoring Olivia's yelp of surprise, he quickly set her aside as he continued after Carolina—who had run to the opposite end of the island. "I swear by all that's holy that I'll lock *you* in your room for the next three days. You do not run out in the middle of an argument to go after reinforcements."

Olivia scrambled around Mac to put herself between him and his sister, and then had to brace her hand on his big broad chest to get him to stop. "Give it a rest already!" she snapped as he came to an abrupt halt, his eyes widening in surprise. "What in hell sort of crime could Henry have committed that warrants *three days* of being locked in his room?" She gave his big broad chest a poke. "The kid's *six*. And at that age three days is three *years*."

"You will stay out of this."

"No, I won't. You're paying a fortune to be here, and if you don't like what we teach then you're free to pack up and leave."

He folded his arms over his chest. "At a full refund?"

Damn, she hated it when people called her bluff. "What did Henry do, Mac?" Olivia suddenly gasped. "This better not be about my conversation with him yesterday," she said, raising her hand to poke him again. "Because that was between him and *me*."

Only he caught her finger before it connected, and refolded his arms—taking her hand with him. "If you must know, we heard something stalking us on our walk last night and I fell behind to see what it was," he told her. "Only Henry pulled away from Carolina when they reached the cabin, and disappeared into the woods before she could catch him." Up went that imperial brow. "Do you expect me to ignore that he could have been mauled by a bear or that he gave his aunt a terrible fright?"

Okay, he had a point. "But don't you think three days is a bit extreme?"

"With only bread and water," Carolina added from the safety of the island.

Mac looked past Olivia at his sister. "*You* will get only water, which might do you some good, considering how winded you became last night trying to catch Henry."

"Ohmigod, my eggs!" Olivia cried, jerking free before he could realize what she was doing and running to the stove. She turned off the burner and flipped on the range fan, then turned to Mac and Carolina. "Oh, come on, you two, hug and make up." She walked back over to Mac. "Carolina's just being an aunt trying to save her nephew from an *unreasonably* punitive ogre." She turned to Carolina. "And Mac, now that he's slept on it," she told the wide-eyed woman, who apparently had never heard anyone call her brother an ogre to his face, "is going to sit down with Henry and explain how dangerous the woods can be at night, and tell the child he needs to spend the *morning* in his room thinking about what a scare he gave everyone." She turned back to Mac. "Right?"

His arms still folded over his big broad chest and his eyes no longer gleaming, Mac shook his head. "Three days, with only bread and water. And one week of making up to his aunt by catering to her every need." He reached out and closed Olivia's gaping mouth. "And if you two ladies don't wish to join Henry in his room, you will leave my son's discipline to me and put your energies into finding something to feed the albatrosses."

He then walked over and grabbed the loaf of bread, and strode out the door.

"You're not going to let him get away with that, are you?" Carolina asked into the silence, gripping the counter as she stared at Olivia. She suddenly sighed. "Damn; I was so sure you had what it takes to stand up to my brother."

"I do." Olivia gestured toward the door. "But not today. He's scared, Carolina. Can't you see Mac's so frightened something bad could have happened to Henry last night that he's directing his anger at us because he knows we can handle it?" She walked over and touched Carolina's hand. "Trust me, the next three days are going to be a lot harder on Mac than on Henry. My guess is, he caves before Henry does."

"But Henry is so disheartened that his father is mad at him," Carolina whispered. "The child is devastated."

"He'll survive, Carolina. And you need to understand that Henry is discovering something very important about his dad." Olivia gave her an encouraging smile. "I'm guessing this is the first time Henry's made Mac truly angry, and the child needs to learn that even though his father might go overboard with his punishment, Mac won't ever stop loving him." She nodded at Carolina's look of surprise. "Personally, I think they've both been tiptoeing around each other since the moment they met, dreading this day. And now that it's finally here and they each realize they'll actually survive it, their relationship will be solid granite from here on out."

Carolina suddenly threw herself at Olivia, giving her a fierce hug. "Oh please, please fall in love with my brother. Mackie so desperately needs someone like you to keep him grounded."

Olivia felt her cheeks prickle with heat as she gave up trying to pull away, and hugged Carolina back with a sigh. "I think you and Henry are the ones who need to keep your feet on the ground. All I want is to have just one passionate affair with a sexy man before I die," she muttered, trying but again failing to pull free.

"Is this some sort of Inglenook ritual for the employees to start off each day?" Peg asked. "Because I got to tell you, I'm not really into group hugs."

Carolina let Olivia go with a gasp.

"Peg, you're early," Olivia said with a laugh.

"I told you I'd be here bright-eyed and bushy-tailed first thing this morning." She took off her jacket and set it and her purse on one of the chairs at the table. "And look," she said, lifting her arms and letting them drop. "I'm totally childless for the entire day."

"Where's Peter and Jacob?" Olivia asked, leading Carolina over to meet Peg.

"Billy's mom was so excited I got this job, she offered to watch them until Inglenook's back up and running so I can spend the next two weeks making myself indispensible to you." Peg's cheeks darkened. "She was afraid I'd get fired my first day if you didn't have any activities to keep Pete and Repeat out of everyone's hair."

"Peg, this is Mac's sister, Carolina," Olivia said. "And Carolina, this is Peg Thompson, my new counselor-slash-mother-in-residence. Peg's an expert on staying calm through all sorts of chaos, since she has four children of her own."

Peg shook Carolina's hand with a laugh. "My specific expertise is runny noses and crowd control."

"And Pete and Repeat are?" Carolina asked.

"My four-year-old twin boys." Peg looked at Olivia. "I'm ready to be put to work."

"And not a moment too soon," Olivia said, taking off her apron and handing it to her. "Only I'm afraid I'm abandoning you. So after you cook breakfast for everyone you can spend the day making yourself familiar with Inglenook." She grabbed her jacket and purse off the peg and turned back to the women. "I need to drive to Bangor today to . . . um, do stuff. So Peg, you check out all the cabins and outbuildings and everything here at the main lodge. Oh, and start a list of anything you might think needs to be addressed." She shook her head. "There's nothing like a new set of eyes to see something I've been overlooking for years. And you'll have to make lunch, but the freezer and the pantry are full, so help yourself to what you need."

She looked at Carolina, giving her a crooked smile. "And if I can be so bold as to suggest it, you might want to stay away from Mac today." She looked at her watch, then back at Peg. "If I leave now I should make it home by the time the school bus gets here. But if not, could you throw a stew in the slow cooker for supper?"

"Wow," Peg said, slipping on the apron. "I don't think I've ever heard you talk that much all at once," she said with a cheeky smile. "And you're so . . . bossy. Who knew duck-out-the-back-door-Baldwin had it in her?" Peg picked up the spatula and used it to salute her. "I'll hold down the fort while you're gone, boss."

Olivia groaned as she opened the door. "I'm docking you a day's pay every time you call me *boss*," she warned, stepping onto the porch only to run into *Sam's* chest.

"Oh, sorry," he said, quickly stepping back.

"Good morning, Sam."

"Olivia," he said with a nod. "You have anything in particular you want me to do today? The horses are all settled in, so I'm free."

"You could check out the tack and make a list of anything you need. And if that doesn't keep you busy enough, you could— Wait, Caleb said you were in the military. You know anything about obstacle courses?"

That got a hesitant smile from him. "A little bit."

Olivia gestured over her shoulder. "In the main room of the lodge there's a map of Inglenook on the wall, and you'll see where we've got an obstacle course laid out on a mile-and-a-half-long path." The smile she gave him was sheepish. "Well, it's our version of a family-friendly obstacle course. I was going to have Mac check out the stations to make sure there wasn't any winter damage we need to repair, but maybe I should have you go with him. I think Mac's expertise is more corporate than military."

Just for a fleeting second, Olivia would swear Sam looked a little incredulous before he went back to smiling. "Sure, I'd love to check out the course with him," he said tightly.

"You can carry any tools or materials you'll need on the older one of the golf carts parked in the machine shed. That way you . . . you won't have to walk the entire course," she finished weakly, feeling her damn cheeks heat up again.

"It's okay, Olivia. It's not exactly like I can hide my limp. And I'm supposed to walk to rebuild my back muscles. I guess you could say Inglenook's like therapy to me."

"Okay," she said, going down the steps but turning back when he said her name.

"You won't be here today?" he asked, gesturing at her purse and jacket.

"No, I'm driving to Bangor. You need me to pick up anything for you?"

"No. I'm good. But I could go with you to help handle whatever supplies you're going after, if you want. It would give us a chance to get to know each other better before the campers arrive."

"I'm afraid you'd get to know me better than you care to, Sam," she drawled. "I'm going clothes shopping."

The man actually took a step back before he caught himself. "Maybe another time, then," he said with a wave, heading inside before she changed her mind.

Olivia headed for the van parked in front of the lodge garage, feeling confident Sam was going to work out after all. She'd always figured kids had a way of reading grownups far better than most adults, and Sophie had done nothing but sing Sam's praises last night after everyone had left the campfire. Olivia tossed her purse and jacket on the opposite seat of the van and climbed in, but when she reached to close her door while checking to make sure the key was in the ignition, her hand touched a big broad chest instead of the door handle.

"Oh! You scared me!"

"Going somewhere?" Mac asked.

She collapsed against her seat with a laugh. "Gee, I haven't had so many people asking me to account for my whereabouts since I was sixteen. If you *must* know, I'm driving to Bangor. To . . . um, do stuff," she tacked on when he merely arched a brow.

"Maybe I'll come with you."

"Maybe you won't. I'm doing girl stuff."

He stepped closer. "What sort of *girl* stuff?"

Olivia stared at the top button on his shirt. Should she or shouldn't she tell him?

"Olivia."

Well, she supposed he'd have to know eventually, wouldn't he?

"Olivia."

But he didn't have to know right now, because . . . well,

because he might not be the one she was doing it for anymore.

She gasped when he leaned in and kissed her.

Oh yeah, she *needed* him to be the one, she thought, sighing into his very talented mouth. And if she didn't start the van and get out of here, she really might take him with her. They had hotel rooms in Bangor, didn't they?

He pulled slightly away. "What sort of girl stuff?"

"I'm going to have an IUD put in."

He straightened away, and Olivia actually leaned back from the look in his eyes. "No," he growled.

She smoothed down her blouse. "I don't believe that's your decision to make."

He took hold of her chin to make her look at him. "Let me deal with that concern."

"No," she said, pulling free. "That's very noble of you, but I'm the one who has to live with the consequences if . . . if we happen to get caught up in the throes of wild, passionate abandon and forget." There, she could talk poetry, too. She touched his arm. "I've had one before, Mac, and found I liked it. It's simple and . . . idiotproof."

"I don't like the idea of you having something foreign inside you."

"But *my* liking the idea is all that really matters. And I'm not really asking your permission; I'm just giving you a heads-up." She shrugged, just to bug him. "Besides, you're a bit presumptuous assuming this has anything to do with you, considering not five minutes ago you threatened to lock me in a room."

He caught her chin and leaned in close. "Did I fail to mention that I would be in that room with you?" he asked—just before he kissed her again.

Oh yeah, he definitely was the reason she was going to Bangor today.

God, the guy could kiss.

"Take my truck," he said when he pulled away.

She laughed at that. "Your truck doesn't like me, remember?" She slipped the seat belt around her and snapped it shut, then unsnapped it to make sure it released before sliding it back into place. "See, that's how seat belts are *supposed* to work."

He merely smiled.

"Um, Mac," she said when he started to close her door. "I'm really not one to stick my nose in other people's business, but your little rebellion against your father appears to indirectly be involving me. So I think you should know that I've already been one man's means of getting a meddling parent off his back, and I consider myself smart enough not to repeat my mistakes."

He said nothing, his expression unreadable.

She blew out a heavy sigh. "So you need to reassure Henry that you won't marry a woman unless she also loves *him.* And that she'll also love animals and the ocean and cookouts," she added, trying to lighten the mood. She set her hand on his arm. "He's been through so much in such a short time, and . . . well, he can handle being punished for running off into the woods, but it would devastate him if you got upset with him just for having a heart-to-heart talk with me."

"Henry told me about your conversation," Mac said quietly. "And that he asked you to fall in love with me."

Olivia stared out the windshield. "Don't worry, I turned him down gently." She looked at Mac again, giving him a smile she wasn't quite feeling. "But I also promised him that neither I nor Carolina would let you do anything so foolish as to marry a woman you only like well enough to satisfy your father."

Mac dropped his head, shielding his eyes from her.

Olivia touched his arm again, but he still wouldn't look at her. "I've been . . . I don't . . ." She put both hands on the wheel to stare out the windshield and took a really, really deep breath. "I thought maybe we shouldn't see each other anymore because of our children, but then . . . I don't . . ."

"*Say it*, Olivia."

"I don't want to stop seeing you." She finally worked up the courage to look at him again. "If we both can just remember where this is going, I'd like for us to keep seeing each other—very discreetly, of course, for Henry and Sophie's sakes."

"So you wish to continue our affair and part ways in September, and not look back," he softly clarified. "Discreetly, of course."

She nodded. "And I want you to also give me your word that you won't marry Godzilla just to shut up your father."

His eyes turned unreadable again. "You have my word of honor, *marita*."

She beamed him a sassy smile and started the van, because she really needed to get out of here before she invited him to come with her. "Then while I'm in Bangor I just might go shopping for an appropriate token of my affection for *you*." She canted her head. "You into handcuffs? No wait, I better not," she said, slapping her forehead with the palm of her hand. "Because I'd probably end up being the one wearing them." She shrugged. "Maybe I'll just get you an ankle bracelet that you can't *take off*. Now what are you smiling at?"

"I much prefer it when you have the conversations with yourself out loud," he said, softly closing her door.

He gave a slight bow then strode away, leaving Olivia frowning at his back. But when she tried to go after him to ask what in hell he was talking about, her damn seat belt wouldn't release.

Chapter Twenty

Mac stood in the shadows of the moonlit trees outside Olivia's kitchen window, and frowned when he saw her snap a lid on the bowl she'd just filled with stew. Sweet Prometheus, between what Caro had sneaked to Henry today and what Olivia appeared to be preparing to take to him now, the boy was eating better than ever.

Olivia placed a good half-dozen cookies in a small plastic bag and set it on top of the bowl, then walked to the table. She took a book out of one of the shopping bags Mac had seen her carrying in from the van earlier, and then started pulling small, lacy clothing out of one of the others. She suddenly stopped and held up an ocean-blue bra, and Mac went back to smiling. That is, until she looked around—specifically at the door and windows—before she pulled her sweater off over her head. Next the bra she was wearing came off, and every muscle in Mac's body responded to the sight of her naked, rose-tipped, beautifully feminine breasts.

She tore off the tag and put on the bra, then headed down the hall. She stopped to peek in her daughter's bedroom, then continued out of sight, only to reappear wearing his leather jacket that she was just zipping up to her chin—with no sign of a shirt beneath it.

She was also wearing a provocative smile that nearly brought Mac to his knees.

She put Henry's dinner and the book inside the small bag she'd emptied, then took something out of one of the other bags and shoved it into the jacket pocket.

Mac stepped behind a tree when the door opened and she came out and stood on the stoop looking around, now carrying two bags. She suddenly pressed a hand to her belly with a small groan, and Mac realized not everything Olivia had gotten in Bangor had come home in a shopping bag. He quietly sighed at the realization that he wouldn't be able to act on his urges this evening, but then stiffened at the realization that she was out for a bit of lusty revenge this evening.

Why else would the woman have dressed provocatively knowing they couldn't make love? So, the little minx intended to pay him back for telling her to mind her own business this morning, did she? And for giving her jewelry she couldn't take off, for picking her up and lugging her around everywhere, for his truck not liking her, and for . . . hell, for any one of a hundred transgressions she felt he'd committed against her.

Which told Mac two things: Olivia wasn't the least bit afraid of him, and she would indeed make a good theurgist's wife—whether she thought so or not.

Mac silently groaned. Sweet Prometheus, now he was having conversations with himself. He quietly followed her through the old-growth pines as she made her way from tree to tree toward cabin ten, even as he wondered if she'd found him a token of her affection on her shopping trip today.

"Pssst, Henry," she whispered, tapping on the boy's bedroom window. "Henry, come over here."

Olivia set her bags on the ground and pried off the wooden screen just as the window opened, then pulled Henry halfway out to give the surprised child a big noisy kiss on his forehead. "Hey there, sport. How you holding up?"

"Miss Olivia!" His son leaned out the window to look around. "You can't be here. If Dad finds out he's going to be mad at you, too."

"You want to know a secret, Henry?" She gestured for him to lean closer. "I'm not afraid of your dad."

Mac saw the boy's eyes widen in surprise. "You're not? Not even a little?"

"Not even this much," she whispered, holding her thumb and finger slightly apart. "In fact, I'm so *not* afraid of your big strong father, look," she said, holding out the front of Mac's leather jacket. "See this; I stole it from him."

Henry's eyes widened again. "You *stole* it? But Miss Olivia, why?"

She twisted back and forth to show it off. "Because I think it looks better on me than it does on him. And you know what? I'm not so sure I'm going to give it back."

Henry shook his head. "He's going to be upset when he discovers you took it, and *really* upset if you don't give it back."

"Oh yeah? What do you think he'll do? Punch me in the nose?"

"No!" Henry cried, only to slap his hand to his mouth and glance at his bedroom door. "Dad wouldn't ever hit a woman."

"Then I guess I don't need to be afraid of him, do I?" She smoothed down the front of the jacket. "Unless . . . unless you think he'll stop liking me because I was foolish for not thinking things through before I stole his jacket."

Mac folded his arms over his chest to lean his shoulder against the tree, and smiled at his son's look of surprise. "Dad won't stop liking you for making one silly mistake, Miss Olivia; he likes you way too much."

"I don't know," she said, shaking her head as she gestured toward the darkened room behind him. "Look what he did to you. He sent you to your bedroom for three whole days. And now I'm afraid he'll probably stop liking me, too, even if I tell him I'm sorry for taking his jacket and give it back to him."

"But his punishing me doesn't mean he doesn't love me anymore," Henry cried in a whisper. "He's just making sure I don't ever run off like that again."

"So you think I should give back his jacket and tell him I'm sorry?"

Henry set his hand on her shoulder. "I think that would be wise. And I bet if you asked him if you could have it, he would give it to you."

Olivia took his hand in hers. "You want to know another secret?"

He nodded.

"Last night your father wasn't nearly as upset with you as he was scared."

"But my dad's not afraid of *anything*."

"Oh, yes he is. He's scared to death something bad could happen to you. All moms and dads get scared if they feel their children are in danger, and when the danger is past all that fear turns to anger." She waved at the room behind him again. "And the punishment usually ends up being way out of proportion to the crime. Tell me, do you love your daddy any less for punishing you?"

"No!"

She nodded. "That's what I figured. So, you're good about all this?" she asked, waving at the bedroom again. "You'll survive the next two days?"

Mac nearly laughed out loud when Henry arched a brow. "I'm an Oceanus; I can survive anything."

Olivia grabbed the boy and gave him another noisy kiss on the forehead. But instead of letting him go, she held his nose only inches from hers. "Wouldn't you like to get just an itsy bitsy, tiny bit of revenge for this ridiculous punishment?"

Mac straightened away from the tree when Henry nodded.

"Okay then, here's what you do. When the three days are up and you walk out of your room a free man, you run up to your dad and throw your arms around him, and tell him he's the very best father in the whole wide world and that you love him to pieces."

The boy looked skeptical. "How's that revenge?"

"It'll drive him nuts, I promise," she said with a snicker. "The nicer you are to someone who's being unreasonable, the guiltier they feel. And the next time you and your dad cross swords—*figuratively*, Henry—he'll think twice before doling out such an outrageous punishment."

Sweet Prometheus, since he'd arrived here Olivia had been encouraging Henry to challenge his authority, and now she was telling him to get revenge.

For the love of Zeus, *why*?

Mac got his answer almost immediately.

"It might be your father's job to keep you safe and give you the tools you'll need as an adult," she explained to the confused child, "but it's *your* job to constantly be testing your own limits as well as his. If you keep doing everything you're told without question, and always worry about not upsetting people, then you're going to stay a little boy inside forever," she said, touching his chest. "Pushing boundaries is the *growing* part of growing up, Henry."

Mac held out his hand to see if that wasn't a pearl of wisdom sprinkling down on him, for wasn't Olivia telling the truth? Didn't women have a need to nurture and keep their babies close, whereas men seemed only determined to mold them into the adults they needed to become?

And children, no matter what century it was, rebelled against both.

Mac stilled. Was that why *he* had constantly been at odds with his father? Titus Oceanus hadn't seen a four- or ten- or even sixteen-year-old child; he had seen the *man* Mac needed to become. And the great and powerful king of the drùidhs had actually been scared to death to fail as a father.

Exactly as Mac was now.

Mac silently growled into his hands as he scrubbed his face. Hell, he was an ass. All these centuries he'd been battling what he'd thought was his father's desire to turn him into a mirror image of himself, and Titus had been fighting equally hard to make sure his son grew up strong and wise and powerful enough to handle his destiny.

And that's why Mac had spent today with his gut in a knot for keeping Henry in his room—and had in truth become his old man. He remembered his mother watching him pack to leave home after another heated argument with his father, and how she'd said that one day he'd have a child of his own who would send him running home to apologize for being such a difficult son.

Only instead of returning to Atlantis to beg his father's forgiveness, in just a few days Mac intended to start a battle between them that would likely make it impossible for him to go home ever again.

Although home was wherever his heart belonged, he'd just recently discovered.

"Here," Olivia said, picking up the smaller of the two shopping bags. "I brought you supper and some cookies to save for later, and a book."

Since Henry was likely full from the basket of food Caro had brought him, the boy immediately went for the book. "Oh, wow! What's it about, Miss Olivia?"

"It's called *Where the Wild Things Are*, and the little boy in the story—his name is Max—gets sent to his room for being bad." She tapped the cover. "And I thought you might enjoy how Max spends his time." She gave a soft laugh. "There's no gods lopping off heads or having sex with everyone, but I think you'll like it anyway. Um, if you can't read the words, I'm sure your auntie Caro can sneak in sometime tomorrow and read it to you the first time. Then you can keep repeating the story out loud to yourself by following the pictures."

"Oh, I can read this," Henry said, holding it out to the moonlight as he scanned some of the pages. "And I really like the monsters; they're not nearly as scary as demons." He closed the book and clutched it to his chest. "Thank you, Miss Olivia. I will cherish your gift forever."

"Yes . . . well," Olivia said thickly, bending down to pick

up the other bag. "And while I was shopping, I just happened to find some pajamas for you and your dad."

Mac straightened away from the tree again.

"You got *Dad* pajamas?"

Olivia reached in and pulled out a handful of material, then set the bag on the ground in order to hold an oversized shirt up to her body. "He can't go around naked when you have friends sleeping over any more than you can, Henry. Well?" she asked, smoothing the shirt over her chest so the boy could see what was on the front. "Do you think he'll like them?"

"What is . . . Is that an animal wearing a long robe and funny hat?"

"Henry, it's *Mickey Mouse*," she said, looking down at her chest as she pointed at the shirt. "You honestly don't know who Mickey Mouse is? What about Donald Duck? Or Goofy? Pluto? *Disneyland?*"

"I know Pluto, only his real name is Hades."

Olivia sighed loud enough that Sam probably heard it down in the bunkhouse. "Never mind Pluto," she muttered, poking the shirt on her chest. "This is Mickey Mouse. And see his magic wand? Mickey's a *wizard*. Or as you might call him, a theurgist."

"Oh no," Henry said as he shook his head, utterly serious. "Mickey's hat is all wrong, and Dad's staff is usually a tri—" Seeing where the conversation was heading, Mac picked up a rock and lobbed it toward the lake, where it hit the shoreline then bounced out onto the rotting ice in echoing thuds.

"Ohmigod, here!" Olivia cried in a whisper, shoving the shirt at Henry, then tossing the shopping bag through the window. She grabbed the boy and gave him another quick kiss. "Hang tight, sport. I'll be back tomorrow." She frantically looked toward the lake as Henry closed the curtains, then darted toward the closest tree.

Mac stepped around behind her and swept Olivia off her feet, and strode off with her in his arms toward the lake.

"Dammit, you scared ten years off my life," she

growled—though he noticed she settled against him quickly enough. "How long were you standing there?"

"Long enough to hear that for every step I take closer to Henry, you're encouraging him to take three steps away from me."

She rested her head in the crook of his neck, apparently not at all disgruntled at being lugged around. "I do believe that's why you're paying me the big bucks."

Mac sat down next to the shoreline and leaned his back against a tree, then positioned Olivia on his lap so that her face was washed in moonlight.

And then he started unzipping his jacket.

Her hand shot up to stop him. "W-what are you doing?"

"I'm letting you return my property. Isn't that why you're wearing it?"

She pushed his hand away and slid the zipper back up to her chin, the moonlight showing her blush. "I'll give it back tomorrow. I'm kind of chilled right now."

"I will keep you warm, *marita*," he whispered, urging her to relax against him. "Did you get everything you wanted in Bangor today?" he asked. "Or did you decide to let me take care of that concern?"

"I took care of it." She picked up his hand and wove her fingers through his. "But the doctor said we shouldn't . . . we can't be together for a couple of days. Mac, are you as rich and powerful as Henry thinks you are?" she asked quietly.

But he could feel the tension humming through her. "Yes. Did you bring me back a token of your affection?"

She hesitated, clearly not liking his redirecting the conversation. "Actually, I did," she said with a sigh. She untwined their fingers to reach in the pocket of his jacket, her hand emerging with a small black rectangular sheath. She held it up for him to see. "You're a very hard man to buy for, you know." She arched a delicate brow. "Though I did try to find you a manly bracelet, but they all had *clasps*. So I got you this instead."

She flipped open the pouch and pulled out a metal . . . something. "It's a multitool," she explained, spreading its two halves apart. "It has a serrated and a smooth knife blade, a file, two screwdrivers, needle-nose pliers, and . . . well, I don't know what some of these things do. But I do know every red-blooded male living around here wears a multitool on his belt." She handed it to him. "So I thought that every time you used it, you'd think of me. Or at the very least you'd think of my creative use for a condom because you didn't have anything to cut off the tops of the water bottles."

Mac reached his arms around her in order to open and close Olivia's gift as he studied its many tools, feeling touched in a way that was unfamiliar to him. "This is perfect, Olivia," he said, hearing the thickness in his own voice. "I will wear it all the time, everywhere." He leaned around to smile at her. "Except in bed, as I don't believe my new pajamas have a belt." He kissed her cheek, letting his lips linger on the heat of her blush. "Thank you, *marita.* I will cherish this for always."

He saw her blush brighten. "It's nothing special, just a silly tool." She reached out and turned it in his hand. "I had it inscribed." And then she gave him a smug smile. "Only it's in a foreign language." She relaxed against him again with a soft snort. "And I promise I'll tell you what it says one day soon," she drawled, throwing his words back at him from when she'd asked what *marita* meant.

Not wanting to spoil her fun by telling her there wasn't a language or dialect he didn't speak, Mac held her gift up to the moonlight and pretended to try to read what he realized was a French inscription—or more specifically, French-Canadian. Mac guessed that was the only language Olivia had immediate access to here in Maine, with Canada and the Atlantic Ocean being close neighbors.

Real magic has the power to rock the world, as you have rocked mine.

He ran his thumb over the inscription, wondering why she'd chosen such peculiar words, even as he hoped she still held the same sentiment a few days from now.

"You really don't have to wear it if you don't want," she

whispered, and Mac felt her slipping away into her shadows. She shrugged, giving a self-conscious laugh. "Especially not to your board meet—"

He draped her backward over his arm and kissed her, and didn't stop until he felt her shiver in response. And having figured out her gift now that he'd held it awhile, Mac flicked it open to expose the tool he wanted, and then placed the pliers on the zipper pull of his jacket.

"I believe this will be handy for a variety of tasks," he said, lowering the zipper.

That certainly brought her out of her shadows. Ignoring her squeak of protest, Mac kissed one plump breast spilling over the top of the Atlantic-blue bra.

"Um . . . I don't think . . . maybe you better not . . . ohhhh," she moaned when he closed his mouth over her beaded nipple straining against the lace and gently suckled. "You really can't do that," she said in a strangled growl, grabbing his head and pushing him away. She immediately covered her breast, her other hand going to her belly. "Oh God, I think there's a string that runs straight from my boobs to my womb."

"I'm sorry for hurting you," he said, instantly contrite.

She pressed her hands to his jaw, rubbing her thumb over his lip. "No, it's okay. It's just that my insides get all . . . when you . . . and I get . . ." She covered her face with her hands. "Ohmigod, this is embarrassing."

"Then why did you wear only my jacket over your bra tonight?" he asked, zipping it up as far as he could, considering her hands were still hiding her face.

She snorted. "Because once again I didn't think things through first."

He shifted her facing forward to lean back against him, and stared out at the lake, content just to hold her.

"But I'll bet *you're* going to think twice before you dish out your next punishment to Henry," she said, apparently unable to handle the silence.

At least she was including him in her conversation this time.

"Because," she continued, "now you know that *you* have to serve the sentence right along with him. How did your gut do today, Mac?"

"I imagine it felt similar to how yours felt coming out of the doctor's office." He sighed. "By the gods, I don't want to go through this again for a good thousand years." He gave her a gentle squeeze. "So stop encouraging Henry to question my authority, or I swear I will—"

"Don't even think of threatening me," she sputtered on a laugh. "Because I've got more tricks up my sleeve I could show that boy than you've got up yours, Mr. Abracadabra." She grabbed his hands and slid them into the pockets of his jacket, then held them splayed over her belly. "Mmmm, the heat feels good. Trust me, Mac," she continued, "your biggest fear should be if Henry *doesn't* push your buttons occasionally. Do you want him to grow up to be a mouse or a lion?"

"Who's asking this question: Olivia the tigress or Olivia the mouse who runs and hides from what she doesn't want to deal with?" He kissed her cheek when she canted her head to frown up at him. "Or are you making sure he doesn't repeat *your* childhood mistakes?"

"Hey, I pushed my share of buttons when I was a kid." She turned back to face the lake. "I'll have you know that when I was only ten years old, I ran off to Ezra and Doris's house after my foster parents announced to me and Tommy, another kid they'd taken in, that they were having a baby of their own. I got grounded for four consecutive weekends for scaring the bejeezus out of everyone, because Ezra and Doris lived sixteen miles away and it took me two days to get there on foot."

Mac nudged her to the side to see her face. "Ezra the store owner? You knew him before you moved here?"

She beamed him a smile and nodded. "He and Doris moved to Spellbound Falls about a month after I did. When they came up for my wedding, they instantly fell in love with the lake and the people here. Within two weeks they'd bought the trading post and a house on Bent Mountain, and two weeks after that they were all moved in and running the store." She suddenly turned sad. "Only a year ago this Memorial Day weekend Doris's heart just quit and she died in her sleep."

"I'm sorry," Mac said, nudging her back around as he frowned over her head. "So you knew Ezra and his wife from when you were a child? And they kept in touch with you all through the years?"

"The Dodds used to own the duplex where I lived with my mom, only they sold it about a month or so after she died. But in a funny coincidence, they ended up buying a house just two streets away from the foster home I went to live at. And after seeing me riding my bike one day, Doris came over with a bunch of fresh baked whoopie pies for me and the other girl living there. She told my foster mother she knew me quite well, and that she'd love to watch me and Susan if she ever needed a babysitter."

Olivia turned and smiled up at him. "It's strange how it kept working out, because I swear I ended up living less than twenty miles away from Ezra and Doris all the time I was growing up except for the two years I was in college. And then I always stayed with them during school breaks." She turned back around with a snort. "They were more like my grandparents than my mom's parents were. The Naglemeyers didn't want anything to do with me. Hell, Doris made every birthday cake I ever had, and my real grandparents never even sent me a card. And Doris was my matron of honor at my wedding, and Ezra walked me down the aisle."

And that, Mac realized, was exactly how Sam knew the color of the frosting on Olivia's cakes. "I'm surprised the Dodds simply didn't adopt you."

"Actually, when Mom died they tried to be foster parents for me, but I think the state felt they were too old. And the social worker told me they prefer to place kids with families, and Ezra and Doris didn't have any children. Well, they'd had a son, but he died in his early twenties. They rarely talked about him and didn't even keep pictures of him around the house, so I didn't bring up the subject because I didn't want to open old wounds."

Mac rested his cheek against Olivia's hair, soaking in her wonderful scent as he marveled at the lengths Sam had gone to in order to keep watch over his daughter. Hell, the man had even gone so far as to move an aging couple from home to home to be near her.

Mac stilled. No, not just any couple; his *parents*.

Ezra and Doris were Olivia's paternal grandparents.

Sweet Prometheus, Sam Waters—which sure as hell wasn't his real name anymore than Dodd was Ezra's—had orchestrated a massive deception that had spanned thirty-three years. Because he couldn't hold Olivia in his arms for fear of her safety, or kiss her scraped knee, or walk her down the aisle at her wedding, Sam had given that privilege to his parents instead.

Except the one thing the man hadn't been able to do was protect his daughter from herself. He couldn't stop Olivia from believing she'd been abandoned, or stop her from hiding in the shadows, or keep her from marrying the wrong man. And now he couldn't stop the Baldwins' or Mac's impending storms, either.

"If I ask you a sincere question," Mac whispered against her cheek, "will you give me a sincere answer?"

"I . . . I guess that would depend on the question."

"I would ask what it is you're wanting from our affair." He brushed his mouth over her heated skin. "What is it that you want from me, Olivia?"

She hesitated long enough that Mac didn't think she was going to answer. But then he felt her draw in a deep breath and press his hands into her belly.

"The short answer is that I crave the feel of a man's strength."

"And the long answer?"

She hesitated again, then took another fortifying breath. "The moment I met you, your confidence and sheer . . . solidness knocked me completely off center," she softly admitted. "And I thought if you focused just a tiny bit of that wonderful power on me, that maybe some of it would rub off and I would become confident and solid, too." She dropped her head away from his and stared down at their hands inside his jacket. "I want to stop always being on the outside looking in." She pressed back against him on another deep breath. "So I guess that means I want to be five years old again, when I thought that love alone could move mountains. Because if I could just believe in that kind of power again, then I'd know there was a chance love would find me, even in . . . the shadows."

Mac touched his lips to her hair. "And if the day ever comes that the mountains actually move, what will you do? Will you run out to greet them, or run in the opposite direction to hide in the safety of the shadows?"

She pulled his hands out of the pockets to fold his arms around her, and Mac tightened his embrace when she shuddered. "If they ever move, then I will believe in magic again," she whispered, "and run out to greet them." She gave a soft snort. "If only to ask what in hell took them so long."

Immensely pleased with both her long and short answers, Mac tucked her head under his chin with a sigh of contentment. "Then let's sit here in silence," he said, "and feel one another's strengths. No conversations inside our heads or out loud; let's simply feel the earth breathing, and move our hearts to beat with it as one."

"You really are a romantic, aren't you?"

He gave her a squeeze. "No talking. And no thinking," he reminded her. "Just *feel*, Olivia. And for this moment in time, simply be here with me."

She tucked her hands back in the jacket pockets, going boneless against him with a sigh. Mac closed his eyes to focus completely on Olivia: slowly bringing his heartbeat into step with hers, then gently urging both their hearts to beat in rhythm with the universe.

He smiled at her soft gasp of surprise, and tightened his embrace when she tensed. "I've got you," he whispered. "You will always be completely safe with me. Do you feel the earth breathing in and out as it slowly awakens from its winter sleep? It's responding to your dreams, Olivia, asking you to believe in the magic again."

Sensing her relaxed state after several minutes of silence, Mac brought Olivia with him as his mind retraced the path his finger had made on the map of Maine in the lodge last night. Only instead of starting at the ocean he began their journey at Bottomless Lake, stopping at several other lakes along the way to carefully examine their depths and suitability before continuing on.

They eventually reached the Gulf of Maine, and Mac felt Olivia's heart lurch at the sight of a massive breaching whale. "That's my old friend, Leviathan," he told her. "He's trying to get a good look at you so he can race home and tell the others. He says you're beautiful, *marita*, and that he can't wait to meet you in person."

Though he could have stayed basking in the power of the ocean all night, Mac feared overwhelming Olivia, and pulled just enough energy for his journey with the albatrosses. He then turned his mind toward land and followed the same semistraight route back to Spellbound Falls, only this time taking note of the towns and highways and the rising terrain leading to the mountains guarding Bottomless Lake.

Mac settled back on the shoreline and smiled at the slow, rhythmic breathing of the woman sleeping in his arms. He hadn't intended to take Olivia on his exploratory journey, but her sincerely given answer had made him wonder if a glimpse of the magic might not help her weather the coming storms. And maybe selfishly, he'd wanted to point out that there was a *man* inside the beast about to literally rock her world.

Mac sensed Sophie stirring in her bed and decided he should probably get Olivia in her own bed as well. "Wake up, cinnamon eyes," he whispered, kissing her cheek. He chuckled when she muttered something and tried to brush him away. "Are you thinking me a bothersome pest? Come on, wake up so I can take you home."

It seemed her lids were too heavy to open, and she wiggled around to cuddle against him. "Just carry me, Mac."

"No, I need you awake to hear what I have to tell you." He sat up just enough for him to stand, then lifted her to her feet.

Her eyes finally blinked open. "H-how long were we sitting here?"

"Long enough for a frost to set in; a couple of hours, maybe."

She rubbed her eyes with her fists, then looked around. "Wow, you're like a blast furnace," she said, looking at him with a sleepy smile. "I'm not even cold."

"Are you steady enough to walk?" he asked, reaching out to her.

She slipped her hand into his and they started toward her cottage. "I can't believe I fell asleep, but I must have because I had the strangest dream. I went down to the coast and out into the ocean, stopping at some lakes along the way, only I wasn't actually flying or anything. I just saw everything like I was simply . . . there. And you were there, too," she added with a smile.

She suddenly stopped walking, her eyes opening wide, and stepped back as far as their clasped hands would allow. "You look different. Taller. *Bigger.*" She let go of him to take another step back. "And your eyes are . . . they're very bright."

Mac held his hand out to her again, saying nothing.

He saw her have what appeared to be a brief conversation with herself as she stared at his chest, and then her shoulders went back and she reached out to curl her fingers around his. Mac started leading her toward her home again.

"You're going away, aren't you? And you're taking the albatrosses."

"Yes. I won't be here when you wake up in the morning."

"Will you be gone long?"

"I estimate two or three days."

"And Henry?"

"He'll stay here with Carolina. And with you."

She stepped up onto her stoop and turned to him, though she still had to look up to make eye contact, and Mac saw her concern. "You won't do anything . . . foolish, will you?" she whispered.

He smiled. "You mean like marry Godzilla?"

She didn't return his smile. "I mean like have a monstrous fight with your father."

"Not on purpose." He touched a finger to her lips when she tried to speak. "When next I meet my father it will be as a father myself, Olivia, thanks to you."

Her mouth curled up behind his finger. "You do know that I'm springing Henry out of jail first thing in the morning."

Mac shook his head. "Good luck with that."

She braced a hand on his chest and stood on tiptoe, he presumed to better glare at him. "I will take an ax to his bedroom door if that stupid doorknob suddenly decides not to work."

"You'd have to take the ax to Henry, as his own sense of honor will keep him in that room for two more days."

"Wanna bet?"

He lifted her hand and kissed her fingers. "I accept your wager; I will put up my cell phone against you letting me take you home to meet my father."

"What?" she said in a strangled squeak.

He nodded. "You persuade Henry to leave his room before his punishment is up and I'll give you my cell phone—which appears to work here in your mountains. But if Henry stays the entire three days, then you must come face my father with me."

She sputtered on a choked laugh. "Why, so he can make *me* marry Godzilla?" But she sobered when she realized he was serious, and she tugged her hand free. "I told you I'm not interested in getting between another man and his domineering parent."

"You're going to have to meet him eventually, *marita.* And it's my hope you'll share with him one or two pearls of wisdom on grandparenting." He arched a brow at her glare. "As I'm certain you have several he should probably hear."

She snorted. "Trust me, Eileen's the expert on that, too." She shoved her hands in his jacket pockets and went back to looking at his chest again. "I don't want to meet him, Mac." She looked up and smiled tightly. "The two male Oceanuses I have now are enough to handle. I can't even deal with my own mother-in-law most of the time without hiding from her more than I care to admit."

Mac folded his arms over his chest. "Did you ever consider moving away after your husband died?"

"I couldn't abandon Ezra and Doris, since they moved here to be near me."

Now there was a revelation; Olivia had stayed for the *Dodds*, not for John and Eileen. Only Mac wasn't sure if she'd be overjoyed to learn that Ezra and Doris were her paternal grandparents, or hurt that they'd never told her.

He pulled her into his arms. "I would have your promise that if you need anything while I'm gone, you'll go to Sam."

She tilted her head back. "Why would I go to Sam just because you're gone? I'm pretty sure I've been taking care of myself for quite a few years now."

He gave her a quick kiss on her lips and then let her go to reach in his pocket. "Just a suggestion. Here, you keep this while I'm gone," he said, handing her his cell phone. "It will work when and where you need it to. Trace Huntsman's number is programmed into it, as well as Carolina's and my father's."

She shoved the phone in her pocket with a smug smile. "You already know you're going to lose our bet, don't you?"

"No. Unlike my jacket, I expect you to give it back when I return. But maybe I will bring you back a cell phone of your own."

She pressed her hands to his face and stood on tiptoe to kiss him. "Have a good trip," she said when she pulled away. She opened her door and stepped inside. "And bring *yourself* back a new cell phone because this one's mine now." She started to close the door but pointed a threatening finger at him instead. "And you better stop at the place you bought that stupid truck and have the seat belt and door locks fixed."

"Sleep well, *marita*," Mac said as she softly closed the door.

He walked over to the shadows outside her kitchen window and stifled a laugh as he watched Olivia struggling to take off his jacket. But when the zipper wouldn't go down, Mac heard her soft growl of frustration as she tried to pull it off over her head, only to get it stuck on her nose.

And with the knowledge that even if she couldn't sleep in his arms tonight Olivia would at least be sleeping in his jacket, Mac vanished into the darkness.

Chapter Twenty-one

Olivia sat at her office desk staring at Mac's cell phone in her hands, wondering why in tarnation it had a full signal. She'd even tried calling Inglenook just to prove it didn't work, but the damn thing had actually rung through. Only it shouldn't have, because the closest cell tower was more than fifty miles south of here, with any number of mountains between it and Spellbound Falls. Even Turtleback got only sketchy service at best, and they were thirty miles closer to the tower.

Not having cell phone reception was probably the number two complaint from guests when they arrived at Inglenook and discovered they really were camping in the wilderness. The number one complaint was the lack of televisions other than in the dining hall and main lodge, and then those only had DVD players for movie night.

But in the packet sent to families signed up for camp, it was clearly stated that laptops, iPods, and handheld computer games were *not* allowed. Which meant that for once Olivia agreed with Eileen: If parents wanted to connect with their kids, first everyone needed to disconnect from personal electronics.

John and Eileen had satellite in their private quarters, though, and Olivia had it at her cottage because they had to stay in touch with the real world somehow. She had argued, however, that the lodge and dining hall sets should also be hooked up to satellite in case there was breaking news everyone should know about, but she'd lost that battle to Eileen.

Olivia looked up, then sat back in surprise when Ezra walked in and plopped down in the chair across from her. "Slacking off as usual, I see," he said in way of greeting. The cell phone caught his eye and he sat up. "Hey, what have you got there? You going techno on us, Olivia?" But then he frowned. "I didn't know they made satellite phones that small."

"I'm pretty sure it's just an ordinary cell," she said, holding it up. "But it's got a full signal, and I'm just sitting here wondering why. It's Mac's." She shrugged. "Maybe they really are making satellite phones this small now."

"Why don't you show it to Sam," Ezra suggested. "He seems to know electronics. He got my store computer running so fast I can't keep up with it now."

"How do you know Sam?" she asked in surprise.

"He was sitting in front of the trading post yesterday morning when I arrived to open up. The idiot walked all the way to town." He shook his head. "Someone really ought to tell that fella he's got a pretty bad limp."

"Oh no, I can't believe I forgot to mention he can borrow the van if he needs to go somewhere. Or he could have at least checked to see if Peg or I was going to town."

Ezra shrugged. "He seems like an independent cuss to me. He asked if I knew of any four-wheel drives for sale in the area." His eyes grew concerned. "And I . . . I've decided to sell him Doris's SUV, if it's okay with you." He scooted forward on his chair and leaned on the desk to place his hand over hers. "But if it's going to bother you to see that truck every day, then I won't sell it to him," he said thickly.

She turned her hand palm up to clasp his. "But what

about you? Aren't you afraid your heart's going to skip a beat when *you* see it in town?"

"It can't hurt any more than when I pull into my garage every night to find it sitting there, knowing Doris isn't in the house with supper waiting."

Olivia dropped her head onto their clasped hands, her heart so heavy it hurt to breathe. "God, I miss her."

"Now, come on," Ezra said gruffly, standing up and coming around the desk. He pulled her to her feet and wrapped her up in his frail arms. "You know Doris would have something to say about us getting all teary-eyed over some damned truck she didn't even like. Hell, she especially hated that it was green." He chuckled against her hair. "She always wanted a candy-apple-red pickup with big fat tires, stack pipes, and flames painted on the fenders." He patted her back. "But if it's gonna bother you to see that truck, I'll take it down to Bangor and trade it in on a new boat or something."

"You'll lose your shirt trading it," she said, straightening to wipe her eyes.

He snorted. "I got more shirts in the closet."

"Is there a problem?" Sam asked from the office doorway, his gaze locked on Olivia. "Did something happen that I could help with?"

"No, everything's okay," she said, wiping her face with her sleeve, then running her fingers through her hair. "Ezra's here to see you, actually. He wants to sell you his late wife's truck. Only you don't need to buy a vehicle, Sam," she said, drawing his concern from Ezra back to her. "Our employees are always welcome to use the van when they want to go into town or down to Turtleback."

"I need to buy transportation anyway. Only that still doesn't explain what's wrong," he said, gesturing at her.

Ezra walked back around the desk. "I was just making sure that seeing my wife's truck here every day wasn't going to bother Olivia, since she and Doris were so close."

Sam went a bit pale, his gaze shooting to her. "Hell, I

don't need it that bad," he said, looking at Ezra. "Thanks anyway, but I'll wait and find something else."

"No, it's just a dumb truck," Olivia said. She smiled warmly at Ezra. "And you're right; Doris never did like the color. I remember how she kept saying it wasn't nearly flashy enough for her."

"She didn't like it?" Sam asked, addressing Ezra even as Olivia wondered at the odd tone in his voice. "I mean, it's not pink or anything, is it?"

"It's the dark green SUV parked out in the driveway," Ezra said. "I drove it out here today to turn it over to you—that is, assuming we can come to terms on a price."

Sam looked at Olivia, his eyes unreadable. "I can find another vehicle."

"No, really. I'm good." She gave him a sincere smile. "Because if you don't buy it, then Ezra's trading it for a boat or something, and he'll lose his shirt."

Peg poked her head in the door, then put a large stack of mail on the desk when Olivia waved her in. "Is there a reason the television in the lobby doesn't work?" Peg asked. "I just heard something strange on the radio on my way back from town, and I want to watch CNN."

"What's happening?" Olivia asked.

Peg shook her head. "It was breaking news on every radio station; something about some strange . . . they're calling it a phenomenon. All sorts of old nets and fishing gear are washing up on beaches all over the world."

Olivia looked at Sam. "If I get my satellite receiver from home, can you hook it up to the television in the main room? I had the technician run a cable into the closet when they hooked up John and Eileen's dish—without Eileen's knowledge, of course. So we just have to make sure everything's back in place before they get home."

"I can hook it up," Sam said, heading toward the main room.

"Peg, why don't you go get Carolina and Henry so they can watch with us," Olivia said. "You tell Henry he can come out of his room for a couple of hours and tack on the extra time at the end of his sentence."

"I really need to have a talk with that boy," Peg muttered, heading after Sam. "It's just not normal for a kid to stay in his room when his jailer is gone."

"Is Doreen watching the store, Ezra?" Olivia asked.

He nodded. "I took today off, figuring to drive Sam to Turtleback to get the truck title changed to his name. And Grundy's coming in later to help Doreen until closing."

"Then you might as well pour yourself a mug of coffee and watch the news with us," she said, waving him out ahead of her. Only she stopped and grabbed Mac's cell phone off the desk and slipped it into her pocket.

Olivia then sprinted through the main room and out onto the porch, but nearly tripped on the stairs when she saw Doris's SUV parked in the driveway. She continued on at a more careful pace, fighting back tears again.

Doris and Ezra had been the one constant in her life, the only anchors keeping her from disappearing completely. But when Doris had died, Olivia had felt herself starting to drift even closer to the shadows. And God help her, if anything happened to Ezra she was afraid she'd end up clinging to Sophie so tightly that she'd never let go.

And that was wrong on so many levels. Sophie needed to grow strong and independent and find her place in the world, not be tied to a needy mother. And that was exactly why Olivia was buying Inglenook: because unlike her father, she would do whatever it took for Sophie and Ezra to have a place to call home.

She went into her living room, pulled out the TV and unhooked the wire running from the satellite box, then unplugged the box and pulled it off the shelf. She ran back outside and caught up with Carolina and Peg. "Where's Henry?" she asked.

"He went down to the barn to give his horse an apple before he comes to the lodge," Carolina said, "claiming he's going to make the most of his temporary freedom."

They continued into the lodge, and Sam already had the TV pulled away from the wall and was looking in the closet. "Here," Olivia said, setting the box on the stand. "You hook the box to the TV and I'll get the cable. I have it taped to the bottom of one of the shelves so Eileen wouldn't find it."

Ezra sat down on one of the leather couches with his mug of coffee, and Peg sat down beside him and patted his knee. "Is this the most exciting place you can think of going on your day off?" she drawled.

"That you, Peg?" Ezra asked. "I didn't recognize you without your kids."

Henry came running in and hopped up on Carolina's lap when she sat down next to Ezra. "Where are Peter and Jacob?" he asked Peg. "I thought I was going to get to play with them for a while before I have to go back to my room."

"Sorry, half-pint, they're at their Memere's until Inglenook starts back up."

"Oh, shoot," Olivia muttered. "I forgot the remote."

"Don't bother going after it," Sam said. He straightened to push a few buttons on the satellite box. "I'll do it manually. Do you know what channel the news is on?"

"In the two hundreds," she told him, sitting down in one of the overstuffed chairs.

Everyone suddenly went silent and Sam stepped away in surprise at the images on the screen of sandy beaches littered with massive nets and fishing gear.

"Sweet Athena," Carolina whispered, clutching Henry. "What has he done?"

"No one can explain the phenomenon," the news commentator said as the camera zoomed in on one particularly gruesome tangle of fishing line. The lens panned up the length of it, showing dead and dying fish, birds, and a large sea turtle undulating in a macabre dance as each wave pushed them farther up on shore. "But this scene at a resort in Rio de Janeiro is being repeated in just about every coastal country across the globe, from the northern Pacific to the southern Atlantic to the Indian Ocean. And now you're seeing the view from an affiliate's traffic helicopter as it flies along the beach south of Miami. And that's the white cliffs of Dover. And now San Francisco Bay . . . Borneo . . . Japan . . . India; it's the same everywhere. Broken and abandoned monofilament longlines and nets, and crab and lobster traps teeming with almost every species of fish, bird, and ocean mammal are washing onto the beaches, with more being carried ashore on each incoming tide."

The image went back to a close-up of a large white bird, its mouth gaping open in death as a thin fishing line disappeared down its throat. "Oceanographers," the commentator continued, "are trying to understand what's happening. We have Frank Dieter, an expert on ocean currents, here with us now. Dr. Dieter, can you tell us how something like this can be happening at the same time all over the globe?"

"That's just it," he said, shaking his head as he stared at the images on the monitor in front of him. "It *can't* be happening. Ocean currents are for the most part circular. This junk—some of which shouldn't even float—would travel parallel to the shoreline instead of toward it. Unless there was a hurricane or typhoon that brought debris in with the storm surge, this shouldn't be happening, especially not on so many beaches, all within the last twenty-four hours. It's simply impossible."

"Apparently not," the newsman said against the backdrop of a group of people trying to free a live dolphin. The poor animal was stuck in a tattered old net, its flesh cut and bleeding in places as others poured seawater over its body.

"Excuse me," Olivia whispered, standing up and rushing to the kitchen. And then she just barely made it outside before she threw up behind one of the bushes beside the porch. She stumbled over to the outside spigot and splashed water on her face and rinsed her mouth, then used her sleeve to shakily dry off.

She usually had an iron-clad stomach, except she'd swear that the dead bird with the gaping pink beak had been an albatross. And all those poor fish and dolphins and turtles caught in nets that had broken free to continue fishing unattended.

"Are you okay?" Carolina asked as she approached with Henry, their expressions somber.

"I'm fine," Olivia said, giving her face another wipe. She winced. "I guess I don't have the stomach to watch any more of that."

"This is actually a good thing," Carolina said. "I believe people are being made aware of what's been going on far out at sea for a very long time now, and this may finally force new fishing techniques to be put in place." She snorted. "There's nothing like the stench of dead fish littering posh resort beaches to raise public outcry for something to be done. It's my understanding they can make fishing gear that simply dissolves after a certain time instead of continuing to ghost fish."

"The oceans will become safe now, Miss Olivia," Henry said, his deep green eyes looking far too old for his innocent face. "It often requires something unpleasant to make people take the appropriate action." He gave a slight bow. "If you're truly okay, I believe I should return to my room so I don't have to extend my stay."

"I'm fine now, Henry," Olivia said with a forced smile as she waved him away. "Carolina, could I talk to you a minute?"

"Go on, Henry," Carolina said. "Set up the chessboard so I can trounce you again." She turned to Olivia and clasped her arm. "Please try to see what's happening as a good thing, because it is. To paraphrase Henry, sometimes it requires a good slap in the face to fight complacency."

"Where did Mac go?"

"I believe he took the albatrosses back home."

"But how?" Olivia waved toward the cabin. "His truck's still here."

Carolina lowered her lids, hooding her eyes. "I was asleep when he left, so I assume Trace Huntsman must have come up from Midnight Bay and gotten him."

"Is Mac going to see his father?"

Carolina turned away with a snort. "Not if he can help it. I believe I'll have dinner with Henry in his room tonight."

She turned and continued walking backward. "Don't worry; there's still plenty of food left over from what everyone, including Sam, sneaked to him yesterday. We'll eat like royalty for a week," she said, pivoting to jog up the lane.

Olivia shoved her hands in her pockets, only to feel Mac's cell phone. She pulled it out and stared down at it, trying to decide what she was feeling. Because if what she suspected was happening on those beaches was causing her gut to react the way it was, she should be scared to death.

But oddly, she wasn't. Instead she felt sort of prickly all over; like something . . . extraordinary was about to happen.

Rather like Mac's ESP.

But unlike Mac's ability to sense specific things like a storm coming or the ice being thin, she had no idea why she couldn't stop shivering.

What has he done? she'd heard Carolina whisper. Did Carolina also believe Mac had something to do with what was happening on the beaches? Because really, it wasn't scientifically much less humanly possible to manipulate ocean currents like that.

Olivia flipped open the phone and studied the buttons. She'd thought Mac had left her his cell phone so he could call her, but he'd been gone a day and a half now and it hadn't rung once. Hell, she'd even slept with it under her pillow.

Olivia glanced toward the lodge, then walked around the side of the garage to be out of sight. She pushed the button labeled *Contacts* and only three names appeared; Trace Huntsman, Carolina, and Father. Except there weren't any numbers for the last two names, so she couldn't even tell what state—or country—his father was in.

She stared toward Mac's truck, which she knew had Maine plates, and then slid her gaze to his cabin. What could make two grown siblings and a child fear one man so much? Titus Oceanus was their father and grandfather, for crying out loud. And really, he couldn't be that big an ogre, considering how nice Carolina and Mac had turned out.

Well, nice but really strange.

How in hell had Carolina gotten here in the middle of a snowstorm? And how had Mac left when Olivia hadn't heard a vehicle drive in or out night before last?

And where in hell were they from, anyway?

It had been one mystery after another since Mac had arrived: seat belts and doors and zippers with minds of their own, albatrosses acting as if they'd come here *looking* for Mac, and the Oceanuses' unusual fascination with magic and mythology.

And what was up with that dream she'd had, anyway? Because she'd swear she really had felt the earth breathing. And why would she have imagined a whale named Leviathan? Who named anything in their dreams? But scariest of all, why did she have this overwhelming feeling that her life was about to change forever?

You will always be completely safe with me, Mac had told her just before he'd vanished into thin air.

And she did feel safe with him. Even though he'd tilted her world completely off-center, Olivia was pretty sure he'd sent it tumbling in the right direction. And just maybe some of his confidence and solidness *had* rubbed off on her, because honestly, the last time she'd felt this certain everything was going to be okay had been when her father had shown up and swept her into his arms after her mom had died.

Rather like Mac had the day Mark Briar had attacked her.

But would Mac vanish into thin air in September just as her father had twenty-eight years ago? Olivia looked down at the cell phone in her hand again.

Was she ready to trust another man with her heart?

Because really, what was the worst that could happen? Well, other than getting her heart broken again. But hadn't she become an expert on repairing a broken heart, seeing how hers was still thumping along? Heck, it was even healthy enough to start racing whenever Mac looked at her with those imposingly deep green eyes of his, and nearly pound out of her chest whenever he touched her.

So . . . did she want to keep acting the mouse forever, or was she finally ready to let the tigress off its leash once and for all?

Olivia peeked around the corner of the garage, took a fortifying breath as she stared down at the phone, and pushed the button that said *Father*.

Because she just loved sticking her nose in other people's business.

It didn't even make it through a second ring. "By the gods, Maximilian, what in the name of Zeus *are you doing*?" a deep, eerily familiar voice boomed against her ear, making Olivia wince. "I swear by all that's holy I will send you to Hades with my own bare hands! You *know* to consult me before you orchestrate anything on such an epic scale. So forget explaining how you got your hands on that kind of power and just tell me where you got the gonads to do something so outrageous!"

"Um . . . I'm guessing from you," Olivia whispered.

Stark, absolute silence was all she heard for several pounding heartbeats.

"Who is this?"

"Olivia Baldwin, Mr. Oceanus. Mac and your grandson are staying at my camp for parents and their children up here in the mountains of Maine."

Silence again, and then, "May I ask what you're doing with Maximilian's phone?"

"He asked me to hold on to it while he left to go do . . . something important."

She heard a muffled snort, as if he'd covered the mike with a hand, and then all she heard was silence again.

Olivia took another deep breath. "And since I found your number programmed into his phone, I decided this would be my opportunity to invite you and your wife to come to Inglenook, so the two of you can see what we do here."

"Does Maximilian know you're inviting us?"

Olivia snorted, and she didn't even try to cover it up. "Not exactly. But Henry's quite eager to meet his grandmother, and personally, I'm quite eager to meet you."

She heard a choking sputter, and Olivia took a relieved breath. Because really, Mac's father didn't seem all that scary. "We encourage grandparents to come for the last few days of our two-week sessions, but I think you and Mrs. Oceanus might enjoy attending a *full* session with Mac and Henry and Carolina. The cabin we've given them is certainly big enough to accommodate all of you. Unless Mac has other brothers and sisters he hasn't told me about?"

"No," he said gruffly, "there's just the four of . . . I mean the *five* of us. Er, you expect us all to share the same cabin?"

"Of course. Isn't that the very essence of family? And we have all sorts of fun activities you can do together; horseback riding, canoeing, an amazing obstacle course, arts and crafts, and campfires with sing-alongs. It's a wonderful way for children and parents—and grandparents—to truly bond. Oh, and hiking. Did I mention we have some beautiful hiking trails? I especially enjoy taking families into the wilderness. So, can I put you and Mrs. Oceanus down for a session in—no, wait; I think maybe you should come to Inglenook a few days *before* camp starts up again, so we can have some private time together before the chaos starts."

He hesitated. "I would need to speak with Rana first."

"From what I understand, I believe your wife is looking forward to *finally* meeting Henry. I'm sure she'll start packing the moment you mention my invitation. *Rana* is a beautiful name. Would it happen to be Greek by any chance?"

"It's Sanskrit, actually; it means *queen*."

"How lovely. Hey, do you happen to know what *ma-REE-tah* means, or even what language it is?"

There was another long, disquieting pause. "Why do you wish to know?"

"Well, your son keeps calling me *ma-REE-tah*, only he refuses to tell me what it means. And I would at least like to know if it's a compliment or not, because honestly, he doesn't always say it like an endearment. So, have you heard it before? Or if I knew what language it is or even how to spell it, I could look it up on the Internet. And that way I could find something equally nice to call him."

"Hello?" she said when he didn't say anything. "Did we get cut off? Mr. Oceanus, are you still there?"

"My wife and I will be arriving at Inglenook tomorrow."

"Will you be arriving by *car*?" she asked, only to realize she was talking to dead air. "Or by broom?" she muttered, snapping the phone shut.

Olivia took another deep breath and threw back her shoulders, and headed back around the garage. She supposed that had gone well, considering the conversation had started out with Mac's father threatening to send him to hell with his own bare hands for orchestrating something so outrageous on such an . . . epic scale.

She stopped next to Doris's truck when she saw Ezra and Sam coming down the porch steps, both men looking troubled. "Sam," she said as they approached, "Caleb told me you spent quite a few years traveling the world. So I imagine you've heard a lot of languages?"

Because she really needed to know what *ma-REE-tah* meant before Mac got back, so she'd know whether to kiss him or punch him in his sensitive gut.

"Caleb sure does talk a lot," Sam said, his eyes suddenly guarded. "Why? You have a question about languages?"

"I was wondering if you knew what *ma-REE-tah* means, or what language it is."

His eyes narrowed as he appeared to repeat the word in his mind. "Actually, it sounds to me like it could be Latin. Which means you can look at English words that sound like it, as most of our language has Latin as its basis. Do you know its spelling?"

She shook her head. "No, I've only heard it spoken."

"Probably *m-a-r-i-t-a*, or *a-e*. Like in *marital*." He shrugged. "It likely has something to do with marriage. Where'd you hear it? In what context was it used?"

Olivia felt the hairs on the back of her neck stir in alarm. "It was just something I heard on TV. This guy kept calling a woman *ma-REE-tah*." She also shrugged, though it felt more like a shiver to her. "I hate it when they do stuff like that on television and don't bother to translate it for us."

"If you've got Internet, then Google it," Sam suggested, his eyes narrowed on her.

"Thanks, I'll do that." She gave him a forced smile. "And you be careful of Ezra here," she said, gesturing toward her friend. "Because he'll likely try to make you pay for whatever gas is still in the tank."

Ezra muttered something she couldn't quite make out before speaking up. "You going to show Sam that phone you got from Mac?" he asked. "Because I'd like to know if we really do have cell phone service up here now, so I can get my own."

"We don't," Sam said, still studying Olivia. "Mine stopped getting a signal around Turtleback Station when we came through with the horses. And I've checked out a couple of places up here on high ground, and still nothing." He held out his hand. "Let me see the phone. Ezra said he thought it was too small to be satellite, but I've seen some that were pretty compact."

Good Lord, what had this guy done in the military? "That's okay," she said, stuffing her hands in her pockets. "I'll just ask Mac when he gets back."

"Olivia," Sam said when she started toward the lodge. "If Oceanus is bothering you, I can have a little talk with him," he said quietly, his steely eyes unreadable again.

"No, I'm good." She started walking backward. "But I do thank you for offering, considering that Mac said if I needed anything while he was gone to go see you."

She certainly didn't have any problem reading Sam's surprise. "He told you to come see me?"

She shrugged. "I guess you two working on the obstacle course together the other day gave him the impression you're a go-to guy. Ezra, you'll stay for supper when you get back from Turtleback, won't you? Sophie and I will give you a ride home after."

"That would depend on what you're cooking."

"We've been barbecuing all week while Eileen's gone. How does a big juicy steak with potatoes slow-roasted in hot embers sound?"

"Wrap up a potato for me, then," Ezra said, rubbing his belly. "And Sam and I will stop and get one of Vanetta's strawberry-rhubarb pies for dessert."

Olivia turned and headed back into the lodge, wondering if the receding wave she'd been standing in since she'd met Mac wasn't about to finally suck her out to sea—even as she tried to decide if she should break the news to Carolina that her mom and dad were arriving tomorrow.

No . . . maybe she'd just let it be a surprise.

Chapter Twenty-two

Dawn cracked so loud that the windows rattled and the walls shook with the sonic boom. Sophie screamed from her bed, and Olivia raced down the hall—shedding Mac's jacket just before she ran into the bedroom.

"You're okay, sweetie," she said, sitting on the bed to hug her daughter. "That was probably just a fighter jet doing low-flight training." She smoothed down Sophie's hair, giving her a lopsided smile. "And I bet Missy Maher is already on the phone with the Pentagon, reading them the riot act again. It's still early; do you think you can catch another half hour of sleep, or would you like me to make us some oatmeal and toast?"

Sophie flopped back on her pillow and pulled the blankets up to her chin. "Can't I just stay home today? I . . . I think I'm coming down with something."

Olivia held her hand to her daughter's forehead and nodded solemnly. "Yes, I do believe you're developing a bad case of spring fever."

"Please, Mom?" Sophie whined even as she rolled her eyes. "I haven't missed one day of school since Christmas vacation. And Henry's getting out of his room this morning, and I haven't seen him for three whole days. Mr. Sam said when Henry's done doing hard time that he'd take us riding so I can show him some of the trails." The girl even went so far as to bat her eyelashes. "And you and I could go on a picnic, just the two of us, before Gram and Grampy get home today."

Olivia sighed, wishing Henry were here to see another pro in action. She tucked Sophie's blankets snugly around her, then used them to pin her in place. "I'll let you miss school just today, just this *once*." She canted her head. "In fact, I hereby declare two days each year—one in the fall and one in the spring—as official Sophie Gets to Skip School Days."

The girl's eyes widened. "Honestly really? I can skip school twice a year without even being sick?"

"Yup. And you get to pick the days, and we'll do anything you want."

"Um . . . since I didn't get a free day last fall, can I have another one this spring?"

Olivia stood up with a laugh. "Sorry, only one official skip day a semester. So decide if you want it to be today or not. If you do, we can take a couple hours to go on a picnic, and Carolina and Henry can go with us if you want. But I'm expecting some mystery guests to arrive this afternoon, so we need to be back by . . . oh, I'd say by three at the latest. Gram and Grampy should get home around then, too."

"Then I declare *today* my official Sophie Gets to Skip School Day," the girl said, snuggling back under the covers. "And so is it okay for Henry and me to go riding with Sam this morning?"

"Yes, as long as you invite Carolina to go with you."

"Mom," Sophie said, stopping Olivia at the hallway. "I declare that you're the best mom in the whole wide world."

Olivia's heart started thumping so hard it hurt. "Thanks, sweetie. That means a lot coming from the best daughter in the whole wide world."

She picked up the jacket she'd shed in the hall and headed to the kitchen, Sophie's words making her feel warm and fuzzy and prickly all over—much the same way she felt in Mac's arms. Olivia stopped in the middle of the kitchen and slipped on his jacket with a shiver, being careful *not* to zip it as she remembered how she'd gone on the Internet last night and looked up *marita.*

Then, somewhat dazed by what she'd found, she'd typed in *theurgist.*

Sweet Prometheus and Athena, she was in big, big trouble, because she had absolutely no business falling in love with an honest-to-God seat belt- and zipper- and tide-commanding supernatural agent of human affairs—better known as a wizard.

Except she already was so deeply and passionately in love with Mac, Olivia didn't even care if he could only just *like* her enough to get married, because she had more than enough love for the both of them.

And that was a good thing, seeing how Mac was already calling her *wife*—which, come to think of it, was really quite arrogant of him since she couldn't remember his ever proposing. But she did remember telling him—twice, actually—that she wasn't interested in being another man's means of getting a demanding parent off his back.

So now what was she supposed to do? Should she pretend to keep her promise not to fall in love with him, and hope he didn't hear her heart shattering when he left in September? Though she was pretty sure she'd spend the summer making a complete fool of herself by wearing her big old sappy heart on her sleeve. She really wasn't much of an actress and Mac *was* a theurgist, so if the man couldn't even figure out she was passionately in love with him, then he might want to start looking for a new profession.

Oh yeah, she was in really big trouble, because if Mac asked her to marry him and move to Midnight Bay . . . well, she was going to say yes.

After all, there wasn't any reason she couldn't open up a family camp on the coast, was there? And when push came to shove, wasn't *she* what constituted a home for Sophie, not some tract of land and a bunch of crooked old buildings?

Only she couldn't leave unless Ezra was willing to sell his store and move to Midnight Bay with them. But if picking up and starting over again at his age was going to be too much for the old poop . . . well, she'd just have to—

The bell at the gate clanged loudly, making Olivia jump in surprise. She ran to the door and looked out the window, then turned to press her back up against the wall with a gasp. "Ohmigod," she whispered, clutching her chest. She leaned over to peek out the window again and groaned. That had to be Mr. and Mrs. Oceanus, because only Mac and Carolina's parents could be that beautiful.

What in hell were they doing here at the crack of dawn?

She stilled. That hadn't been a sonic boom; that had been her guests arriving!

Olivia flinched when the bell clanged again, only louder and for a really long time.

Since she couldn't very well leave them standing out there, she opened the door, stepped out onto her stoop with a welcoming smile, and calmly walked toward them.

God, they were beautiful. And if Mac was tall and imposing and commanding, Titus Oceanus was flat-out scary. Rana, however, was simply drop-dead stunning.

Olivia's smile faltered under their intense scrutiny, as she figured Titus probably already had her pegged as a gold digger, and Rana was trying to find out if Olivia was worthy of her son. Why in heaven's name had she asked Mac's father if he knew why his son called her *marita*? No wonder the man had dropped everything to be here today; he needed to check out the woman Mac had obviously chosen to replace his hand-chosen bride.

"Good morning," she said, extending her hand. "I'm Olivia Baldwin. And I can see by the resemblance that you are Mr. and Mrs. Oceanus."

Mr. Oceanus didn't so much as move a muscle, his arms remaining folded over his chest as he merely arched a brow—rather like Mac did way too often.

Mrs. Oceanus grabbed Olivia's hand, only instead of shaking it she clasped it between her own. "Please call us

Rana and Titus, Olivia," she said warmly, her smile genuine. "I'm so glad you invited us to visit. I'm really excited to meet Henry."

"You're in for quite a treat. Your grandson is positively precious."

"Where is he?" Rana asked, still clutching Olivia's hand as she looked around.

"Over there, in cabin ten," she said, gesturing through the trees. "Probably still sleeping." She slapped her forehead, looking directly at Titus. "What am I saying; dawn just cracked loud enough to wake the dead."

And there was it was: that distinct Oceanus gleam in those vivid green eyes—despite his attempt to give her a threatening glower. "Please have someone get our luggage," he said, turning away. "It's sitting on the front steps of your main building."

And why was she surprised it wasn't sitting in the trunk of a car?

Olivia shot out through the gate to cut him off. "We don't have bellhops at Inglenook," she said, having to walk backward when he didn't stop.

But just as she lifted her hand to physically stop him, Olivia cried out when her foot landed on a sharp pebble, and she would have fallen if Titus hadn't caught her. "Ohmigod," she squeaked when he swept her into his arms and plastered her up against his big broad chest.

He sighed hard enough to actually move her hair. "Do you not have the sense to put on shoes before coming outside?" He reversed direction and started carrying her back toward her house. "And what is this you're wearing?" he asked, his gaze moving over her flannel pajama pants to Mac's jacket—which she'd nervously zipped up as she'd walked out to greet them.

"This old thing?" she said, plucking at the leather. "It's your son's jacket. He's letting me . . . um, borrow it while he's gone."

He stopped, presumably because he couldn't walk and

talk and lift a brow at the same time. "It would appear you've been enjoying Maximilian's generosity."

"Oh yeah, your son's the gift that keeps on giving even when he's not here. See," she said, straightening her right leg to pull up her pajama pant. "He gave me this on our first date. You don't happen to know how the clasp works, do you?"

Olivia felt him stiffen, and half expected a bolt of lightning to shoot out of the sky and strike her dead. But really, having lived practically in Eileen's pocket for eleven years, she had no intention of ever tiptoeing around another in-law again.

Titus demanded her attention by giving her a good squeeze—only now his dark, imposing green eyes were completely unreadable.

Olivia lifted her leg again. "Would you happen to know *why* it hasn't got a clasp?"

It was Rana who finally gave her an answer. "It's a symbol of Maximilian's protection," she explained with a warm smile. "As long as you're wearing it, no one would dare harm you."

Oh God, Mac had enemies? "Thank . . . thank you for telling me."

But then Olivia became contrite. This poor woman was dying to meet her grandson, and here she was trying to get a handle on Mac's father. "You can put me down now," she told Titus, drawing his scowl away from his wife. She smiled. "I know you're big and strong like your son, but I also happen to know I weigh slightly more than a feather." She sighed when he didn't move. "Or you can finish carrying me home and I'll toss on some boots and take you to your cabin so your wife can *finally* meet Henry."

"Titus," Rana said quietly.

He started walking again, only instead of heading toward her house he turned and headed for the cabin.

God, she hoped Mac's father didn't throw out his back carrying her.

"Olivia. Wait up."

Titus stopped and turned again, and Olivia saw Sam making his way toward them at a limping run. "Please put me down," she asked. "I'll watch where I'm walking."

He finally set her on her feet just as Sam reached them. "You need to get everyone to the lodge," Sam said, surprisingly not the least bit winded. "It seems to be the sturdiest building here and it's on the highest ground. Don't let Sophie go to school, and call Peg and tell her to bring all her kids to Inglenook. Then call Ezra and tell him to forget about opening the store and just come here."

Olivia grabbed his sleeve. "But what's going on?"

"I was listening to the radio in the barn and it seems there's a bad storm headed this way. The weatherman said it slammed into the coast around midnight last night, and is already about fifty miles north of Bangor. They're saying it's the most powerful nor'easter they've ever seen, and it's moving inland at about thirty miles an hour. That gives us only a few hours to prepare. When you get to the lodge, turn on the television and see what they're saying on the news."

Sam then looked at Titus and Rana, Rana now clutching her husband's arm as Titus had grown unusually still. "You're Mac's parents," Sam said in surprise. He looked around, then back at Titus. "How'd you get here? I've been in the barn since before sunrise and I didn't see or hear anyone drive up the road."

"You must have been occupied when we arrived," Titus said quietly. "This storm, was it not predicted?"

Sam shook his head. "The weatherman said it just suddenly appeared on their radar, forming in the Gulf of Maine instead of farther south like usual." He looked at Olivia. "I'm going to make sure everything's battened down, and I'll put the van in the garage. There's a good chance we'll lose power for several days if it's as bad as they're claiming. Most of the downeast coast has been without power for hours now."

"Sweet Athena! Mama! Father!" Carolina cried from the

porch of her cabin. She ran down the stairs as she belted her robe. "What are you doing here?" she whispered when she reached them. She clutched her mother's arm. "Why didn't you war—tell me you were coming?"

"We wanted to surprise Henry," Rana explained. "Is he awake? Oh, please, take me to him, Caro."

"Wife," Titus said as the two women started off. "You will not dally. Get the boy up and just as soon as he and Carolina are dressed, you go to the lodge as Olivia's father has instructed."

Olivia gave a startled laugh when she saw Sam go deathly pale. "Oh, I'm sorry," she told Titus. "This isn't my father; he's our horse wrangler, Sam Waters. Sam, this is Mac's father, Titus. And . . . um, that's his mother, Rana," she said, waving toward the cabin just as the two women disappeared inside.

"This isn't your father?" Titus asked tightly, his gaze narrowing on Sam.

"No," she said. "I've been an orphan since my mother died when I was four."

Titus slid his gaze to her, his eyes unreadable again, and gave a slight bow. "If you will excuse me then, I believe I will go hurry my family down to the main house. Mr. Waters," he added with a nod before turning away.

"Sorry about that, Sam," Olivia said, giving his arm a playful nudge. She started toward home. "I wonder if John and Eileen will be able to make it back from Boston ahead of the storm," she said conversationally when he merely fell into step beside her.

He glanced over at her. "They told you they were going to Boston?"

"Eileen went there looking for interns. She and John usually check out different universities every year around this time."

He stopped at the gate. "If you don't mind, I'm going to go use the lodge phone and call Ezra and give him a heads-up on the storm. But you can call Peg." Sam shook his head.

"After seeing her house when we took her home the other night, I'd feel better if she brought her family here."

Olivia looked through the trees toward the upper parking lot, trying to see the horizon. "Do you really believe the storm is going to get that bad?"

"I have no idea, but I'm in the habit of preparing for worst-case scenarios. You really think your old man is dead?"

She looked at him in surprise then shrugged. "I figure he must be, since I haven't heard from him since I was five."

"But you told Titus you've been an orphan since you were *four*."

"My mom died when I was four, and I was raised by foster parents." She grinned. "And by Ezra and Doris Dodd. They've been more like parents to me than anyone else for as long as I can remember. In fact, when I turned eighteen and was no longer a ward of the state, they opened their home to me. Doris decorated a bedroom up all fancy and girly, and I spent every Christmas and Thanksgiving and all my school breaks with them. And then, because they just couldn't live without me, they sold their home and moved to Spellbound Falls when I married Keith Baldwin."

"Ezra mentioned you've been the apple of his eye all your life."

"And he'll be mine until the day he dies, just like Doris was," she said thickly. She looked around and blew out a heavy sigh. "He's the only reason I'm staying in Spellbound Falls."

She saw Sam stiffen again. "You're here for Ezra? Not for Inglenook and Sophie and your in-laws?"

She snorted. "Yeah, I just love living a stone's throw away from my mother-in-law." She shook her head. "Look, don't let my bias influence your dealings with Eileen, okay? I simply don't see eye to eye with her on several things."

"Is that your late husband's jacket?" he asked, nodding at her.

"No," she said with a surprised laugh, "it's Mac's. And I *swear* I'm going to return it the minute he gets back. I just grabbed it off the peg when I ran out the door this morning." She started toward home, walking backward. "Oh, and just so you know, Sam: You don't need to stop at the gate. That's for guests. You want to see me, you come to my door. I'll get Sophie up and go start breakfast right after I call Peg. The keys are in the van ignition. And thanks for caring about Inglenook enough to batten down the hatches."

"I'm not doing it for Inglenook," he muttered, waving over his shoulder as he limped away.

Chapter Twenty-three

The storm slammed into Inglenook with the force of a small hurricane around midmorning, but the earthquakes were what really had everyone rattled. Up until half an hour ago when the power had gone out, the small band of refugees had all been sitting in the main room of the lodge watching the news. Everyone, even the children, had listened in shock to the reports on what appeared to be one long series of earthquakes that had started at the coast and were slowly rumbling inland toward the mountains. But for some unexplained reason, the newsman had said, the only shifting the scientists could detect was deep underground.

Well, except for several lakes in the earthquake's path. As images of the storm flashed across the screen, the newsman had gone on to say that four lakes appeared to have turned salty. He'd then brought on a panel of experts who speculated that the earthquake seemed to have split open the bottom of each of the lakes in succession. And like a plug being pulled on a bathtub all the fresh water had drained out, only to be replaced by an underground river surging in from the Gulf of Maine. Then just before the power had flickered off for the last time, they'd reported that the earthquake had just claimed a fifth lake not thirty miles south of Bottomless.

Peg and her children, Ezra, Sam, the Oceanuses, and Olivia and Sophie had sat motionless in the storm-darkened room for several minutes, the silence broken only by the gale-force winds battering the windows with rain.

And that was when the lodge had first shivered on its foundation.

Within twenty minutes those shivers had turned to deep rumbling tremors that rattled the dishes in the cupboards and made the pine-log walls creak and groan with increasing frequency.

Olivia wondered if the Oceanuses were enjoying their visit. "Well," she said into the silence, standing up. "I think we should build a fire in the hearth so Henry can teach his Gram and Grampy how to make s'mores." She looked at Sam. "There's firewood on the back porch."

Sam also stood up. "If the tremors crack the mortar on that old stone chimney and it crumbles, we could end up burning this place down."

Olivia sighed. "Good point. Okay then," she said, rubbing her hands together excitedly as she smiled at the unusually quiet, wide-eyed children sitting in every available adult lap. "I guess we'll have to make the s'mores on the kitchen range."

"We can take turns," Peg said, setting Peter—or Jacob—on his feet and standing up. "And while we're each waiting our turn, we can sit at the kitchen table and color. Didn't I see paper and crayons in the closet?" she asked Olivia.

Olivia nodded and held her hand out to Henry, who was cuddled up on his grandmother's lap on the couch. "Come on, young Mr. Oceanus. Let's show your Gram how to make your new favorite treat."

He clung to Rana, his eyes filling with terror when the lodge gave another violent shudder. "I want my dad," he whispered. "He promised to protect me from the demons."

Olivia dropped to her knees in front of him. "Oh, baby, nothing's going to get you. You're perfectly safe here with us. And don't forget your Grampy's here. Didn't you tell me he's just as big and strong and powerful as your dad?"

Henry darted a worried glance at Titus and then threw himself at Olivia. "But I want *Dad*!" he wailed, hugging her tightly. "He promised."

"Easy, honey," she crooned, cupping his head buried in her neck. "Your daddy's on his way here right now." She leaned back but had to pry him away so he'd see her smile. "Didn't I tell you he would move heaven and earth and any mountains that got in his way to get to you?" she asked. "That's what all this shaking is about, Henry. It's just your dad coming for you."

He blinked at her. "You think it's *him*?"

She nodded. "And you know why he's putting on this ridiculous show?"

"Why?" he asked, his eyes now wide with awe instead of terror.

"Because he feels so bad about making you stay in your room for three days, he's out there rearranging a few of the mountains just to prove how much he loves you."

Henry went back to clutching her neck when the house shook again. "But he just has to *tell* me he loves me! He's never said it once." He reared back when the shaking stopped, and darted another quick glance at his grandfather before looking at her again. "He doesn't have to waste his powers on moving mountains, Miss Olivia; he just has to *say it*. Mama used to tell me she loved me all the time."

Olivia gave him a lopsided grin. "That's a mama thing, Henry. Dads are better at *showing* their love." She stood up and took his hand and headed for the kitchen. "So every time the house shakes, you'll know he's one step closer to you."

"Gram, come on," Henry said over his shoulder. "We're going to make s'mores. You come too, Grampy. I just know you're going to love them."

"Henry," Carolina hissed as she caught up with them. "You need to address him as *Grandfather*."

"No, I don't. Dad said I should call him *Grampy*."

Olivia stopped inside the pantry and started handing him

supplies. "You want to know a secret, Henry?" she whispered even as she winked at Carolina standing in the doorway. "He just pretends he doesn't like for you to call him *Grampy* because he doesn't want people to know he's got a big old sappy heart."

"But what's wrong with having a big heart?"

"Well, I think theurgists have to *act* scary so people won't keep pestering them to use their magic for all sorts of meaningless things."

"I hadn't thought of that." Henry gave Carolina an uncertain look. "Do you think that's why Grampy scowls so much?"

"You know, little man, I believe it is," Carolina said, lifting her gaze to Olivia. "And it seems to have worked quite well for him for a very long time."

"Then maybe we shouldn't tell anyone he's really nice," Henry whispered. "And I'll call him *Grandfather* when other people are around and *Grampy* when it's just us."

Peg popped her head around the corner. "I just realized why everyone's falling all over themselves to come to Inglenook," she said, shaking her head. "I can't believe you just turned a scary situation into something exciting for the kids. Now Pete and Repeat and Isabel have their noses glued to the windows, hoping to be the first one to see the mountains moving."

"Yup, that's why they pay us the big bucks," Olivia said with a laugh, shooing everyone out of the pantry ahead of her.

Other than the escalating storm and the tremors that grew more frequent as the morning dragged into afternoon, it could have been an ordinary day at Inglenook as everyone settled down at the large kitchen table to color and eat popcorn while taking turns making s'mores. Well, everyone except Sam, who kept going out to check the horses and make sure none of the cabins had blown away. At least that was what he told Olivia he was doing. But she suspected Sam felt better equipped to handle the weather outside than the boisterous storm of children inside, especially after Isabel asked him to help her fold a newspaper into a hat.

Apparently they didn't teach arts and crafts in Sam's branch of the military.

And seeing that everyone was fully occupied, Olivia finally escaped into one of the back meeting rooms to have herself a good little cry. Because really, she didn't know which disconcerted her more: that it might truly be Mac raising havoc on Maine, or that she missed him so much her heart hurt.

How in hell could she have fallen in love with him so quickly?

Unless . . . ohmigod, what if he'd used his *magic* on her!

No, that was just plain foolish. If Mac had that kind of dastardly power he'd have used it a long time ago and on a more beautiful, more confident, sexier, and hell of a lot braver woman than she was.

"Olivia."

And why in hell was he messing with Mother Nature, anyway? Lakes were supposed to be full of *fresh* water, not little oceans. He was going to completely ruin the area's already precarious tourist industry. People went to the coast to see whales, and to the mountains to hike and camp and hunt.

"Olivia."

Really, someone had to go out there and stop the crazy man.

Olivia turned to head back to the main room, only to run straight into a big broad chest. She turned away with a gasp, afraid Mac's father would see she'd been crying. "Um . . . if you're looking for the restroom it's two more doors down," she said, trying to surreptitiously wipe her face with her sleeve.

"I was looking for you. I would ask if you happen to know what Maximilian is doing, and why."

Fairly certain she'd wiped away all her tears, Olivia turned back to him. "Here's the thing: I don't know who or what he *is* much less what he's doing."

"My son may have his flaws, but lack of honor is not one of them. He would never marry a woman without explaining to her not only who he is but *what* he is."

"Yeah, well, that's another thing. You see, despite his calling me *marita*, I'm not actually his wife."

Up went that imperial brow. "Then what are you to him, actually?"

Olivia hugged herself. "I thought I was his girlfriend," she said, wondering how a person went about having such an intimate discussion with her lover's father. "I thought my deal with Mac was to have a no-strings affair that would end in September when he went back to Midnight Bay. He's supposed to buy a house there and get serious about searching for a wife he only has to *like* well enough to win your approval."

"And you?" Titus quietly asked. "Were you simply going to thank my son for his time and attention, and wish him well as he walked away?"

Feeling tears threatening again, Olivia turned to stare out the rain-spattered window. "That was our deal."

"Only you fell in love with him instead."

She pulled in a shuddering breath. "I promised him I wouldn't."

He turned her around, his warm, solid hands on her shoulders. "Would you care for some advice from a supposedly wise old man, Olivia?" he asked. "As I would like to suggest that you close off your mind long enough to hear what your heart has to say about all this." He lifted her chin. "I assure you that Maximilian is letting his own heart guide him right now. No man moves heaven and earth because he only *likes* a woman well enough to marry her."

Olivia gasped. "He's not doing this for *me*." She pulled away and turned to face the window again. "This has something to do with three lost albatrosses and the fishing gear on the beaches, and—" She spun to face him. "This has nothing to do with me." She gestured at the windows. "Who in their right mind destroys an entire state for somebody? My God, he's turned freshwater lakes into *oceans*." She shook her head. "He's trying to make a point about something, so everyone will sit up and take notice."

"He's definitely trying to make someone take notice,"

he murmured, heading for the door. "Come, Olivia. I believe there are more people arriving."

Olivia stared at the door he disappeared through, wondering if Titus wasn't as crazy as his son. Because instead of just sitting here while the world was collapsing around them, why wasn't he out there *stopping* Mac?

"Gram! Grampy! You made it home," she heard Sophie holler.

Olivia headed down the hall at a run, equally surprised that they'd made it back to Inglenook. Only she came to a screeching halt when she saw the woman standing beside John and Eileen—as well as the little boy in John's arms.

Eileen straightened from hugging Sophie and turned the girl toward John. "Sophie, I want you to meet—"

"No!" Olivia shouted, rushing over and pulling her daughter away while giving Eileen a warning glare. "Not one word," she growled to her shocked mother-in-law.

Olivia turned to look for Ezra, only to flinch when Sam stepped forward and wrapped his arm around her shoulders—his dark steely eyes locked on hers. "I guess you do know," he said tightly. "Ezra, take Sophie into one of the back rooms and stay with her," he instructed. "Sophie, you go with him, okay?" he said more gently. "Your mom will be along in a couple of minutes."

"But I don't under—"

"Go with Ezra, baby," Olivia said, giving her a nudge. "I'll explain later."

"Really, Livy," Eileen hissed, grabbing Olivia's shoulder to turn her around.

Only Sam stepped between them. "You've got some balls bringing her here without warning," he said, nodding at the woman all but hiding behind John now.

Eileen flushed with anger. "Who do you think you are, speaking to me like that?"

So shocked by what Sam was doing, it took Olivia a few seconds to gather her wits before she stepped around him and got right in Eileen's face. "I'm the one who should be asking that question. What in hell were you *thinking*? You don't introduce an eight-year-old child to a half brother she didn't even know existed without preparing her first. And you sure as hell don't do it without consulting her *mother*," she said, slapping her own chest. "I'm the one who decides when and how to tell Sophie that her precious daddy wasn't quite the hero she thought he was. And you, John," she said, rounding on him. "You should be ashamed of yourself for letting Eileen do this to Sophie and me."

Olivia then looked at the boy in John's arms—who had Keith Baldwin's bright blue eyes and sandy-brown hair—and started shaking again. She slid her gaze to Jessica Pilsner. "I suggest you take your son upstairs before he becomes anymore confused." And then she rounded on Sam. "Who *are* you? And how in hell do you know anything about this?"

But before he could answer, the cell phone in Olivia's pocket rang, making her nearly jump out of her skin. She pulled it out and flipped it open. "Hello," she snapped.

There were several heartbeats of silence. "I want you to come to me, Olivia."

"Yeah well, I'm sort of busy right now, Mac. So I guess you're going to have to come to me."

There was a longer, more ominous pause. "Now, *marita*," he quietly growled.

"You know what, you sound just like your *father*. And by the way, did you happen to notice there's a hurricane and an earthquake going on right *now*," she growled right back at him.

Another pause, this one so loaded with tension she'd swear she could hear Mac's heart beating. "How would you know what my father sounds like?"

Olivia darted a glance at Titus, only to see him . . . good Lord, the man was smiling. She turned away from her gaping audience. "The next time you leave me your cell phone, you might want to erase any contacts you don't want me calling. Who is Sam, Mac? Because telling me to go to him if I need help implies you know more about him than I do."

"I'm sort of busy right now," he drawled—though she

could hear the edge in his voice. "We will discuss this when you get here."

Olivia took a calming breath. "Where are you?"

"On top of the cliff that rises up from Whisper Lake to overlook Bottomless."

"Are you insane?" she cried into the phone, only to dart a glance over her shoulder before shielding her mouth with her hand. "Mac, there's a *hurricane* going on outside. And it'll be dark by the time I get there—assuming a tree doesn't fall on me."

"Are you still wearing the bracelet?"

She merely snorted.

"Then you will get here safely. But I need for you to come to me, *marita*."

Olivia closed her eyes on a sigh. Really, men were so damned *needy*.

"Be brave, Olivia, and come watch me truly rock your world."

"Ohmigod, you translated my inscription. Hello? Mac? Dammit, don't you dare hang up on me!"

Olivia slowly turned around as she closed the phone and slipped it into her pocket. "Um . . . Peg, do you think you could hold down the fort for a little while?"

Her eyes filled with confusion, Peg silently nodded.

"John, I think you better take Miss Pilsner and her son and Eileen upstairs to wait out the rest of the storm. We'll talk when I get back."

She started for the hallway leading to the meeting rooms, but had to grab the back of a chair when a deep rumbling tremor shook the house, causing the timber trusses supporting the roof to groan. Something crashed to the floor in the kitchen, sending the children scrambling into the main room with cries for their mother.

"No, you don't have to be afraid," Henry said, running into the room after them. "It's just my dad coming for me."

"Come on, you little heathens," Peg said, herding them back into the kitchen with Carolina and Rana's help. "Let's go make some more popcorn."

"Will someone please tell me what's going on here?" Eileen demanded, though it was Olivia she was glaring at. "Whoever heard of a storm and an earthquake hitting at the same time?" She angrily gestured toward the ceiling. "The last thing we need is for this place to fall apart before the new owners take possession."

Olivia had to grab the chair again, but suspected she was the only one who'd just felt the earth move. "You . . . you *sold* Inglenook?"

"Well, we didn't think we'd find a buyer so soon," Eileen said, her face flushing with chagrin. "And we planned to tell you as soon as we got back from our trip, so you could start sending out résumés to facilities like this one in California. I've found several camps that aren't too far from where we'll be living."

"California?" Olivia whispered, looking at Jessica Pilsner, then back at Eileen. "You're moving to California?"

Eileen nodded. "We planned to leave in September whether Inglenook sold or not, but the real estate agent said the new owners want to take immediate possession so they can start construction as soon as the ground is ready. So we're going to have to start calling our guests to tell them we're closing." She shrugged. "It'll be tight in the house we've rented, but you and Sophie can stay with us until you find a—"

"Enough," Olivia snapped, holding up her hand. "One, I have no intention of moving to California with you. And two, I don't have time to deal with any of this right now. Go upstairs, Eileen." She pointed at her gaping mother-in-law. "And you stay away from my daughter."

That said, Olivia turned and walked down the hall, glancing in each door before finding Ezra and Sophie in the last meeting room.

"Mom," Sophie cried, throwing herself at Olivia. "What's going on? How come you got so mad at Gram and made me leave?"

Olivia gave Ezra a thankful smile and got down on her knees to be at eye level with Sophie. "First, I want to thank you for going with Ezra without making a fuss. You're becoming a very wise young woman, sweetie, to know when to stand and fight and when to quietly slip away. And second, I was angry at Gram because she was going to tell you something you should be hearing from me. So that's why I shouted at her to stop, and then asked you to come back here with Ezra."

"What are you supposed to tell me?"

Olivia hugged Sophie to her. "I'm afraid it's going to have to wait until I get back, baby." She leaned away to smile at her. "But I promise it's not something bad or anything to worry about." She canted her head. "Actually, knowing you, I think you're going to find some of it way cool. But the third thing I want to tell you is that I have to go away for a few hours. I should be back by midnight at the latest."

"But it's storming out and the ground keeps shaking. A tree could fall on the van or something. Can't you wait until the storm is over?"

"I can't, sweetie. Mac's stuck up in the woods and I need to go help him find his way back." She smoothed down Sophie's hair. "He's just on the other side of Whisper Lake, and I know the path really well and there's still plenty of daylight left." She bobbed her eyebrows. "And I'm not going to melt from a little rain. But I need you to help Peg. You're going to have to be *me* while I'm gone, and play hostess to the Oceanuses." She gave the girl's shoulders a squeeze. "And you don't go upstairs to see Gram, and you do whatever Ezra says. Understand? Can you be patient just a little while longer?"

The girl nodded hesitantly, her eyes concerned and very confused.

Olivia hugged her again. "I promise, when I get back you and I are going home and making hot cocoa, and we'll cuddle up on the couch and have a nice little mother-daughter chat," she whispered, giving her a ferocious squeeze. "Everything's going to be okay, Sophie, because you and I are an unbeatable team."

"You'll be careful going after Mr. Mac?" she asked against Olivia's hair. "And you promise not to get lost?"

"I lose campers," Olivia said with a laugh, pulling away and standing up. "But I always know *my* way home." She walked to Sam standing at the door, his rain slicker on and holding another one in his hand, and shook her head. "I'm going alone."

"I go with you or you're not going at all." He stepped closer. "I'll lock you in the cellar if I have to."

She looked directly into his steel-gray eyes. "I have no idea who you are or what you're doing here, much less why you're so concerned about me and Soph—" Olivia took a step back, so dizzy she had to grab Ezra to steady herself. "Ohmigod, no!" she cried, stumbling away from the suddenly familiar eyes of the man who had abandoned her twenty-eight years ago. She turned to go after her daughter. "Sophie—"

Only she was spun back around, Sam's grip unbreakable. "It's not what you think," he said tightly. "*I loved you too much* to come back for you. My job made our being together impossible and could have gotten you killed."

"You think being raised by strangers and feeling abandoned was *better*?"

His grip tightened against her struggles. "I didn't leave you with strangers; I left you with my parents," he said thickly, nodding toward Ezra.

Olivia's knees buckled. Sam kept her from falling and helped her to a nearby chair, where she buried her face in her hands, utterly insensate.

"Mom?" Sophie said, making Olivia flinch. "What's he talking about?"

"Ohmigod, baby," she said, turning her back to the men as she pulled Sophie protectively against her. "It's okay. Really. I just had a bit of a shock. Change of plans, Sophie. Henry's grandparents are going to look after you, okay?"

She stood up and stiffly led her daughter past Sam without looking at him. Reeling from the realization that Ezra and Doris were her *grandparents*, she continued into the hall even as Ezra whispered her name, fearing she'd lose what little control she had left.

She found Titus standing alone in the main room, watching the door closing on the stairs leading up to John and Eileen's private quarters, and walked over to him. "I have a few favors to ask of you," she said without preamble, drawing his concern. "First, would you and your wife look after my daughter while I go get Mac?"

"Certainly," he said with a slight bow, giving Sophie a warm smile.

Olivia bent to hug her daughter. "Sweetie, go in the kitchen and help Miss Peg and Carolina now, okay? Remember, you're the hostess while I'm gone. You know where everything is and how everything works." She kissed her cheek. "I won't be gone long, I promise."

Sophie threw her arms around her. "You have to stop at home first and put on your hiking boots. And take your headlamp in case you don't get back before dark."

"Good idea. I'll do that. Now go on. I need to talk to Mac's dad. I love you, baby," she said, nudging the girl on her way. She straightened, waiting until Sophie disappeared into the kitchen before turning to Titus. "Two more favors and a question."

He silently nodded.

"I assume you can manipulate locks like your son can, so could you please make sure Sam doesn't follow me?"

"It's already done, Olivia. They'll be in that same room when you get back."

"Okay. Thanks. And could you make sure Eileen doesn't get anywhere near Sophie while I'm gone?"

"Done. And your question?"

God, the man was scary calm. "Um, I guess I'm just curious as to why you aren't stopping Mac from doing what he's doing."

"Because I've been waiting centuries for a woman like you to come into his life. And truthfully, I was beginning to fear it would never happen."

"A woman like me?"

"I'm not stopping Maximilian because I would be doing the same thing in his shoes." He chuckled, nodding toward the kitchen. "I pulled more than one crazy stunt to impress that beautiful woman in there, trying to persuade her to marry me." He touched Olivia's hair. "And now, for the first time in his life, Maximilian is experiencing the full force of true passion. My son has spent his entire life fighting his destiny, drifting in a sea of indifference in search of a reason to care. That is until he met you."

"But I'm *nobody*."

"Ah, Olivia, it's the perceived nobodies who have the power to move mountains."

"But Mac is destroying an entire state with his . . . his passion. You don't think ruining beautiful lakes and a good part of Maine's economy is a little extreme?"

Titus shrugged. "Change is the one constant in the universe and the price of progress. There's nothing to say altering the ecosystems of a few lakes won't in fact prove beneficial in the long run."

The lodge shook on its foundations violently enough that books fell off shelves.

Titus grasped her shoulders. "Be brave, Olivia. Have the courage to love my son for *what* he is as well as who he is. Now go," he said, leading her to the front door and opening it. "I will keep all of your loved ones safe."

Olivia reached up and pulled his head down as she stood on tiptoe, and gave him a big noisy kiss on the cheek. She turned away from the startled man with a laugh and stepped out onto the porch. "Anything you want me to tell Mac when I see him?"

"Yes. Tell him . . . tell Maximilian that I'm proud of him," he said gruffly as he softly closed the door.

Olivia immediately grabbed the knob to tell Titus that *he* should be the one telling Mac he was proud of him, only to find it was locked.

"You sappy old poop," she muttered. She turned to face the storm, took a fortifying breath, and ran toward home to get her hiking boots and rain gear and headlamp.

Because really, she wasn't putting *all* her faith in a piece of jewelry.

Chapter Twenty-four

His arms stretched upward to hold back the energy pulsing to be freed, Mac kept his mind's eye on Olivia making her way up the cliff path toward him. He smiled at her curse to Poseidon when she slipped in the mud, then scowled when she started muttering curses at *him*. Yet she bravely continued putting one foot in front of the other despite the storm and ground-shaking tremors, her fierce determination to reach the precipice overlooking Bottomless making him wonder if she wasn't more anxious to give him hell than return his jacket—which he knew she was wearing under her rain slicker.

Mac was forced to turn his focus to the raging energy when it began attacking the very mountain he was standing on as it attempted to reach the lake. Wrestling it back under control, he then returned his attention to Olivia to see what was taking her so long. Sweet Prometheus, getting the woman to stay on the path was like trying to herd mackerel. If he didn't know better he'd swear she was deliberately daring the wind-whipped trees to fall on her, as if she were testing the bracelet's protection.

Mac sighed, realizing Olivia was so busy having a conversation with herself that she wasn't watching where she was going. She was also bawling so hard it was a wonder she could see at all. Yet Mac sensed she wasn't crying because of him, but that something else had a dark grip on Olivia's tender heart.

Had his old man said something to deeply wound her feelings?

Or Eileen? He knew the Baldwins had returned; had they already told Olivia they'd sold Inglenook? Or had Eileen finally exposed the full extent of her son's deceit?

Then again, maybe Sam had revealed who he really was.

Dammit to Hades; Mac needed Olivia to focus on *him* right now.

A rogue burst of powerful energy suddenly broke free, flinging Mac off his feet and forcing him to drop what was left of his mortal façade to wrestle it back under control. Which is why when he stood, not even the feet he planted firmly on the trembling ledge were recognizable as he lifted beastly arms to redirect the energy down through the ice covering Bottomless. He forced it into a narrow laser of heat, aiming it toward the deepest basin, and cut a twenty-mile-long seam in the bottom of the lake.

The vast expanse of freshwater rushed free, and Mac sent it splintering in a multitude of directions, making sure the gushing streams sucked all the fish with them to bubble up in several surrounding lakes. The thick ice the water had been supporting collapsed in a series of long thunderous booms, and the underground river cutting a relentless path toward the south end of Bottomless finally burst into the empty basin.

Mac watched in satisfaction as the lake began to refill with frothing ocean water that lifted the shattered ice to float like miniature icebergs. He then turned his attention to Inglenook. Capturing some of the swirling energy, he directed it toward the end of the peninsula. Being careful of the cabins, not wanting to so much as crack a window, he commanded the stream bed that separated the two lakes to lift, creating a waterfall that allowed the freshwater from Whisper to gently spill into Bottomless.

Satisfied that the small lake would remain fresh, he turned back to the inland sea he'd created. Once again calling forth the powers that be, Mac carefully pushed apart two of the nearest mountains to form a long, deep fiord, then directed the powerful river of seawater downward again. Guiding it northward deep below ground, he allowed the massive surge to resurface only one last time in a remote Canadian lake before finally letting it break into the Gulf of St. Lawrence.

Its journey complete, Mac focused on the ebb and flow of the great subterranean river, carefully adjusting the tides and currents to regularly replenish the various inland seas he'd created, ensuring a healthy environment for the ocean creatures that would soon inhabit them. He then stood quietly with his arms stretched upward again and began dispersing the remaining energy, commanding the gale-force wind to become a gentle breeze even as the rumbles of thunder grew to distant echoes. The late-afternoon sun suddenly broke through the parting clouds, revealing the placid waters of the newly created Bottomless Sea.

"Oh. My. God."

Mac stiffened, not turning around, and closed his eyes at the realization that he was still trapped inside the beast. "Go away, Olivia. Go back down the path a few hundred yards and I will join you in twenty minutes."

He heard her snort a few paces behind him.

"Now, wife!" he snarled. "Go away!"

"Oh, will you get over yourself!" she cried, throwing herself against him to wrap her arms around his beastly torso. "This hasn't exactly been one of my better days," she sobbed, her voice thick with tears.

"Olivia." He pulled her hands away to step out of her desperate embrace. "Go back down the path."

Only she threw herself right back at him the moment he turned, wrapping her arms around him again and burying her face in his beastly chest. "It's just been one thing after another today! From the moment dawn cracked with your parents' arrival to Eileen bringing home Jessica Pilsner and her son—who is Keith's son and Sophie's half brother—to finding out that Sam's my father and Ezra's my *grandfather.* Oh God, Mac, they *sold* Inglenook to developers before I could buy it!"

He tried to gently break her hold. "Olivia."

Her arms tightened. "You have some nerve ordering me to leave like a good little *wife*, when you should be down on your knees apologizing to me."

Holding his hands out, he stood stiffly in shock. "Apologize for what?"

She leaned back to glare up at him, apparently too distraught to realize *what* she was hugging. "Really, Mac, did you once consider that a simple 'I love you' might be easier than destroying my beautiful state?"

"Olivia," he hissed, trying to peel her off him so he could turn away. "Go down the path and wait for me."

She stepped back, giving an angry gesture. "Why, so you can make yourself all perfectly handsome again?" She swiped at the tears rolling down her face, then bent at the waist to hug herself. "P-please don't send me away. I *need* you right now. My whole world is falling apart and you're the only solid thing I have to hold on to."

Mac dropped to his knees and opened his arms. "Then come to me," he whispered, folding her into his embrace when she hurled herself at him again. "Shhh, it's okay. I've got you now." He pressed his face to her hair. "Your world is only changing, not falling apart."

"Ezra's my grandfather!" she wailed. "And Doris was my grandmother, and . . . and all these years I didn't even *know.*" She leaned away and swiped at her eyes. "And Sam's not really Sam because he's my *father.* And without thinking I asked your dad if he knew what *marita* meant, and he made dawn crack like a sonic boom to get here because he thought I was a gold digger. Only he's not mean and scary like everyone makes him out to be, because he's got a big old sappy heart." She waved at the ocean below them. "And now he's all excited because he thinks you did this crazy thing to *impress* me."

"I did," he quietly rasped, holding her trembling body as tightly as he dared. "I did it all for you, *marita*."

Her fingers dug into his neck. "Stop calling me that. We're not even *married*." She reared back with a glare, though he doubted she could see him because she was crying so hard. "You have to *ask* me to marry you, and I have to say *yes*, and we have to have an actual *wedding*."

Mac pulled her back to his chest and adjusted his hold to prepare for the coming explosion. "Actually, I have the power to simply declare that we're married."

Only instead of exploding, Olivia went perfectly still in his arms.

"But you," he rushed to assure her, "have the right to reject me." He touched his lips to her hair. "One time," he said quietly. "Once you accept me as your husband of your own free will, it will be forever." His arms involuntarily tightened around her. "But your rejection frees only *you* to marry another, not me. My fate was sealed the moment I claimed you."

She started trembling again. "Oh, Mac, what have you done?"

"I've handed you my heart, Olivia."

"But I'm nobody!"

A chuckle escaped the tight fist squeezing his chest. "By the gods, there will be days you'll *wish* you were nobody if you accept our marriage." He smoothed down her hair, only to notice that his hand was shaking almost as much as she was. "Please be brave enough to love me, Olivia. Ask me to be your husband. I promise I'll say yes."

She leaned away to blink up at him. "Now? I have to decide right *now*?"

Not able to handle her looking at him, Mac sat on the ground and settled her in front of him facing Bottomless. "We walk down this mountain as husband and wife, or you walk down alone," he told her. "But if you do, we will never see each other again."

She said nothing, though he felt her give a small shudder.

"I prefer that you have your conversations out loud, wife," he whispered. "Tell me your thoughts."

She started running her fingers over his nearly once-again-human arm. "I'm just wondering why you couldn't have just asked." She waved toward Bottomless again. "Why all the . . . drama?" Only before he could answer she turned with a gasp, her beautiful cinnamon eyes locking on his for several pounding heartbeats. And then she just as suddenly melted against him, but not quickly enough to hide her smile.

"Will you marry me, Mac?"

He took hold of her chin to make her to look at him again. "Do you understand what you're agreeing to, Olivia? That it's *forever*?"

The woman actually shrugged. "I'm game for forever if you are."

"Why?" he blurted before he could stop himself. Mac closed his eyes to block the light shining from hers. "Why would you bind yourself to a man—no, to a *beast* of a man—who doesn't even have the courage to ask you to be his wife?"

He snapped open his eyes when she pressed her hands to his ugly face. "Do you have any idea how hard it is to be around a perfectly handsome, confident, sexy-as-hell man?" She patted his ugly cheek. "Maximilian the beast is way easier to love, because . . . well, honestly? I find the real you far less intimidating."

She snuggled back against him with a sigh. "And I probably shouldn't tell you this because it will probably go straight to your already oversized head, but I really do have a thing for masculine strength." She folded his arms under her breasts and glanced up with a brilliant smile. "And if you made my palms sweat and my heart race before, there's a very good chance I really will faint the next time we get naked together, now that I know the real you." She turned to face forward again. "If I tell you a secret, will you promise not to hold it against me?"

"My word of honor," he whispered. "You can always tell me anything."

"I flat-out lied when I promised never to fall in love with you, because it was already too late." Mac felt her take a shuddering breath. "I'm pretty sure I fell in love with you the moment you swept me off my feet the day you saved me from Mark, only it took my brain a while to realize what my heart knew instantly." And then Mac felt a tear fall onto his arm. "I don't need you to say the words," she whispered thickly. "I'll just look up at the mountains when I need a reminder. I only wish there were some grand and dramatic way for *me* to show *you* how passionately I love you."

"Ah, Olivia," he said on a sigh, pulling her more tightly to him. "You did that when you hugged the beast." He kissed her cheek. "Which again leads me to ask why you decided so quickly not to reject me as your husband?"

She actually chuckled. "Because I suddenly realized how scared you are."

Mac stiffened. "Excuse me?"

"Oh, come on," she scoffed, waving toward Bottomless. "You weren't trying to impress me by moving heaven and earth and a few little mountains; you were making sure I was so overwhelmed by your gesture that I wouldn't notice how desperate you were." She craned her head around to raise a brow at him. "And that, *husband*, is why I don't need you to say the words. Only a deeply-in-love man who's obviously afraid of being rejected would set such a diabolical trap," she said, turning to face the lake again.

But not quickly enough to hide her smug smile.

"I am not afraid. I simply decided that if I have to live up here in the mountains, then I would bring the ocean to me."

She scrambled off his lap so fast that Mac barely had time to protect his groin, and he hadn't even made it to his feet before she gave him a sharp poke in the chest.

"If you *have* to live up here?" she repeated ever so softly. "Are you implying that I'm forcing you to stay here?"

He pulled her against him with a laugh. "Sheathe your claws, little tigress, and tell me again that you accept our marriage."

She stared at his fully human chest. "If I do, will you put all the lakes and mountains back the way they were?"

Mac stiffened. "I can't, Olivia. I just used up the last of my powers making all this happen. And Henry and I really do need to be near the ocean to survive."

"Are you serious? Mac! You destroyed Bottomless!" She grabbed his hand and started leading him off the ledge. "By God, if you can't fix this then your father sure as hell better be able to."

"Olivia."

"You can't just go around moving mountains simply because you want to go swimming in salt water. People's livelihoods depend on this lake." She came to an abrupt halt when he refused to follow, and spun around with a glare fierce enough to stop a bear in its tracks.

Mac swept her off her feet and, ignoring her gasp of outrage, carried her back onto the precipice and sat down. She immediately stopped struggling and clung to him when he let his feet dangle over the edge, and then he had to pry her arms from around his neck in order to settle her facing forward on his lap.

"Look, Olivia. Does Bottomless appear destroyed to you?"

"It . . . it's . . ." She blew out a heavy sigh. "Okay, it looks pretty much like it did before, except for that new channel carved between those two mountains," she said, pointing to the north. She turned to look up at him. "But it's *salt water*."

He nudged her back around and tightened his embrace. "And what do you think will happen to Turtleback Station and Spellbound Falls," he asked, "when word gets out that there's a beautiful inland sea tucked up here in the mountains?"

Mac felt her breath catch. "We . . . we'll become a tourist

destination. Ohmigod," she whispered, leaning away to look at him. "We'll be swarmed by tourists from all over the world. But that's even worse! People from away are going to buy up all the land around Bottomless and start building fancy vacation houses all over the place. Property values are going to skyrocket and the locals are going to be taxed out of their homes!"

"No, they won't, because I'm not going to let that happen." He waved toward the mountains. "Right after I purchased Inglenook, I also bought most of the timberland surrounding Bottomless all the way to the Canadian border. Except for the resort you're going to build over there," he explained, pointing to one of the mountains, "all of the land will remain wilderness."

She leaned away again, only this time to gape at him.

"It will no longer be Inglenook, Olivia, but the resort will be *yours*."

"But—"

He gave her a gentle squeeze. "All my resources are at your disposal, wife, be they money or magic. Whatever you need to make your resort successful you will have, including my support."

"But I don't want a fancy resort; I want a camp for *families*."

"Then build both. Design a resort that will cater to all lifestyles, from a spa-type retreat for couples to an intimate camp for families to wilderness camping for hikers. You have the land to create whatever you want, limited only by your imagination."

"But I don't know anything about building that kind of resort much less running it."

He smiled. "Then hire someone who does. Or if you wish, I happen to know someone who's quite skilled in building a microcommunity. And I'm sure if you ask for his help, my father would be happy to advise you."

"Y-your father?" she squeaked.

Mac tightened his hold on her, afraid she was about to

gasp so hard she'd fall off the ledge. "Who better to ask than the man who created Atlantis?"

Only she gasped hard enough that *he* nearly fell off the ledge. "As in the lost *continent* of Atlantis?"

He nodded.

"But that's a *myth*."

He shrugged. "Then I guess I must also be a myth, since I was born there."

"But—"

He pressed a finger to her lips. "A long, long time ago," he began quietly, "when the gods were so busy trying to wrestle control of the world from each other that they were nearly destroying it, Titus Oceanus stepped forward to champion mankind." Mac settled his once-again-gaping wife back against his chest and stared over her head at his new home. "And so he built the beautiful island of Atlantis on which to plant a very special grove of Trees. He then chose a handful of trustworthy mortals to train as drùidhs, and charged them with protecting the Trees."

"What was so special about them?"

"The Trees of Life hold all the knowledge of the universe. Only when the gods realized what my father was doing, Titus was forced to sink Atlantis to keep it hidden. But before sinking it he scattered his small army of drùidhs—each of them carrying one of his Trees—all over the world." He dropped his head beside hers. "As a matter of fact, there's a Tree of Life growing right here in Maine. Matt and Winter Gregor are two powerful drùidhs who live on Bear Mountain at the southeastern end of Pine Lake, and their combined energies are responsible for an entirely new species of Tree that will ensure mankind's survival for many millennia."

"You realize what you're saying is flat-out fantastical, don't you?" she whispered. "Forget that you claim Atlantis exists; you also expect me to believe there are drùidhs living not a hundred miles from here? And that they're protecting some magical Tree of Knowledge from *mythological* gods?"

Mac kissed her cheek. "Actually, the only thing I need is for you to love me," he said against her flushed skin. "Everything else pales in comparison to the power of love, Olivia." He moved his mouth next to her ear. "And the true magic that happened here today, as far as I'm concerned, is that we'll be walking down this mountain together as husband and wife."

Her grip on his arms tightened. "Yeah, about that. Do you think we could have an actual ceremony, preferably in a church with an actual minister, and a best man and maid of honor, and guests and a reception and everything? Because I really need for Sophie and Henry to *see* us get married. And so does everyone in town."

"You have one week to plan your wedding," he said even as he tightened his embrace. "And maybe this time your father will have the honor of walking you down the aisle."

"Oh God," she sobbed, burying her face in her hands. "What am I supposed to do about Sam?"

"I would suggest you ask yourself what lengths *you* would go to in order to protect Sophie if you found yourself in the position Sam was in twenty-eight years ago. Would you risk your daughter's life to be with her, Olivia? Or would you give her up to the only people in the world you trusted to keep her safe?"

She dropped her hands to stare out at Bottomless again. "You expect me to just pretend I didn't wait years for him to come for me?"

"I don't expect anything from you, Olivia, as this particular matter is between you and your father. I'm merely suggesting that you might try to put yourself in Sam's place long enough to hear what your heart has to say."

She turned to bury her face in his chest. "He broke my heart twenty-eight years ago," she sobbed.

"I know he did," Mac whispered, smoothing down her hair. "But only because he loved you enough to walk away."

"But it's so unfair."

"Life is neither fair nor unfair, Olivia; it merely *is*. In fact, it's completely neutral. But," he said, giving her a gentle squeeze, "we are all free to choose how we deal with our trials and tribulations as well as our joys." He lifted her chin to look at him, and used his thumb to brush a tear off her cheek. "Sam chose not to come back for you, but please don't mistake that for abandonment. If you but ask him, I believe you'll discover he knows more about you than most fathers know about their children."

"But why couldn't Ezra and Doris tell me who they were? Why all those years of lying to me, when I could have known them as grandparents? And now it's too late. Doris is gone, and I never once got to call her G-Grammy."

"And would you have loved her any more if you had known?"

"Of course not."

Mac kissed her forehead. "And do you love Ezra any less now?"

She stilled, and her eyes widened. "No."

Mac pulled her to him. "I didn't think so. Which means the only question is, can you find room in your heart for your father?" He gave her a gentle squeeze. "Assuming it's not already filled to capacity with your love for me and our two children."

She blinked in surprise. "Ohmigod, we're a *family* now." She pressed her hands to his very human face and gave him a rather noisy kiss on his lips—only to suddenly scramble off his lap before he realized what she was doing.

"Be careful," he yelped when she not only nearly unmanned him but nearly made them both fall off the cliff.

"Come on, we have to go tell Henry and Sophie," she said, dragging him to his feet. She stopped and pivoted toward him. "Only we're not telling anyone anything until you *tell* Henry that you love him. Got that?" she said, poking him in the chest even as she smiled smugly. "And the moment you do, you may consider yourself officially graduated from Inglenook."

He grabbed her poking hand and started leading her down the mountain again.

"What's so funny?" she asked when he chuckled.

"Oh, I was just wondering if you're going to keep encouraging Henry to question authority, now that *you* will be on the receiving end of his whining and pouting."

Olivia didn't chuckle, she snickered. "I figure I can't do any worse than you're going to when Sophie starts batting her big long eyelashes at you." She pulled him to a stop. "How about we make a deal? I'll handle Henry's whining and you handle Sophie's pouting? And just when the little manipulators think they've got us wrapped around their little fingers, we'll switch."

He started walking again. "I have a better idea. How about we simply send them both off to visit Grampy Titus and Grammy Rana for a couple of weeks three or four times a year?"

She pulled him to a stop. "To *Atlantis*?"

Mac sighed, and started walking again. "You realize that if we don't send their grandbabies to them, they'll keep coming to visit, don't you?" He snorted. "Hell, you might as well build them a permanent wing on your resort, seeing how I unconsciously built a fiord deep enough to hide my father's ship."

She stopped again, and Mac figured that at the rate they were going, Henry and Sophie would be adults before they made it back. Only when he looked at her it was to find that the woman was smiling.

"You mean they can *sail* here like normal people instead of arriving on a sonic boom or in a blizzard?"

"Well, they can now that I opened up a saltwater channel. Only it's not a sailing ship; it's a submarine."

"Please don't tell me it's yellow," she muttered, heading down the mountain again. She slipped her hand into his when he fell into step beside her. "Are you seriously going to build a resort here?"

"I'm serious about you building a resort." He grinned over at her. "At least one of us has to earn an honest living." She tried to stop again, but Mac pulled her along when he finally realized why she was stalling. "It will be okay,

Olivia. I will be at your side as you deal with all that is waiting for you back at the lodge." Only this time he stopped them and grasped her shoulders to steady her for one last bit of news. "But I would warn you that young Riley is in desperate need of a bone marrow transplant, and that Sophie is a perfect match."

"Ohmigod, no!" she cried. "Is that why Eileen brought him here? Mac, I can't put Sophie through something like that."

"So you would deny your daughter the right to save her brother's life?" He pulled her into his arms. "Sophie is a strong, wise young woman just like her mother, Olivia, who will embrace this chance to be a hero. And you should also know," he whispered, "the procedure will be successful, and little Riley will live a full and exciting life thanks to his very brave sister."

"C-can't you just make him better without involving Sophie?"

"Yes." He touched his finger to her lips when she tried to speak. "But I would suggest you think before asking me to, Olivia. Have you not been teaching me that it's our place to help our children embrace life rather than protect them from it?"

"But she's only eight."

"And weren't you only four when your world collapsed around you? And yet you not only survived, you managed to turn into the woman I moved mountains to marry. Empower your daughter to do the same, Olivia, by giving her the chance to do this."

Though he could tell she was very much afraid, she blew out a resigned sigh. "I hate it when you turn my words back on me." She arched a brow. "Since when did you start sprinkling little pearls of wisdom around like rain? That's supposed to be my claim to fame."

He kissed the tip of her cute little nose and started walking down the mountain again. "Do you not know that every teacher is in danger of being outsmarted by their student?"

Giving her a reassuring squeeze when she silently slipped her hand back into his, Mac sighed loudly. "Am I ever going to get my jacket back?"

"This old thing?" she said, plucking at the collar sticking out of the top of her rain slicker. "Why would you want a jacket with a finicky zipper that only works when it wants to? Speaking of which," she said, stopping again, "*you* might think it's expedient to manipulate locks and zippers and stuff, but I have no intention of being married to a controlling husband. So you better stop using your fancy tricks on me."

"Or else . . . what?" he asked with a laugh. "What are you going to do, wife? Lock me in my room? Burn my dinners? Withhold *sex*?"

One delicate brow arched into her hairline. "Oh, I rarely get mad, but I *always* get even. And just so you know, you're not the only member of this family with a few tricks hidden up his or *her* sleeve."

"At the risk of bursting my apparently nefarious bubble, I'm afraid your seat belt and door locks and zippers not working were more your doing than mine. Each time you found yourself trapped, it was because you were right where you wanted to be." He shrugged. "I can't help it if that also happened to be exactly where I wanted you."

She reached up and pulled his face down to within an inch of hers. "Then I guess it's a good thing you married a woman brave enough to love you," she whispered as she started to kiss him.

Only Mac held back, needing to give her the words he knew she so desperately needed to hear. "A woman I am so deeply and passionately in love with that I will continue to move heaven and earth and any mountains in my way to be with her."

"Ohmigod, is that a promise or a threat?"

"That, my little tigress wife, is both," he said quietly, capturing her gasp in his mouth as he decided to finally reclaim his jacket—only to discover it was *all* she was wearing under her rain slicker.

Epilogue

Olivia sat on the steps of the lodge, her arm slipped through Ezra's as she watched John and Eileen's car—which was also carrying Jessica Pilsner and little Riley—disappear over the knoll behind their moving van.

"Now there's a sight I was afraid I wouldn't live long enough to see," Ezra said as he tried to stand up. "So come on, girl, let's get you moved into the main lodge where you belong."

Olivia held him sitting beside her. "I'm in no hurry. I'm still getting used to the idea that it's really mine."

He patted her knee, giving a soft snort. "You didn't exactly get Inglenook the way you were expecting, but Sam told me he checked and the deed is definitely in your name." He shot her a confounded look. "Or rather it's in Olivia Oceanus's name. You gonna tell me exactly when you ran off and got married?"

Olivia leaned her head on his shoulder to hide her smile, and twined her fingers through his. "The wedding's this Saturday, actually. Mac just put my *married* name on the deed to make sure I said yes."

Ezra's fingers tightened around hers. "You . . . um, you

don't think the Oceanuses are a . . . that they're sort of . . . aw, hell, Olivia, they're strange people." She felt him shudder. "And that Titus fellow is downright spooky." He lifted his shoulder to get her to sit up. "Rana's about as far from Eileen as they come, but are you sure you're not trading in a pain-in-the-ass mother-in-law for an even scarier *father*-in-law?"

She rested her head on his shoulder again with a laugh. "Titus is a bigger cupcake than you are, you old . . . Grampy," she whispered. She leaned up and gave him a kiss on his startled cheek. "Thank you for being the best grandfather in the whole wide world. I never would have survived without you and Dor . . . Grammy. Will you give me away to Mac on Saturday? I promise it'll be the last time you'll have to walk me down a church aisle."

His clouded eyes grew misty as he clutched her fingers between his trembling hands. "Can you find it in your heart to give Sam that privilege, Olivia? Now I know you feel like he abandoned you," he rushed on, squeezing her hand when she tried to speak. "But I swear Sam did what he did because he loves you more than life itself. And I also know the only reason he made it back from some of his missions was because he needed to be around to watch over you. Maybe not in the way you would have liked, but . . . aw, hell," he said, his shoulders slumping as he lowered his gaze to their hands. "From the day you were born that boy did everything in his power to give you whatever you needed."

"I know," she managed to whisper past the growing lump in her throat.

"Please let him walk you down the aisle. If not for Sam, then would you consider doing it for me?" He reached up and pressed her face against his shoulder, stroking a trembling thumb over her damp cheek. "I'm getting too old to keep giving you away."

"It's kind of difficult to ask him anything, seeing how he disappeared the moment Mac let you two out of that room."

Ezra snorted. "Sam was just about to try *burning* his way out of there when Mac showed up. That door could have been made of steel for the way it wouldn't give, and Sam said even bulletproof glass wasn't that indestructible. Nothing he tried worked." He shook his head. "I swear I ain't never seen that boy lose his cool like that. And I hope to hell I don't live long enough to see it again." His eyes grew misty again as he clung to her. "He was scared to death for you, Olivia. And though he won't admit it, Sam's getting too old to keep playing his games. He risked everything to be here for you this time, because I think after Doris died he . . . he's worried that if anything happens to me that you'd be all alone."

"Nothing's going to happen to you."

"Well jumped-up old monkey poop, I know that," he said gruffly. "I intend to still be here when *Sophie* walks down the aisle."

Olivia wiped her eyes. "If you have any way of contacting Sam, you tell your son that if he wants to see me, he knows where I am."

"Why don't you tell him yourself?" he said, his gaze moving past her shoulder.

Olivia went utterly still.

"I'm sorry for disappearing the other day," Sam said to her back. "But I needed some time alone to . . . sort things out." She felt more than heard him step closer. "If it's any consolation, I didn't go far. I've been staying with Dad for the last three days." He moved to the bottom of the stairs and Olivia turned to face him, the lump in her throat nearly strangling her when she saw the utter defeat in his eyes. "I'll understand if you don't want anything to do with me," he continued, stepping closer. "But I need to tell you that I was able to find a bone marrow donor in France for little Riley. I can have the woman in California a week from next Monday, and keep Sophie out of it completely."

Olivia stared at him in silence. He was going to remain on the outside looking in, she realized; always working in the shadows where it was safe.

Probably because he'd been doing it so long, he didn't know any other way.

"Thank you, but Sophie wants to save her half brother's life."

Sam smiled sadly. "Your little girl comes by her courage honestly."

"My birth certificate says my father is unknown. What's your real name?"

He hesitated, then shrugged. "I've grown pretty used to Sam."

She could actually see him disappearing right before her eyes, slipping away from her and Sophie and his father. And suddenly everything fell into place: the prom dress that was too expensive for a foster girl to even dream of wearing that Doris had bought her, her first car—a sturdy full-sized truck—that Ezra had gotten her for her eighteenth birthday, the college scholarship she'd received out of the blue, and her small but elegant wedding the Dodds had insisted on giving her. All of it—everything—had come from Sam. Even the substantial savings Doris had left her, and the money Ezra seemed to always have too much of; Sam had been supporting his parents, who in turn had been supporting her.

And what money couldn't buy, he'd provide some other way.

Even as she tried to wrap her mind around all he'd secretly done for her, Olivia wondered when the last time was that he'd slept with both eyes closed.

"Well," he said gruffly, turning to slowly limp away. "I guess I should be going."

"Did you know I broke my elbow when I was seven?"

He stopped and stood stiffly, not turning around. "I know."

"And that when I was nine, on my first day at a new school, Frankie Turner walked up and kissed me right on the mouth?"

"I know you sent him home with a bloody nose." He turned to her. "And that you spent an hour in detention every day after school for the rest of the week."

Olivia patted Ezra's knee and stood up, then walked

down the stairs and over to Sam. "Stay," she whispered. "Stay here in the light with me, Sam, and with your granddaughter and with your dad."

"I can't, Olivia. I'd be putting all of you in danger."

She smiled, even as she gestured toward Bottomless. "I just found out that mountains really do move, sometimes as easily as wishing them to. You tell me which ones are casting their shadows on you, and I'll see what I can do about getting them out of your way." She pressed her palm to his pounding heart. "Stay and walk me down the aisle Saturday. Be here to hold Sophie's hand while they draw her marrow. And keep Ezra from rattling around in his empty house." She wrapped her arms around him and rested her head on his pounding heart. "Stay."

Olivia closed her eyes with a sigh of pure pleasure when he hesitantly folded her into his embrace. "I'm not sure I want to give you away to Oceanus," he said thickly. "Because near as I can tell, he doesn't actually exist."

"Oh, he exists, all right." She leaned back just enough to smile up at him, not quite ready to step out of her father's arms—not that he seemed to mind. "Mac's just as real as . . ." She patted his chest. "Well, he's as real as you are. And I love him, and he loves me. And come Saturday at noon sharp, I'm going to find myself with more honest-to-God *family* than I know what to do with."

She turned serious, staring up into his deep liquid gray eyes. "Come home, Dad. Spend the next thirty-three years with us, and let *me* keep *you* safe for a change." She smiled at his surprise. "I'm a lot stronger than I look. And I have it on good authority that wisdom beats brute strength, hands down."

Olivia stepped out of his arms and took hold of his hand, and started leading him back to the steps just as Sophie and Henry came running up from the barn and plopped down beside Ezra. "Hey, you two, why the glum faces?" she asked, stopping at the bottom of the stairs but continuing to hold Sam's hand so he couldn't disappear again.

"Sophie told me Mr. Caleb's going to take the horses

back when he comes to our wedding on Saturday," Henry said. "And when I asked Dad why we couldn't just buy them, he told me that his satchel of money was empty because he just bought us a really big wedding present."

"I see. And you don't have any money of your own?" Olivia asked in mock surprise. "You haven't saved *any* of your allowance?"

The boy frowned at her. "What's an allowance?"

Sophie jumped to her feet. "Wait! I've got forty-three dollars and seventy-five cents in my piggy bank. Would that be enough to buy Pegasus?"

"Well, I don't know," Olivia said. "I guess that's something you'd have to ask our horse wrangler." She held out her hand to Sophie even as she tightened her grip on Sam's. "But first, I think I should properly introduce you to each other." She gave her confused daughter a squeeze when the girl slipped her tiny hand inside hers. "Because seeing how maturely you've handled all the surprises you've gotten over the last few days, I thought you might be ready for a couple more. Sophie, I would like to introduce you to my dad and your granddad, Sam."

Sophie gasped so hard she actually clasped her chest as her gaze darted to Olivia. "He . . . he's your dad?" she squeaked, her big brown eyes going to Sam. "And my *grandfather*?" She looked back at Olivia, clearly confused. "But you said your dad was dead," she whispered.

"I thought he was," Olivia whispered back, tightening her grip on Sam when she felt him take a deep breath. "But it turns out he was just having a really hard time getting back to me." Olivia crouched down to be at eye level with her daughter, only to discover Sophie had grown more than she realized. "You want to hear something else that's way cool, sweetie? Instead of calling him *Mr. Ezra*," she said, nodding toward the stairs. "From now on you can call him *Great-Grampy*, because Ezra is Sam's daddy—which makes him *my* Grampy and your Great-Grampy."

Sophie went back to clutching her chest, utterly speechless as her gaze darted from Olivia to Sam to Ezra, then back to Olivia. "Honestly really?" she whispered.

Olivia nodded. "Honestly really." She stood up. "So, Grampy Sam, do you think Caleb will sell Pegasus for forty-three dollars?"

"And seventy-five cents," Sophie interjected.

Being a tad over six feet tall, Sam started to crouch down to the girl, only to falter because of his stiff back.

"I've got you," Olivia said, using her grip to steady him even as she chuckled. "See, I told you I'm stronger than I look.

"I'm not ready for a wheelchair yet," he muttered, obviously more confounded than embarrassed. He looked at Sophie, narrowing his eyes as he tapped his chin in thought. "Well, I suppose with a little haggling, you might get Caleb down to forty-three dollars and seventy-five cents."

"Oh, Sophie," Henry cried, leaping off the steps and running to her. "You're going to get to buy Pegasus!"

"But, Mom," Sophie said. "What about Henry? It's no fun to go on trail rides all by myself. He needs to buy a horse, too."

"Hmmm." Olivia also tapped her chin. "Let me think. Grampy Ezra," she said, looking toward the stairs. "Isn't there some old tradition that says the bride is supposed to give her new stepson a wedding present?"

Ezra's eyes lit with laughter. "The way I recall it, she's supposed to give the *entire* family a present. Especially if she happens to find herself with a sizable savings account she doesn't need anymore."

Olivia was suddenly a tad confounded herself. She'd scrimped and saved for more than six years to buy Inglenook, and she was afraid it was going to be a tad harder parting with her savings than it had been amassing it.

Wait; if Mac's satchel of money was empty, exactly how were they supposed to build a fancy resort?

She was suddenly glad that a small army of oceanographers and geologists were arriving tomorrow to study Thursday's phenomenon; renting them her cabins would at least keep food on the table and make payroll for the skeleton crew she was keeping.

"It's okay, Miss Olivia," Henry said. "Just your marrying us is gift enough."

Olivia immediately crouched in front of him. "But I want to buy you a horse, Henry, because Sophie's right; not only isn't it any fun riding alone, it's not safe, either. So you'd really be doing me a favor by going along to watch out for her."

She would swear his young chest expanded a good two inches. "I believe that would be very wise. And to repay you, I will get up every morning at the crack of dawn to water and feed the horses."

"I'm afraid it's going to have to be *before* dawn, sport," she said, standing up and ruffling his hair. "Because first thing Monday morning, your daddy and I are signing you up for school."

He gasped so hard he nearly fell over. "I'm going to *school*?"

"Oh no, Henry," Sophie said, "you're going to be in Isabel's class."

Henry started backing away, shaking his head. "I'm really not sure I'm ready for school, Miss Olivia," he whispered, bumping into the steps and sitting down with a thud.

Sophie went over and sat down beside him, and patted his knee. "Don't worry; Isabel can't bug you in the classroom, and I'll protect you during lunch and recess."

Henry looked downright horrified as he stared at Sophie. "Girls don't protect boys! It's supposed to be the other way around."

"Sure they do, young man," Sam interjected, sitting down on the step above them beside Ezra. "Why, in some parts of the world, women . . ."

Olivia stopped listening to the conversation in favor of backing away to take in the entire scene, not stopping until she bumped into a big broad chest. She sighed when a pair of big strong arms encircled her, and melted against him. "Do you realize that in a matter of only a few days," she said, smiling at the lodge steps, "I went from being an orphan to having a huge family?" She glanced up at Mac, then back at the lodge. "Can you keep Sam safe, so he can stay?"

"It's already done, Olivia. If his enemies continue pursuing Sam, the trail will lead them to a death certificate issued for Sergeant Kelly Waterhouse three years ago, and then to his grave in Arlington. And," he said quietly when she sighed, "if you request a copy of your birth certificate, you will find Sam Waters Dodd listed as your father."

She leaned her head back to look up at him. "You told me you used up all your magic moving the mountains."

He shrugged, shrugging her with him. "Not all of it."

She faced the lodge again, only to see Titus and Rana and Carolina emerge from the path leading from their cabin to join Sam and Ezra and the children on the steps. "I think we should give your parents the main lodge."

"Why?" Mac asked, a slight growl in his voice. "Are you *deliberately* encouraging them to stay longer?"

"I can't have your parents sleeping in a leaky cabin, Mac. All your mom's clothes got wet during the hurricane because the roof needs to be reshingled."

"Then give them your cottage. After Saturday, we're going to be a family of *four*."

Olivia laughed. "No, we're going to be a family of *nine*." She tilted her head back to smile up at him. "And that, husband, is the real magic that came to Spellbound Falls."

LETTER FROM LAKEWATCH

Winter of 2012

Dear Readers,

Fairly early on in our marriage, my husband found out that a big strong hug cured just about any ailment a woman might have. Sadness, anger, frustration, fear, low self-esteem, hopelessness, bad hair—nothing stands a chance against a powerful hug.

Now I can't imagine it's easy to step up and hug an angry woman, but from the perspective of the person being hugged, I can tell you that love trumps anger every time—even when it's the hugger the huggee is angry at.

It wasn't long, however, before I discovered that I had unwittingly handed my husband a tool that has gotten him out of more than one uncomfortable situation, many of them not involving me. "Wow, this is powerful stuff," Robbie told me one day, looking two inches taller as I suspiciously eyed the wet spot on his shirt. "She started crying and I didn't know what to do, so I just hugged her."

This particular her *was our next-door neighbor who also happened to be our tenant at the time. She was a single woman with two dogs that had once again just frightened some children walking to the school bus, and the woman had finally reached the conclusion that the overly aggressive and very old dogs had to be put down before they ended up biting someone—hence the tears that had precipitated the hug.*

And with that revelation forever etched into his psyche, Robbie has since gone on to hug eighty-year-old women, babies with boo-boos, total strangers at a yard sale, widows, orphans, nuns, and even the waitress who dumped dinner all over me. *(Now, in case you're worried about my husband going around hugging other women, he's very careful not to hug the same one twice, lest* she *get the wrong idea and hugs him back, because . . . well, he claims taking care of me is a full-time job and he really doesn't actively go looking for more trouble.)*

But I feel I should caution you that hugging only works in one direction, because everyone knows that when a man hugs a woman she sees it as an emotional thing, but have a woman hug a man and he immediately thinks, "Hey, she's touching me, so that must mean she wants to have sex with me right now.*" Ladies, they're* guys; *a smile means you want to have sex with them.*

So, where am I going with this? Well, those of you who've read my books may have noticed that my big, strong, intimidating heroes give my heroines quite a lot of hugs. That's because being the smart men they are, it isn't long before they realize how well hugging works. And personally, I like men who are just that smart, so I write them that way because I can. Judging by the letters I get from readers, women the world over share the fantasy of big tough men being brought to their knees by the one woman who in turn is smart enough to love them for the guys *they are.*

Teach your man to hug. I promise it will be the best thing you ever do for your relationship. Just realize that once you give him such a powerful weapon, he's liable to use it—preferably on you—every chance he gets.

Until later, from LakeWatch, you keep reading—and hugging—and I'll keep writing.

Janet

Read on for a special preview
of Janet Chapman's next
Spellbound Falls romance

Charmed by His Love

Available June 2012 from Jove

Peg rounded a curve in the peninsula's winding lane and gasped in surprise when she spotted the strange man striding across the parking lot with Jacob thrown over his shoulder. Even from this distance she could see the sheer terror in her son's eyes as Isabel skipped backward in front of them, trying to get the man to stop. Peg started running even as she sized up her adversary: tall, athletic build, short dark hair. Yeah, well, instead of traumatizing defenseless little children, Claude the mad scientist was about to find himself on the receiving end of a healthy dose of fear.

"I swear I'll kick you if you don't put him down, mister," Peg heard Isabel threaten. "He wasn't hurting your stupid machine none. He's just a baby!" And then the six-year-old actually did kick out when the guy didn't stop, only to stumble backward as he merely sidestepped around her. "Charlotte! Peter!" Isabel screamed as she scrambled in front of him again. "Come help me save Jacob from the scary man!"

When she saw him hesitate, Peg was alarmed that the guy intended to go after her daughter. Without even stopping to think, she lunged onto his back. "Put him down!"

she shouted, wrapping her arm around the bastard's neck as she tried to pull Jacob off his shoulder with her other hand. "Or I swear I'll rip out your eyes!"

The guy gave his own shout of surprise and suddenly dropped like a stone when Peter slammed into his right knee. "You leave my brother alone, you scary bastard!" Peter shouted as he rolled out of the way, dragging Jacob with him.

Peg reared up to avoid Charlotte's foot, which was swinging toward the guy's ribs, although she didn't dare loosen her grip or take her weight off him, fearing he'd lash out at her children. He suddenly curled into the fetal position with a grunt when Peter landed on him beside her.

"Get away from him!" she screamed over her shouting children, trying to push them off when they all started pummeling him. "Run to the—" Peg gave a startled yelp when an arm came around her waist and suddenly lifted her away.

"Sweet Zeus," Mac muttered, dragging her up against his chest as he took several steps back. "You will calm down, Peg, and control your children," he quietly commanded even as he tightened his grip against her struggles.

"Ohmigod, Jacob, come here!" she cried, holding out her arms. Jacob and Isabel threw themselves at her, actually making Mac step back when he didn't let her go. "You're okay, Jacob. You're safe now," she whispered, squeezing both trembling children. "You're a brave girl, Isabel, and a good sister."

Charlotte called out, and Peg saw the girl pull away from Mac's father just as he also released Peter. Both children ran to her, giving the bastard rising to his hands and knees a wide berth. Peg took a shuddering breath, trying to get her emotions under control. "You can let me go," she told Mac over the pounding in her chest. Holy hell, she couldn't believe they'd all just attacked the giant!

Mac hesitated, then relaxed his hold, letting her slip free to protectively hug all four of her children. "Mind telling me what incited this little riot?" he asked the man who was now standing and wiping his bleeding cheek with the back of his hand.

The guy gestured toward the lower parking lot. "I was taking the boy to find his parents, because I caught him inside my excavator not five minutes after I'd just pulled him off it and told him to go play someplace else." He shrugged. "I figured his mother or father could explain how dangerous earth-moving equipment is, since he didn't seem to want to listen to me." He suddenly stiffened, his gaze darting from Jacob to Peter and then to Peg. "They're twins." His eyes narrowed on the boys again. "Identical."

Pushing her children behind her, Peg stepped toward him. "I don't care if they're sextuplets and were *driving* your excavator or stupid submarine." She pointed an unsteady finger at him. "You have no business manhandling my kids. And if you ever touch one of them again, I swear to God I'll—"

"Take it easy, mama bear," Mac said, dragging her back against him again. "He was only concerned for Jacob's safety. As well as yours, apparently," Mac said quietly next to her ear. "Did you not notice he didn't defend himself when you and your children were attacking him? Duncan's intentions were good."

Peg stilled, a feeling of dread clenching her stomach. "D-Duncan?" she whispered, craning to look at Mac. "He . . . he's not Claude, the scientist?" She lifted her hands to cover her face. "Ohmigod, I thought he was the guy who scolded Jacob for climbing on the submarine yesterday."

She peeked through her fingers at the man she and her kids had just attacked, horror washing through her when she saw the blood on his cheek and scratches on his neck. "Ohmigod, I'm *sorry*," she cried, jerking away from Mac and rushing to her children. Even though he was over half as tall as she was, Peg picked up Jacob and set him on her hip as she herded the others ahead of her, wanting to flee the scene of their crime before she burst into tears. "C-come on, guys," she whispered roughly, her heart pounding so hard it hurt. "Let's go to the van."

Mac's father plucked Jacob out of her arms and settled him against his chest, giving the boy a warm smile as he smoothed down his hair. "That was quite a battle you waged, young Mr. Thompson," Titus Oceanus said jovially, shooting Peg a wink as he took over herding her children away when Mac pulled her to a stop. "I'll have to remember to call on you young people if I ever find myself in a scary situation," Titus continued, his voice trailing off as he redirected them toward the main lodge.

Damn. Why couldn't Mac let her slink away like the humiliated idiot she was?

"It will be easier to face him now rather than later," Mac said, giving her trembling hand a squeeze as he led her back to the scene of her crime. "Duncan's a good man, Peg, and you're going to be seeing a lot of him in the next couple of years."

Wonderful. How pleasant for the *both* of them.

"Duncan," Mac said as he stopped in front of the battered and bleeding giant. "This beautiful, protective mama bear is Peg Thompson."

God, she wished he'd quit calling her that.

"She's not only Olivia's good friend, but Peg is in charge of keeping the chaos to a minimum here at Inglenook." He chuckled. "That is, when she's not creating it. Peg, this is Duncan MacKeage. First thing Monday morning, he and his crew are going to start building a road up the mountain to the site of our new resort."

MacKeage. MacKeage. Why did that name sound familiar to her?

All Peg could do was stare at the hand her victim was holding out to her, feeling her cheeks fill with heat when she saw the blood on it. Which he obviously only just noticed, since he suddenly wiped his hand on his pants, then held it out again.

Peg finally found the nerve to reach out, saw his blood on *her* hand, and immediately tucked both her hands behind her back. "I'm sorry," she whispered, unable to lift her gaze above the second button on his shirt—which she noticed was missing. "We . . . I thought you were the man who scared Jacob yesterday. He had nightmares all night and I barely got him back here today."

He dropped his hand to his side. "I'm the one who needs to apologize, Mrs. Thompson, as I believe you're correct that I shouldn't have touched your son." She saw him shift his weight to one leg and noticed the dirt on his pants and small tear on one knee. "I assumed he was the boy I'd just told to get off the excavator. And having a large family of young cousins, I thought nothing of lugging him off in search of his mother or father." He held out his hand again. "So I guess I deserved that thrashing."

Damn. She was going to have to touch him or risk looking petty. Mac nudged her with his elbow. After wiping her fingers on her pants, Peg finally reached out, and then watched her hand disappear when Duncan MacKeage gently folded his long, calloused fingers around it.

Oh yeah; she had been a raving lunatic to attack this giant of a man. Not that she wouldn't do it again if she thought her kids were being threatened.

Okay, maybe she *was* a protective mama bear.

It seemed he had no intention of giving back her hand until she said something. But what? *Nice to meet you? I look forward to bumping into you again? Have we met before? Because I'm sure I know someone named MacKeage.*

Damn. She should at least look him in the eye when she apologized—again.

But Peg figured the first three times hadn't counted, since she'd mostly been sorry that she'd made a complete fool of herself trying to gouge out his eyes with her *bear* hands. But looking any higher than that missing shirt button was beyond her. "I'm sorry!" she cried, jerking her hand from his and bolting for the main lodge, her face blistering with shame when she heard Mac's heavy sigh.

Duncan stood leaning against the wall of Inglenook's crowded dining hall, shifting his weight off his wrenched knee as he took another sip of the foulest kick-in-the-ass ale he'd ever had the misfortune to taste. He wondered if Mac was trying to impress his guests by serving the rotgut or making sure they never darkened his doorstep again. He did have to admit the ancient mead certainly took some of the sting out of the claw marks on his neck, although it did nothing to soothe his dented pride at being blindsided by a mere slip of a woman and her kids.

Hell, if Mac and Titus hadn't intervened, he'd probably still be getting pummeled.

Duncan slid his gaze to the bridesmaid sitting at one of the side tables with her four perfectly behaved children, and watched another poor chump looking for a dance walk away empty-handed. Peg Thompson appeared to be a study of innate grace, quiet poise, and an understated beauty of wavy blond hair framing a delicate face and dark blue eyes—which was one hell of a disguise, he'd discovered this morning. He couldn't remember the last time a woman had left her mark on him, much less taken him by surprise, which perversely made him wonder what the hellcat was like in bed.

She was a local woman and a widow, raising her four children single-handedly for the last three years, Mac had told Duncan just before leaving him standing in the parking lot bleeding all over his good shirt. After, that is, Mac had subtly explained that he also felt quite protective of his wife's friend. A warning Duncan didn't take lightly, considering Maximilian Oceanus had the power to move mountains, create inland seas, and alter the very fabric of life for anyone foolish enough to piss him off.

But having been raised with the magic, Duncan wasn't inclined to let the powerful wizard intimidate him overly much. He was a MacKeage, after all, born into a clan of twelfth-century highland warriors brought to modern-day Maine by a bumbling and now—thank God—powerless old drùidh.

And since his father, Callum, was one of the original five displaced warriors, not only had Duncan been raised to respect the magic, he'd been taught from birth not to fear it, either. In fact, the sons and daughters and now the grandchildren of the original MacKeage and MacBain time-travelers had learned to use the magic to their advantage even while discovering many of them had some rather unique gifts of their own.

Hell, his cousin, Winter, was an actual drùidh married to Matt Gregor, also known as Cùram de Gairn, who was one of the most powerful magic-makers ever to exist. And Robbie MacBain, another cousin whose father had also come from twelfth-century Scotland, was Guardian of their clans and could actually travel through time at will. In fact, all his MacKeage and MacBain and Gregor cousins, whose numbers were increasing exponentially with each passing year, had varying degrees of magical powers. For some it might only be the ability to light a candle with their finger, whereas others could heal, control the power of mountains, and even shape-shift.

Duncan had spent the last thirty-five years wondering what his particular gift was. Not that he was in any hurry to find out, having several childhood scars from when more than one cousin's attempts to work the magic had backfired.

That's why what had happened here last week wasn't the least bit of a mystery to the clans, just an unpleasant shock to realize that Maximilian Oceanus had decided to make his home in Maine when the wizard had started rearranging the mountains and lakes to satisfy his desire to be near salt water and the woman he loved.

Duncan sure as hell wasn't complaining, since he was benefiting financially. Mac was building his bride a fancy resort up on one of the mountains he'd moved and had hired MacKeage Construction to do a little earth-moving of its own by building the road and prepping the resort site. Duncan figured the project would keep his fifteen-man crew and machinery working for at least two years.

And in this economy, that was *true* magic.

Spellbound Falls and Turtleback Station would certainly reap the rewards of Mac's epic stunt, since there wasn't much else around to bolster people's standard of living. Not only would the resort keep the locals employed, but stores and restaurants and artisan shops would soon follow the influx of tourists.

It would be much like what the MacKeage family business, TarStone Mountain Ski Resort, had done for Pine Creek, which was another small town about a hundred miles south as the crow flies. Only it was too bad Mac hadn't parted a few more mountains to make a direct route from Pine Creek to Spellbound, so Duncan wouldn't have to build a temporary camp for his crew to stay at through the week. As it was now, they had to drive halfway to Bangor before turning north and west again, making it a three-hour trip.

Then again, maybe Mac didn't want a direct route, since the clans had recently learned the wizard was actually allergic to the energy the drùidhs he commanded gave off. And that had everyone wondering why Mac had decided to live so close to Matt and Winter Gregor, who were two of the most powerful drùidhs on earth.

Apparently the wizard's love for Olivia was greater than his desire to breathe.

Not that Duncan really cared why Mac was here; only that the money in his reputed bottomless satchel was green.

"Have ye recovered from your trouncing this morning, MacKeage?" Kenzie Gregor asked. He looked toward the Thompson family sitting quietly at their table and chuckled. "I can see why ye were so soundly defeated, as together the five of them must outweigh you by at least two stone."

Wonderful; help a man rebuild his home after it was nearly destroyed by a demonic coastal storm, and the guy felt the need to get in a shot of his own. But then, Kenzie was an eleventh-century highlander who'd only arrived in this time a few years ago, so Duncan figured the warrior didn't know better than to poke fun at a MacKeage. Kenzie might have his drùidh brother Matt to back him up, but the sheer number of MacKeages was usually enough to keep even good-natured ribbing to a minimum.

"If you're needing a lesson on defending yourself," William Killkenny said as he walked up, a large tankard of mead in the ninth-century Irishman's fist, "we could go find a clearing in the woods. I have my sword in the truck, and I'm more than willing to show another one of you moderns the art of proper fighting." He looked toward the Thompson table, then back at Duncan and shook his head. "It pains me to see a man defeated by a wee slip of a woman and a few bairns."

"I think Duncan is probably more in need of dance lessons," Trace Huntsman said, joining the group. "Have I taught you nothing of modern warfare, Killkenny?" Trace slapped Duncan on the shoulder even as he eyed William, making Duncan shift his weight back onto his wrenched knee. "Our friend here knows the only way he's going to defeat the Thompson army is to lure their leader over to his side. And women today prefer a little wooing to feeling the flat of a sword on their backsides."

William arched a brow. "Then someone should have explained that to his cousin, don't ye think? Hamish kidnapped Susan Wakely right out of Kenzie's dooryard in broad daylight, and rumor has it he wouldn't let the woman leave the mountain cabin he took her to until she agreed to marry him."

Trace gave Duncan a slow grin. "So I guess it's true that you first-generation MacKeages inherited many of your fathers' bad habits?" He shook his head. "You do know you're giving us moderns a bad reputation with women, don't you?" He nodded toward the Thompson table. "Maybe you should go ask her to dance and show these two throwbacks a better way to win the battle of the sexes."

"And let her trounce me twice in one day?" Duncan gestured in Peg's direction. "I believe that's bachelor number five walking away now, looking more shell-shocked than I was this morning."

"Sweet Christ," William muttered. "The woman just refused to dance with a fourteenth-century king of Prussia."

"Who in hell are all these people?" Duncan asked, looking around Inglenook's crowded dining hall.

"Friends of Titus, mostly," William said, "who aren't about to incur old man Oceanus's wrath by not showing up to his only son's wedding."

"I can't believe he dared to put time-travelers in the same room with modern locals," Trace said, also glancing around.

"And serve liquor," Duncan added, just before taking another sip of mead—because he really needed another good kick in the ass. His knee was throbbing, the scratches on his neck were burning under his collar, and social gatherings weren't exactly his idea of a good time. But like most everyone else here today—the small party from Midnight Bay plaguing him now likely the only exception—Duncan wasn't about to insult the younger Oceanus, either, considering Mac was his meal ticket for the next two years.

"Uh-oh, your target is on the move," William said, his gaze following Peg Thompson and her ambushing children as they headed for the buffet table. He nudged Duncan. "Now's your chance to show us how it's done, MacKeage. Go strike up a conversation with the lass."

"Maybe you could offer to let her children sit in your earth-moving machine," Kenzie suggested. "That would show her ye don't have any hard feelings."

"Kids and heavy equipment are a dangerous mix," Duncan growled, glaring at the three of them. "Don't you gentlemen have wives and a girlfriend you should be pestering?" He elbowed William. "Isn't that Maddy dancing with the king of Prussia?"

"Oh, Christ," William muttered, striding off to go reclaim his woman.

Kenzie also rushed off with a muttered curse when he saw his wife, Eve, start to breast-feed their young infant son under a blanket thrown over her shoulder.

Trace Huntsman, however, didn't appear to be in any hurry to leave. "If it's any consolation," Trace said, "Peg Thompson was more rattled by this morning's attack than you were. Maddy and Eve and my girlfriend, Fiona, were there when Peg came to Olivia's cottage. Fiona told me it took the four of them over twenty minutes to calm her down." He shot Duncan a grin. "The women all promised Peg they would have done the exact same thing if they'd caught a stranger manhandling their child. Can I ask what you were thinking?"

"I wasn't thinking," Duncan said. "I manhandle dozens of children every time my family gets together. Everyone looks out for everyone's kids, making sure the little heathens don't kill themselves or each other. Hell, that's the definition of *clan*."

Duncan tugged his collar away from his neck as he eyed the widow Thompson leading her gaggle of children back to their table, each trying to reach it without spilling their plates of food. He sighed, figuring he probably better apologize to her again, seeing how she owned the only working gravel pit in the area.

Just as soon as Mac had hired him to do the resort's site work, Duncan had started calling around to find the closest gravel pit to Spellbound Falls. He would eventually dig his own pit farther up the mountain, but he needed immediate access to gravel to start building the road. Duncan had been relieved to discover that the Thompson pit was just a mile from where the resort road would start, and that it had a horseback of good bank run gravel. He'd also learned Bill Thompson had been killed in a construction accident three years ago.

Which is why a feather could have knocked him over this morning as he'd stood beside his truck in the parking lot changing his shirt, when he'd finally put two and two together and realized he'd just pissed off the person he wanted to buy gravel from. He hoped she'd still sell to him now. And then even if she did, he'd likely be paying an arm and a leg for every last rock and grain of sand.

"Which branch of the military were you in?" Trace asked.

Duncan looked down at himself in surprise. "Funny; I could have sworn I left my uniform in Iraq."

Trace chuckled. "You forgot to leave that guarded look

with it." He shrugged. "It's common knowledge that every MacKeage and MacBain serves a stint in the military." He suddenly frowned. "Only I've never heard it said that any of the women in your families have served."

"And they won't as long as Greylen MacKeage and Michael MacBain are still lairds of our clans," Duncan said with a grin. "It'll take a few more generations before we let our women deliberately put themselves in harm's way."

Trace shook his head. "You really are all throwbacks. You must have a hell of a time finding wives. Or is that why some of you resort to kidnapping?"

Duncan decided he liked Trace Huntsman. "There's no 'resorting' to it; we're merely continuing a family tradition that actually seems to work more often than it backfires. And besides, it beats the hell out of wasting time dating a woman for two or three years once we've found the right one."

"You don't think the woman might like to make sure *you're* the right one before she finds herself walking down the aisle, wondering how she got there?"

Duncan shifted his weight off his knee with a shrug. "Not according to my father. Dad claims time is the enemy when it comes to courting; that if a man takes too long wooing a woman, then he might as well hand her his manhood on a platter."

Trace eyed him suspiciously. "Are you serious?"

"Tell me, Huntsman; how's courting Fiona been working for you?"

"We're not talking about me," he growled. "We're talking about you MacKeages and your habit of scaring women into marrying you."

"I did notice you managed to get an engagement ring on her finger," Duncan pressed on. "So when's the wedding?"

Trace relaxed back on his hips and folded his arms over his chest with a heavy sigh. "You don't happen to have an available cabin in Pine Creek, do you?"

Duncan slapped Trace on the back and started them toward the refreshment table. "Considering Fiona is Matt Gregor's baby sister, I think you might want to look for a cabin a little farther away. Hell, everyone within twenty miles of Pine Creek heard Matt's roar when he learned she was openly living with you without benefit of marriage."

Trace stopped in front of the large bowl of dark ale and glared at Duncan. "A fact that has brought us full circle back to women being warriors. The only reason I'm still alive is because Fiona puts the fear of God into her brothers if they so much as frown at me." He looked at Peg Thompson, then back at Duncan—specifically at the scratch on his cheek. "Trust me; the strong-arm approach won't work on any woman who can handle children. Not if a man values his hide."

Duncan refilled his tankard. "Which is exactly why I'm still a bachelor," he said, just before gulping down his third kick-in-the-ass like a true highlander.

An enchanting new novel of richly drawn romance.

From *New York Times* Bestselling Author
JANET CHAPMAN

Highlander for the Holidays

After a brutal attack, Jessie Pringle moved to the small mountain town of Pine Creek, Maine, to start over. But she never expected to meet Ian MacKeage, who had seemingly stepped right out of the Scottish Highlands. As drawn to Ian as he is to her, Jessie finds it more and more difficult to deny her own desires—until a chance encounter gives her a way to let go of the past . . .

penguin.com

M986T0911